P9-CFB-268

STONE ANGEL

CAROL O'CONNELL

JOVE BOOKS, NEW YORK

STONE ANGEL

A Jove Book / published by arrangement with
Hutchinson, a division of Random House U.S. Limited

PRINTING HISTORY
G. P. Putnam's Sons edition published July 1997
Jove edition / July 1998

The Penguin Putnam Inc. World Wide Web site address is
http://www.penguinputnam.com

ISBN: 0-515-12298-X

A JOVE BOOK®
Jove Books are published by The Berkley Publishing Group,
a member of Penguin Putnam Inc.,
200 Madison Avenue, New York, New York 10016.
JOVE and the "J" design are trademarks belonging to
Jove Publications, Inc.

PRINTED IN THE UNITED STATES OF AMERICA

10 9 8 7 6 5 4 3 2 1

ACKNOWLEDGMENTS

Dianne Burke, Search and Rescue Research, Tempe, AZ
lfqy01a@prodigy.com

Yvonne Finley, Chief Civil Deputy, Tensas Sheriff's Department, LA

Norman Herland, Computer Consultant, White Plains, NY
hfdb01a@prodigy.com

Kitt Peak Observatory

Ellsworth Pilíe, Jr., Hydraulics Branch of U.S. Army Corps of Engineers

Bob Rholi, Ph.D., Climatologist, Southern Regional Climate Center, LSU, Baton Rouge, LA

PROLOGUE

IN THE IDIOT'S philosophy, a cloud could never be *just* a cloud. Seeking portent, he read much into the shapeshifting. This particular cloud was bereft of any wind to drive it. Thwarted in its forward movement, it billowed upward in a silent explosion of form, pluming high and angry, boiling over the face of the midday sun and killing its light.

Now the cloud was alone in the sky.

The town square flickered in and out of the dark as a succession of quick bright flashes of gaseous green lit the cloud from within. Then came a low rumble—prelude to the main event.

All dark now, like a stage.

It was coming; it was surely coming. He knew a jagged bolt of lightning would hit the earth, and soon, for the air was primed—electrified. The idiot's flesh tingled. He felt an exquisite, unbearable tension as he waited for the strike.

And the cloud let him wait.

It loomed above him, massing higher and darker, as he counted off the seconds. *One, two—*

•   •   •

THE YOUNG STRANGER came to town just past twelve noon.

Within an hour, the idiot had been assaulted, hands bloodied and broken; Deputy Travis suffered a massive stroke at the wheel of his patrol car; and Babe Laurie was found murdered.

The young stranger who had preceded all of these events was sitting in a jail cell.

Sheriff Jessop made out a receipt for the prisoner's possessions, which were fewer than the average woman carried: one .357 Smith & Wesson revolver and one handed-down pocket watch. Inside the cover of the watch were the names of the generations: David Rubin Markowitz, Jonathan Rupert Markowitz, Louis Simon Markowitz and, last to inherit, Mallory—just Mallory.

CHAPTER
1

THE RAIN HAD finally ended, and the sky was a noisy circus of life on the wing, birds getting off to a late start on the day. Every fish hawk was screaming after its supper, and the woman wondered if the fish could hear them coming.

One osprey flopped its catch onto the grass. The fish struggled under the bird's talons; its silver scales were striped with watery blood. The fish hawk was so intent on tearing flesh from bone, he paid the woman no mind as she drew closer, smiling benignly on the creature and his bloody, living meal, nodding her approval of a good catch.

If reincarnated, Augusta knew she could depend on coming back to the earth with feathers, for she had the ruthless makings of a fine bird, and God was not one to waste talent.

A breeze off the river whipped the faded green cotton dress around her bare legs, and long waves of hair streamed back over her shoulders. The finer detail of cornflower-blue eyes would be lost from the distance of the town below, but any citizen of Dayborn would have recognized her tall and slender silhouette striding along the top of the levee, that great sloping barrier which was the high ground for the lands along the mighty Mississippi.

A sudden cloud break made her tresses into a brilliant flowing shock of white, wildly upstaging the few remaining strands of black hair. She winced at a twinge of bursitis in her left shoulder and shifted the weight of her grocery bag onto one hip as she moved down the steep incline of dirt and spotty clumps of Bermuda grass.

When she stepped onto level ground, she walked slowly toward her house perched behind distant trees. One dark window, round like an eye, could see and be seen through the choke of foliage. It watched her progress from the base of the levee to a narrow dirt road.

The mansion of forty-seven rooms had been standing for nearly a hundred and fifty years. She wished it would finally crumble back into the earth. Toward that end, she had made no repairs on the place in the half century since her father's death. She had done nothing to abet her incarceration, nor anything to free herself. For the majority of her seventy years, she had been known by the titles of Miss Augusta Trebec, spinster of Dayborn and professional prisoner.

She paused in front of Henry Roth's cottage, a small one-story affair of red brick walls and a fine slate roof. The garden was ablaze with exotic flowers growing in wavy bands of brilliant primary colors. She had always coveted this house for its simplicity of form and manageable space. If it had been hers, she would have let the garden go to a more natural state of untended wildflowers. But Henry was an artist who could not help but improve upon nature. Every day of his life, he improved blocks of stone with his chisel to create beautiful and most unnatural things.

A stranger was standing at Henry's door, and a silver car was parked in the driveway. Augusta did not know the style of one car from another, but she could recognize a Mercedes hood ornament when she saw one. The license plate was obscured by shrubs and could not tell her where the man and his vehicle had come from.

Henry's visitor was a tall one, well over six foot, and a good figure of a man by the back of him. As he turned away from the door, she was struck with admiration for his profile. That nose was a thing to behold, right formidable, nearly a weapon in its size and length.

The man turned around to face her. His eyes were large and heavy-lidded, with small blue irises. They put her in mind of a fairy-tale frog who had not quite completed the transition to a prince by way of a kiss from a beautiful maiden. Perhaps he had not been properly kissed, or maybe the maiden was flawed.

Augusta walked up the flagstone path to Henry's door. The visitor nodded to her in the modern version of a gentleman's bow.

Respectful—she liked that.

He was not a very young man, but there was no gray in the longish brown hair to help her fix his place in time. He might be in that awkward phase before the onset of middle age. She was near enough to note the fabric of his three-piece suit, and by that heavy material she made him a northerner from a colder state of autumn.

"Hello," he said, with a smile that was at once loony and beguiling.

Augusta smiled back before she realized what she was doing. Now she pressed her lips together in a more dignified and noncommittal line. "Henry's not expected back from New Orleans till early evening."

"Thank you, I'll come back later." He handed her a white business card.

She was charmed by this small gesture. It reminded her of the gentleman's calling card, a custom from her father's generation.

He pointed to her grocery bag. "May I help you with that? It looks rather heavy."

Apparently, he was from good family, or at least his mother had raised him right. By his accent, she narrowed his compass points to the northeastern corner of the country.

Augusta placed her brown paper sack in the crook of his arm, slyly reveling in his look of surprise as he realized how heavy the bag really was. She had carried greater weights. Beneath the light cotton dress was a well-toned body, kept in good order by spurning any form of transportation but her own good legs, and by carrying all her own burdens.

She scrutinized his business card. "Charles Butler, consultant." A line of academic credentials trailed after his name, like boxcars on a train.

Could any man be that overeducated?

And now she learned that Mr. Butler had carelessly misplaced a very good friend. "Perhaps you've seen her." With his free hand, he pulled the folded page of a newspaper from his inside pocket and handed it to her.

Augusta opened the sheet and looked down at a large, grainy photograph of a stone angel. She recognized the page from last Sunday's edition of the *Louisiana Herald,* which had featured famous plantation gardens along the River Road. The caption gave a credit line to the sculptor, Dayborn's own Henry Roth.

"That statue was commissioned five months ago," he said. "It looks so much like my friend, I think she must have posed for it." Now he produced a wallet photograph of a young woman with blond hair and green eyes. Both the carved angel and the glossy portrait of a living woman were good likenesses of an unforgettable face.

"She was here. I knew her." Augusta refolded the sheet of newspaper and handed it back to him. "She's gone now. It was a sudden death."

During the long silence, she watched questions welling behind the man's eyes, crowding up against his lips, mad to find an exit. But she had just wounded him, deliberately and severely; he was incapable of speech. His head tilted to one side, as though to empty out her words and cure himself this way.

Well, obviously, he was not good at death.

"You can leave your car here." She turned back to the road and motioned him to come along with her. "My house is only a short walk through the cemetery."

He was slow to follow her, moving mechanically as he carried her groceries along the path leading into a broad circle of trees and a city of small whitewashed houses, each one home to a corpse. The roofs of the tombs were topped by crosses of stone and crucifixes of wrought iron. Less impressive graves were slabs made of concrete to prevent the dead from rising in the buoyancy of sodden ground.

Many a grave was spotted with the colors of dying blooms. The wilted bouquets were remnants of All Saints' Day, when the local people had left flowers for dead relations—the very day the young stranger had arrived, and Babe Laurie had violently departed from the world, leaving a nasty red stain by the side of the road.

The crunch of shoes on the gravel path was masked by the incessant music of birds as Augusta's tall companion walked beside her, still speechless. And all the while, she was measuring his state of shock as a sign of good character. Evidently, he had been telling the truth. He was merely a man in search of a friend, and that friend was certainly beloved.

Ah, but one could never be too sure of anything, she cautioned herself as she guided him toward a statue with the same face as the one in his newspaper clipping. But this one held a different pose, and she didn't carry a sword.

"Now this is her monument," said Augusta as they approached the back of an angel poised for flight, stone wings spread on the air. "There isn't a corpse, though."

The sheriff had never found her body.

The young woman had not gone into sacred ground, but certainly to her death. Her lost blood had grown to the dimensions of a river in the talk of townspeople. And a child had also vanished, gone to that famed place of Only God Knew Where.

As they rounded the monument, Augusta pointed to the angel's face. "Now that's a real good likeness of her. Is that your friend?"

She looked up at the stranger beside her. His face was a

waffling confusion of anguish and relief as he read the date of death, seventeen years in the past.

YET IT WAS undeniably Mallory's face.

Charles Butler stared up at the delicately sculpted features, the long slants of her eyes, the high cheekbones and full lips. The wings were unfurled in the disturbing and masterful illusion of levitating stone. In her arms, the angel carried a smaller version of herself, a child.

He felt a tug at his sleeve and looked down into the old woman's dispassionate blue eyes. "Is that your missing friend?"

"No. My friend would have been a little girl when this woman died."

The old woman pointed to the stone child in the angel's arms. "Well now, that's Cass's daughter. The girl ran away, or was carried off—we don't know which."

The carved child was perhaps six or seven years old. The age was right. Yes, the child was Mallory; he was certain of it now. So, after all the months of searching for her, he had stumbled onto the beginning of the road and not the end of it. "You have no idea what happened to the little girl?"

"No," she said. "Those seventeen years between the day the child disappeared and the day she came back to town—well, that's a total mystery to everyone."

"She came back?"

"Three days ago."

"And she's *alive*?"

"Oh, yes. By all accounts, she's very healthy."

He looked into the old woman's cunning eyes, only now realizing what a cruel joke she had spun out for him. He glared at her in silent accusation, and her foxy smile offered no denial whatever.

The agony she had put him through, knowing all the while that Mallory was alive.

"Perhaps that was a nasty trick," she said. "But I'm

old. I have to get my fun where I can.'' Her smile slowly spread into a glorious grin.

She was at least thirty years his senior, but he was not entirely immune to what beauty survived in her. His mind's eye worked backward in time, undoing her wrinkles and restoring the dark glory of her waist-long gray hair. In his imagined reconstruction, she astonished him.

The woman pointed to the roof and round window of a house, all that was visible over the trees beyond the rim of the cemetery. ''That's my place, up there on the hill.''

''What hill?'' In his travels along the west bank of the Mississippi River, he had yet to see a hillock or even a bump on the Louisiana landscape.

''According to the surveyor's report, my house sits ten feet above sea level.'' Her tone bordered on combative. ''In these parts, that qualifies as a damn mountain.''

She threaded her arm into his, and they walked along the path leading out of the graveyard and toward the imperceptible hill, which he was taking purely on faith. ''Where can I find my friend? Do you know where she's staying?''

''Oh, yes. The whole town knows where she's staying. I hear she's called Mallory, but I don't recall if that's her last name or her first.''

''Her first name is Kathy, but Mallory is the only name she answers to.'' He glanced back to the angel and her child. So Mallory had finally found her way home.

''That cinches it,'' said the old woman in the spirit of *eureka*. ''Kathy is the name of Cass Shelley's daughter. But Sheriff Jessop only knows your friend as Mallory. He found that name inside an old pocket watch she was carrying. When you see the sheriff, don't you tell him any different.''

''Why not?'' And what did a sheriff have to do with—

''Don't help him. He's no friend of hers. So, don't give him anything useful. Oh, perhaps I should have mentioned that a local man was found murdered, and your friend was put in jail shortly thereafter.''

Charles stopped dead on the path, and his eyes rolled up to the sky. *What next?* What new torture might this woman be fashioning for him? He looked down at her and caught the smile that was just stealing off.

"All right, let's have it—all of it." It was a fight to keep civility in his voice. "I assume the murder and her jailing are connected, but I don't want to take anything for granted—not with you. What happened?"

She drew out the silence, eyes squinting at that middle ground of focus, as though reading the small print of a contract. Charles popped off the balls of his feet and settled down again, inclining his head to prompt her.

"What happened?" she echoed him, and held a pause for a few more maddening seconds. "Well, I guess a number of odd things happened the day Kathy came back. The deputy nearly died of a heart attack. And then they found Babe Laurie's body, his head all stove in with a rock. Oh, but wait—I'm misremembering the day. First, the idiot got his hands broken, but that was done with a piano."

"A piano. Right. And Mallory is supposed to have accomplished all this in one day?" *Not likely*. Though she was capable of frightening a man into a heart attack, she was fanatically neat, hardly the most likely suspect for a messy homicide by rock. And as for the idiot's broken hands, though Mallory was a highly original creature, if she were merely assaulting someone, she would probably not use a piano.

With light pressure on his arm, the woman moved him forward again. "Well, we're pretty sure she had something to do with the deputy's heart attack. He had a dickey pump. It wouldn't have taken much of a fright. Your friend startled a whole lot of people, showing up the way she did."

Well, that fit. Startling people was Mallory's forte. She had an unparalleled talent for it. "After we drop off your groceries, perhaps you could give me directions to the jail?"

The woman's face was stark-naked incredulity. *Oh, you rube*, said her eyes. "So you're gonna go strutting in there and demand to see her, is that it?"

"That's my plan, yes." It was a nice straightforward plan, no flaws, no holes in it.

"The sheriff's bound to ask what you know about her. If she'd wanted him to know anything at all, I guess *she* would've told him."

But, according to this woman, who now introduced herself as Augusta Trebec, Mallory had refused to say anything at all. Miss Trebec had this on the word of the cafe proprietress who delivered the prisoner's meals. For three days, Mallory had sat on the edge of her bed, staring at the jail cell wall and driving Sheriff Jessop wild. She never moved, never said a word. Except once or twice, Jane, of Jane's Cafe, had seen Mallory smile while the sheriff was pitching a fit. "Jane says the girl is making him a little crazier every day. So if you go in there all—"

"I see the problem." It might create complications for Mallory, and it would certainly ruin her fun.

When they cleared the cemetery, the path changed from gravel to hard-packed dirt. As they drew closer to the house, he was told that jail visits were limited to the morning hours. Charles also learned that Mallory had not been blamed for breaking the idiot's hands. The murdered man had done that particular piece of damage.

Well, that was encouraging.

He paused at the foot of a wide lane flanked by stands of ancient trees. Their dark twisty limbs reached out across space to form a green canopy high above them. The ground was dappled with bright patches of late afternoon sun streaming through the leaves.

"These are live oaks—*Quercus virginiana,*" said Miss Trebec, in the manner of a tour guide. "And the house at the end of the lane was built in 1850."

He had seen centurion oaks before, but never one approaching the enormous girth of these giants. Surely the trees were older by—

"The trees are three hundred years old," said Miss Trebec. "Give or take a few decades."

Charles shook off the idea that she was reading his

thoughts. She could no more do that than could the men who regularly beat him at poker. It was his face that spoke to everyone. Even his most private thoughts were on display in every change of expression. She must have noted his confusion and followed the swing of his eyes from manse to tree trunks.

"So the oak alley was planted for another house?"

She nodded. "And it was built by a real tree-planting fool. There's fourteen varieties of trees back there." She gestured back over her shoulder. He turned to scan the woods extending out from the cemetery, east and west of the oaken lane.

"Now that first house was destroyed in a flood, and my house sits on top of its remains."

He smiled. "Hence the ten-foot hill?"

"Right you are, Mr. Butler. My place, however, has never shown any structural weakness. It's harder to destroy." By her tone, she seemed to take this as a challenge.

Looking westward through the spaces between the massive tree trunks, he could see an open field of green grass stretching out to the levee. He watched the slow flight of a bird in a glide, a free ride on the wind. There were birds everywhere—singing, and some were screaming. Everything was in motion. Drapes of Spanish moss swayed in the boughs of the oaks, and shade-loving ferns waved in the breeze. There were nods from blooming shrubs and deep bows from independent flowers.

When they had come to the end of the covered lane, he had his first unobstructed view of Trebec House. The basement level was a gray brick wall with deep-set windows and a small door. Rising above this foundation was a massive structure very like a Grecian temple. He counted eight white fluted columns soaring up past two flights of windows. The breakneck flow of their lines was not disrupted by the ornate railing on the gallery, which served as a roof to the wide veranda. The scrolled capitals supported the massive triangle of a pitched roof with a round attic window.

Thick foliage surrounded the foundation wall and climbed the brick to wind strong green tendrils around one column, threatening to pull the shaft from pedestal and lintel, and thus to bring down the house. But this was only illusion. The structure was elegant, yet bold enough in its design to withstand every assault of nature.

Two graceful staircases curved upward from the grass, and inward to embrace on the main level above the brick foundation. A massive carved door was set well back on the veranda.

"Those are courting staircases," said Augusta. "In my grandfather's day, a young lady never preceded a gentleman on the stairs. That was for the gentleman's protection. One sight of a woman's ankle and he was as good as engaged. So they each took a separate staircase and met up there at the front door."

The house was so beautiful, even in its ruination—like the woman who walked beside him. The exterior had once been white and smooth, but now was weathered by the elements and extreme age.

He had to bow slightly to follow her through the small wooden door set into the foundation between the staircases. They passed down a dimly lit hall, which suddenly broadened into a wide, bright room.

"This kitchen only dates back to 1883," she said. "The original was in a separate building out there where the paddock is now." She gestured to a tall window which framed a white horse at the center of a fenced enclosure. The entire wall was a bank of such windows.

Charles loved kitchens, and this one was a sunlit marvel. Absent was the neglect of the exterior. The room was in perfect order and contained all the creature comforts of a twentieth-century Hobbit—microwave and dishwasher, coffee machine and bean grinder. Polished copper-bottom pots and pans hung from the mantel of a stone hearth large enough to accommodate a roasting ox on a spit.

A broad table was laid with a red-and-white checked cloth. At its center was a sketchbook, which lay open to a

rather good drawing of a white owl. Beside this book was
a set of galleys with the red marks of a proofreader's pencil.

Augusta caught his eye. "I write monographs on local
birds."

As he set the grocery bag down on a slab of butcher
block, a hiss called his attention to the top of the refrigerator and the narrowed eyes of a large yellow cat.

"You just sit yourself down." Miss Trebec gave Charles
a gentle push in the direction of the table.

The cat on the refrigerator followed his every move. He
stared at the animal as he spoke to the woman. "This man
Mallory's accused of murdering—"

"Babe Laurie?" She put the cans of orange juice in the
freezer compartment, brushing the cat's tail aside to open
and close the refrigerator door.

"Babe?" He raised his voice to be heard above the
noise, for she had quickly moved on to the chore of grinding coffee beans by touching one finger to a state-of-the-
art machine.

"He used to be called *Baby* Laurie—that's the name on
the birth certificate. He was the last of eleven children by
the same woman. When the doctor put the newborn in the
mother's arms, he asked what she would call this one. She
said, 'I'd call it a baby,' and then she died. And that's the
truth."

While she set out the coffee cups, he was told that Babe
Laurie had started out as a child evangelist on the tent-show
circuit through the prairie states. Charles volunteered that
his cousin Max had once journeyed across the country with
a tent show, but Max had done a magic act. According to
Miss Trebec, Babe Laurie had done much the same thing.

He watched the hot water from the coffee machine drip
into a carafe as she explained that the murdered man was
the figurehead of the New Church, which was not so new
anymore, having been started thirty years ago when Babe
was only five or six years old and still called Baby.

"Wouldn't be too surprised if your friend did kill him.
Didn't like him none myself." She put a sugar bowl and a

cream pitcher on the table. Each belonged to a different pattern of china, and both were familiar to him as priceless museum pieces.

"You'll be staying in town at the Dayborn Bed and Breakfast—am I right?"

He nodded, pulling out the newspaper photo of the stone angel and unfolding it. He stared down at the likeness of Mallory's mother. "This sculptor, Mr. Roth? I gather he knew Cass Shelley very well."

"Yes, he did. And Kathy too. That child spent as much time in Henry's studio as she did at her own place. Did I mention that the dead man was found near the old Shelley house?"

"Who found the body?"

"Your friend did. She found Babe by the side of the road while she was driving the deputy back to town in his own patrol car. Oh, I didn't tell you that? She saved the deputy's worthless life—delivered him to the paramedics at the volunteer fire department. Travis is in the hospital now. I hear he's in critical condition."

"But if the deputy was with her when she found the body—"

"The deputy was driving toward town when he had his heart attack. Babe was found further up the road on ground your friend had already covered. She could have killed him before she met up with the deputy."

A moment ago, the golden cat had been perched on the refrigerator. Charles had only blinked once or twice, and now the cat was standing on the table a short distance from his right hand. How like Mallory was that trick of disappearing from one place and appearing in another.

"You said she drove the deputy's car to town. She was on foot?"

The woman nodded. "She was walking in the direction of her old house. It's on this side of the bridge, but not that much of a walk from the town square."

Miss Trebec poured coffee into his cup and then turned

back to the half-emptied grocery bag and unpacked the rest of the canned goods.

The cat hissed and arched its back as Charles's hand moved toward the sugar bowl. Apparently, he had violated some house rule of table manners. Slowly, his hand withdrew from the bowl and came to rest on the table by his cup. The cat lay down, stretching her lean body across the checkered cloth, and the tail ceased to switch and beat the wood. When his hand moved again, she bunched her muscles, set to spring, relaxing only while his hand was still. The cat controlled him.

Now who did that remind him of?

The old woman was back at the table. "Don't touch that cat. She doesn't like people—barely tolerates them. She's wild—raised in the woods. When I found her, she was too set in her ways to ever be anybody's idea of tame. She had buckshot all through her pelt and chicken feathers in her mouth. Now that told me, right off, she was a thief. And she is perversity incarnate. Sometimes she purrs just before she strikes."

Charles nodded while the woman spoke, and he ticked off the familiar character flaws as she listed them. Now he peered into the cat's slanted eyes. *Mallory, are you in there?*

Miss Trebec bent down to speak to the cat, to explain politely that an animal did not belong on the table when company was calling. The cat seemed to be considering this information, but she left the table in her own time, as though it were her own idea. The tail waved high as she disappeared over the edge.

It was disconcerting that the animal made no sound when she hit the floor. It crossed his mind to look under the table, to reassure himself that the cat did not float there, waiting to catch him in some new breach of etiquette. Instead, he peered into his cup as he stirred the sugar in his coffee. When he looked up to ask his hostess a question, the cat was riding the woman's shoulders.

"So, have you thought of a story to give the sheriff?"

He shook his head. Making up stories was not his long suit. Under Mallory's bad influence, his few attempts at lying had been disasters. "Could you take a message to Mallory? Tell her I'm here and I want to help?"

"I'm your worst possible choice," she said. "Me and Tom Jessop—he's the sheriff—we've been sticking pins and needles in one another for years and years. He wouldn't leave me alone with that girl for a minute."

"I have to see Mallory, but I don't want to create any problems for her." He tapped the newspaper clipping spread out on the table. "Do you think Henry Roth would help me?"

"Well, Mr. Butler—"

"Charles, please."

"Charles, then. And you must call me Augusta. Yes, he might help you. Henry's a mute, so be sure you got a paper and pencil on you. He doesn't always carry his notebook."

"My father was a deaf mute. Does Mr. Roth use sign language?"

"Yes, he does. Kathy and her mother used to be the only ones in town he could talk to with his hands. Well, you and Henry should get along just fine."

So, like himself, Mallory had been fluent in sign language as a child. In the past thirty minutes, Charles had discovered more about her early childhood than his old friend, the late Louis Markowitz, had learned over the years of raising her. For all poor Louis knew, his foster child had sprung to life as a full-blown ten-year-old thief on the streets of New York City.

And now, because Augusta Trebec wanted to keep an eye out for an expected visitor, he picked up his coffee cup and followed the old woman back down the hall toward the small door in the brick wall. He was wondering where the cat had gone. Then he saw the animal's bright eyes gleaming in the shadow of an ancient porcelain umbrella stand. She was set to spring, and her gaze was fixed on him.

"Be sure you don't let that cat out," said Augusta, as

she passed by the umbrella stand. ''I can't have that poor animal getting her hopes up, thinking she might catch a bird for supper.''

''I thought cats were rather good at that.'' He would have bet his life that this one was particularly good at bloody violence.

''She shows real talent with mice, 'cause that's a foot-race, and the quickest wins. But the birds usually see her coming in time to fly off. It's that bright yellow fur. She's like a little bonfire in the grass.''

Charles nodded. Mallory had much the same problem. So she had certainly not been in Dayborn all these months—not if one appearance could cause the commotion of a heart attack, a beating and a death. Surely she would have wiped out the entire town by now. The sign which had welcomed him to Dayborn had only boasted a population of eleven hundred people.

He was closing the door, when through the crack, he saw the cat bounding down the hallway, her lips pulled back over sharp white fangs and her eyes outraged. He pulled the door shut, and heard the angry cat's body hitting the wood three feet off the ground.

CHARLES WAS BREAKING the tradition of courting staircases, admiring Augusta's fine legs and trim ankles as she led him up to the wide veranda. Black birds perched on the curving wrought-iron rail, unperturbed by the old woman's presence. But, one by one, they took flight as he climbed the stone steps behind her.

When he was eye-level with the massive base of one column, he could see patches of encroaching moss. At the top of the stairs, he stepped over a thick vine, which had crawled up from the yard and now reached out for the front door in bursts of new sprouts. He could almost hear it growing, creeping across the boards. Autumnal wildflowers bloomed all around the house, and their perfume was layered over the heady aroma of chicory coffee wafting up from the cup in his hand.

"I'm waiting on a relative," said Augusta, walking to the far side of the veranda. "Her parents phoned me this morning to say she was coming to town. Lilith's father would have told her to pay a courtesy call before she even thought of sitting down to dinner."

She settled into a high-backed throne chair, the sturdiest

piece among the collection of aging wicker. As he sat down
beside her and gazed across the wide expanse of tall grass,
he understood why the porch furniture was clustered here
at the far end. *Now* he believed in Augusta's invisible ten-
foot hill. According to his guidebook, the levee was nearly
thirty feet high along this stretch of the river. Only the rise
of Augusta's land and the added footage of the brick foundation below them would have afforded this panoramic
view across the barrier.

Sea gulls dipped and soared, screamed and swooped
above the surging Mississippi. A majestic white steamboat
was heading downriver toward New Orleans and churning
the muddy water with her paddle wheel. He could see all
three tiers of the vessel's superstructure. For one moment
of magic, the great ship seemed to glide with perfect balance along the top of the earthen dike. He followed its slow
progress until he was distracted by the runner on the levee.

Against the backdrop of bright light reflected on the water, she was a lean, dark silhouette with the long legs of a
colt and the speed of a long-distance runner. She turned
down the steep incline of the embankment and was lost
behind the trees near Henry Roth's cottage.

"That would be Lilith Beaudare, my cousin's child,"
said Augusta.

He caught sight of the runner's shadow sprinting through
an exposed sliver of the cemetery and then disappearing
behind the cover of encircling trees.

The running woman had cleared that ground with amazing speed, appearing again at the foot of the oak alley to
his right. She had settled into a slower gait, jogging up the
dirt path toward the house. Charles could see the runner's
true colors now: the red of her T-shirt, the purple shorts—
the black skin.

He turned to the pale woman beside him.

In the manner of delivering the last line of a fine joke,
she said, "The world has changed, Charles. You must try
to keep up."

Augusta laughed, and he liked the sound of it, no matter that she was laughing at him.

"My cousin, Guy Beaudare, moved his family to New Orleans when Lilith was a little girl. They used to come back every summer for a visit—but no more. I haven't seen that child in years. It's strange that Lilith should turn up in Dayborn just after your friend was jailed." There was a caution in her voice as she leaned closer. "You should find it odd, too."

The young woman was walking toward them with an easy confident stride. Charles noted the detail of the serious competitor's track shoes. While the young woman was still out of earshot, Augusta smiled at him. "You think *Lilith* is dark? Her mother is so black she's blue—pure Africa."

As the introductions were made, Charles believed he saw African suns in Lilith Beaudare's eyes, twin orbs of yellow on the rise as she looked up to his face. Her black hair was cropped close to a finely shaped skull, and her lips were the color of plum wine. It was an intoxicating array of hue and form. She was a bit taller than her elder cousin, and he guessed her height as closer to Mallory's five foot ten.

After kissing Augusta on both cheeks, Lilith took his hand in hers, and she kept it a few moments too long for a first handshake. She was smiling, but not with her eyes.

"Lilith is on loan to Sheriff Jessop," said Augusta. "I think I mentioned that his deputy was in the hospital."

Charles detected a warning note in Augusta's tone. But six blunt questions into the conversation, he would have guessed Lilith's occupation anyway. Her style of conversation might have been off-balancing for some. The young woman never phrased a sentence that did not elicit—*demand*—information, and she left him no room for return volleys. But she had no edge, no leverage with him. Charles was long accustomed to the interrogation mode. Sometimes Mallory could not turn it off.

"How long have you known Augusta, Mr. Butler?"

"We met this afternoon."

Lilith leaned toward him to press her next question.

"And exactly what is your business with my cousin?"

Augusta waved her hands behind Lilith's back to stop his mouth. "Will you *listen* to that? She graduated from the police academy not two weeks ago, and she's already interrogating people." Augusta paused to glare at her young relation before the next rush of words. "Not that it's any of your business, Lilith—I hired him to investigate a woman who might be Cass Shelley's daughter. If she is, then it's time to turn over her mother's estate."

Augusta rose from her chair, and Charles stood up, taking this as his cue to leave.

The old woman lowered her eyes like gun sights. "In case your daddy never mentioned it, I'm the executrix. I've been collecting rents and paying taxes on the house since Cass died—and I'm tired of it. So as soon as Mr. Butler nails down the line of inheritance, I can get rid of that chore."

The young woman nodded and turned back to Charles. "Are you licensed in the state of—"

"That's enough, Lilith. Don't mess with my affairs again."

The two women locked eyes, and in this peculiar form of wrestling, the younger woman's gaze was beaten back—not sufficient experience in the world to outglare the old one, not yet.

"I expect you'll be wanting to get on with your business." Augusta reached out to shake his hand in farewell.

Charles said good evening to the women and walked back the way he had come, down the covered lane of oaks. A bird screamed after him, and other birds flew overhead as he crossed the open ground and entered the wide circle of trees.

A fat black starling perched on the roof of a tomb and followed him with its eyes and the cock of its head. As he walked on through the cemetery, he heard the flap of pursuing wings and felt a rush of air as the starling lit on a marble monument level with Charles's head. The creature pointed its sharp beak at his face. Its eyes were cold, showing no more emotion than a reptile.

He could well believe the theory that the dinosaur had not died off, but had taken wings and lived on in the smaller form of modern birds. A memory of majesty must survive in this one, for it looked upon Charles as no threat whatever—merely a man, an upstart creature in the scheme of time on earth.

He watched the black bird fly off toward the low-riding sun, and now he noticed that all the graves and monuments were aligned east to west. Perhaps local custom arranged the dead to face the sunrise, ancient symbol of resurrection.

Only one tomb was facing north.

Curious.

He went back to the rim of the cemetery and walked around this structure to stand before a door gated with intricate designs of ironwork and flanked by narrow windows of exquisite stained glass. At first, he placed the tomb in the colonial period, for it was showing the wear of ages: corners rounding and fissures running through the walls. And then he realized that it was constructed with a soft, porous stone. Given the fine craftsmanship of the tomb, this use of shoddy material made no sense at all.

Above the door was the bas-relief carving of a man's face, minus the nose which had crumbled to dust. The stone eyes were gazing through a break in the trees which allowed a view of Trebec House. The first name engraved over the door was lost to erosion, and the surname was barely legible.

Trebec?

Yes, that was it. Well, what would Mr. Trebec think of his ruined mansion now?

Charles walked around the tomb and headed for the path back to Henry Roth's house. Before leaving the ring of trees, he remembered one more anomaly and turned to Cass Shelley's monument, visible through a narrow alley of tombs. The stone angel was facing south.

And what was *she* looking at?

A gust of wind came ripping through the trees, tearing leaves away, and sighing off with them to the other end of the cemetery. The soft racket of thrashing branches stopped suddenly, as though the wind had closed a door behind it. The air was colder now and unnaturally still. No sound of insects, no birdcall. The stones were casting their longest shadows toward the close of day.

He felt a light breeze on his skin, as though someone unseen had just walked by, caressing his face in passing. His involuntary shiver was delicious.

Oh, what Cousin Max could have done with a stage like this.

Cemeteries were primed for the illusionist's art. The atmosphere alone would have done half the magician's work for him.

As Charles left the circle of trees and drew closer to Henry Roth's yard, he heard the sound of an engine. His own car sat in the wide driveway, its silver metal gleaming, throwing back light from the sunset sky. There was no other vehicle in sight. He approached the front door, already sensing the stillness of no one home. The sound of the engine stopped now, but suddenly, not tapering off down some road in the distance. It must be close by.

He followed the curving driveway as it wound around the house and past a large chicken coop attached to an empty garage. The meandering road led him into the trees and ended at the heart of a grove. A brace of heavy branches concealed the upper portion of an old chapel made of large, rough-hewn blocks of gray. Only the religious arches of the windows and the open doors were not obscured by leaves. A large and blocky tarpaulined shape lay in the bed of a red pickup truck parked in front of the building.

Charles rounded the truck and walked up a short flight of steps. He paused on the threshold and peered inside. Two massive skylights were set into the steep pitch of the high ceiling. Slow floating clouds of pink and gold seemed within grazing distance of the glass.

The vast room was full of day's end shadows. The pews and religious trappings were gone. At the back of the church, ghostly shapes in white drapes formed a circle on the raised floor where the altar had been. Uncovered sculptures stood about the room in a more casual arrangement and varying states of emergence from granite and marble. Many of these figures had wings and appeared to be flying out of their uncarved sections.

A small, delicate man came out of the shadows to dance with the tall statue of a woman. The strange couple glided past a long worktable, and now Charles could see the feet of the man and the wheeled pallet beneath his stone partner as he rolled her to the wall.

Charles would have called out, but remembered that Henry Roth only conversed in sign language and written notes. He came up behind the man as he was arranging a drape around the statue. With no hint of surprise, the sculptor turned to face his uninvited guest. Charles assumed the man had felt the warning vibrations of approaching footfalls on the wooden floorboards.

This person was neither white nor black, but a stunning new race of golden skin and light brown eyes with sparks of green. His hair was pure white and tightly kinked about his crown. The sculptor truly belonged in this company of angels, for his smile was charming and gentle as he spread his hands on the air. His face was an open question.

Charles fumbled for a moment, but the movements came back to him quickly enough. As a toddler, he had signed his words before he had ever spoken aloud. This was his first language, though he had abandoned it over the twenty years since his father's death. With broad gestures and finger spelling, his hands said, *"My name is Charles Butler. You are Mr. Roth?"*

The man nodded. Charles made more signs, his hands curving and pointing. When memory failed him, he spelled what he could not sign in a fluid movement. Here and there, he made a slip of the fingers and erred, but all the intricate nuances of tense and adverb were coming back to him as he stabbed the air and danced one hand in a circle. Facial expression gave depth to his feeling when he described his relationship to Kathy Mallory, whom Henry Roth would remember as young Kathy Shelley. He raised his brows to punctuate with a question mark when he asked for help. He tightened his lips for the sense of an emphatic exclamation point when he explained his dire need to see her again.

Only the ignorant believed that sign language was dumb show, simple mime. This graceful three-dimensional voice of hands flying through space, *this* was the true art of conversation. One gesture flowed smoothly into the flight of a bird, and then he finger-stepped across the stage of midair to describe the details of Augusta's ruse with Lilith—his role as Augusta's agent. And then, after one last plea for aid, Charles's hands fell silent.

Throughout the long and involved explanation of events, Henry Roth had been extremely attentive and patient. Now the man smiled broadly, and his hands said, *"I'm not deaf—only mute."* And then he laughed in silence as though this were a great joke, and Charles supposed it was.

"Sorry." Charles spoke aloud this time. "I shouldn't have assumed—"

"Everyone does," signed the mute. *"People in town have been assuming that for sixty-five years."* He went on to explain that he didn't mind, because people would say the most amazing things when they believed he couldn't hear them. *"I live in an eavesdropper's paradise."*

When the conversation came back to Mallory, Charles said, "I don't want to alarm her by barging in with no warning. She might be afraid I'd given something away to the sheriff."

Actually, she would just *assume* he had done that. Mallory knew she had wasted her time tutoring him in the sister arts of lies and poker. Despite his freakish IQ, she regarded him as learning disabled.

"So, would you prepare her for my visit? You could tell her Augusta will back up the story that I'm working for the estate. Will you help me?"

The sculptor used both hands, upturned and open, alternately moving them up and down, weighing one thing against another to say, *"Maybe."* He went on to say he *might* speak with Mallory, *perhaps* tomorrow—but only if it could be done without the sheriff asking questions, and that was unlikely. He did not enjoy the idea of lying to a man he had known for so many years, and Charles should not count on his help. Then his hands dropped back to his sides and hung there with nothing more to say.

Charles's hands rose, as though to speak, but instead, they splayed wide in helpless frustration. He lowered his eyes and nodded. "I understand." Of course he did. This man had no reason to trust him, to help him or lie for him.

Henry Roth shrugged to say that he could offer nothing more solid. And then his hands explained that he had work to do, and he must get on with it.

Charles followed the sculptor to the door and watched him unfold a metal ramp, extending it over the stone stairs to the back end of the truck. Now Roth unhinged two metal legs to level the ramp. He moved a rolling pallet in place near the open truck gate, and began to work the large canvas-covered shape from the flat bed, patiently rocking the massive stone and pulling it toward him.

Charles guessed, by metallic sounds, the pads beneath the stone must ride on ball bearings. Still, it was a tremendous weight, and this would be slow work for a man not much over five feet tall. Now he grasped the sculptor's problem of weight, balance and leverage. In a moment, he had doffed his suitcoat and rolled up his sleeves. "Allow me, please."

Henry Roth stood aside, and Charles pulled on the block until half of it jutted out from the bed of the truck. He eased it into an incline, and the bottom edge of the stone was sliding down toward the rolling pallet. As it touched the edge of the pallet, quickly, with one foot, he moved the rolling platform underneath it. Braced against the truck bed, the block was leveraged into an upright position. Next, he put his shoulder to the stone and pushed it along the ramp until it was housed inside the sculptor's studio.

The man smiled his thanks, then signed, *"It takes me an hour to unload a block that size."*

Roth locked the doors, and the two men walked away from the chapel and back toward the house. Now the sculptor made a firm date to meet at the town square in the morning, for he had thought of a way to avoid the sheriff and his questions.

Charles was still smiling as his Mercedes pulled out of the driveway. He traveled back along the dirt road, circling around the cemetery. Near the bridge was a signpost topped by a board in the shape of an arrow and weathered to blank, gray wood. All that remained of its lettering was an ironic *y* at the edge of the board. The mystery arrow pointed down a side road, a dark and narrow tunnel through dense woods of low-hanging branches. A notice posted on a near tree warned him not to enter the swamp by Finger Bayou, a narrow waterway running alongside the nameless road.

The sign for Upland Bayou was freshly painted and fixed to the metal girders of the bridge. This wider body of slow moving water was black in the evening hour and edged with a lace of pale green algae. Along the banks, the tree limbs were draped with gray beards of Spanish moss. On the far shore, wooden houses perched on feet of brick, and small flat-bottom boats were moored to gray wharves standing over the water on stilts.

At the other end of the bayou bridge, he was offered a choice of paved roads. To his right was the turnoff for the main highway and green fields of sugarcane extending out to the horizon line. He turned hard left toward the town. On both sides of Dayborn Avenue, the houses sat on conventional foundations, children played in the front yards, and windows lighted, one by one, as people returned home from work. Except for the warm weather and the occasional banana tree, he might be anywhere in America at the close of an autumn day.

When he rolled into the town square, his vista widened and perception altered radically. He was back in time. It

was everything the brochure from the Dayborn Bed and
Breakfast had promised—a collage of architectural history.
The formal Georgian structure at the far end of the square
must be the municipal building. Its walls were painted Federal green, and the white rooftop cupola mimicked a capitol
dome.

The square was flanked by Italianate row houses of brick
and mortar in hues of purple, pink, blue and yellow. Graceful galleries of ornate iron lace supported flowerpots in a
smaller riot of colors above the ground-level storefronts.

He pulled his car to the curb in front of the hotel. There
were private homes of Gothic Revival on either side, but
this massive Colonial before him was the oldest building
of all. The slanted roof of the bed and breakfast sported
five gables and a chimney at either end, and its dark shingles sloped down to the support posts of the front porch.

He carried his suitcases up the stairs and met his hostess,
Betty Hale, a white-haired woman of generous size and a
more than generous smile. After the formality of checking
in and depositing the bags in his room, she led him back
out to the front porch and gently pressured him to sit down
alongside the other guests, whose chairs were lined up by
the rail like spectators at a sporting event. They were all
facing north and holding field glasses to their eyes.

Betty unstrapped her own binoculars and put them in his
hand. "Mr. Butler, I'm so sorry you missed the evening
bat races. But if you look real quick, you can still see some
of the losers."

He followed the point of her finger to the triangular peak
of Augusta Trebec's house above the distant trees. He focussed the twin lenses on the tiny silhouettes of three bats
flying upward from the roof. They were backlit by clouds
which had lost all their color after sundown.

"Now look across the square, above the sheriff's office," said Betty, speaking to the larger audience and di-
recting them to the south side of the municipal building.
All heads turned in unison. "You see that light that just
came on? See the bars on the window? That's where they

keep the woman who murdered Babe Laurie, though that's not her window. Hers faces the alley between the sheriff's office and the fire department.''

She tapped Charles on the shoulder, speaking only to him. ''You can see a real good likeness of her in the cemetery tomorrow morning—if you want to take the tour with the other guests. It's included in the cost of your room.''

Charles was so startled, he only caught the odd word in Betty Hale's ongoing monologue of breakfast and checkout times. This was even more inconceivable than the murder charge—Mallory had become a tourist attraction.

He slumped low in his chair, and stared at the window above the sheriff's office.

So there you are. So close.

He remained on the porch long after the other guests had retired to their rooms, or gone off in search of evening meals with Betty's advice on local cuisine. Long after nightfall, when the house lights had gone out, he was still sitting in the same chair, fixated on the light in the window across the square, until that too flickered out.

Good night, Mallory.

CHAPTER

3

THE HOUR WAS late, but Lilith Beaudare remained with her elder cousin until they were caught up on family stories to fill in all the years since the last visit.

The old woman's face glowed in the flame of a match. She lit a cheroot and exhaled blue smoke into the night air.

"You know," said Lilith, in the lecture mode, "you shouldn't smoke. You want to be wheezing with emphysema in the golden years of your life?"

"You're absolutely right," said Augusta. "I would quit this minute if I had any sense." Smoke swirled around her as she spoke. "I should practice discipline and self-denial."

Lilith nodded.

Augusta continued. "Then, when I'm ninety years old and blind with cataracts, when I'm crippled with arthritis and my breasts have been hacked off for tumors—I'll be able to say, well thank God I don't have *emphysema*." Augusta threw back her head and laughed. Her bubbling voice had a wicked young character.

All the wrinkles, the deep lines, every detail of Augusta's age was lost in the dark. Here was the lean, unbowed body and long, flowing hair of the famed beauty who, shot for shot, had drunk many a young man under the table—the better to take advantage of them in the love affair and the equally bloody war of a business transaction.

Augusta had also been a legendary horsewoman. As a small child, Lilith had been enthralled by the sight of her elder cousin riding bareback along the top of the levee. And best of all was that moment when Augusta had turned her horse down the steep slope of the dike, riding home to earth. The horse's massive body had obscured the action of its legs, and the animal appeared to fly down from the road in the sky. Whenever Lilith thought back on that day, she remembered the horse with wings.

Now Augusta's laughter subsided.

"I saw the angel when I passed through the cemetery," said the younger woman, casually, as though this might be idle conversation. It was not.

"There are *sixteen* angels in that cemetery." Augusta tipped back the last of her coffee and reached for the pot on the small wicker table by her chair.

Lilith repressed an urge to caution her cousin on the dangers of caffeine. "I mean *the* angel. I forgot how beautiful Cass Shelley was. So the prisoner is really Kathy?"

"If I knew that, I wouldn't need Mr. Butler's help, would I?"

Augusta was betraying a trace of temper, and Lilith knew she was onto something. "But you've heard talk in town. You think it—"

"Don't insult me," said Augusta, and the subtext of her sarcasm was clear—Idle conversation my *ass*.

"I'm just curious is all," Lilith lied.

"*Fine*. We'll just pretend I *am* the addled old woman you take me for." Augusta settled back in her chair, but the tension between them was strung tight. "Let's say the prisoner *is* Kathy. Remember, she was born in Louisiana, and I do believe the strategy of a woman comes with the mother's milk. But I'm told she talks like a northerner. Must have been up there all this time. So now the southern woman and the northern woman meet in one brain and one body.'' She turned to Lilith and smiled with no intention of kindness. "Now there's a hellish piece of work. Does that scare you, Lilith? It should."

The younger woman pressed her lips together in a hard line to stifle the remark that would put her on Augusta's bad side.

The old woman went on. "Oh, I know what you're up to. But if I had to bet on the outcome, I wouldn't give even money for your chances."

Lilith began to hum a tune as she pushed off with her feet to rock on the back legs of her chair, working off the angry energy. She watched her cousin out of the corner of one eye, and then she smiled to see Augusta looking back in the same way. She sought out safer ground for conversation. "You still ride your horse along the top of the levee?"

"No, I never ride anymore." Augusta said this with the rare tone of defeat. "I had a bad fall one year. Broke my leg, and it took forever to mend. I don't have time to be laid up with another injury. Time is precious."

The sudden howl of an animal made Lilith tuck in a breath and sit up a little straighter. "That was the wolf."

"Oh, *stop,* Lilith." The red coal of the cheroot made an impatient streak in the dark as Augusta waved her hand. "You're too old for that game."

"I know that howl." Indeed, this was the strongest memory of her early childhood in Dayborn. "That was Daddy's wolf."

"It was nothing of the kind—only an old dog." There was a tired smile in Augusta's voice. "Your father was pulling your leg when he told you that story. You *know* that."

Yes, she did. In one pragmatic room of Lilith's mind, she knew her father had created the wolf for her. But there was another room where she kept her father's gifts: his poetic blind faith in things unseen, and the power of that faith.

"There has never been a wolf in these parts—not ever," said Augusta.

And Lilith knew this was fact. But in that room, her father's gentle voice was saying, *"Lil, if you can only catch that wolf, he will infinitely increase your life."*

As though Augusta were arguing against this inner voice, she said, "He only told you that tall tale when he had it in mind to raise him a little track star."

"When you catch him, when that moment comes, your life will be changed."

"Oh Lord, how you did run to see that wolf."

"Hear him howl, Lil? Isn't he magnificent?"

"But all the time, it was only Kathy's dog," said Augusta. "And that's him wailing now."

And it did sound more like a wail for the dead, tapering off to a mournful crooning, ending with a whimper. The animal was crying.

"But he can't be alive. No way. He'd be more than *twenty* years old." Lilith had kept faith with a winged horse and a wolf she had yet to see, but she could not believe that a common dog had lived well past the century mark in the canine's translation to human years.

"It *is* an indecent age for a dog." Augusta exhaled a perfect smoke ring. "Every time I leased out Cass's house, I always told the old story of the murder and how the dog missed little Kathy. All the renters were good sports. They even fed him. And I might've kept that house occupied. But after a while, the renters began to realize that the dog was insane."

Lilith turned away, preferring her father's wolf to the half-dead dog haunting the yard of the old Shelley house.

Augusta's voice droned on in the background of her thoughts.

"In any case, you never want to chase down a wolf, Lilith. Ever think of what you'd do when you caught up with it?"

·   ·   ·

THE OLD BLACK dog's hind leg was working as he ran through his dream, pacing himself to the towheaded child with green eyes. It was toward the violent end of the dream that he moaned and rolled over in the dirt to expose all his old scars to the moon, every wound that was not concealed by his pelt. The pain of old injuries woke him again, and he felt the real and solid world all around him.

He was alone.

His head dropped low as he did the dog's version of bitter tears. Then came a fresh spate of howling. It was one of those rare phases of weather when the wind carried his night music everywhere, even into Owltown.

AT THE EDGE of Dayborn was its unacknowledged spawn, a crescent cluster of shacks and mobile homes on blocks, a main street of neon lights that glowed all night, and drunks who did not fall down until the first light of dawn. Though it was a legal partition of Dayborn, the older residents pretended it was not. When they had occasion to refer to the sprawling blight on the lower bayou, they called it Owltown.

Alma Furgueson, who lived in this place, rose in her bed and listened to the dog's voice. She wished someone would put that demented creature out of his misery and hers. She would do it herself, but she could not bear to go back to the Shelley house again.

She gripped the edge of her blanket and drew it up over her face. Though she was past fifty, she reacted to her fears with the solutions of a child. She left her bed and went to the closet, hiding herself away at the back and pulling the door shut.

Alma sat very still, but her body was hard at work, a damned factory of emotions, slopping great dollops of tears through her eyes, pouring acid into her stomach and churning up the bile. A scream was rising in her throat, and a heavy weight of guilt was resting on her breast, like a lump of something cancerous, inciting fear and daring her to look at it. And so, though she sat in the blackness of a closet, she shut her eyes.

But fear would not be deterred, and it flooded her brain with ugly pictures. There was no place to hide.

IN THE TOWN square of Dayborn, in the house next to the bed and breakfast, Darlene Wooley listened to her son screaming in the next room. It was not the pain in his broken hands; he had taken pills for that.

Kathy's dog ceased to wail, and Ira's screaming stopped. Her son had moved on to a hiding place in some other dream.

That was a small mercy, for whenever she had to wake him from a nightmare, to put her hands on him and shake him out of the dream, the fear in his eyes destroyed her. He would always push her away, batting at her hands, repulsed by every demonstration of mother love. And that was the worst of it, because she loved him so.

She stood by her bedroom window, sending silent prayers to the dog, asking him not to howl anymore, please, not tonight.

Let him be. Let my child alone.

There was no way to comfort Ira without knowing what had happened to him all those years ago. He could never tell her. From the age of six, her child's communication had been mostly musical—ripples of piano keys and snatches of sung songs. But she was not a musical woman, and all of Ira's conversations remained one-sided.

So many questions had gone unanswered, and they continued to nag at her. Sometimes Darlene half expected the vanished Cass Shelley to come back, to knock on her door, to sit down with her over a cup of coffee and explain away each dark shadow on Darlene's life and the content of Ira's dreams.

Her son screamed again. She could hear the thrashing in the next room. Oh, he was awake now and beating his head against the bedstead.

Darlene ran into Ira's room. As she came toward him, he stopped his frantic motions and stared at her with big eyes, the child's unconscious signal to be held and hugged out of his fears. This was a perversity that drove her crazy, for if she tried to hold him, he would scream again, as though she had stabbed him.

He was full-grown now, but his body was small and slender. His face was thin, making his eyes seem larger, more vulnerable in their plea for comfort. She longed to cradle him in her arms, but instead, she clasped her hands behind her back to reassure him that she would not. She only stood by his bed until he felt safe again, until he drifted back to sleep and escaped from Kathy's dog.

Long after Darlene had returned to her own bed, she lay awake.

THE OTHER WOMAN, on the floor of the closet in Owltown, was also awake. Her fists were grinding into her eye sockets, madly at work erasing the pictures in her mind. Alma Furgueson only wanted to forget. She had been there; she had seen it all from beginning to end; but she had understood it no better than Darlene Wooley, who had seen nothing at all.

LILITH BEAUDARE SAID good night and left Augusta to her chronic insomnia.

Running down the covered lane of oaks and into the woods, her feet pounded on the hard dirt until she entered the cemetery. She sprinted across the sacred ground, keeping to the soft grass, crunching gravel when she crossed a path. She was running on packed dirt again as she sped along the road by Henry Roth's cottage and climbed up to the top of the levee. Her long legs were flowing across the high road as she looked down at Dayborn. The glowing streetlamps mapped out the town beyond the trees.

Running was her passion, always chasing the wolf—not

an old, half-blind dog, but something sleek and powerful. She had evolved a personal mythology around this animal: He was the metaphor for a moment just ahead of her in time, "the powerful, the uncommon"—Rilke's "awakening of stones."

Tonight, Augusta had voiced Lilith's greatest fear. When she did catch up to the wolf, what then? If she failed to recognize the moment, it would be just another tick of the clock, and she would be condemned to an ordinary life.

In successive scenarios, she plotted out her strategy: *The wolf is slowly turning round. What now?*

Lilith was deep in the euphoria of the runner's high, and in the bizarre contradiction of a devout atheist, she believed she could reach out and touch the face of God and His gleaming white fangs. While in this state of grace, the strain and effort fell away from her body. She lost the awareness of feet lighting to ground; the earth itself fell away, and she was flying down the side of the levee.

The dog cried out again, and Lilith's epiphany was shattered.

Her feet touched down on the hard-packed dirt of level ground. She looked into the blackness of the trees ahead and shivered when a breeze slipped up behind her in the dark to lick the sweat off her skin.

THE PRISONER LAY on her back, staring up at the ceiling. Golden rectangles floated there, a play of shadows and the yellow light of a streetlamp bouncing off an alley wall to shine on the window bars.

Mallory was listening to her dog howling, reminding her that she had not yet made it all the way home.

CHAPTER

4

AT EIGHT O'CLOCK in the morning, Lilith Beaudare was officially sworn in as a deputy of St. Jude Parish, but her new job title was "girl." This was what Sheriff Tom Jessop called her, sometimes using the variation "Hey, girl."

At half past the hour, a gray-haired, beefy woman named Jane, of Jane's Cafe, had expanded on this theme, saying, "Hey, little girl, I guess I can find the cell by myself. I don't need no escort." Jane had then brushed by Lilith to trundle the prisoner's breakfast tray up the stairs to the holding cells, leaving the brand-new deputy with no way to stop the woman—short of a bullet in the back.

Oh, hadn't *that* been a temptation.

And there were other disappointments. Lilith glared at an antique telephone, which predated push buttons by fifty years. This toy-size police department was a damn museum. Not one stick of furniture belonged to the current century, and there were only a few pieces of semimodern equipment.

Like everything else on her desk, the early-model computer was covered with a film of dust. The fax had scrolled out a dozen pages, and by their dates, she knew the machine had gone ignored since Deputy Travis's heart attack. Apparently, the computer and the fax had been Travis's domain, and now it was hers.

She had yet to see the famous prisoner. Sheriff Jessop was still upstairs in the small cell block, while Lilith was tied to a telephone that never rang.

Her desk faced the open door to the sheriff's private office. The St. Jude Parish Historical Society had not spared this room either. The ornate mahogany desk was handcrafted. Antique guns of the early 1800s hung in glass display cases. The yellowed map on the back wall was made long before the levee was built; the winding Mississippi flowed on a different course, and the land was free of the chemical plants in the column of pollution that marched up the River Road to Baton Rouge. And every building framed in the office window was antebellum, offering a view on the past, when cotton was king and the unforgiven Civil War had yet to be waged and lost.

Lilith decided that Dayborn was definitely a town in denial—bad losers on a grand scale.

Beyond the sheriff's cluttered desk was a credenza piled high with papers, books and a black leather duffel bag which threatened to slide to the floor at any moment. She recognized the bright orange identification tag which marked the bag as evidence. This must be the prisoner's property, surrendered by the hotelkeeper, Betty Hale, on the day of Babe Laurie's murder.

Lilith glanced at the staircase to her right. The ancient steps could be depended upon to creak when the sheriff came down again. She softly padded into his office and opened the duffel. Inside was a .357 Smith & Wesson revolver. It had been placed in a clear plastic bag, though her law enforcement handbook clearly stated paper was the best way to protect fingerprints on a slick surface.

She shook her head in a sad commentary on the state of the older generation.

Now she examined the clothes. The running shoes were top of the line, and the blue jeans bore a designer label on the pocket. The blazer had all the fine detail of a hand-tailored garment, but there was only a rectangle of tiny holes in the lining where the maker's label should be. Except for the silk underwear, there were no personal items, nothing to pin the prisoner to a name or a place.

In the side compartment, she found a bundle of wires and a small metal box the size of a pack of cigarettes. There was a silver pick clipped to one side to work a miniature keyboard, but it couldn't be a palm computer. Without a light display, what good was it? Yet it had computer ports at the base. Perhaps it was a component for the laptop resting in the next pocket. She pulled out the more conventional computer and powered up, but when she tried to enter a file, the main directory dissolved, not even offering her one try at the lockout password.

Clever.

So the prisoner was computer oriented, fancied guns with maximum killing power, shopped in better stores than a deputy could afford, and she had taken some care to avoid being traced.

Lilith restored all the items to the duffel bag and returned to her desk. At precisely nine o'clock, as the sheriff had requested, she contacted the FBI to ask if they had made any progress on tracing the gun's serial number. An FBI agent said no. After a few seconds of silence, she asked if they had gotten anywhere with the comparisons on the test bullet. Again, the agent said no, and there were other words to the effect of "Don't call us, we'll call you." On the pretext of delivering this latest bulletin of no value whatever, she climbed the staircase to the three holding cells, only one of which was occupied.

Lilith hesitated by the door at the top of the stairs. She opened it carefully, not wanting to squeak the hinge. She had already annoyed the sheriff once this morning with the squeal of the unoiled joints in her swivel chair. He had thrown a can of oil at her and shouted instructions for its use, as if she might be only half bright.

She had no memories of the sheriff from her childhood in Dayborn. His friendship with her father had been conducted over bottles in the Dayborn Bar and Grill. But this was surely not the same Tom Jessop her father liked to remember as a better man and a bigger one. Guy Beaudare had described him as a personality larger than life. All those years ago, even the sheriff's blue eyes had been different— brighter—like onrushing headlights. Or so said her father, the storyteller, the mythmaker.

Somehow, Sheriff Jessop had regressed into a smaller man, or maybe he had become just another man like any other. Over the years since her family had moved away, there had been more profound departures from her father's memories.

When she opened the door, the sheriff was standing in the narrow corridor before the middle cell. His gut paunched over his belt, and his once thick black hair had gone to the iron-gray widow's peak of a receding hairline. Where his Stetson had protected his high forehead, it was ivory white in sharp contrast to his sunburnt nose and jowls.

The sheriff moved away from the cell to lean his back against the wall of the small corridor, and she had her first look at the prisoner called Mallory, who wore a gingham dress with "St. Jude Parish Jail" stamped on the pocket.

Lilith sucked in her breath.

This was the cemetery angel come to life. The young woman's hair grazed her shoulders in curls of burnished gold. Lilith could swear the blond aureole was leaching light from every quarter of the small cell, and growing brighter still. The eyes were an unnatural shade of green with the concentration of a stalking animal. The prisoner's gaze fixed on Lilith—as though the new deputy might be lunch. But then Mallory's eyes passed her over, apparently not that hungry—not yet anyway.

Though the prisoner was caged, Lilith's hand reflexively touched her holstered gun, for she had erred. This woman was far removed from the stone angel. This one belonged to an entirely different god.

The sheriff was speaking to Mallory in the voice that adults reserved for innocent children.

Fool. Didn't he have eyes to see?

And now she realized that the sheriff was not seeing Mallory at all, but looking inward at a memory of little Kathy Shelley, who was not quite seven years old.

"So, Kathy," said the sheriff, taking a cigarette out of his pocket and fitting it into the side of his mouth. "Tell me something." With no hurried motions, he opened a box of matches, lit the cigarette and watched the smoke rise and curl into the bars of the cell. "What's it like coming home again after all these years?"

"It's not so bad," said Mallory. "If you don't mind waiting around all day for people to finish their sentences." And now she said to the wall, "Don't call me Kathy."

Sheriff Jessop's head snapped right. He was suddenly aware of Lilith standing at the end of the corridor. "What is it? Speak up!"

"I called the FBI, sir." Lilith's voice had come out small and weak.

Shit.

She squared off her shoulders, and, louder, she said, "They don't know where the gun came from, but they're still working on it, sir."

"Well, missy, thank you very much for dragging yourself all the way up here to give me that worthless piece of news. Now get back down there where you belong. Watch those phones."

She bit down on her lip, lest some smartass remark escape. It wouldn't do to get fired off the job on the first day. As Cousin Augusta had surmised, Lilith was a woman with ambitions.

The sheriff's face was reddening, an early warning sign of foul temper. "What the hell are you waiting on, girl?"

And now the prisoner had her attention again. Mallory was smiling. It was not a happy smile, but disquieting and full of contempt. She was staring at Lilith when she leaned into the bars and said, "You shouldn't let him call you *girl*, unless you get to call him *fat boy*."

The sheriff pointed his finger at the deputy and said, "Move, girl! Now!"

And Lilith moved, slamming the door behind her and taking the steps two at a time in her descent.

When she hit the bottom of the stairs, she found herself staring into the angry eyes of a middle-aged woman with a gray suit and an attitude problem. The woman yelled at her and jabbed the air with one finger, as if it were the barrel of a loaded gun leveled at the new deputy's face.

Beyond the yelling woman was a slight young man near Lilith's own age. He had the yelling woman's same hazel eyes, rimmed with thick lashes, and the light brown hair was her coloring too. But, unlike her, his expression was utterly peaceful—too peaceful. Both his hands were bandaged.

Could he be on medication?

Then he began to move his hands in slow circles, one rolling over the other. This simple activity seemed to capture his whole attention.

I know you, don't I?

Yes. He was still dressing in his trademark red socks and a red shirt neatly tucked into his blue jeans. Much of the familiar child still hung about him in the aspect of innocence and in this old habit of the rolling hands. The other children had called him the idiot, and at the age of six, she had believed this was his name. Her father had roughly corrected her, applying his large hand to the seat of her pants until she learned to call the boy by his true name.

"Hello, Ira," said Lilith. "How are you?"

The yelling woman was suddenly mollified by this small courtesy. Her angry face relaxed into a smile, and she was almost pretty when she turned to her son. "Say hello to the deputy, Ira."

"Say hello to the deputy," Ira said.

CHAPTER

CHARLES BUTLER STARED at the drugstore window display. Stacks of multicolored T-shirts were emblazoned with the name and likeness of the murdered evangelist. One bit of T-shirt art depicted the Virgin Mary holding an infant with Babe Laurie's adult face. Beyond this novel heresy was a rack of paperback books and shelves crowded with sunglasses and dental floss. Toothbrushes kept company with cellophane-packaged voodoo dolls and all the other little things that tourists might have forgotten to bring with them.

Charles turned back to the alley between the sheriff's office and the fire department. The mute sculptor had located Mallory's cell. Henry Roth was staring up at the second-floor window and making conversation with his hands. Charles walked across the square to listen in with his eyes.

As he neared the municipal building, his gaze was pulled toward another man seated on a wooden bench in front of the sheriff's office. Charles noted the resemblance to the face on the T-shirts. The general features were the same, but not so dramatic. And unlike the wild-eyed Babe Laurie, intelligence was more in evidence here. He was perhaps thirty-five years old. His long hair was the color of sand, and it brushed the collar of his denim shirt. His eyes were blue and serene as he nodded a greeting in the familiar way of an old friend.

Charles found himself drifting toward this man, for the invitation was clear and compelling. *Come to me,* said the tranquil expression. *Sit and talk awhile,* said his glance to the empty side of the bench.

Then Charles remembered that he had business elsewhere, very pressing business, and he turned away with the slightly disoriented feeling of awakening. In the next moment, the man on the bench was forgotten as he moved closer to the mouth of the alley and concentrated on reading the silent language of Henry Roth.

The sculptor's eyes were fixed on the second-floor window. A pair of white hands appeared at the bars, signaling back to him. Charles read the words off her fingers. *"Tell him to go away."*

Henry Roth glanced at him and shrugged, then turned his face up to her window, hands flying in conversation.

Charles was staring at his shoes. *Go away?* He had traveled more than a thousand miles for *that*?

He turned his back on them and walked off to the fountain at the center of the square. Water flowed from ornate spigots and splashed into a large basin. Atop the fountain pranced a saddled but riderless bronze stallion. Charles was facing the horse's rear end.

How fitting.

He paced one turn around the wide pool of water, ruminating over all the sleep he had lost on her account, all the anxiety she had caused. Done with feeling sorry for himself, anger won out over deeply ingrained good manners. He decided to disregard her wishes, and he fairly flew up the stairs to the sheriff's office and pushed through the front door.

When he entered the reception area, the first person he saw was Augusta's young cousin. Her short-sleeved tan uniform was so crisply starched, he knew the fabric would crack before it wrinkled. Lilith Beaudare was wiping the screen of her desktop computer. The dust cloth moved in listless circles, for her attention was focussed on the scene in the private office at the far side of the room. And now Charles also looked through this open doorway.

A woman in a gray suit was standing before a man in rolled-up shirtsleeves and jeans. A six-pointed golden star was pinned to the lapel of a wrinkled linen blazer which lay carelessly draped on a chair back. Though he was more casually dressed than the woman, he exuded authority. His arms folded across his chest to tell her that whatever she wanted, she wasn't getting it. The woman's hands were placed on her hips to say she would not be moved until she had satisfaction from this man.

Standing near this couple was a young man with vacuous eyes and no apparent relationship to either of them. He was slender with an innocent, unlined face and bandages on both his hands.

As Charles drew nearer to the office door, Deputy Lilith Beaudare glanced up at him, but she said nothing. They eavesdropped in easy companionship.

"I have a statement from Malcolm," said the sheriff, addressing the woman with the light brown hair. "Malcolm says Babe asked your boy, real polite, if he would please stop playing the same damn five notes over and over again. The boy went wild and attacked Babe. Malcolm says his brother just defended himself."

The woman stared at the sheriff as if he had just flown down from the moon, an alien land of strange custom and law. "Babe *defended* himself? By breaking Ira's fingers with a *piano lid*?"

Exasperated, she threw up her hands, perhaps wondering if these words had the same meaning in Lunarspeak. "When did you ever know my boy to do any violence? Ira hates any kind of physical contact, and you damn well know it! That should have been your first clue that Malcolm Laurie was lying."

The young man with the bandaged hands stood just outside the fray in body and mind, utterly captivated by the slow-moving blades of the ceiling fan directly above him. Head tilted back, eyes trancegazing, his body moved in a circular sway. He seemed unconcerned with his mother's complaint, or even aware that she was in the room.

"Well, seeing that Babe is dead," the sheriff countered, "it doesn't make much sense to file charges against him, now does it, Darlene?"

"That's not what I come about." Darlene was rummaging in a black purse hanging off her shoulder by a thin strap. "That young girl you arrested? I want to pay her bail. If she did kill that little bastard, it's the least I can do to thank her." Darlene produced a checkbook and a pen.

The sheriff waved her off. "There's no bail for the prisoner."

"Tom Jessop, you have no right to keep that child in jail. You don't know she did it. For all you know, *I* could have killed him. You never thought of that, did you?"

Sheriff Jessop smiled. "Well now, Darlene, that just isn't true. I thought so much of your prospects, I had you at the top of my suspect list—right in front of Babe Laurie's widow and that youngster in the cell. Hell, I ain't got around to suspecting a single man *yet*. That's how highly I prize a woman as killer material. The Dayborn Women's Club is gonna make me damn Feminist of the Year."

The sheriff sat down in the green leather armchair behind what was possibly the messiest desk Charles had ever seen. The man swiveled his chair to face the window, saying goodbye to Darlene with his back.

But she would not be dismissed. She walked around the desk to stand by the window and call his attention back to her. "Nobody asked where *I* was when Babe Laurie was murdered."

"Didn't need to." His words were distracted, but now he smiled again and seemed to be gathering the energy he needed for one more round with her. "I know your car took off in the same direction as Malcolm and Babe. But they stopped at the gas station—you went flying toward the hospital. And I do mean flying.''

He swiveled around to face his desk and the sprawling loose piles of papers and folders. He reached into the mess, plucked out a sheet of handwritten text and held it up to her, waving it like a flag. ''Manny, the gas jockey? This is his statement. He was just real impressed with your driving.''

The sheriff reached into the middle of another loose arrangement of paper and pulled out a second sheet. Charles wondered how he had managed that, for there was no discernible order to this paper storm which resembled the aftermath of vandalism.

''Now this is the doctor's statement. He said you left the hospital sometime after dark.'' The sheriff let this sheet waft back to the desk. Then he sat back and splayed his hands in the air, perhaps to show her that he had nothing up his sleeves—though Charles was convinced that the desktop filing system was a magic act.

''I *am* sorry, Darlene. Your alibi is solid. However, I do admire your competitive spirit.''

Though she did not stamp her foot, anyone could see that she wanted to. ''Tom, you got to allow bail—that's the law!''

''Not in a murder case I don't. She was carrying a concealed weapon, a damn cannon of a gun.''

Darlene leaned down until her face was within a few inches of the sheriff's, and now it was her turn to smile. ''Exactly how many times was the victim shot with the *rock*?''

''Shit.'' And the sheriff did look as though he had just stepped on a dog turd. ''Is there anybody in town that doesn't know about that damn rock?''

Tom Jessop stood up now, the better to look down at Darlene. From this high ground, he said, ''Rock or gun, it doesn't matter—it was a very thorough job with clear intent to kill. I have to figure she had some purpose for that gun, whether she used it on him or not.''

Darlene folded her arms. "It's all supposition. You don't even have a motive. You can't hold her."

The sheriff countered, "Clerking for a lawyer don't make you one, Darlene. It so happens I can hold her as a material witness. She's already demonstrated willingness of flight."

"If that *is* Kathy in there, then you know damn well she was a month shy of seven years old when she made that flight."

"It still fits the criteria. But don't you worry—I'm keeping an open mind. Haven't charged anybody yet. So I'll give some more thought to *your* alibi, if you like. Hell, I'd be happy to put you in a cell just to pacify you, but who'd look after Ira?"

Darlene smashed her checkbook back into her purse, and turned to her son. "Ira, we're leaving!"

The young man continued to stare at the ceiling. Darlene moved one hand across Ira's line of vision, dislodging his gaze from the blades of the fan. She was not touching him, but gesturing with both hands to herd him across the room.

Suddenly, she was caught up short by the sight of Charles filling out the doorway—all six feet, four inches of him. No one could help but notice him. It was like trying to avoid a Kodiak bear in the shower stall.

"Good afternoon. My name is Charles Butler." He felt almost apologetic for looming over these people of normal size. "I'm here to see a woman called Mallory."

"I would never have guessed that."

But, by the sheriff's tone, Charles gathered the man had grown weary of Mallory's visitors.

"Now don't tell me," said the sheriff, closing the door behind the retreating Darlene and her son. "You're from New York City, right?"

"Yes," said Charles, standing before him in a Savile Row suit, handmade Italian shoes, an oxford shirt, and a silk tie from Galeries Lafayette in Paris. "How did you know?"

"Saw the license plate on your car outside of Betty's.

Had to be your car—it goes with that three-piece suit.'' Sheriff Jessop sat down and motioned Charles to take a seat in the chair by his desk.

The sheriff picked up a stack of papers to expose an aged manila envelope with writing in faded blue ink. He opened it and pulled out a sheet of yellowed paper. Attached was a photograph which Charles easily recognized as Mallory the child. Her foster father, Louis Markowitz, had carried a similar portrait in his wallet until the day he died.

''When she was a little kid, her name was Kathy Shelley.'' The sheriff dipped one hand into his shirt pocket and grasped a gold chain. ''The only name we got for her now is Mallory. That's the name engraved inside this watch, following a slew of Markowitzes.''

He was holding up Louis's pocket watch—Mallory's inheritance. It twirled on the chain, precious metal softly gleaming in the morning light. Charles would have known it from a thousand other timepieces. On the cover of its case was the familiar figure of a solitary wanderer crossing open country. Clouds had been wrought on the golden sky; a master engraver had given them motion and direction, and it was possible to see that the wanderer was walking against the wind.

''So, Mr. Butler,'' said the sheriff, calling him out of his fugue. ''Is she using Mallory for her first name or her last?''

''Oh, I'm sorry. You misunderstand. I'm not here at the request of the prisoner.'' That was true enough—too true. ''I represent Augusta Trebec, the executrix of the Shelley estate.''

The sheriff sat well back in his chair, more wary now. ''So what are you then—a lawyer or a private investigator?'' It was more an accusation than a question.

''Neither one. I'm only doing a favor for Miss Trebec.'' Knowing that Mallory, the consummate liar, would have cautioned him to mix in more than equal parts of truth with every lie, he said, ''Generally, I work with government agencies and universities. I evaluate people with odd talents, and then I find applications for their gifts.''

''Odd talents? Well, you come to the right place.'' The sheriff pointed to the window beside his desk. Charles could see the woman and her son crossing the square and heading for the cafe.

''That boy, Ira Wooley? He's an idiot savant and a world-class piano player. He can rip off any tune he hears but once. Oh, but you should hear him sing. He has perfect pitch and a voice like a damn angel. Now what do you make of that, Mr. Butler?''

''Well, his mother mentioned a revulsion for physical contact. And then there was his preoccupation with the ceiling fan.'' Charles leaned closer to the window to watch the boy's progress across the square. ''Judging by his rather good coordination, and without any evidence of retardation—I would have guessed he was autistic. So the correct term is '*autistic* savant.' ''

And now Charles realized he had been telling the sheriff what he already knew. He had also passed a test of sorts and allayed this man's suspicions.

The sheriff seemed less interested in his visitor as he turned back to the window. Ira and his mother were passing through a doorway under the sign for Jane's Cafe. ''Years ago, a damn schoolteacher pronounced Ira an idiot savant, and the words stuck to him. Most people shortened it to 'the idiot,' like they forgot Ira ever had a name. Bastards.''

He turned back to Charles, his mood more affable now. ''We did have one other odd talent you might've liked even better. The late Babe Laurie was a born orator. He was preaching the gospel at the age of five. I'll bet you've never come across a gift like that.''

Oh, but he had. In the prairie states, it was a talent as common as cornstalks. The rarer, more impressive gift was Ira's. Charles had always been fascinated with savants. But he was even more intrigued with Ira's connection to Mallory, his part in the chain of odd events occurring within the hour of Mallory's homecoming.

Lilith Beaudare entered the room with a handful of faxes.

She did not even glance at Charles to let on that they had met before. Now that was another odd thing, and he filed it away in his growing collection.

"The extradition on Mrs. Laurie has gone through," said Lilith, setting the faxes on the sheriff's desk. "She caved in and waived rights. The Georgia State Police say we can pick her up at the airport day after tomorrow. If you plan to hold her overnight, I have to call social services to take her son."

"No need. I don't plan to spend more than five minutes with Sally Laurie. I just hauled her back because she pissed me off leaving town that way." The sheriff rustled the faxes and handed them back to her. "File these or burn 'em."

She hesitated, looking for something to say, but finding no way to prolong her presence here, she turned and left the room.

"And close that door!" the sheriff hollered after her. He smiled at Charles. "Babe's widow left town with her kid the day of the murder. I tracked her down inside of a morning. Not bad for a hick sheriff, is it?"

Charles ignored this opportunity to flatter the sheriff with a predictable denial of the man's hickdom. Mallory would not have approved of that tactic. "Never suck up" was a Mallory constant. "So the dead man had a wife and child."

"Well, the dead man's widow has a son—that part's a fact."

"Not Babe Laurie's son?"

"That's the rumor. Babe and his wife have big blue eyes, and the boy's got little slitty brown ones. Just by coincidence, Babe's brother Fred has those same slitty brown eyes."

"Well, you know, genetically it's possible if there's a factor of—"

"No, it isn't possible, Mr. Butler. This is too small a town to make room for hard science. The sign at the highway says population eleven hundred, but that's pure bragging—more like nine hundred."

And the stranger in a small town was always first to be suspected of a crime. Charles refrained from jumping to Mallory's defense, though he did long to point out that, for many reasons, she was the least likely suspect.

"You must be under a lot of pressure, Sheriff."

"Pressure?"

"The news media?"

The sheriff seemed to find that funny. "A man's head connected with a rock. You can't make the evening news with a murder like that. Those reporters are looking for *inspired* killing, real talent."

"But he was a religious leader."

"He was the freak headliner in a road show called the New Church. Babe's only publicity is a mention in Betty Hale's tour ramble for the guests at the bed and breakfast. Now that does sell a few souvenirs at the drugstore, and I'm sure Betty gets her cut."

How embarrassing for Mallory to be embroiled in a mediocre murder. "I'd like to see this woman now, if you don't mind."

The sheriff accompanied him out to the reception room and handed him into Lilith's care. Charles followed her up the stairs and broke the uncomfortable silence as she opened the door for him. "Aren't you going to check me for dangerous weapons?"

Her expression was insulting, only because it obviously never occurred to her that he would know the barrel of a gun from its butt end. The deputy hung back by the door at the end of the cell block as he walked down the narrow corridor.

He had been prepared to see Mallory languishing in a cold impersonal cell; he had never imagined anything like this. On one wall was the print of a quaint landscape in a gilded frame, and a braided rug sat at the foot of a stuffed armchair. Her bed was decked with a colorful patchwork quilt, and fresh violets sat in a mason jar on a small chest of drawers. But for the iron bars of door and window, it was all rather charming.

How she must hate this.

Her own tastes ran to stark simplicity in her surroundings and superb tailoring in the blazers she wore with her blue jeans. That gingham dress must be humiliating. But when she looked up at him, she was only angry.

He stood with his back to Lilith Beaudare, his body blocking her sight of Mallory. "Augusta Trebec has asked me to ascertain whether or not you're the legal heir of Cass Shelley." His hands said, *"I only want to help. Tell me what I can do for you."*

"Go away," Mallory said. And then her hands said, *"Go away."*

"I'd appreciate it if you'd at least hear me out." He restricted his sign language to finger spelling to conceal the movements from the deputy at his back. *"Let me call Riker or Jack Coffey. They can do something."*

"No," she said, and *"No way,"* said her hands and her angry face. *"Are you nuts? They're both cops."*

"But, you're a cop." Or was she? Though she had neglected to do the proper paperwork for separating from the police department, she had left her badge behind in New York City, along with the police-issue .38 revolver. She had always preferred to carry her own personal weapon, the cannon of a gun that so intrigued the sheriff. If she was not a cop anymore, then what was she?

The term "rogue" came to mind. The word suited her on so many levels.

"Just go away and leave me alone," she said.

"No, I won't leave you sitting in a jail cell."

"I won't be here for long. Go away."

Aloud, he said, "I could hire an attorney for you."

"I don't need one. Get out," she said, rising, walking to the bars. *"They can't prove motive. But I think the sheriff might be working on that. He's smart. Don't underestimate him. I don't."*

"Well, that's high praise, coming from you." He handed her the garage bill for an oil change and the warranty on his car's new transmission. "This is the paperwork on your

estate. It's an affidavit of inheritance. Will you please read through it and sign it?''

She put the papers down the front of her dress to free her hands for speech. *"You have to go now. You can't help me. Everything will go sour if you stay in Dayborn."*

He knew what she meant. Mallory was predicting that he would botch every attempt at deception with the inexperience of an honest man. So she didn't trust him to do anything base or even remotely shady, but he was not offended by her confidence in his good character.

"I just put a lie past the sheriff," he signed hopefully, offering this act of gross wrongdoing as a sign of improvement.

Mallory winced, going beyond mere skepticism to near pain. She was probably wondering how much damage he had already done.

She handed the papers back to him. "I've read it, okay? Now get out!" She brought her face closer to the bars, her hands extending through them to touch his own hand, and then she signed, *"You haven't asked me if I killed that man."*

In her expression, there was the slight suggestion that she might have done it. Perhaps it was that unwholesome smile of hers. And now there was a question in her eyes.

One would not say of Mallory, she couldn't possibly do murder. However, because he took his friendships so seriously, if she had set fire to a school bus full of nuns and orphans and pushed it off a cliff, he would have assumed that she was merely having a bad day.

CHARLES WAS LEAVING the municipal building when he saw the woman emerge from the alley and stop a few feet from the stone steps. Her hair was what he noticed first. It was a black dye job gone awry and turned to purple in the highlights. The thin middle-aged woman revolved slowly, eyes wide with confusion, looking now to heaven for some sign to point her in the right direction. There was time to note that her slip hung below the hem of a dress that needed washing; that her face was wet with tears and deep etched with agony lines. Her mouth hung open in an eerie prelude to a scream as she bolted to the far side of the square.

A tall stocky woman, wearing an apron and carrying a covered tray, appeared on the steps of the municipal building beside Charles.

"Alma!" she called out to the running woman, but the purple-haired Alma never looked back. The stocky woman shrugged and carried her tray across the square to Jane's Cafe, where Darlene had gone with Ira.

Charles turned back to the alley in time to see Henry Roth emerge. The mute was smiling at the running woman's back, as though pleased with some handiwork of his own. Charles had the feeling of something gone terribly wrong with the universe today. In the face of that woman's extreme distress, Henry Roth's smile was unnerving. This was simply not in the artist's character, or what Charles had surmised of it.

Henry discreetly signed his farewell to Charles and walked off in the direction of his truck. And now it was the sculptor's back that was marked. His departure was followed by the eyes of the man on the bench, the one who so resembled the late Babe Laurie. This man now turned his gaze back to Charles, and with only a nod, he renewed his invitation to sit down and pass the time.

But something was different. The man's aspect had altered. Now the eyes were far from serene; they were alive with light. He wore the winning smile of a wild and handsome child. A lock of hair strayed over one eye, and he grinned to say he had a card trick Charles might like to see, or a secret he might want to know. *Come to me,* said the disarming face of a charming, barefoot boy of ten. *We've got games to play, places to go.*

So compelling was this silent call, Charles was made young again, and he was moving slowly toward the bench.

Then he stopped, as though he had met with a wall.

This was no shoeless, artless boy, but a grown man with

heavy boots and an agenda involving subterfuge. Here was a polished actor with at least two personas.

Charles thought he had done well against the sheriff, but elected not to press his luck with a man who made an art form out of guile. So he nodded an acknowledgment, shrugged his apology, and turned toward Jane's Cafe.

ABOVEGROUND PHONE LINES and power cables were tucked away at the rear of the building. No jarring reminder of modern times marred its historical character. Even the wavy distortions in the window glass of Jane's Cafe were true to the period. Near this window, the mother and son were seated at a table laid with a wine-red cloth and sparkling white napkins.

Charming.

However, when Charles entered the cafe, he found himself back in the correct era. A giant coffee machine gurgled in time to the music of soft rock. A gleaming metal and glass counter lined the back wall. Deep stainless-steel wells were filled with an amazing variety of salads, breads and cold cuts to be loaded on trays and paid for at the electronic cash register. All the white napkins were paper, and all the red tablecloths were washable, late twentieth-century plastic.

He collected a broad array of sandwich makings, condiments and salad greens on his tray. After paying for it, he settled down at the table next to Darlene and Ira Wooley. The woman was speaking to her son in a soothing mother voice, but the young man wasn't listening. He was absorbed in constructing a tower of food on top of a slab of rye bread.

In a soft-spoken, one-sided argument, Darlene pointed to the items that would set off Ira's allergies, and then she pulled out the offending layers. The boy stared at the mutilated sandwich for a moment, and Charles braced himself for the screaming fit common to autism. But Ira was very calm as he quietly disassembled the sandwich and began again with a new slice of bread from his mother's tray. He worked deftly, despite bandaged hands and the splints on two fingers. Charles determined that there was nothing wrong with any of the motor skills, as Ira laid a precise line of sardines across a bed of mustard-slathered bread.

Darlene Wooley was looking at Charles with the suspicion common to overprotective mothers.

"Forgive me for staring," said Charles. "Sandwiches are my hobby."

Ira looked up for a moment as Charles spread mustard on pumpernickel and then embellished it with stripes of red from a pointed squeeze bottle of catsup.

Ira reached into his mother's salad bowl and carefully picked out the carrot sticks and arranged them in a crosshatch over his sardines.

Charles made a perfect circle of croutons on his stripes of catsup. Ira noted this and added a squared slice of ham on top of his carrots. Charles laid down two slices of bright yellow cheese, one layered askew over the other to form an eight-point star. Ira countered with a dollop of cream cheese spread over the ham in the rough smear of a triangle.

Though Darlene Wooley seemed very tired, she was smiling at the pair of them as they engaged in this conversation of sandwiches.

Charles stacked his ingredients faster and higher. Ira took up the challenge, finishing his own design first and crowning it with a slice of white bread.

Charles applauded the winner, and Ira's laughing mother joined in, taking unreasonable delight in the moment. It must be an oasis in her day. He noted her bitten nails, the red veins of her eyes and the vertical worry line etched between her eyebrows. All the telling signs of life with an autistic child.

Well, her son's mind was certainly alive. Wheels were turning, and quickly. Charles wondered if Ira was articulate. Many autistic people were not. They were as diverse as snowflake patterns in their behaviors; few generalizations would hold for all.

Ira was again absorbed in his food, and never looked up when his mother exchanged names with Charles and introduced her son. Ira's eyes were looking elsewhere, not fixed on any point in the immediate universe.

When Charles had explained his interest in autism, he learned that eating lunch in the cafe was part of Ira's behavior therapy, and he approved. This daily exercise would account for the lack of stress, despite the babble of conversation, the comings and goings, and the company of strangers.

"There's no local program for autism, so four mornings a week, Ira goes to a state school for the mentally retarded."

"Well, it's miles better than no therapy at all," said Charles. And it was common practice. A sympathetic doctor would alter the diagnosis of autism to that of retardation in order to utilize whatever program was available. "I imagine they use many of the same methods, learning skills through repetitive tasks?"

"Yes, and they do make a special effort with Ira. I tried to get him into a private program in New Orleans," said Darlene. "But he couldn't pass the screening test."

Finally, the conversation turned to Charles's business with the sheriff. "Augusta Trebec believes the young woman in custody might be Cass Shelley's daughter. As the executrix—"

"Well, who else could that girl be, Mr. Butler?"

When she became comfortable with calling him Charles, she recounted Mallory's arrival in Dayborn on the day of the murder. "She stepped out of a cab in front of the bed and breakfast."

Darlene had been sitting on the front porch, talking to her friend and neighbor, Betty Hale. "The girl was the very image of her mother. You couldn't forget a face like that, even without the reminder of Cass's angel in the cemetery."

Babe Laurie had also seen Mallory, and reeled like a drunk, his eyes grown to the size of saucers. "So Babe sat there on the edge of the fountain while the girl was checking into Betty's. Then his brother Malcolm came for him in the car. But Babe wouldn't leave the square, and they got to arguing."

Her son had slipped away and gone home to his house next door. "And then I hear Ira at the piano, and he's playing this same little handful of notes, over and over. It drove Babe wild. He stormed into my house, with his brother right behind him. Well, I could not believe they had done that—just barged into my house. I was up from my chair and heading that way when the music stopped. And then my boy was screaming. The Lauries came out the door as I was going in. I found Ira at the piano with his hands smashed and blood running over the piano keys."

Charles glanced at Ira to see how he was reacting to Darlene's replay of a traumatic day. The boy seemed not to hear them. Charles surmised that Ira was shutting out the noise, not perceiving it as meaningful. His primary thoughts would probably be a cascade of images, not words. The perception of spoken words would require the concentration and effort of discerning a second language. Food was more alluring to Ira just now, but he might be responsive to music, another language more natural to him than the spoken word.

In the spirit of an ongoing examination, he turned to Ira. "Could you hum the tune you were playing on the piano?"

It was his mother who answered. "He won't hold normal conversations with people anymore. He used to talk a lot when he was a little boy. But now he just repeats things.

It's called echolalia. That's why he can't pass the screening test for the program in New Orleans.''

Well, that was reasonable. An advanced program would make a prerequisite of communication skills. Though the echolalia sometimes passed for response to conversation, a kind of shortcut. "Perhaps *you* could remember the notes?"

"Oh, no," she said, throwing up her hands in mock helplessness. "I got a tin ear. My boy has all the musical talent in the family. If you sit him down at the piano, he'll play, but he won't do requests. Just plays what he wants. And sometimes he'll sing for you—if he wants to. He has the most beautiful voice you ever heard." She looked down at her hands and their ruined fingernails. "You think that's just a mother talking."

"No, not at all. The sheriff spoke very highly of Ira's talent."

She smiled with some embarrassment and hid her hands under the table. "Sometimes, if the windows are open, every living thing in the square stops to listen to my boy when he sings. They just stand there, so still and quiet you'd think they were all in church. And I have seen people cry when Ira's song is over."

He could ask for no better corroboration. So the sheriff had given an accurate account of Ira's gifts, and now Charles was doubly intrigued. This was something very rare, well beyond the odd case of multiple talents in the savant. The gift of song was unrelated to quirks and mysteries in the autistic brain. The origin of autism was unknown; its symptoms developed after birth. But song came from the egg.

Done with his sandwich, Ira stared at his hands and moved them in circles as he rocked back and forth in his chair. Charles knew the young man was using this activity to calm himself, but why? He had not been agitated a moment ago.

Darlene covered Ira's rolling hands with her own, not touching flesh to flesh, but only threatening contact to get her son's attention. "What's wrong, honey?"

"What's wrong," said Ira, staring at the door.

Charles and Darlene both turned to see a figure standing in the doorway. It was the man with two faces, the artist of altered states, and he was smiling at Darlene, one hand rising in a greeting.

Her face was rigid as she quickly gathered up her purse and her son and departed with a strained goodbye.

The man engaged Charles's eyes as Darlene and Ira passed by him. Walking toward the table, he extended his hand. "My name is Malcolm Laurie. But you call me Malcolm." This was stronger than a suggestion. "May I join you?"

"Of course." Charles reached out to grasp the proffered hand. "I noticed your resemblance to Babe Laurie."

"He was my brother." Malcolm Laurie sat down with a comfortable attitude, as though he were in his own personal dining room.

"My condolences on your loss," said Charles.

"Thank you, Mr.—?"

"Butler." He neglected to mention his given name, as he usually did, for he felt the need of polite distance. As Malcolm leaned forward, Charles was mentally backing up, saying, "I understand your brother toured the country as an evangelist."

"We all did. The road show is a family enterprise." The winning smile was back. Perhaps the man sensed that this was the face that elicited the most favorable response. "Ever seen a real tent show?"

"Yes, when I was a child—" Charles stopped himself from mentioning his summer with Maximillian's Traveling Magic Show, but he could not have said why. "I expect they're all gone now. All the evangelists have television shows."

"Not all of 'em. Our family still tours with a tent. Bought it off a bankrupt circus when Babe was a little boy."

"A circus? So it's one of the *great* tents?" He had not

seen one of those beauties since he was a child. "How big is it?"

"Biggest you've ever seen—I guarantee that. It's going up tomorrow for Babe's memorial service. No girders—all single shafts and raised with muscle and line. It's a thing to behold. If you wanna see that tent raising, you'll have to get out to the fairground early. Round eight in the morning?"

"I'll be there." Charles was elated. He would have given anything for this chance. He had never expected to see such a sight again. "Thank you, so much."

"My pleasure."

Though it could not be true, Charles had the impression that Malcolm never blinked. His eyes were bright and riveting. Charles felt self-conscious for staring into them. The other man seemed to sense this and pulled back with his body, leaning into the slats of his chair, and perhaps his eyes had pulled back on their brilliance, for now they were merely the color blue.

"I understand you have some business with the prisoner," said Malcolm.

Was that her name now—the prisoner?

"If she's a friend of yours, I want you to know I've forgiven her for murdering my brother."

"Jumping the gun, aren't you? She hasn't been charged with murder. She's being held as a material witness."

And now Charles realized that he had given this man something of significance. It was clear by Malcolm's surprise.

Charles cast his eyes down. It was surely no great secret he had given away, or the sheriff wouldn't have mentioned it. However, he *had* violated Augusta Trebec's caution not to give any useful information to the opposition, and this man was surely not a supporter of Mallory's. In an effort to lead the conversation away from her, he said, "I'm not familiar with your religion. Is the New Church close to Baptist?"

"No, you're confusing your southerners, sir. This part of

the map is wall-to-wall Catholics. We tour with the biggest damn crucifix you ever did see. Now that bleeding, twisting torture on the cross, that's the Catholic stress on His dying for our sins. The Protestants like to see an empty cross as a reminder that He rose again.'' Malcolm shook his head in amused reproval. "No passion. Those Protestants are real boring—no offense if that's your poison."

"So the New Church is a Catholic sect?"

"I'd say we're a bit of one thing and another, a little something for everybody. Come see for yourself. Gonna be a big turnout for the show tomorrow night, but I could save you a front-row seat."

"Thank you, I'd like that. So, exactly what sort of ideology do you practice?"

"Awareness. When you learn to see things as they really are, you can participate in the energy flow. You follow the New Church steps to awareness, and soon you begin to notice that everything that happens to you was meant to happen. Each event, however small, is moving you closer to your destiny."

Charles recognized the corrupted, reworded prophecy of a hippie philosopher from the early seventies. The original work had been recently appropriated and regurgitated by an ungifted author on the bestseller list.

"I've seen the destitute led to riches and the weak led to power." And now Malcolm shifted to a poor man's version of Zen from another bestseller. "You don't even have to work at it. The less you strive, the closer you come to getting what you want—everything you want, and everyone."

This man had obviously researched the New Age promise of enlightenment, lucre and instant, everlasting love— all on sale at any bookstore. So the New Church was yet another shoppers' outlet for a larger life, a hipper soul and every tactile desire. And it was pain-free, labor-free and best of all—tax free, for this was a religious enterprise.

"There is a lacking in your life, isn't there?" The brightness was back in Malcolm's eyes. "What you have is not enough. You want something more. Am I right?''

"Of course," said Charles. Who did not?

"The kingdom of heaven is all around them and men do not see it." In keeping with New Age style, Malcolm had failed to give Jesus Christ a credit line. "Shall I tell you how to get the thing you prize the most?"

Somehow, Charles doubted that he could, but he waved his hand as an invitation to continue.

"It's a woman you want, isn't it?" And now the man was nodding, in answer to his own question, as though he had just seen the word "yes" lighting up in the center of Charles's forehead, in a splash of neon light. "A woman—that's it!" More confidential now, he asked, "The prisoner in Sheriff Jessop's cell is a beautiful woman, isn't she?"

Charles said nothing, yet he knew he had given a reply of sorts, for Malcolm was aglow with satisfaction over his discovery of this raw nerve, this emotional admission of a very personal link to Mallory.

How to fix this? And how to avoid betraying her with every change of expression? Mallory had once reminded him that unartful deception was the downfall of a man with something to hide. More precisely, she had said: "You shouldn't be allowed to play poker without a bag over your head."

Sudden inspiration made him smile broadly, well aware that this expression gave him the unwitting appearance of a cheerful, but harmless lunatic. It was the only deception he could pull off with any great success, for he had been born with this foolish feature. But until this moment, he had found no practical use for it.

"I see where you're going with this, Mr. Laurie," said Charles, disregarding the invitation to use the man's given name. "Yes, I suppose attractive women are beyond the man who is decidedly unattractive."

"I never meant—"

"No, that's all right. Every mirror reminds me of it. I can well understand your making that connection. You're right—my fantasy is a beautiful woman I can never have.

But anyone who'd seen my face would've guessed that. So while your observation is accurate, it's not particularly astute." And this was the truth, mightier than the lie.

Now Malcolm's own smile wavered. "But there is *one* woman you want." He said this with a rising inflection, close to a question, not quite so self-assured.

"New York is full of beautiful women, and not one of them has the slightest romantic interest in me. Perhaps it's the nose that puts them off. Hard to ignore it, lunging out in space as it does. But I'm worse off than you know. I also require intelligence. A woman with that combination can have any man on the planet. She won't pick an ugly one. I'm nothing if not a realist."

Malcolm sat back in his chair, and Charles watched the blue eyes making reassessments and finally fixing on a course. "I believe I've isolated the problem. Your enemy is your ego. It anticipates reaction to everything you do. It creates fear and kills all your forward motions."

"I must be careful about my forward motions. I wouldn't like to accidentally batter a woman with my nose."

This time, Malcolm grinned with spontaneity. "So, in your mind, it would take a miracle to get that woman."

"I would say so."

"What a coincidence. Miracles are my business."

"Business implies a price tag."

"I like you, Mr. Butler. Your money's no good with me. I'm going to see that you get what you want. I look on it as karma in the bank." Malcolm lightly slapped one hand on the table. He was smiling with purpose, metaphysically rolling up his sleeves to go to work in earnest. "Forget the past and every failure, every rejection. Don't think about the future." The commands were soft-spoken, but they *were* commands. "Accept the moment for what it is. Surrender to it, and then you can observe the problem with some detachment."

Detachment? But his largest problem was hanging off the end of his face.

"Not your nose," said Malcolm, following the track of

Charles's eyes to that peninsula of flesh at the center of his visual field. "The *woman*."

And now Malcolm ceased the plagiarism of an Indian twelve-step program to universal insight. He leaned forward on the prop of his folded arms, and the conversation became a more personal conspiracy of men against that other sex. Charles soon discovered that a beautiful woman had certain expectations, which Malcolm listed as the attention, admiration and dogged devotion of males.

"So don't be predictable. She expects you to follow after her," said Malcolm. "Don't do that. Just walk away. That'll tie her up in knots for a while, and then *she* will come to *you*."

"But why?"

"All of a sudden, you're the unattainable one. She'll assume you've found some fault with her. It'll drive her crazy until she figures out what it is."

"So, by moving away from her, I've created an equal but opposite reaction?"

Malcolm nodded. "And remember, a beautiful woman has no experience in failure. That's where you have the edge."

"And now my drawbacks have become advantages." Charles was rather enjoying this. From his early years, as a child among grown college students, to his adulthood in the think tanks, he had met no one who could competently discuss women. He had made his most intimate friends late in life, too late for adolescent questions like—How do you get a woman?

"All right," said Charles. "Now she's following me. How do I close the gap without reversing her forward motion?"

"Let her do that. Women are the ones who make the contract, lay down the rules, create the relationship. That's their job. Your job is to grudgingly allow her to bind you to her. Just remember, as she's dragging you off—you're only humoring her to be polite."

There was good logic here. But would any of it apply to

Mallory? Some malformation in her psyche had created a disfigured mirror, which neatly killed the concept of beauty's expectations. Yet his own behavior was still predictable to her, for every time she turned around, there he was. Perhaps that was why she had not said a word about her plans to leave New York. It would have been predictable that he would follow her, creating problems by giving up all her secrets with his naked face.

"You have some doubts, Mr. Butler?"

Charles met the eyes of the mind reader—more accurately, the face reader. Evidently, his raised eyebrow had expressed a doubt, and he had punctuated the thought with downcast eyes. He resorted to the old conjuror's trick of substitution. "Mr. Laurie, what do you suppose women really want?"

"It doesn't matter." He grinned, accepting this doubt in place of the other. "If you work this right, you'll never be troubled with that question again."

Against his will and better judgment, Charles liked this man and found himself smiling more and more. He was leaning into the conversation, drawn to Malcolm. The charismatic quality put Charles in mind of Louis Markowitz. He had seen his old friend draw strangers close enough to bind them up in toasty warm intimacy on only ten minutes' acquaintance. And now he made a mental note to write his next paper on charm as a true gift.

A half hour later, when Malcolm rose from the table, Charles shook his hand with genuine warmth. Shortly after the door closed, the sense of energized well-being died off, and regret settled in with a feeling of loss. Charles was left alone at the table with an untouched sandwich, one last question and no witnesses to the worried state of his face.

What did Mallory really want—what had brought her back to this place? Homesickness was not in his bag of possibilities. Even if she were not devoid of sentiment, there was no longer a family tie to this place. Her mother was dead—a sudden death, according to Augusta Trebec.

•   •   •

THE SHERIFF GRIPPED the bars of Mallory's cell. "You haven't changed so much. Taller, that's all. How well do you remember me?"

Very well. Her last memory of Sheriff Jessop was betrayal. Though she had buried it deep, the act had come back in bits and pieces of unguarded thoughts and violent dreams.

In the early days, Louis Markowitz had rescued her from every screaming childhood nightmare. He had flooded her bedroom with light and held his foster child close until her dreaming feet ceased to run from the bloodbath, and she awakened to touch down on safe and solid ground. When Markowitz died, her life had begun to unravel. Ugly images had plagued her every day since she had laid the old man in the ground.

Mallory waited for Tom Jessop to tire of being ignored, to go away and leave her in peace. But he was a stubborn man. He hugged the bars. She was tempted to rush the cell door and rake him with her nails. Her hands balled into fists, and her long red fingernails pressed into the flesh until she felt real pain.

She stared down at the indentations in her palms. Was she getting a little crazy? Hadn't she been moving in that direction for more than a year? Markowitz was gone, and now she didn't even have his pocket watch anymore. The sheriff had it, and Mallory added this to the list of Tom Jessop's crimes against her.

"Do you know how your mother died?"

As if you didn't. And didn't the sheriff know another song? She was so tired of hearing the same words every day. Mallory stared at the wall in silence. She heard him sigh.

"When you were a kid, you didn't talk much," he said. "But you laughed all the time. You were a little copy of your mother. I miss her, too. Maybe we could help each other, Kathy."

"Don't call me that." And now she turned to him. Her face conveyed solid hate.

Startled, his hands dropped away from the cell bars. "I can guess what you're thinking."

Can you? Then why don't you die? She continued to stare at him until he looked away.

"You think I should have closed the case by now, arrested every one of them." He turned his face back to hers. "Don't you think I wanted to?"

No, I don't.

And now he looked into her eyes again, and it seemed to cause him some pain. "I wanted to do a lot worse to them."

Yeah, right.

"What the hell happened to you out there?" He grasped the bars again. "You were the sunniest child. Look at you now. You got the coldest eyes I've ever seen. If I knew who did this to you, I swear I'd kill him."

He wanted to touch her; she could sense that. She had an old memory of this man tossing her high in the air and catching her in a bear hug. How old was she that first time? Three or four? She had screamed in delight. Every time she saw him after that, she had run into his arms for the chance to be airborne again.

And then the world changed. Four days ago, she had wanted to shoot him dead the moment she recognized him.

"When are you going to charge me, Sheriff?"

"With murder? Never. You're a material witness in protective custody."

"Give me my gun. I'll protect myself."

"Maybe it's the town I'm protecting. I don't care if you killed Babe. I wouldn't touch you for that. But what about the rest of them? I can't let you go after them all."

Mallory waited out this last long silence, and then, finally, she heard his footsteps leaving her, walking down the corridor. She spun around, pressed her face to the bars and whistled a short phrase of familiar music.

He faltered in his steps, and one hand went to the wall, as though he suddenly needed its support. The sheriff walked on, but his stride had changed. He was less sure of his legs now, and his head was bowed.

CHAPTER
7

AUGUSTA FISHED DEEP in the pockets of her dress. "I can't think what I did with those keys. I know I had them on me this morning."

The white horse lowered his huge head over the paddock fence to nudge her shoulder.

"Oh, I remember. I gave them to Henry Roth. He said he'd look at a pipe joint for me. The local plumber is a thief."

"I don't want to disturb Mr. Roth while he's working." Charles stroked the horse's silky muzzle. The stallion was a bit long in the tooth, but still a fine-looking animal.

"That's no problem." Augusta held the paddock gate open, and the horse walked out to nuzzle her neck until she waved him off, annoyed and pleased at once. "We'll give Henry a call after supper."

They crossed the open ground between the fenced enclosure and an old carriage house in need of paint. The horse wore no halter, but trailed behind them, docile as an old dog.

"So, Charles, how do you find our small town? Does it bore you?"

"Hardly. I met Malcolm Laurie today. He's a fascinating man."

Augusta pulled on the latch of a wide arched door, and it swung open on a dark and cool interior, pungent with the smells of hay and horse. The sound of running water came from a trough at the rear of an open stall, and the horse was on his way to it.

When the stall gate was closed and latched, Augusta turned a stern face on Charles. "Don't you go falling in love with Malcolm."

That was an order.

"I beg your pardon?" Did she think that he was—

"You know, it's been years since I made a man blush like that. Come along."

His eyes had no sooner adjusted to the dimness than she was leading him into the bright light. He was blinking, making all the readjustments to his eyes and his head.

Fall in love with Malcolm?

She motioned him to follow her back to the house. He walked alongside of her, hands jammed in his pockets as he picked his words. He was searching for just the right phrase to protest—but not too much, when she took his arm, as she had done on the day they first met.

"Settle down, Charles. I'm not implying anything carnal. Men are always falling in love with other men. What with their war heroes and sports heroes, I believe the love for another man is much more potent than the love for a woman. Though *any* man would be shocked if you threw that up to him."

"It's not *quite* the same thing," he said, and perhaps he said it a bit too fast.

"Not like sex, you mean? Well, of course it is. Malcolm uses sex just like a woman does. He's shameless. And men succumb to him the same as women do."

Charles squared his shoulders and drove his hands deeper into his pockets. "The leader of a cult religion has the devotion of his *followers*. I'll grant you that." He wondered if his tone of voice was too defensive. "But based on a psychiatric profile of the typical cult member—''

''Forget the psychiatric voodoo.'' Her grip on his arm tightened, and she scowled at him as if he were an errant child. ''Get your mind out from behind that zipper in your pants, and pay attention. You're going through a bad patch, Charles. You're vulnerable now—easily led or misled. We've all been there. Man or woman, sometimes we all feel that need to be swept up in strong arms. Malcolm invited you to the show tomorrow night, didn't he?''

''The memorial service? Yes.'' Why did he feel as though he had just confessed to a lovers' tryst?

''When you see Malcolm on that stage, he'll be larger than you remembered. He'll swoop down on you with his eyes, and he'll carry you away with promises of heaven on earth.''

And this Malcolm had already done. *The kingdom of heaven is all around them and men do not see it.*

''And you'll believe in him because you want to, you *need* to.'' Augusta opened the door between the staircases and paused with her hand on the knob. ''Malcolm will show you a vision of paradise so real you can go live in it for a while. You'll be spellbound—and grateful.''

She stared at him now, as though she had intuited his conversation of the morning. She was shaking her head, disapproving of whatever knowledge she had gained from his telltale face. She went into the house and down the hall to the kitchen. He followed close behind her, just as the horse had done.

Walking to the stove, her back was turned on him when she spoke again. ''Then he'll ask you for something—probably a small thing compared to his own gift of the moon and the stars. And you'll be glad to give it to him . . . this small thing.'' She lit the flame under the burner. ''That's how it begins. Maybe you don't get between the sheets with the man, but it's a consummation. When you yield to him that first time?—it *is* a surrender.''

She was facing him now, gesturing with slow swirls of a wooden spoon. ''In a sense, you're on your back, eyes all full of love and trust. He can do whatever he likes with you—and you will *want* him to. So, Charles, don't go falling in love with that man.''

Though he had just been rather imaginatively raped, Charles was nodding. The spell she spoke of was within his experience. He could have used the old woman's frightening counsel when he was falling in love with Mallory.

Too late now.

He sat down at the table and watched Augusta's back as she stirred the contents of the pot. Though he had missed his lunch, he was nearly immune to the aromas of chicken, vegetables and spice scents he couldn't name. Hunger had been displaced by high anxiety.

On the bright side, he was perfectly safe from the likes of Malcolm. That most excellent thief, Mallory, had already taken everything of value—his pride, his self-respect. He had traveled more than a thousand miles for a rude brush-off. How pathetic was that?

Malcolm was right. If he wanted Mallory, he must not pursue her anymore. He would not try to see her again. She always found him so predictable, she would not know what to make of that. It would definitely disconcert her. Well, good. If it gave her a few bad moments, she well deserved it.

Thank you, Malcolm.

Two fragrant bowls of thick gumbo and rice were set on the table. He looked up and met Augusta's eyes. She stared at him with such intensity, he wondered if she was tracking his thoughts. Had he simply become conditioned to this paranoia? Or was she even more skilled than Malcolm Laurie?

Ah, but it was all in his face, wasn't it?—the anger, the petulance, the plotting. Augusta, a master of human nature, was watching his slow fall into the dangerous pit she had just mapped out for him. She had drawn a huge sign and set flares by the side of the road, hadn't she? But he had gone off the edge, stone blind and foolish.

''I do understand,'' he said, and this was finally true. He

would not be seduced by the evangelist. Mallory was his friend. Whatever she needed from him, it was hers, whether she wanted his help or not. If he had been in trouble, Mallory would have done the same for him. How could he have forgotten that?

Having restored his priorities and prevented his fall from grace, Augusta sat down at the table with him and bent over her bowl. Though they ate in silence, there was much going on between them. He smiled and inclined his head to acknowledge his admiration for her dark science of human behavior. She smiled back, approving his good sense in following her advice, however slow he might have been to catch on.

By the time their meal was done and they were working on the second round of coffee, Charles's mood had changed radically. The food had done wonders for his state of mind. In fact, he was feeling slightly euphoric.

Augusta eyed him over the rim of her cup. Her expression could only be described as good-natured evil. ''I bet you're feeling better now.''

''Miles better. Your cooking has worked a miracle.''

She nodded. ''That's the Saint-John's-wort talking.''

''Pardon?''

''*Hypericum perforatum.*'' She pointed to one of the small herb gardens along the windowsills. ''It's that pretty little yellow flower. I gave it to my mother to treat her depression. 'Course she died. But I seem to be having better luck with you.''

''You drugged my food?''

''Oh, not much. That silly looking grin on your face will wear off in a little while. Now *that* side effect comes from one of my hybrids.''

''You *drugged* me?''

''Time to call Henry,'' she said, pushing her chair away from the table and politely ignoring the fact that he was repeating himself.

Charles's smile would not leave his face, but it had

grown a bit tense as he followed her out of the kitchen and into another doorway off the hall.

This larger room was a century removed from the modern kitchen. Diffused light softly illuminated hand-colored Audubon prints on every wall. On a round table with delicate wood inlays and intricately carved legs, her sketchbook lay open at the foot of a rare white owl. Around the room, a score of other birds fixed him with their bright eyes, their bodies frozen in that tense moment before the flight, or the attack. They were all artful compliments to the craftsmanship of Augusta's taxidermist.

So she had followed Audubon's custom of using dead models for the drawings.

The ceiling was low, creating the atmosphere of a cottage. The tables and odd pieces were a mix of periods and styles; all were in fabulous condition. It was a cluttered but comfortable room with a narrow bed built into the window alcove. Against one wall, an armoire was flanked by two French Régence bookcases, and volumes with ornithology titles were stacked on every surface. Apparently, this single room served as her living quarters. Why had she retired into this small portion of a mansion?

He had no sooner sat down on the couch than the cat joined him on the brocade and forced him to move off the center cushion by advancing on him only an inch or two—with her lips curled back over a mouthful of pointed teeth. She arranged herself on the vacated cushion and continued to stare at him in silent contempt.

Augusta was speaking into a telephone which he could date to the first decade of the century. "I counted twelve taps. Tap again if I got that right, Henry." She turned to Charles. "Is twelve noon all right with you?"

"Yes." He was looking at a narrow staircase leading up to the main floor above them.

"Well, fine. Thank you, Henry." She set the antique phone receiver back on its cradle. "He'll meet you at the house. Now the large key will unlock the front door, and the smaller one will let you into the attic where I stored Cass's personal things.''

Charles waved his hand to include the entire room. ''This is an amazing collection of antiques. I love your house.''

''But there's forty-odd rooms you haven't seen. Would you like a tour of the place?''

''Oh, yes, please.''

And now he noticed the neighboring cushion was cat-free. He turned to see the animal stealing up the staircase. Clever creature; she had anticipated them. She was waiting, purring, when they reached the top of the stairs. Augusta stood on the landing and hissed in the cat's own language. The animal backtracked to stand on the stair behind Charles.

''Be sure you don't let her out.'' Augusta passed through the door and left Charles to fend off the wild thing with one shoe. He escaped with only minor damage to one pant-leg.

He stepped into a long gallery, and space expanded in all directions. Every flat plane was a far distance and every vertical line soared. He judged the ceilings to be at least eighteen feet high, and the doorframes were made for eleven-foot giants.

Augusta's hand rested on a Dresden china doorknob as she pointed up to the ornate friezes at the ceiling molding. The upper wall was studded with delicate roses. ''The flowers were made from a mixture of Spanish moss and plaster.''

She guided him into a room of even more generous proportion. Tall windows extended from floor to ceiling and provided light enough to see delicate tapestries falling to tatters on the walls, and mold gathering on the furniture. All the pieces in this room might have been worthy of a museum, but now they were beyond restoration. The cracked windowpanes had allowed rain damage. A chair-backed settee was kneeling on broken forelegs. The thick Oriental rug, which should have lasted centuries, was rotting on the floor. Threads gave way under his shoes and beetles ran out from underfoot.

So poverty was not the cause of the neglect. The sale of these pieces would have paid for maintenance on the house. He averted his eyes as they passed by a cracking landscape of foggy moon and ghostly trees. It had been worth a fortune—once. They passed into the vast dining room, where other precious paintings were warping and cracking on water-stained walls.

"Why has it all gone to ruin?" He hadn't meant to ask that aloud, but he could not contain himself.

"Well, I had to let the house rot. That was a promise I made to my father as he was dying."

Had the man been demented? That probably *would* be a rude question, and Charles kept it to himself as he followed her back to the long gallery, where another set of doors opened onto a grand ballroom.

Now this was glorious, luminous. The white walls and floor reflected all the light at the end of the day and dazzled him into a wide smile. But now his smile waned as he stared at the ruined marble floor. Each tile bore a crack and some were nearly pounded to dust.

"You can blame that damage on one of my horses," said Augusta. "That Appaloosa was a good strong animal, but you'd be amazed how much punishment the tiles can take before they crack." And then in the afterthought of a tour guide, she said, "It's all Italian marble."

This was almost too much for Charles. His parents had never allowed him to run indoors, lest he damage some old and valuable piece of china or glass—Augusta had ridden a horse through the house.

He followed her up the grand staircase, and as they passed by the open doors along the hallway, she gave him a running commentary. There were precious clocks in every room, all stopped at the same time, the hour of her father's death.

Augusta said, somewhat disgusted, "The house is made of cypress. Termites cannot penetrate it. The walls will not fall down. These floors are made of heart pine, and there's hardly a patch of wood rot. However, I am making some headway with the roof. It's got some prominent holes that'll let you see daylight. The poor bats, though. They don't take too well to direct sun. Some of them are migrating to the lower floors.''

He peered into the last room before the next staircase. The carpet was spotted with dung. Bats had indeed taken up residence here. Against one wall was an elaborately carved canopy bed. He had only seen one like it at a New York auction house. Mosquito netting partially covered the bed in a wreckage of gauzy spiderwebs and woven rotted threads of cotton. A dead bat lay on the mattress, its molding body fusing with the material.

They continued up the stairs and into the attic, where he found more antiques serving as homes to spiders. At his feet lay a broken Federal bull's-eye mirror.

"Wait here a minute," said Augusta. "I'll make sure they've all cleared out. There's only been a handful of bat rabies cases in the past thirty years, but you never know.'' She disappeared through a doorway, and the scent of something foul came wafting through the brief opening.

He turned to the only source of light and air. This was not the round window facing the town. This one afforded a view of the land at the back of the house. A pair of field glasses lay on the broad sill.

Looking down, in the hour of dusk, he could still make out what once had been a carefully planned maze and stepped terraces of lush vegetation. This was the good bone structure of a ruined garden. He could imagine it in bygone days when the shrubs had been carefully trimmed and the flowers confined to their beds. A flagstone path wound through the grounds, disappearing in places where it was overgrown with plants reverting to the wild, blooming in random bouquets of blue and red. More exotic flames of orange were—   .

Oh, but now two bright-colored blossoms took flight, and all the flowers called out to one another. Birds—the garden was alive with birds. In a chain reaction of motion, all the colors were rising from the foliage in a brilliant wave, fluttering on the air and singing songs.

He picked up the binoculars and trained them on the small pecan trees and shrubs. Here and there, he picked out the conical tops of bird feeders spread throughout the avian sanctuary.

This was no side effect of Augusta's neglect; it was an act of creation.

She was back again, standing beside him, and the flowers continued to fly and sing.

"My compliments, Augusta. It's the most beautiful garden I've ever seen."

"Let me show you the view from the other side while we still got some light. Hold your nose when you pass through that door."

He did as she suggested, but the stench of dung and urine was overwhelming, and his eyes stung. He could feel the crunch of bugs beneath the soles of his shoes, as she led him around the stalagmites of droppings with the beam of her flashlight.

Not all the bats had flown at sunset. A pair of tiny eyes gleamed with reflected light. He turned away quickly, not wanting to alarm the creature into sudden flight. When they had cleared the midsection of the attic and passed under an archway, a breeze of fresh air alleviated the smell. Light penetrated the roof through a gaping hole between the wooden ribs of the ceiling. Foliage had attached itself to sod trapped by the wind in the cross wood of exposed beams. Ironically, he recognized the encroaching plant as resurrection fern.

And now he noticed that another bat had been left behind. The animal was revolving in circles on the floor, trailing a torn wing in the dust.

"I wonder if that cat's been up here." Augusta looked down at the poor beast and shook her head. "Now that one—see the red metal on his leg? He was banded fifteen years ago. The government man wanted to mark a lot more of them that way, but he had clumsy hands and crippled as many bats as he did right, so I run him off the place. That bat is the old man of the colony.''

And now it was at the end of its life. The injury to its wing fit well with a cat's claw. If the bat could not fly, it could not feed.

"What's the name of the bat?''

"Charles, if you ever hear me giving pet names to flying rodents, you can tell them it's time to put the old woman away.''

"Sorry, I meant the species. Brown bat? Serotine?''

"The government man who checks the bands, he calls them *big* brown bats or sometimes *Genus Eptesicus*. I call them owl food.'' The old woman was standing at another round window overlooking the town. A telescope stood on a tripod, its long barrel pointed down to the earth. A notebook lay open on the sill and bore a crude map recording the sites of nests.

This was what the bird in flight must see. The whole countryside was laid out before him. Augusta pointed to a Victorian house on the other side of the cemetery. A wide dirt-colored ribbon led away from the building, and he recognized it as the mystery road along Finger Bayou, the one with the blank sign.

"That's Cass Shelley's place.'' She moved the telescope closer to the glass and focussed it. "Here, take a look.''

He put one eye to the lens. The Shelley house bore a recent coat of paint. The shrubs had been cut back, and all the flowers kept to the perimeters of rock gardens surrounding the trees in the front yard. There were no signs of neglect, and that was odd for a property in Augusta's stewardship.

Beyond the boundary of wide Upland Bayou were the homes and shops of Dayborn. Augusta was pointing to the line of trees beyond the town square.

"Now you see that windbreak of trees? That's the end of Dayborn's proper limits and the beginning of Owltown.

That's where the New Church roadies live in their cracker box houses and mobile homes.''

He followed her pointing finger to a crescent of neon lights bounded on its far side by another bayou.

"Owltown never sleeps,'' said Augusta. "Twenty-four hours a day, you can buy liquor and drugs. Gambling goes on till daybreak. That's the Lauries' work. Almost everyone in that place is related to the Lauries by blood or marriage. Don't you go there after dark, unless you take a gun.''

"Why is it called Owltown?''

"Oh, it's had that name forever. Up till thirty years ago, we used to have quite a population of rare owls on that plot of land. That was before the damn Lauries took over the habitat and cleared the horseshoe bend on the lower bayou to make a fairground. Damn waste.''

"I gather you dislike these people.''

"It wouldn't bother me if the whole place burned to the ground. I don't trust myself to go to Owltown with matches in my pocket.'' She moved the telescope back to the side of the window. "Well, now you've seen it all.''

"Thank you for the tour.''

"My pleasure, Charles. Anything else I can do for you?''

"You can tell me how Cass Shelley died.''

She was genuinely surprised. "I thought Henry or Betty would've told you that by now.''

"I never thought to ask them. So, how did Mallory's mother die?''

"I believe the attack was outside the house. That's where Henry found Kathy's dog. Poor beast was half dead. Cass's bloody handprints were all over a good portion of one side of the house where she must have been driven back to the wall. The grass was covered with her blood, and they found two of her teeth there. And there were rocks scattered around—lots of rocks. They had bits of her skin and blood on them.''

"Are you saying this woman was stoned to death?''

•   •   •

JIMMY SIMMS BORE the Laurie family resemblance in a girl-ish delicacy of bone structure. And though he had turned thirty this year, his unshaven face was still spotty with the straggly silken hairs of an adolescent beard.

Jimmy's father would no longer speak to his small half-finished son, and neither would the man allow him in the house anymore. But over the long years of estrangement, Jimmy's mother had continued to slip him her husband's castoff clothes. He could roll up the legs of his father's long pants, but the shoes were so big, even with newspaper stuffed in the toes, he always limped with a blister on one foot or the other.

He shambled up the path to the Shelley house. The old black Labrador retriever knew his footsteps, despite the al-ternating limp. The animal raised his regal head in the usual greeting, a look of tolerance but no great interest.

Jimmy reached into the pocket of his oversized wind-breaker and pulled out a bulky package. Unfolding the pa-per wrapping, he displayed the half-eaten fish fillet for the dog's approval. He had recently retrieved it from the trash bin behind Jane's Cafe, and now he set it down on the dirt in front of the black Lab. Years ago, he had brought offer-ings of red meat, but the dog had since lost his chewing teeth, and now Jimmy's gifts were made of softer foods.

"Babe Laurie is dead," he said to the dog for the fifth day in a row, as if by repetition he could make himself understood. He sat down in the dirt and stroked the ani-mal's neck.

The dog only sniffed at the fish, and then rested his mas-sive graying head on his paws.

The sun had set, and the light was going fast. It had been Jimmy's long habit never to be caught out after dark, but tonight he decided to remain until the moon had risen. There was no telling how much time was left for the ancient dog.

The animal slept for a while. From the low growls and the frantic movement of a hind leg, Jimmy surmised that the old black Lab did not like his dreams. Now the dog snapped awake, raised his head and turned his face upward until the waxing moon was reflected in his eyes. Jimmy jumped in his skin, believing the eyes had begun to glow.

The dog stood up with great effort. He yelped, then crooned, his voice slowly swelling to a full-throated howling.

The old lab still had magnificent moments. One day soon, the animal would die, and Jimmy would miss his company and their common bond of despair, which the dog expressed so eloquently in his song to the moon.

THE DOG BELIEVED his own name was a long high note and two whistling ripples of music from a child's mouth. No one had called him by this sound since the child went away. She had done the unthinkable. She had left him behind, broken and bleeding. And she continued to do this to him night after night, in every dream, eroding his sanity a little more each time he closed his eyes.

He parted his lips and bared his remaining teeth to the little man beside him, growling low, until the man scrambled to his feet and limped away.

Now the dog began to wail in earnest, sharing his dementia with Alma Furgueson down in Owltown. The dog howled and Alma cried. Her neighbors pretended not to hear. The strange duet went on for hours.

Alma pulled the covers up over her head, but still she could see the rocks flying and hear the sickening sound of their impact on human flesh and bone and teeth. She could hear the sound of Cass's body breaking.

Alma's nearest neighbor was long accustomed to this racket. But now he removed the sound-baffling pillow from his head. He woke his wife, and they both listened, for this was something they had never heard before. Alma had begun to harmonize with the dog.

•　•　•

LYING ON HER bed in the Dayborn jail, Mallory was also listening. She turned her face to the bars that kept her apart from the dog.

One fist rose high in the air and crashed down on her pillow with enough force to burst the case and send the feathers flying all around her cell, like small freed birds. Throwing off the covers, she stood up and walked barefoot to the window, the better to hear her dog's mad serenade.

After a time, the old black Lab fell into an exhausted silence. Mallory returned to her bed and to sleep, lying under a blanket dusted with feathers and resembling a sheltering wing.

CHAPTER

8

THE EARLY MORNING sky was an outrageous shade of deep blue. The air was crisp and breezy, filled with ever present birdsong, as Charles passed through the long stand of trees which served as windbreak and borderland between Day-born and Owltown. He made his way along the well-worn path to join up with a paved road curving into Owltown's small commercial district.

This main street was lined with simple structures, one and two levels of weathered gray board. Though obviously decades old, they had the temporary character of hastily constructed carnival booths. The telephone poles and street-lamps had a greater sense of permanence. A neon sign in every third storefront window advertised liquor by the shot or the quart.

A car sped by, whipping up trash and dust in its wake. Bottles lay against the curbs; some were shattered, and one was still grasped in the hand of a slumbering drunk. Half of him lay on the walkway, and the rest of him sprawled in the street. Aromas of stale whiskey and vomit hung cloudlike over the man's body. He snored contentedly as Charles passed him by.

A woman was coming toward him, hobbling as if one leg might be a good three inches shorter than the other. And now Charles could see that it was, for she held a broken shoe in her hand and limped along on one bare foot and one stiletto heel. Her brassy hair had the texture of slept-in cotton candy, and the dress of dark blue sequins threw off a million brilliant sparks of sunlight. She had wept her mascara into a raccoon's mask.

He was about to ask her if he could help, putting out one hand to hail her, when a car pulled to the curb beside him, and a familiar voice commanded, "Don't touch anything in Owltown, Mr. Butler. You don't know where it's been."

The weeping woman turned abruptly to face the car marked with the official star and legend of the sheriff's office. Her face was in a panic as she hurried down the street, moving faster now that she had lost her one good shoe in a race to be gone.

The car's curbside door opened in invitation, and Charles got into the front seat with Tom Jessop. The interior smelled of aftershave and cigarettes. The dashboard was a clutter of loose papers, envelopes and handwritten notes on napkins and matchbook covers.

"Good morning," said Charles.

The sheriff touched the brim of his brown Stetson in a return salutation. "Where you headed, Mr. Butler?"

"I'm hoping to get out to the fairgrounds before the tent goes up." And he also hoped the sheriff had no time-consuming business with him. Charles had waited all his adult life for this event.

"Yeah, that tent raising is a rare sight." The sheriff put the car in gear and they glided away from the curb. "You get a great view of the lower bayou from the horseshoe bend. The Lauries cleared that bend by fire—killed every root system on the near shore."

"Not very sound ecology. Wouldn't that tend to speed up the erosion of the land?"

"Yeah." The sheriff smiled. "One day, all of Owltown will be under water. It may take the better part of a century, but I'm a patient man." And his patience was evident in the slow crawl of the car.

"I take it you don't care much for Owltown."

"Let me give you the tour, and we'll see how well *you* like this place."

They stopped at a cross street. The sheriff pointed to a line of gray shacks along an unpaved road. "You go that way, and you can see something real nasty at the peep shows." He turned to the rear-window view of the road already traveled. "Go back that way, and you can buy drink, drugs and a woman at the same establishment—one-stop shopping." The car began to crawl again. "When I was a kid, we didn't have all those good things—there was nothing out here but Ed Laurie's bar and a pack of owls."

They proceeded down the main street, and Charles observed more signs of liquor for sale. "I wouldn't have thought a place this size could support so many bars."

"Those're all New Church hospitality houses," said the sheriff. "There's not one liquor license in the pack. No money changes hands, no tax revenues. But you need a church voucher to get a drink."

The sheriff slowed the car to a roll and pointed out a two-story house on the left side of the street. "That's a real landmark there—Ed Laurie's old bar. Thirty years ago, the only Lauries in this parish all lived on the second floor."

It was like the other buildings, naked wood and spare in form, but older than the rest. The sunporch roof sagged in an evil smile, and bright-glowing beer logos blinked on and off in the window. And now Charles noticed the relative quiet. He could hear the noise of distant car engines, but no birds. He had become accustomed to their music everywhere he went. Apparently, birds did not sing in Owltown.

The sheriff stopped the car in front of the bar. "That's where Babe got his start when he was five years old. He was called Baby Laurie then. His daddy would sit him on top of the jukebox so the boy could preach scripture, and worse. If you wanted live theater, you went to Ed's bar to see who Baby Laurie was gonna hex that night."

"Hex? Are we talking about voodoo?"

"Nothing that sophisticated, Mr. Butler. But the little bastard was real good at predictions. If he said your wife would have a stillborn child, she might accidentally connect with a baseball bat in the gut before she come to term. 'Course you could ask Baby Laurie to pray you and yours away from the wrath of the Lord. And if you made a contribution to the ministry, then lo and behold, your baby would be born alive."

"A protection racket? So the father was—"

"Or one of Babe's big brothers did the work. The other boys were full-grown by then. Their father was the most hated man in St. Jude Parish. If Ed hadn't died of a drunk's liver, eventually we would've found him floating facedown in the bayou. And don't you know, Babe was just the image of his father."

"So you're saying there's more than a few people who wanted to see Babe dead?"

But the sheriff said nothing at all as he set the car in motion once more. Either the man was evading the question, or he simply didn't care who killed Babe Laurie.

"Sheriff, you said Babe's brothers were full-grown when he was five. But that was thirty years ago. Surely Malcolm couldn't be much over thirty."

"Malcolm is fifty-one. Just a few years younger than I am."

Charles stared at the lines and jowls of the sheriff's face, and the graying hair that Malcolm didn't have. This was not possible. He couldn't have been so far from the mark in—

"Malcolm is a strange one," said the sheriff. "He encourages rumors that he's even older. Makes people think he's onto a secret, and maybe he is." But Jessop's tone lacked conviction and bordered on sarcasm. "Years back, Babe and Malcolm looked almost like twins. But when Babe died at thirty-six, he looked ten years older. Could be Malcolm used his brother like that magic portrait of Dorian

Gray's. Babe becomes debauched, and Malcolm stays young forever.''

Charles was still stunned by the age factor, but the sheriff misunderstood the surprise in his eyes.

"Don't get excited, Mr. Butler. I'm sure I got that literary reference off the back of one of my bubble gum cards.''

"I remember bubble gum," said Charles, not missing a beat, not rising to the bait. "It was wonderful. Do they still make it?''

"Why you poor ignorant man." Jessop pointed to the glove compartment. "In there. Help yourself.''

Charles opened the small door in the dashboard, and a pile of card-size packets spilled out with the rich timeless smell of gum and an Officer Friendly logo printed on the wrappers.

"We give them out to the kids." Sheriff Jessop pulled a few packets from the pile that Charles was stuffing back into the glove compartment.

"So Babe was debauched?" The landscape crawled by the car window, and Charles looked at his watch. Still lots of time. "Not leading the exemplary life of an evangelist?''

"Babe was no saint—that's a fact. These past few years, he was stoned on drugs or drink every time I saw him. That sorry, diseased son of a bitch.''

"Diseased?''

"You bet. Every last soul in Dayborn remembers his party at the Dayborn Bar and Grill. It was his nineteenth birthday, but the Lauries were really celebrating Babe's first case of the clap. That VD party was a legend. It went on for three days." He put his hand into the pile of clutter on the dashboard and extricated a folded sheaf of papers bearing today's date and the seal of a medical examiner. He handed it to Charles. "Cut to the second page, top of the sheet.''

Charles scanned the lines. According to the autopsy report, Babe Laurie had died in an advanced stage of venereal disease. Various drugs and alcohol were listed in the contents of the stomach. Charles turned to the sheriff, who was nodding, saying, "Yeah, he was diseased all right."

Approaching the fairgrounds, they traveled by a cluster of trailers. Men in sleeveless T-shirts were standing in groups, drinking beer for their breakfast. Now a shoving match ensued and one man hit the ground in a hurry. He was kicked in the ribs by another man, and the content of a beer can was poured over the fallen man's prone body. But the sheriff seemed not to care about this infraction of the law against assaulting one's fellow citizen.

Charles unwrapped the packet in his hand and released the spicy aroma of bubble gum. He discarded the baseball trading card and held the bright piece of gum to his nose, seriously assessing the bouquet. It even *smelled* pink. When he popped it into his mouth, the taste evoked a flood of memories. That summer on the road with Cousin Max, bubble gum had been a staple of his diet.

Before they pulled into the parking lot, he had outdone himself by blowing a larger bubble than the sheriff could manage with twice the chewy pink waddage. Then Charles did a bit of showboating by blowing a bubble within a bubble. The grand finale was a resounding pop, and the sheriff took his hands off the wheel to applaud.

The car rolled to a stop in a dirt parking lot, and the two men sat companionably for a few minutes of highly competitive chewing and bubble blowing.

"You know, Sheriff." *Pop.* "I haven't seen a single child in Owltown."

Pop. "The families with kids live in Dayborn. Most of this roadie trash around here is drunks, junkies, hookers and the odd pervert—the staff and clientele of the Owltown business district."

Pop. "How many Lauries are there?"

"With cousins, second cousins, and relations by marriage? I guess a few hundred people. When the family business got too big for Mal and his brothers to manage it, they brought in relatives from Texas and the Carolinas. Now the whole pack of them work for the New Church."

Pop. Pop.

"How does a church support so many people?"

"When the tent show's touring up north in the Bible Belt, they pull in at least thirty grand on a bad night. The Lauries who stay behind in Owltown make even more money running the mail-order business."

Charles aborted a bubble. "Mail-order religion?"

Pop. "Oh, yeah. For a five-dollar donation you can have an envelope full of dirt from the Holy Land. I'm afraid I crunched up a lot of that holy dirt when I pulled into this parking lot."

Pop. "God forgives you," said Charles. "How much for a piece of the true cross?"

"Twenty dollars. However, those sawdust shavings are laminated in a strip of plastic. You can use them to mark your favorite scripture in the autographed Bible."

Pop. "Autographed by . . . ?"

"The authors, all twelve of 'em."

Charles's last bubble died in a smile. The sheriff had produced the lesser pops but the better punch line. Then Charles was appalled to learn that the sheriff was not joking. There were twelve apostles on the New Church governing board, and the text of the Bible had been substantially rewritten.

As he opened the passenger door of the car, the sheriff leaned toward him and said, "I'm gonna send my deputy back here to pick you up when you're done. I'm not being pushy, Mr. Butler, I'm just real concerned for your health. So you won't mind that?"

"Not at all. I appreciate the concern." And he meant that, for they had just been bonded by gum, hadn't they?

"Have a nice visit," said Jessop, "but don't stray off the fairgrounds. That's just a friendly caution."

Charles stepped out of the car and walked over the open field beyond the parking lot, past the blights of vans and trucks, trailers and food stands. When he stood at the center of the denuded horseshoe bend, he had a spectacular view of cypress trees and their mirror reflections lining the far

shore of the bayou. A snowy egret took flight in the distance, escaping the noise which was growing in volume as
the grounds filled with workers shouting and barking commands.

His eyes followed the flight of the bird. Its wings spread
on the air and long legs flowed back from white feathers.
The sun dappled the bayou in a bright band of sparkling
lights. A fish broke through still water near a string of trap
lines extending out from the bank. Scales shining like silver, it rose out of the bayou as though to fly free. At the
end of the tether of hook and line, it fell back into a foam
of splashing water.

Charles turned his attention to the metal shafts erected
in the middle of the field. Each tall pole waved a bright red
banner, and long ropes trailed down to the ground. The
tallest would be the center pole of the great canvas tent,
which now lay in a huge flat circle spread out at his feet.
Its circumference would make a fair-size dog track.

Off to one side of the bend, a sudden burst of a cappella
music came from a gospel choir in blue jeans. A woman
with a baton stood before the group and waved their voices
up and down with a flick of her wrist. Suddenly, she broke
off the rehearsal to shout obscenities at a man passing close
by with a boom box blaring rock music. There were hollered conversations all around him as men converged on
the massive circle of canvas.

He had come just in time. The tent was going up, being
hoisted on the ropes, rising before his eyes and blotting out
the sky. Each time he blinked, it morphed into some new
shape, sharply pointing at the center and more points at the
outer rim, as the material, anchored in metal rings, was
drawn up the length of the poles. All around the vast circle,
men hauled on the lines, and the pulleys squealed. The
canvas was alive in the wind, whipping and bucking against
the ropes, stressed and straining, finally rearing up into the
familiar form of a gigantic circus tent. Atop the poles, the
red banners snapped in the breeze and then stuck straight
out in forked tongues.

Another man had come to stand beside him, and when Charles turned, he half expected to see the famed magician, Maximillian Candle. But Cousin Max was long dead, and Charles was staring at Malcolm Laurie, a head smaller than himself. But it occurred to him that this man must also be a conjuror of sorts, for he was experiencing the illusion of falling down into Malcolm's eyes.

"I thought you might enjoy this, Charles. I'm glad you came."

So, Malcolm had gone to the trouble to learn his first name, but not asked if he might use it. Though he had always given such permission to anyone who wanted it, he didn't like the sound of his more familiar name in Malcolm's mouth. It felt like an intrusion.

A violation?

Augusta, get out of my head.

Charles turned back to the tent. Four men were raising a neon sign by guide wires to suspend it from a tall steel framework. It was a marquee of green glass tubes rising high in the air above them. The capital letters were very large, and Charles was startled by the bluntness of the words: MIRACLES FOR SALE.

MALLORY SHOOK PILLOW feathers off the blanket and sent them drifting into the corridor outside her cell, where the sheriff was lecturing his new deputy on the fine points of housekeeping and the proper procedure for handling dangerous prisoners.

"Now, at the end of the month, I gotta give you back to the state in the same condition they gave you to me. So follow my orders and stay out of trouble." The sheriff waved one hand in the air to bat away the feathers from the small storm Mallory had created with her blanket shaking. His mood was worsening by the second.

Good. Mallory sat down on the bed and commenced her daily activity of staring at the opposite wall.

"First, have her put her hands through the bars. Then

you cuff the prisoner to the bars before you unlock the door. You got that? And be sure you hang up your gun belt outside the cell.'' He pointed to the hooks on the wall.

Mallory had noticed that the sheriff never took his own advice. During all the hours of questioning, pacing up and down her cell while she sat in silence, he had never taken off his gun belt. He had all but waved it in her face. But she had bided her time, waiting for a slip of words to hang him with.

As a small child, she had believed this man was God with a six-shooter. This morning, the man outside her cell was just an ordinary human, sloppier and slower now, falling short of a god in every way. He was even conforming to Louisiana code and carrying a police-issue automatic. However, his deputy had strayed outside the code to pack a .38 revolver. Now that was promising. The ammo would work in her own .357.

''And then,'' the sheriff was saying to his new deputy, ''you clean all those damn feathers outta that cell. Hear me?''

The deputy took umbrage, dark eyebrows rushing together, lips pouting. Perhaps no one had told her that maid service was part of her job description. All Lilith Beaudare's words came out in a rush. ''I was first in a class of—''

''Girl, that police academy was nothing more than a glorified kindergarten.'' His irritation was showing more, building to a boil.

So the deputy was only a rookie, fresh from a six-week training program which might have taught her how to avoid shooting herself in the foot, but little more than that. Mallory noted another giveaway—the deputy's belt. It was weighted down with Mace, ammo, flashlight, handcuffs, cell phone, speedloader and a nightstick. This woman was all dressed up for a task-force raid, yet she conveyed the credo of the overly prepared Girl Scout.

Mallory ceased to listen to the argument beyond the door of her cell. She was taking further measurements of Lilith

Beaudare, estimating the woman's height as even with her own. Their build and weight were about the same. Beaudare might be a few years younger. The woman seemed secure in her dark skin, moving with an easy physical confidence of the body—but the sheriff was walking all over her.

"When I come back up here, I don't want to see one damn feather in that cell." The sheriff opened a small door to disclose a pantry of shelves bearing cleaning supplies. He pulled out a broom, a dustpan, a cloth and a folded plastic trash bag. He handed off these items to the rookie, who was now subdued by humiliation. "We'll just see if you can do this one job right before we turn you loose on organized crime."

Mallory picked up a handful of feathers from the floor, held them to her lips and blew the sheriff a kiss. Two feathers landed in his hair. Others were delicately balanced on his nose and chin. He removed them with great deliberation, pinching them between his fingers and reducing them to strings.

Lilith Beaudare was working hard at holding back a smile.

Jessop stared at his deputy until her mouth assumed a more respectful line. "Just get on with the housework, girl." His feet were heavy on the floorboards as he stomped down the narrow corridor. The door slammed shut behind him.

The deputy leaned the broom against the cell block wall. It was well within Mallory's reach.

Stupid move, Deputy.

The woman turned to Mallory. "You know why that bastard thinks he can talk to me that way?"

"Because you're a woman? Or because you're black? Pick one. I haven't got all day for this crap." She reached out through the bars to grasp the broom.

The deputy only watched her do this, unconcerned, not realizing that a broom could be a weapon—if Mallory chose to drive it through the bars and into the deputy's gut. If she really wanted to do some damage, she could drive the broom handle into the deputy's throat. It would only take a second. But it was not Lilith Beaudare she wanted to damage.

"It was a mistake to tell him you were at the top of your class," said Mallory, moving the broom along the floor. "He's going to gnaw on that for a while, and then sometime after lunch he just might put it all together." She had fluffed a small pile of feathers up to the bars, and now a sweet light southern drawl crept into her voice. "Hand me that dustpan, will you?"

The deputy's face was fixed in rapt attention as she surrendered the copper dustpan with its nice sharp corners to tear the flesh of a throat with only minimum force.

Oh, Deputy, you have a lot to learn, and I am going to teach you.

"I know your name can't be *girl*." In fact, she knew that Deputy Beaudare's middle name was Mary. Most of Mallory's information came from Jane, who brought her meals three times a day and didn't mind holding up both ends of a conversation.

She brushed the feathers into the dustpan. And some took flight, escaping between the bars.

"My name is Lilith Beaudare." And now, unbidden, the deputy also handed over the large green garbage bag, which would fit so nicely over the dark head if Mallory chose to suffocate the life out of this rookie cop.

"Lilith, this is no place for an up-and-comer like you. First in your class? That would have guaranteed you first pick of assignments." She set the bag and dustpan on the small chest of drawers by her bed. "He'll have to wonder what you're doing here in St. Jude, the smallest parish in the state. And the town's population wouldn't fill two city blocks of New Orleans."

"I was born in this town. It makes sense that I—"

"Well, no it doesn't. It would make sense for you to get as far away as you could. First in your class? Not small-town material. No, there's definitely something wrong with this picture."

Mallory came back to the cell door and got on with the chore of fluffing the feathers along the strip of floor by the bars. "He'll have to figure you for a liar. Or maybe you're a screwup, and this is a punishment detail."

"I am not a—"

"You could be a plant." Well, that shut her mouth. "Yeah, that would work."

Even Jane, of Jane's Cafe, had found it odd that the state police should send the sheriff a deputy. Tom Jessop had been hiring and training his own people for decades. "You've made a lot of mistakes, Lilith. But maybe he's as dumb as you think he is. Maybe he won't put it all together . . . unless *somebody* puts the idea in his head."

The woman said nothing. She was only gaping.

Mallory gestured to the stuffed armchair opposite her bed. "Come into my office and pull up a chair. I'm going to fix your life."

The invitation was delivered so like an order, the rookie nearly followed it. But she stayed the hand that was reaching for the door, the hand with the key. Her arm dropped to her side, and she only stared at her prisoner.

Mallory lowered her eyes in submission. She returned to the bed and knelt down on the floor to move the broom underneath it, stirring a small cloud of feathers into the open. Her back was turned when she heard the clicks of the key working the tumblers of the lock. Footsteps entered the cell, and the door was locked again. When Mallory looked up, the deputy's hand rested on the gun in her holster.

Perfect.

Mallory gestured to the armchair, inviting her guest to sit down. The deputy remained standing, eyes on the prisoner, as though Mallory might be a viper in striking distance. And she was.

"So he humiliated you." Mallory turned her attention back to the feathers at the far corner under the bed. The armchair creaked behind her. "I bet he does that a lot."

She turned to see the deputy sitting in the chair, rigid, hands tightly clutching a dustcloth.

"He's a son of a bitch," said the deputy, teeth clenched. "I could write him up for—"

"No, that's a bad idea." Mallory swept feathers into the dustpan as she went on in an easy tone, low and conspiratorial. "If you ask someone else to solve your problem, they'll write you off as a loser. That's what I'd do."

Oh, the rookie didn't like that at all. *Well, tough.*

"Here's a better idea," said Mallory, emptying the dustpan into the green plastic bag. "Be the kind of cop no one would treat that way." She stood up slowly and swept feathers closer to the armchair. The deputy sat ramrod straight, distrustful in every alerted muscle.

Mallory picked up the dustpan and began to herd the feathers into it. "Shoot better, even if it means putting in overtime and paying for extra practice rounds." She walked to the window of the cell and ran one finger over the sill, staring distastefully at the dust. "Think better—don't be in such a damn hurry to get the words out." Now she strolled back to the deputy's chair. "You don't want to open your mouth unless you have something to say, and then you only say something worth listening to."

The deputy seemed more relaxed now. Her grip on the dustcloth had lightened. Mallory bent down and plucked the cloth from the woman's hand in a natural, easy movement. She began to rub the surface of the chest of drawers. "Never take crap from anybody. If you take it once, you'll take it forever. If it means a fight, then fight—even if you know you can't win."

Mallory made intense eye contact until the other woman found it uncomfortable and dropped her guard to look at the floor. Mallory walked closer to the deputy's chair. She bent low, her fair head next to the dark one, so close— sisters now. "Wear the bastard down." And now she whispered, giving equal weight to every syllable, "Make this your religion."

Mallory moved quickly to rip the gun from the deputy's

holster. She pressed the muzzle to the woman's skull. As a throwaway afterthought, she said, "Oh, and there's nothing quite as stupid as losing your gun to a prisoner."

Lilith Beaudare showed all the signs of deep embarrassment, but no fear. Mallory liked that—she liked it a lot. This rookie cop had promise. She sat down on the edge of her bed and leaned toward the woman. "Now I'll tell you why the sheriff treats you like dirt. It's because you're a useless rookie, green as they come."

And maybe you're also a spy, Lilith Beaudare. State or federal, I wonder?

"Right now you're no help to him at all. You're more likely to get yourself shot." Mallory held the gun a little higher as a show-and-tell exhibit. "Point taken? *Now* do you understand your place in the world?"

The deputy nodded.

Mallory turned the gun around and handed it back to her.

The deputy only stared at it for a second, as if disbelieving it could be within her reach. Then she accepted it and pointed it at her prisoner.

Mallory ignored the gun barrel leveled at her heart. "School's out. I fixed your life. I probably saved it—you won't lose your gun again, will you? You owe me big-time, *girl*."

"Deputy Beaudare, to you."

"Now you've got it. Remember, the sheriff thinks you're worthless. See what you can do to change that."

Mallory had finally concluded that the new deputy had been planted by the feds, and not the state. It was the delayed fingerprint report that decided her. She had no worries about the serial number on her Smith & Wesson. She had altered that computer entry years ago. But results of the fingerprint search should have come back to Sheriff Jessop long before now.

A homicide case would get a high priority. Just the name Mallory, her age and description would have a large array. But she gave the sheriff credit for coupling "Mallory" with

"Kathy," which narrowed the field. So the feds were holding out on Jessop, but why?

When the sheriff returned, his deputy was once again standing in the corridor beyond the bars, holding on to a plastic bag full of feathers. Tom Jessop cast an approving eye over the tidy cell. "Good job. I guess you're ready for something a little more challenging. You remember Mr. Butler, don't you? The giant with the big nose?"

The deputy nodded.

"I want you to drive down to the fairgrounds and wait on him till he's ready to be escorted back to Dayborn. And try not to put any dents in the car. It's all we got till Travis's unit is out of the shop."

When Lilith had quit the cell block, the sheriff turned to Mallory, and she smiled at him. It was her first friendly overture to this man in all the days she had been his prisoner.

He wore the startled look of sudden recognition, and then his face relaxed. "Now that's my Kathy." He said it softly. It was almost a sigh.

And Mallory was still smiling when she said, "Step into my office, Sheriff. Pull up a chair."

"OH, THE SIGN," said Malcolm Laurie, waving it off as though Charles had simply misunderstood the message of miracles for sale. Or perhaps it was a typographical error in four-foot block letters. "It's a commercial world, isn't it, Charles? I have to relate to my flock any way I can." The smile of the charming boy was back.

"So you don't actually sell the miracles?"

"Oh, sure I do. People don't trust what they don't pay for. They're more inclined to believe in things that cost hard cash. In my line of work, belief is ninety percent of the job. Hell, it *is* the job. If Christ came back today and gave His Sermon on the Mount for free, who would turn out for the show?"

"I believe that sermon was catered with magical loaves

and fish to feed the multitude,'' Charles countered. "I'd
turn out for that.''

"Hey, Mal!'' A man with a clipboard was coming toward them. He had the same general features as Malcolm,
except for his eyes, which were small and dark. This man
was being introduced to him as Fred Laurie. While Malcolm attended to the clipboard, Charles was distracted by
the sight of the sheriff's car pulling into the parking lot.
The promised escort had arrived, and he should be saying
goodbye to Malcolm soon.

When Fred Laurie had left them, he asked, "What sort
of miracles do you sell, Malcolm?''

"Whatever you're in the market for.''

Over the head of the smaller man, Charles saw Lilith
Beaudare alight from the car and look around. Now she
had picked him out of the crowd, an easy feat; he was the
only person of abnormal height and wearing a three-piece
suit. As she was striding across the field, a drunk stumbled
into her path and engaged her in conversation. A group of
people passed in front of Charles and blocked her from his
view. "Suppose I bought a miracle that would let me get
away with murder?''

Malcolm's smile hovered in the zone of bemusement.
His eyes flickered with the bright work of running calcu-
lations and taking measurements. "Every miracle comes
with a caution and a guarantee. The scales of heaven and
hell are balanced, and every destructive act exacts a terrible
price. So you may decide you don't want that kind of miracle.''

Now it was Charles who was confused. Was Malcolm
taking the literal meaning of getting away with murder?
Was this a more common request than he had supposed?

The small group of people passed on. Lilith was visible
once more, and in heated conversation. The drunk looked
rather pleased with himself, and even more pleased with
her.

"What if that's the only miracle I want to buy?'' Charles
continued to watch over Lilith as the drunk was moving

closer to her. But she was smiling at the reeling man, and so Charles saw no cause for alarm. He turned back to face Malcolm, and reiterated, "Would you sell me that miracle?"

"Yes, but it would cost you dearly." There was a silence now. Perhaps the salesman of miracles was gearing up for the barter, only waiting on Charles to ask the price so the dickering could begin. But Charles remained silent.

"My guarantees are good as gold," said Malcolm. "Written in the name of the Lord."

Charles smiled at the tie of gold and religion which rather neatly summed up the core philosophy of the New Church—payment first, rapture later.

"But, as I recall, Charles, I already offered you one miracle for free. Have you lost faith in that one—maybe because you didn't have to pay for it?"

Charles ceased to smile, for now the game had become more intricate. He could no longer hazard a guess at this man's strategy.

He looked beyond Malcolm to the unexpected sight of the drunk falling at the feet of the young deputy. Now the man was rolling on the grass, tears streaming down his face, as the deputy knelt beside him, forcing his hands behind his back and cuffing him. A much bigger man was standing over them, screaming at her, "That was a damn kidney punch. You punched him when his back was turned!" The drunk's large champion raised his hands in angry balled fists.

Those fists came down to his sides very quickly, as the deputy rose to her feet in one graceful and fluid motion, her hand lightly touching on the handle of her holstered gun. The trio was too far away for Charles to hear what was not hollered, but the big man raised one hand in the calming gesture of *Okay, enough said*. He then backed away from the deputy with both his hands splayed out to say, *Hey, no harm done*. Obviously, he had decided that Lilith's hitting the drunk when his back was turned was not such a criminal offense after all.

•   •   •

LILITH BEAUDARE WAS smiling as she entered the sheriff's office with her prisoner. She had safely delivered Charles Butler to his hotel in the square, and also bagged this fine, but highly intoxicated trophy. The drunk seemed a bit too docile, though. Perhaps she had punched him too hard. She did wish he would show a bit more life, à little more angry resistance to make a better impression on the sheriff.

She bundled the drunk up the stairs, gripping him by one arm, as much in an effort to keep him from falling down as to direct his steps. When they were through the door and standing in front of the first holding unit, she was searching her pocket for her key ring when she glanced into the middle cell.

Mallory was gone.

The sheriff was standing at the back of the closed cell with an empty holster. He was staring out the bars of the window, hands in his pants pockets, his head angled to watch the foot traffic at the mouth of the alley. He was within easy hailing distance of help, yet not calling out.

Of course not. Neither had Lilith called out when it had been her turn to lose a gun.

Now the sheriff turned and saw her standing there, gripping what he could see of an arm in a red shirt. Lilith looked back at her prisoner. The drunk had seen nothing of the sheriff yet. The man's unfocused eyes were cast up to the ceiling, perhaps looking there for flights of angels to carry him home. She pushed the drunk back to the door at the end of the cell block.

"I'm gonna let you go with a warning this time." She uncuffed him and shook him roughly by the shoulders. "Are you listening to me?" She opened the door and motioned him through it. "Go!" She watched his stumbling, half-falling progress down the stairs, and when he hit bottom, she called after him, "Don't steal anything on the way out!"

She returned to the middle cell and unlocked the door,

resisting the urge to say something sarcastic. *Don't be in a hurry to get the words out.* She suppressed a smile as she looked down to the sheriff's empty holster.

His face reddened and his hand moved quickly to cover the leather as though she had caught him naked. "We don't need to mention this to anybody, do we, girl?

"Girl?"

"Lilith," he corrected himself.

"Deputy," she said, in the manner of striking a bargain.

He nodded and the deal was sealed. She opened the door. He passed into the narrow corridor, as Lilith studied the cell's lock. "Now, how do you suppose she got out? Oh, wait. I see it now."

He looked down as she pointed to the lock.

"You know, Sheriff, that piece of junk must be as old as the building. It's a damn antique, isn't it? Pity the parish didn't increase your budget this year. You might've had that replaced."

Lilith hit the lock once with her nightstick, but it held. She hit it a second time and put some muscle behind it. The old lock began to give.

The sheriff wore the ghost of a smile.

"Damn penny-pinching fools," said Lilith, as she continued to hammer away at the rusted metal. "I'd really make those bastards burn for this, if I were you."

The sheriff's smile was wider now, and Deputy Beaudare took that to mean that he had finally found her useful.

There was only one other possibility—he might be laughing at her.

He did clap her warmly on the back, in the way that men congratulate one another, but she was still unsure of him as they descended the stairs. He disappeared into his office and emerged a few minutes later with another gun in his holster. Through the open door, she saw the credenza behind the desk was missing the black leather duffel bag. So now the escaped prisoner had two guns, the sheriff's 9mm automatic and the .357 revolver.

"I'm going after her," said the sheriff, almost to the

door. "I want you to stay close to that phone in case I need you, all right?" And then he was gone, and the door swung shut behind him.

She sat down at her desk and resumed her job of watching a phone that never rang. Nothing had changed.

Lilith powered up the computer. At the C prompt, she prepared to enter a code, but the machine was writing its own commands. Sitting at the edge of her chair, she watched the unfolding notice of a message in a newly created private file which awaited the deputy's personal password. She entered her password at the next prompt, and her message appeared. By the opening salutation, she knew whose work this was. How long had it taken Mallory to figure out that the password was WOLF?

Dear Rookie,
Not in your best interests if I get caught. I'll tell the
sheriff what you really are. And, Rookie, you don't
even know the whole answer to that one. I'll call
when I want you.

Lilith felt the touch of ice running along her back, fingering her spine from the inside of her skin. As she was deleting Mallory's memo from hell, she glanced down at the disk pack on the desk. The cellophane wrapper had been sealed this morning, but now it was split open and the box was missing two computer disks. So the escapee had taken time from her busy jailbreak-morning to download the files.

CHAPTER
9

DEATH CREATED NO problem for Ira Wooley when the bodies were laid to rest in the vaults of existing tombs. A fresh grave required him to memorize the entire cemetery anew, but this was rare. Generally, sameness prevailed, and so this was a favorite place. The people were silent; their monuments and stone houses never changed. But the dying bouquets of All Saints' Day had been removed from the graves, and now he walked through the alleys of tombs, making minor adjustments in his mind, fixing a new image for this city of the dead, *sans* flowers.

"Hello, Ira," said a voice behind him.

Startled, he turned around to see a tall figure standing at the rim of the tree circle. It was the sandwich man from Jane's Cafe, and he was moving forward with long-legged strides, increasing Ira's fear as he drew closer. The sandwich man was smiling, but facial arrangements for love and anger were all the same to Ira. It was a language he could not read. Now the sandwich man seemed to understand that motion communicated menace, and he stood very still.

Ira ceased to gulp the air, and the rhythm of his heart was slowing, but then he plunged into deep distress. The tall man represented a new object in the cemetery. Ira's body slowly revolved, eyes passing over the ground, the stones and the trees to create a new inventory. The sandwich man played the statue with endless patience until Ira had committed each object to a new schematic which incorporated the man as part of the cemetery.

When Ira was done, the man spoke again, but what he said did not come across as words yet, only noises at the moment, for the fear had not entirely subsided.

"Do you remember me? Charles Butler?"

"Do you remember me," said Ira in a monotone.

"I wonder if you could answer a question about what happened to your hands. Would that upset you?"

"Would that upset you," said Ira. And in the next moment, the noise had become a few words. His hands—upset him? He looked down on the bandages. His hands had done nothing to upset him.

The man was saying more, but his words became noise again, as unintelligible as the wind in the trees, the musical birdcalls and the more mechanical clicks and whirs of insects. Every sound in the cemetery was melding together, all the same noise. Ira focussed on his bandages as he began the work of shutting down the sound. At last, he entered the peaceful zone of white static.

But the man's words came through again, noise insisting on itself, rising in inflection.

Ira cried out, "Yes, yes, yes, yes, yes," until the sandwich man learned that "yes" meant "Shut up! SHUT UP!" and the man fell silent. And now Ira taught the tall stranger to stand motionless again, and to drop his eyes. It took only a little time till the man learned not to look at him directly. Then Ira's attention was captured by a drop of water moving slowly along the leaf of a shrub. He was sliding into a trance when the drop elongated and fell off the leaf to become a perfect sphere in free fall. It splashed on the ground and freed him from fixation.

The sandwich man sat beside him so quietly, he became as the trees and the stones. And now they could talk.

"So you played five notes on the piano, and Babe didn't like that."

"Babe didn't like that," said Ira.

"Can you tell me why?"

"Tell me why." Ira rocked back and forth, and then he began to hum. Babe had broken his hands but not his mouth. Humming soothed him and reduced the terror of a new voice which he had not been properly prepared for. Jane's Cafe was not terrifying because he ate his lunch there every day, and his mother was always beside him. But now he was alone with the very large sandwich man, and this was wrong. The cafe was not supposed to follow him about.

But the man seemed to understand him much better than other people did. He was patient and his voice was calm, asking more questions about Babe.

Babe was dangerous. His mother had told him the man was dead, but Ira had no pictures of a dead Babe, and he had not yet seen Babe's stone added to the cemetery.

Ira looked over the sandwich man's shoulder as he prepared to speak to him. He delved into his store of dialogue for something appropriate. He decided upon an instruction he had received in the kitchen one bright morning, years ago. He remembered that scene best for the play of light on the wall, taking its patterns from white lace curtains. Then the fascination with curtain patterns had been displaced by his attraction to the fire of the stove's front burner, and he had reached for it. His mother had restrained him and spoken to him out of deep concern. Now these were the same words he gave to the sandwich man. "Don't burn yourself."

The man changed his expression and hung his head a little lower. Ira perceived a touch of sadness as the sandwich man stood up, said, "Goodbye," and walked away with his eyes cast down to the gravel path.

"Goodbye," Ira echoed as he watched the tall man disappear into the encircling trees.

A few seconds passed by before he heard the next sound

that did not belong in this place—footsteps so light a cat might have made them. He turned slowly, not wanting to see it, unable to help himself.

Impossible. He sat down on the grass before his knees could buckle underneath him and tumble him to the ground.

It was Dr. Cass.

But she had been made whole again, washed clean of blood. He labored over this a moment more, and worked very hard at his school lessons in an effort to put stored pictures in chronological order.

Cass Shelley was dead. He had attended her funeral service. This was a fragment of early memory which followed the flying stones, the breakage and the blood, Cass's eyes finally closing—closed. This woman before him could not be Dr. Cass.

"Who," said Ira, without inflection. She walked toward him, and looked directly at him. In a sudden onslaught of new fear, the sense of the word escaped him. When he said it again, it was as meaningless as the language of the owl. "Who."

The woman knelt down beside him, her hands rising, reaching out for him. She was going to touch him! He shrank back. *No, no, this is too much! No! Don't touch! Oh, please, no—*

She held him firmly by the shoulders. His body went rigid and his eyes rolled up to solid whites. He wanted to scream. He was afraid of her eyes.

"I know you don't like this," she said so gently, so softly, it was almost music. "But I need you to pay attention, Ira. *Focus.* You did that for my mother, and now you have to do it for me."

The words meant nothing. He was terrified. He wanted to look at her without being seen, and she allowed this, dropping her eyes of intense color. But his fear of her was still so great, it sent her shape into a swirl of bright light that threatened to overload his senses. The sun drenched her hair and set it on fire. Her lips of red jumped out at him, parting to show the perfect rows of her teeth.

She was talking again. "I know you heard the song on the record player, Ira."

Song?

He listened to her voice on the level of music for a while, having no idea what she might be saying. But soon the meaning was forcing its way into his consciousness. Over and over again, the same music, "What did you see?"

He saw the words now, dancing vibrations in the air before his eyes. He watched the rocks fly into Dr. Cass's face and the rocks that doubled her body over. He nodded his head and said, "What did you see." Yes, he was there, he had seen it. "What did you see," he said, nodding again. She released him. He stood up and began to pace in circles.

She walked behind him, golden shadow, thrumming with color, throbbing with energy. He looked up to the sky, because looking at her was unbearable now, too much intensity. She was an explosion of life. His hands began to flutter in circles. His breathing was rapid and shallow—he was suffocating.

"What did you see?"

"She was red!" he screamed, and watched his words burst into colors which made ripples in his perceptions. "No more noise—the dog cried." This second phrase tumbled out in quieter tones of stone gray. "The letter was blue." These last words were dull pebbles thudding on the dirt at her feet.

"The letter?"

"Blue." He shook his head to say it was blue and nothing else; he knew nothing more.

"How many of them, Ira? The people who threw the rocks! How many?"

She said this many times, walking with him around the cemetery, fifty times around the angel, exactly fifty times, and she was always right behind him. "How many?" she asked without tiring, without any sign of ever stopping. His hands rolled one around the other, faster and faster.

"How many?"

"Twenty-seven people! Eighteen rocks!" His count was

exact, he had only to look at the television set inside his
head, which replayed everything, each rock in its own turn,
each body in the crowd vibrating in a separate hue, and an
overall aura of violent energy.

He walked to the statue of Dr. Cass's angel and wrapped
his arms around it. He beat his head against the stone, not
feeling the pain, but wanting to. She pulled him away. Her
soft hand went to the place on his head where the red
flowed.

"She was all red," he said, seeing Dr. Cass in vivid
color.

"I know, Ira. I saw her, too. All red."

She pulled back her hands and sat down in the grass.
After a few moments, he sat down a safe distance away
from her. In her hand was his own handkerchief, plucked
from his pocket and stained with his blood. He never met
her eyes but once and accidentally. She was crooning low
music, an old lullaby; he remembered it well. He rocked
himself, and she was rocking with him. This was so familiar, something beloved that he had carefully stored
away.

He replayed the old pictures of a small girl humming his
songs with him as she walked alongside him. She had been
his only friend and the only child who had never tortured
him.

His old playmate.

Rocking, rocking, calmer now, he leaned his head back
and stared at the clouds. "Kathy."

"Yes, Ira?"

"Kathy," was all he said, and that was quite a lot. It
was said with love.

CHAPTER
10

THERE WERE NO curtains on any of the windows, yet Charles Butler wondered if he had been misinformed. Cass Shelley's house should be vacant, but wasn't the dog a sign of residency?

The black Labrador had come loping from behind the house, favoring one hind leg with a limp. Some of his front teeth were broken and others were missing. Hanging from his graying muzzle and his ears were tags of flesh on strings of skin grown awry in the aging process. The Lab didn't look directly at Charles, but turned his head to the side to study his visitor with the eye that was not clouded by cataract.

Perhaps this was only a stray, or maybe it was Augusta Trebec's idea of a guard dog.

Though Charles knew it was the conceit of humans to see their own emotions in other creatures, he perceived a great disappointment in the dog's aspect and his one good eye. Had this poor beast been expecting someone else?

The animal lowered his large dark head, limped back to the house and disappeared in the bushes at the rear of the yard.

Henry Roth was nowhere in sight. Charles looked at his watch. It was still a quarter to the hour when the artist had agreed to meet him with the keys.

He stood back to admire the elaborate woodwork on the porch of the old Victorian building. The turret rooms on either side had rare barrel glass in the windows. Augusta might be slack with her own house, but she had spared no expense in keeping this one in good order, even to replacing the red shingles and applying a fresh coat of blue-gray paint to the walls.

Charles walked up the short flight of stairs to the front door and tried the knob. The house was unlocked. Henry Roth must have come early and left it open for him. He stepped into a foyer of hardwood floors, calling out, "Hello? Mr. Roth?"

No answer.

He stood at the foot of the staircase and glanced at a set of doors which should open to a wide drawing room. If he correctly recalled the architecture of this period, he would find a narrower servant staircase at the other end of the hall, and that one would lead from the kitchen to the attic. He opened the last door off the hallway and entered an enclosed, airless space. A window at the second-floor landing provided a generous amount of light, and he climbed past it, heading toward the attic, hoping that door would also be unlocked.

More light came flooding down the steps from a top-floor window. As he neared the final landing, he could see the attic door standing open to a darkened room. When his eyes had fully adapted to this space he could see that all but one of the dormer windows were obscured by trunks and furniture. A film of dust had been allowed to settle on every surface. He turned around to see that he had left footprints on the dark wood floor. Nothing had been disturbed in a very long time, but someone had taken care that Cass Shelley's personal papers should be preserved. Clear plastic boxes were stacked up against one wall. Each bore a carefully printed label. At the base of the stack was a doctor's Gladstone bag.

He wiped the dust from a box marked "Business Correspondence," and through the plastic he could see a packet of letters with surprisingly little yellowing. He opened the box and held the first letter to the light of the only clear window. It was addressed to Cass Shelley, the town doctor and parish health officer. And now he found the label for her journals on a lower box. Twenty minutes later, he was deep into her personal notes on Ira Wooley, the boy's progress reports from the age of two years to five. She had also written lengthy impressions of his talents. It was nearly poetry, and in every line there was deep respect for the small child who had been her patient from birth.

Dr. Shelley's appointment book had not been packed in one of the boxes, but rested in a plastic bag bearing an evidence tag from the sheriff's office. Inside the cover of the book, he found a faded carbon of the receipt signed by the executrix, Augusta Trebec. He turned to the last entry, seventeen years in the past, and found Ira's name. But the six year old was expected for a piano lesson, and not a medical appointment. So Cass Shelley was the one who had taught him to play. The entry was dated to the last day of her life.

Suppose Ira had witnessed the murder?

That would explain the block in his progress, the withdrawal and lack of articulation. With seventeen years of ongoing therapy his speech skills should have improved, not declined. Even after the traumatic loss of his primary mentor—there should have been improvement. But if he had seen her murdered, what then?

He held the sheriff's receipt in his hand. The same thought must have occurred to Jessop. Had he interrogated the boy? Depending on how such an interview was carried out, that might have done even more damage.

He was so preoccupied with his thoughts, he never heard a sound until the footsteps were almost on top of him. He was turning to say hello to Henry Roth, but he found him-

self staring into a barrel of blue-black metal a few inches
from his face. He never moved and scarcely breathed for
all the time it took the sheriff's eyes to adjust to the dim
light.

The weapon was returned to its holster. "Afternoon, Mr.
Butler."

"I *do* have a letter of permission from Augusta Trebec."
Charles was reaching to the inside pocket of his suit.

"No need for that. Sorry if I frightened you."

The sheriff did seem genuinely regretful—and relieved.
He was working on a smile when his eye fell on the appointment book in Charles's hand. Now his lips were set
in a tight line, and he stood a little straighter as though he
were bracing for a blow.

"I was expecting Henry Roth," said Charles. "He was
supposed to meet me here."

"Henry's probably out in the yard feeding the dog. He
does that every day." The sheriff was staring at the stacks
of cartons, perhaps looking for other worries in the printed
labels.

Charles stood up, dusting off his pants with his free hand.
"So you took me for a burglar?"

"Light's so bad in here. At first, all I saw was a shadow
bending over the boxes." Now the sheriff was pointing at
the book in Charles's hand. "Find anything interesting?"

"I know Ira had an appointment for a piano lesson the
day Cass Shelley died. I assume the lessons were part of
Ira's behavior therapy."

"You don't need to mention Ira's appointment to anyone
else."

"Does his mother know?"

"I never ran that past Darlene. Her husband was alive
then. I asked him about it. He said he'd canceled the piano
lesson. He had a falling-out with Cass. Said he was planning to change doctors."

"But Cass Shelley didn't mark it as a cancelation. She's
done that with other entries, but not this one. So you never
asked Darlene if—"

"I don't think we need to mention this to Darlene," said the sheriff, as though explaining something to a child for the tenth time and getting damn sick of it.

"Why the secrecy? The mother has a right to know. If the boy was here when—"

"Well, maybe the boy was here." The sheriff's voice was on the rise. "So *what*!" Jessop pressed his lips together tight, damming up his words for a ten count. His tone was lighter, lower, when he said, "Mr. Butler, you've met Darlene. She wouldn't like it much if she were to find out—at this late date. She'd be back in my office shooting off her mouth, and then everyone would know."

"If Ira saw his doctor die, that would explain the problems with his—"

"He'll have more problems if you tell Darlene. No one in Dayborn would ever hurt Ira. Most of those people have known him since he was a baby. But I got all that trash in Owltown to consider. Ignorant fools might take it into their heads that Ira could be dangerous. You know how Cass died?"

"Yes, but Ira was only a little boy when—"

"Ira's a mimic, echoes everything you say. Maybe they'll see Babe's murder as another kind of echo because he was done in with a rock—just like Cass."

Charles thought that was a bit of a stretch.

"All right, you got me." Obviously, the sheriff was adept at reading incredulity. "Let's say Ira's a witness to an unsolved murder. Suppose one of the killers goes after him? Maybe more than one. Remember, it was a mob that stoned Cass to death."

"I understand." Charles paled at any possibility, however remote, that Ira might be harmed. "Augusta tells me you never established a motive for the crime."

"Well, it wasn't a crime of passion." The sheriff picked up a box and stared at the label. "It was a quiet kill—more like an execution."

How was that possible? "A mob killing—with no passion?"

Jessop tilted his head to one side and looked at Charles as though he might be a bit slow. "That's what I said." Disinclined to elaborate, he turned his back and perused the rest of the box labels.

Charles thumbed through the previous entries in the appointment book. He found another familiar name. "Babe Laurie was one of her patients?"

The sheriff seemed almost bored now. "Yeah, but Cass had to drag him in off the street to treat him." Jessop stood beside Charles and glanced down at the page. Then he sat down in an armchair, suddenly appearing very tired. A cloud of dust rose all around him. "That was the day she discovered Babe's syphilis lesions. I told you about the clap party that went on for three days. Babe was just nineteen, and I swear he had no idea what venereal disease was. He was an ignorant little bastard—never went to school a day in his life. I remember once, when he was maybe fifteen, Cass dragged him in to stitch up a head wound—flap of skin hanging loose from a fight. Nobody in that useless family of his ever thought to get him to a doctor."

The sheriff's hand grazed the Gladstone bag, and he smiled at some more pleasant memory. Back in the present and more serious, he said, "There were times when I actually felt sorry for Babe. I suppose Cass did, too. She was the only one ever showed him any kindness and didn't have some more practical use for him."

"So he's not a likely suspect in her murder investigation?"

"I didn't say that." He eased himself out of the chair and walked to the stairs. "I don't know that Babe was all that grateful. She had to chase him down to treat him, and he didn't appreciate that much. Swore at her, as I recall."

Charles walked down the stairs behind the sheriff. They had emerged in the hallway at the back of the first floor before Charles thought to ask, "And what brought you out here, Sheriff?"

"The prisoner broke jail this morning." Jessop walked down the hall, heading toward the front door.

Charles kept his silence, reasoning that if he did grab the sheriff by the lapels of his blazer, if he demanded to know if Mallory had been hurt, it might indicate something more than a passing interest in the erstwhile prisoner. "You were looking for her here?"

The sheriff seemed almost sheepish when he turned around to face Charles. "Maybe you saw that old black Lab outside?"

Charles nodded.

"That was Kathy's dog. I had this silly-ass idea that she might come back for him." He shrugged and smiled. "Well, I'm that kind of a fool."

Charles suspected the sheriff was many things, but not that. However, he had never suspected Mallory of harboring any sentimental feelings for dogs. She was compulsively neat, and dogs left hair on the furniture, didn't they? But now he toyed with the ludicrous idea that the dog had also been expecting Mallory to come back.

"She's armed and dangerous, Mr. Butler. So I'd rather you stayed out of her way if she does show up. And the jailbreak is one more thing I wish you'd keep to yourself. I don't need these woods full of vigilante Lauries and guns. Wouldn't be so bad, but half of 'em can't shoot straight, and they might wipe out an innocent tree."

"Why can't you just let her go? You really had no right to hold her."

"Like I said before, she's a material witness to her mother's murder. It's all legal."

"So it was the mother's murder, not Babe's. I rather doubt that she could have been here when her mother died. Why would the mob let her go if she was a witness to the stoning?"

"I *know* she was here that day. She was supposed to be on a riverboat trip with every other kid in her school. But they crossed her off the boarding list as a no-show. Her teacher said she'd had the sniffles on Friday. So Cass probably kept her home with a cold."

"Mallory could have been truant and elsewhere. You

can't know that she was in the house when the murder occurred.''

"Oh, yes I can. You need a guided tour, Mr. Butler. You can't really appreciate what happened here, not looking at the house the way it is now."

The sheriff opened the double doors to the drawing room and pointed to the side window. "The stoning happened outside the house on that side of the yard. That's where the bastards left her for dead. But she wasn't dead—not yet."

He opened the front door and pointed down at the floor-boards. "Seventeen years ago, Cass's blood was all over those front stairs and the porch.'' The sheriff looked down at the floor of the foyer now. "Where the old carpet used to be, there was a blood trail. You could make out her handprints as she dragged her body into the house."

The sheriff moved over to the banister. "The blood trail led up the stairs—handprints and smears. She was mortally wounded, but she managed a flight of stairs. And do you know why? She was trying to get to her little girl."

He climbed the stairs, and Charles followed him.

"I followed the blood up to Kathy's bedroom.'' Jessop turned into the second door off the hallway. He walked to the center of the room and looked down at the floor. "And this is where the trail just disappeared in a lake of blood. This is where Cass died. So this is the way I see it. When she came into the room, Kathy was locked behind that closet door over there. But Cass just couldn't make it that far."

The sheriff moved over to the closet and opened the door. A shaft of sun streamed down from a high window, a common light source in the closets of old houses predating electricity. "Well, you should have seen the job that little kid did on this door, fighting her way out to get to her mother. Kathy demolished that bottom panel, and it was real solid construction. I figure she had to throw her body into the wood a hundred times to break it. And she cut up her hands pulling the wood out so she could crawl through. That was the worst of it for me, finding those tiny bloody prints inside the closet, and the track of Kathy's own blood to the place where her mother fell. Can you picture that?''

Charles shook his head. "If she was locked in there, she couldn't have seen the stoning or identified the killers." He pointed to the square of light near the top of the closet's rear wall. "That window is too high for a full-grown adult to see anything but blue sky."

"Maybe so. But she knows something. She might know who took Cass's body away. Or maybe her mother was able to tell her something before she died."

"So you're going to hunt Mallory down like an animal. She's the victim, the innocent."

"It's my call. The mob that killed her mother is still out there. And who do you suppose they'd most like to see dead? Unless you give Ira away, the only witness is your good friend, Mallory."

The two men stared at one another in an uneasy silence.

"This is very personal to you, isn't it, Sheriff?"

"You got that one right, Mr. Butler. It's just real damn personal. Let me tell you the other little detail that keeps me awake at night. Cass locked Kathy in the closet and probably told her to keep quiet. Maybe she made a game of it. I figure Cass saw them coming from the bedroom window, and there was just time to save Kathy. The mob figured on Cass being alone in the house. Damn near every kid in town was supposed to be on that riverboat. Now if Kathy had heard her mother screaming, you think she would have kept quiet? Not that kid. So it's a safe bet she didn't hear anything at all."

"What about the noise from the mob?"

"I told you it was a quiet kill. They never made any noise—no yelling—nothing like what you'd expect. Maybe there was some conversation. She might have overheard that. And later there might have been words between Kathy and her mother—I'm hoping for words, but Kathy never heard screams. I figure Cass kept quiet all the time those bastards were taking turns at her with rocks. She didn't want them to know the kid was in the house. Can you picture it? I can. I see it every damn day of my life. I see a woman standing up to a mob, terrified, in pain, and never letting out a sound. I couldn't have done that. Could you?''

The sheriff stepped into the hall. ''One of them came back for the body.'' He pointed toward the back stairs. ''She must have been carried out that way. By the time I got here, those steps had been wiped clean, and the hall carpet was damp between this room and the back stairs, like somebody'd scrubbed it. Odd thing, isn't it? One staircase full of blood, and the other one tidied up.''

In silence, they walked down the main staircase and left the house. The sheriff was standing by the open door of his car when the dog came back to the front yard.

''I couldn't stop what was done to the mother, but no one will get to the kid. I guarantee that. I'll get her back and she'll stay in jail until she talks to me. And remember, Mr. Butler, word about the jailbreak will be out soon enough. Don't speed it up, all right?''

The dog came slow and growling. His teeth were bared, and they seemed longer. He looked larger, too, as he headed for the sheriff, eyes glowing red in a trick of the light. He snarled and snapped at the air, biting a path to the man. The old dog was possessed by a completely different animal, younger, with purpose and teeth. There was a deadly occupation in the stalking stride.

Jessop never moved. He showed no fear of the dog, as though he and the animal had been through this before. The sheriff only waited patiently until the growling subsided.

The dog stopped ten feet from the man. He raised his muzzle and sniffed at the air. Then the old Lab lost his footing in a sorry confusion of missteps and nearly fell. In that moment, he was made old again, gray and slow. He turned and walked away, moving with a pitiful drag of the hind leg.

Charles watched the sheriff's car drive off, soiling the air with clouds of fine brown dust.

A dark figure stood in the shadows at the far side of the house. The man walked slowly into the light, which dappled his golden skin. Henry Roth's smile was dazzling to-day. Absent was the suspicion of yesterday morning, which had probably been reinforced when Mallory told him to send Charles away.

Something had changed.

Charles walked up to the man and shook his hand. In the clearing behind Henry, the black Lab had settled down near a pan of water and a half-finished bowl of food. The animal was sleeping now, and caught up in some chase of an old dog's dreams, one hind leg stirring into movement as he slept.

The sculptor's hands moved into language. He pointed at the sleeping Lab. *"He was near death when Augusta found him. That was the morning after Cass's murder."*

"They stoned the dog?"

Henry nodded. *"Augusta did what she could, but he was so badly broken, she had to call in a vet. The doctor offered to put him down for free. The sheriff would not allow it. He paid a staggering amount of money to keep the dog alive. It was months before the animal could even walk."*

"The dog doesn't seem to like the sheriff."   •

"The car confused him. He hates the sight of it. Tom usually parks it down the road."

The dog rolled in the dirt and moaned. This animal should have died long ago. What kept him alive?

Charles rejected the idea that the dog was waiting for Mallory. Still, the thought kept creeping back to him.

"Why wouldn't the sheriff let the animal die?"

Henry shrugged. More specific with his hands, he said, *"I don't think there was any one reason. It was Kathy's dog, and Tom loved Kathy. But later, he realized the dog was a way to add to his list."*

"List?"

"A list of people who were in the mob—like Travis."

"Travis? The deputy who had the heart attack?"

"The same. The sheriff suspected Travis the first time the dog attacked him. Tom only kept the man on the job so he could torture him. It was Travis's job to take the dog to

*the vet. The dog lost one of its teeth smashing into the glass
window of the car door. In his younger days, he nearly
took a leg off the deputy. Travis screamed like a woman
until I pulled the dog off him."*

"Is it possible that the dog caused the deputy's heart
attack?"

*"No. Travis wouldn't go near the dog unless I was with
him. I was late the day he had his heart attack. He probably
just turned around and drove back to town. I always helped
him load the dog into the car, and then I'd ride along to
the vet's, so I could walk the dog home. The vet says he
needs the exercise. Over seventeen years of walking the
dog, I've added a few people to my own list."*

In answer to Charles's silent query, he added, *"We never
speak of lists, but Tom and I both keep them."*

"So the sheriff figured the dog recognized Travis."

Henry nodded. *"Tom also used the dog to torture Alma
Furgueson. She was the purple-haired woman you saw running through the square yesterday. Alma was a creature of
habit. Every Saturday when she did her grocery shopping
at the Levee Market, the sheriff and the dog would be there
waiting for her."*

"The dog recognized her?"

*"No. Alma recognized the dog, and she was afraid. Tom
and the dog would stare at her for a while and then walk
away. Finally, she went to pieces. She was always a little
crazy, but then she got worse. Talks to herself now—cries
all the time. The sheriff did that to her. Don't make an
enemy of that man."*

"You think he's dangerous?"

*"One day, he caught Fred Laurie shooting at the dog.
The fool missed the dog three times. The sheriff beat the
living hell out of that man."*

"And you added Fred Laurie to the list."

*"That day, two of the Laurie brothers made my list. They
were tight—Fred and Ray. And violent. Maybe that's why
Malcolm never gave them any money—easier to keep them
reined in. But anyone could have bought the pair of them*

for fifty dollars, and it would not be the first time they did rough work for money.''

''And what about Babe?''

''I suppose I never gave much thought to Babe on any account.''

Henry picked up the sack of dog food and carried it in his arms. Charles followed him to the back of the house, where he stored the sack in a garden shed. When his hands were free again, Henry asked, *''Have you seen enough of the house?''*

Charles nodded. Henry was so much more talkative to-day, more forthcoming. The radical change in the man's attitude nagged at him.

''Mallory wants you to go. I think that might be a good idea. This place seems tranquil, but now you understand it can be very dangerous.''

''I won't go.''

''I didn't think you would.''

''You've seen Mallory today, haven't you?''

Henry ignored the question, as they walked by the side of the house. *''It's important that you know what you're dealing with.''* He stopped to look down at the ground. *''This is where Cass was stoned. By the tracks in the wet ground, the sheriff figured around thirty people turned out for this murder.''*

Charles was thinking of the six-year-old child, locked in a closet while a mob killed her mother.

''When I arrived that next morning, I could hear the music inside the house. It was an old record player. The needle was stuck. It played the same five notes over and over.''

''The sheriff believes the stoning was done in silence.''

''Yes, it was very strange.''

''Henry, there's a problem with the logic. The sheriff said it was a silent kill. He reasoned that if Kathy had heard screams or shouting, she would have called out to her mother. They would have found the child and killed her, too.''

Henry was nodding in agreement with this.

"But why didn't the sheriff jump to the conclusion that the noise of the mob muffled the sound of a screaming child? He made such a point of the silent kill. As though he knew it for a fact, but how?"

"He was out of town when Cass died, but he probably knows more details than the people who were here that day."

"But the silence? This was a violent murder—the act of a mob."

Henry pointed to the circular beds of flowers ringed by stones. *"Those flowers were not trampled. The people actually walked around them. No branches were broken on the shrubs. No twigs were snapped on the lower branches of the trees. There were no running prints on the ground. The only signs of violence were the rocks and the blood. They didn't rush her in anger—they assembled here for a killing. And when they were done with Cass and the dog, they quietly walked away. Tom figured that out by the stride of the prints."*

And perhaps Mallory had backed that up. "You know where she is, don't you?"

Henry Roth only looked down at his silent hands, and walked around to the front of the house.

"I know Mallory broke out of jail this morning. Won't you—"

"She's fine. Don't worry about her. She's more concerned about finding a safe place for you. I suggest you check out of Betty's tonight, and we'll put your car in my shed. You can stay with me."

Charles followed him out to the road. "Thank you, but I was planning on going to the tent show tonight, the memorial service for Babe Laurie. Malcolm offered me a front-row seat."

"It would be best to go through Owltown on foot. Many people will be coming for the service. The road will be bumper-to-bumper traffic from the highway. So much easier

to walk. And you don't want anyone to follow your car back to my place.''

Now they left the wider road to take a path into the cemetery, which lay between this house and Henry's.

"Augusta says Owltown is dangerous at night, and the sheriff doesn't think it's safe to go walking there in the daylight."

"Tonight, all the really dangerous people will be in church.''

They were approaching the cemetery when Charles stopped on the path. He was listening to the unaccompanied lyrics of a Puccini aria. The disembodied voice was so beautiful, so delicate in its perfect phrasing, glass-fragile in the highest notes. They rounded the trees and beheld Ira singing to the statue that so resembled Cass Shelley and her daughter.

The young man was all the sheriff had said he was, talented beyond reason. Carved cherubs poised over neighboring graves, wing and body frozen in flight, as though straining to catch each sweet note flowing by on the air as Ira sang to his audience of marble and granite, sandstone and common rock.

Charles well understood the isolation of the wildly gifted child. He had some personal sense of what Ira's early years had been like. And he had sad professional knowledge of what lay in the future. Dr. Shelley's notes had concurred: Ira would never develop subtle social skills, and so he would never understand the flirtations of a girl, for he would be unable to read any expression of tenderness or willingness. That sweet phase would pass him by.

But, according to Cass Shelley, Ira could play complex scores of music, note-perfect. He could follow the slow evolution of clouds with patience beyond a Buddhist master, and he was on intimate terms with the constellations, calling every star by name. The sheriff had said that Ira could sing with the angels. Cass Shelley's journal said he *was* one, ''with wings unseen by the vast majority of beings, who had only the one temporal, solid context for life on earth.''

The concert ended, and Charles found the silence unbearably sad, the loss of the music, the loss of heaven.

The two men watched as Ira folded his body inward and sank to the grass at the foot of the statue. He curled up like an exhausted kitten, pulling his broken hands into the protective circle of his body. After a time, they walked away and left him sleeping in the perfect peace of a winged shadow.

ROUSED FROM SLEEP, the dog opened his eyes to the bright light of day. One shaggy ear rose to attention. Was it an animal he sensed? It came toward him so stealthy, he could barely detect its movement—even with his muzzle pressed to the earth and sensitive to every vibration. Suspicious now, his weary head lifted, and he caught the scent.

Not an animal.

The elderly sentry rose to a stand, his fur coated with the dry smell of dirt. With some regret, he left his patch of shade and padded slowly across the yard and down to the narrow path leading away from the house, his paws kicking up small swirls of dust. His eyes were dry and sore, slow to focus on the figure in the road. He turned his head, the better to see with his good eye.

The stranger whistled to him, an old familiar ripple of music—one long high note and two short bursts—his secret name. It was not a stranger in the road, and neither was this the stuff of his dreams.

She had come home.

As she came closer, his heart beat faster. He moved a few steps into the road, his jaws hanging open in the dog's way of a smile. Enormous waves of emotion pounded his heart, banging out blood to crash through the wreckage of ancient veins, and his mind was lost between shores of disbelief and joy. His steps were slow, but he believed he was running, bounding toward her.

At last, he stood before her, making low loving noises in his throat. He licked her hand, and then his legs betrayed him. He was falling, rolling into the dirt at her feet.

She knelt down to stroke his pelt, and then to hold him in her arms, pressing him close to her body. Her face was wet as she cradled him. One soft and gentle hand was probing that place where his heart was caged by ribs, and together they followed the weakening beats. His gaze was fixed on her face, backlit by the brilliant aureole of the midday sun.

He was shivering now, so very cold.

And then his eyes rolled back; his day was done; the darkness was absolute.

CHAPTER
11

CHARLES BUTLER WALKED on water. Or perhaps this was only the top of the natural water table. His shoes squished with each step across wet grass. The soaked earth was yet another piece of evidence in favor of Augusta's invisible hill, for the land closer to the house had been dry.

"Augusta!" he shouted to the distant figure in the faded cotton dress. She stopped at the edge of the woods and turned to wave.

As he moved toward her, the water level was rising, his shoes were sinking and probably ruined. When he joined her by the trees, he noticed that she was barefoot—an elegant solution to the footwear problem.

She grinned. "Charles, you and I must have a talk about your wardrobe."

He supposed it was ridiculous. The tailored suit and handmade shoes had been of no help blending in with the locals. Blue jeans abounded here. He had not owned a pair since the summer spent with Cousin Max. At home, his parents had always dressed him as a miniature adult on his way to a dress-code office job.

"I came to return the keys to the Shelley house." He

looked down at the small plastic bag in her hand. It was half filled with chicken wings. "Planning a picnic in the swamp?"

"No, but you take off your shoes, roll up those pantlegs, and I'll show you a sight to remember."

"You're on." When he was properly attired in naked feet and showing a bit of leg that had not seen the sun in years, he splashed after her into deeper water which now covered his toes.

"Stay close to me and don't wander off the path." She spoke to him over one shoulder, stern in her warning. "If you go into the bayou, you won't find any purchase. Bottom's real slippery."

They had cleared the semisolid ground and passed into a watery, primeval forest of widely spaced cypress trees and small grassy islands. He could not immediately detect the path she mentioned. Then he saw the chunks of rock, more like man-made mortar, colored green with slime and moss. She was using them as stepping stones.

"These chunks came from the foundation of the original house."

Augusta's feet grasped the rocks like a second pair of hands. He fared less well, but with practice, his toes got the hang of it. Both his arms shot out as balancing beams until he stepped onto soggy but more solid ground, a small rise jutting over a sea of water hyacinth. A pondlike area had been cleared of the choking plant life covering the rest of the water. This must be the narrow tributary which ran alongside the road to Cass Shelley's house.

"This is the tip of Finger Bayou." Augusta's lips curled inward as she sucked in air to make a sound like a child's fingers rubbing the skin of a balloon. She pointed to a log floating toward them, though the dark glass surface of the bayou showed no trace of a current. Augusta made the strange sound again, and he realized that she was summoning the log.

And now Charles could see that it had large reptilian eyes. The beast hung in the water only four feet from his toes, and there was time to remember that this was not a zoo with bars to keep the wild things in their place. This thing went wherever it wanted. In this primordial habitat, Charles had slipped to a humbler notch on the food chain. "Don't you worry about having a flesh eater in the neighborhood?"

"You've been listening to Betty Hale," said Augusta. "Alligators prefer dead humans to live ones. But even if you were three days dead and real tasty, this one wouldn't touch you. It's his hibernation period. He only surfaces every two days. He knows when I'm coming with the chicken. Won't eat but a few pieces, and sometimes nothing at all, but he's gotten used to me over the years, and we never disappoint one another."

"Could Cass's body have been eaten by an alligator?"

"No, there were no gators in those days. They were wiped out before Cass died. You can trust me to know the exact count of every living thing that crawls in the swamp and swims in the bayou. I put this alligator in myself when he was small. That was after I cut off the herbicide to give him shelter from those poaching Laurie brothers."

"Then what could have happened to her body?"

"You won't get the solution to every mystery, Charles. Just let it go."

"But I'm not made that way. I need that solution."

Augusta stepped onto a small man-made platform of rock chunks, some with corners, a wharf of sorts, and she threw the small bits of chicken to the alligator. Its massive jaws opened to expose the sharp teeth, hundreds of them. The jaws clamped down and the water exploded in sudden violence. A tail appeared and Charles could see the enormous size of the monster. The leviathan's tail splashed down, hitting the water with the force of a hammer, raining frothy particles far and wide. The water bubbled and boiled, and when the foam subsided, the alligator had vanished. Large waves slapped the side of the bayou, and the water hyacinth bobbed and rocked in the wake of waves.

As Augusta had promised—a sight to remember.

"Magnificent, isn't he? If that fool Ray Laurie or his brother Fred knew the gator was here, he'd be dead by this time tomorrow. I trust you to keep my secrets, Charles, and I will keep yours."

"Actually, I wouldn't have any secrets if you hadn't told Lilith that I didn't know Mallory. I always meant to ask why you did that."

"Mallory—I can't get used to that name. I always think of her as little Kathy Shelley."

"Perhaps it was her father's name?"

"Can't help you there. Cass never mentioned Kathy's father. I couldn't even say if there was a marriage. Never thought to pry. Cass was pregnant with Kathy and carrying her maiden name when she came back here to practice medicine."

As he followed her out of the swamp, he well understood the need for a guide. He had no sense of direction in this alien world. Things slithered here, and the plant life reached out to him, pointing accusing fronds at his eyes. He swatted the back of his neck where a tiny winged thing had bitten him, and now there was a spot of red on his palm. Blood-sucking insects were so unfair in the month of November.

When the house was in sight, he walked abreast of her to the place he had left his shoes and socks. "Do you think the father might have had something to do with Cass Shelley's death? A love affair gone wrong?"

"No, that doesn't work for me," said Augusta, looking down at his wet socks and ruined leather. "The man who fathered Cass's baby would be a stranger here. Not likely he could bring thirty friends along without someone taking notice. And how would a stranger get thirty locals to go through with a thing like that?"

"The father couldn't have been a Dayborn man?"

Augusta shook her head. "Cass left town when she was eighteen and didn't come back till she was twenty-eight. Most everyone else who went off to school never came back. Tom did, but he was home four or five years before Cass."

"Could there be a connection between Cass's murder and Babe's?"

"Doubt it. Cass had no enemies. Now *her* death was a genuine mystery. But Babe was such a mean-spirited bastard, no one was too surprised when he turned up dead." She waved her hand with impatience to rid herself of this topic, which obviously bored her. "So where are you off to now, Charles?"

He hesitated for a moment. Well, he supposed he could hold her alligator as a hostage against a secret of his own.

"I'm checking out of the bed and breakfast. Henry invited me to stay with him, but I don't think he wants that generally known."

Augusta only nodded, with no curiosity in her face. "Well, that can wait, can't it? I'm just gonna put the horse in his stall, and then I'd be pleased if you'd join me for a meal. It's all cooked—I just have to turn a light under it."

"Thank you."

"And then I'm gonna send you over to Earl's Dry Goods. I know he's got a pair of jeans that would fit you, and maybe some sturdy boots."

They walked together over the sodden ground, which became more solid, less watery with each step toward the mansion. The only approach to Trebec House was the path from the cemetery. Every patch of surrounding ground would be rough going for a car unaccustomed to lakes in the grass and no traction to speak of. And there was only one road into Cass Shelley's house. Beyond that it was swamp and bayou. "I suppose the killer took Cass's body away in a vehicle."

"Well, he didn't dump it here in the swamp. If you put a body into this ground, eventually it will bob up to say, 'Hello again.' "

"Is it possible, just possible, that Cass could have survived?"

"No, it isn't." Augusta was firm in this. "There was so much blood, Tom Jessop even gave up little Kathy for dead. Cass could not be alive." And there was a trace of menace when she said, "Don't you even suggest that to her child."

CASSANDRA SHELLEY'S CHILD turned to the north, where Trebec House crouched behind the oak trees, hidden but for the attic window. Reflected clouds created the illusion of movement and life in that round pane of glass.

Mallory carried the dog's body into the dense foliage at the far side of her mother's house to block any view from the mansion's dark window, so like an eye. In early childhood, she had believed that eye had followed her about. She remembered it well, and somewhere between heightened instinct and imagination, she believed the window-eye also remembered her.

She sat down beside her dog and ran one hand over the scarred pelt, still warm to the touch. It was a comfort, this tactile deception of life. She did not look at his eyes, for with the passage of only a little time, they had lost their roundness and could not fool her anymore. She continued to pet him.

Good dog.

She was alert to every sound, every movement in the trees and the grass. The air was alive with winging insects and birdcalls. The pure blue sky was slowly deepening into the darker shade of nightfall. She could hear the gurgle of the narrow stream tumbling by the house, splashing over rocks and lapping at a floating branch, plucking at twigs like prongs in a music box.

Ripples of phantom music poured through the window at her back, sweet simple notes of a child's piano lesson. When she turned around, remembrance filled the glass pane with a woman she had seen in mirrors. Their countenances did differ, for Mallory's smile was always forced, and the mother at the window of her mind was laughing in absolute delight. Her eyes lit up like green stars as she beheld her child—young Kathy, six years old, almost seven.

Mallory raised her hand to the window, and the woman

waved to her. But it was too hard to sustain the illusion, and she turned away from her own reflection. She was alone again.

The stronger memory of terror and violence stayed with Mallory longer. There was the vision of her mother, hair streaming with blood, inching toward her across the floor, gathering Kathy into her arms, pulling a laundry marker from the pocket of her bloody dress and writing a telephone number on the back of the little girl's hand. "*Run*," Cass Shelley had said to her child. Young Kathy had held on to her mother, terrified, screaming. "*Run!*" yelled her mother. And then she had slapped the child hard to make her go. The first touch that was not gentle.

Mallory turned her face up to the sky. There were lights overhead, tiny lamps turning on one by one. She retrieved an old sheet of canvas from the garden shed and used it as a shroud to wrap the animal's body, which had grown cold. An hour later, when the sky was dark blue and banged with stars, she lifted the dog in her arms and carried him into the woods.

CHARLES WALKED OUT the front door of the Dayborn Bed and Breakfast with his suitcase in hand. The other guests had deserted the porch following the evening bat races. Only Darlene Wooley remained. She was slumped in one of the wicker chairs lining the rail. The porch light was being unkind to her. Harsh shadows deepened all the lines of worry and stress common to the caregiver of a special child. Even Darlene's hair seemed strained and tired, falling to her shoulders in halfhearted attempts at curls.

"Hello again." He had spoken softly, but even so, she was startled into better posture. Her back was stiff and straight when she smiled a wan greeting.

He set his suitcase down beside her chair. "I ran into Ira in the cemetery today. I tried to speak to him, but I'm afraid I may have upset him. I *am* sorry."

"Don't be." She made an effort to sustain her smile, but

it slipped away as she looked down at her folded hands. "I'm so pleased that you did stop to speak to him. Some people in this town don't believe Ira *can* talk anymore, let alone *think*."

"Well, I can tell them different." Betty pushed open the porch door. Neatly balanced on the flat of one hand was a tray laden with a china coffee service. "Ira used to talk a blue streak when he was a little boy."

Betty's white hair had taken on a yellow cast from the porch light. The same lamp which had aged Darlene made the innkeeper seem younger than her sixty-five years. The flesh of her arms jiggled beneath the flower-print sleeves of her dress as she waved off Charles's attempt to help her with the tray. She placed it on a small side table between an empty wicker chair and her own wooden rocker. "I brought an extra cup for you, Mr. Butler." Betty settled into the rocking chair and filled it to overflowing. "No need to run off this minute. Sit yourself down for a bit."

"Thank you, I will." He settled into the chair beside Darlene and addressed the usual problem of what to do with his long legs. He elected to leave them sprawling on the floorboards between the two women. "I understand Cass Shelley was Ira's doctor."

Darlene nodded. "Cass started his therapy when he was two. He could read when he was only five years old."

This was a tribute to a dedicated doctor. And it spoke well of Ira. He must have been highly motivated to participate in the world. "That's amazing progress."

"I thought so. But his behavior wasn't improving quick enough to suit his father. One night, my husband took Ira to a faith-healing service. Have you ever seen one of those sideshows?"

"Yes, a faith healer's tent show." This had been a professional courtesy—the evangelist had been to Cousin Max's tent the night before. The religious showman had put on an extraordinary performance—gospel music and howls of damnation, elements of carnival and magic, voodoo and Christ.

Charles tried to imagine the terror of an autistic child standing up in front of a thousand screaming people, going through the faith healer's laying on of hands. In such a setting, the forced contact alone would have driven the boy wild. "I imagine that experience set Ira back a bit in his therapy."

"More than a bit," said Darlene, with a faint reserve of anger. "If I hadn't been working late that night, I could've stopped it. Ira was never the same after that. And then, after Cass Shelley died, he got worse—never talked at all for the longest time. My husband took him to another doctor in the next parish. That one tried a new therapy—gave him shots for allergies."

"Well, allergies *can* create additional problems for the autistic. They—"

"That may be," Betty interrupted him as she finished pouring out the coffee. "But the shots didn't help one bit. He never did improve until his father died, and Darlene got Ira into a state school program." She spooned cream and sugar into a cup and handed it to Darlene. "I remember the days when Ira would talk your ear off. That child was talking since he was how old, Darlene?"

"Eighteen months. But he would talk *at* you more than *to* you," said Darlene, almost as an apology.

"But he did have a lot to say," said Betty, more magnanimously. "Mostly, he would go on about his lists, and his stars. I believe you take your coffee black, Mr. Butler— and three sugars? Oh, yes, Ira was always counting things and memorizing things."

"One time," said Darlene, more animated now, "he memorized all the stars he could see from the window of his bedroom. He made himself a star map that even showed the window frame and the curtains."

"And the things Ira knew about stars," said Betty. "To this day, I can't get some of Ira's facts out of my head. Do you know about the old stars, the cold stars? Just a *bit* of one in the palm of your hand could weigh as much as a ton." She leaned toward Darlene. "Remember the night the sheriff took down Ira's missing-star report?''

"That was a time, wasn't it?'' Darlene's gaze was focussed on the sheriff's office across the square. One yellow light burned late tonight. "I should go over there and apologize to Tom for blowing up at him. The day he took up Ira's side—''

"Let me tell it, Darlene.'' Betty began to lightly rock her chair. "Ira was just a little thing back then. Was he five years old?''

Darlene nodded, and Betty went on. "We were sitting out here, like we always do after supper. Old Milton Hamlin was here, too. He was a steady boarder in those days. Dead now and good riddance. I never liked that fool. Milton was one of those people who have to advertise their superior education every damn minute of the day. You know the type, Mr. Butler?''

Charles nodded.

"So little Ira was sitting on the steps right there with his star map,'' said Betty. "Suddenly, he looks up at his mother and says one of his stars is missing—winked out in the dark. And he couldn't have been more upset if it was a lost puppy. So then Milton Hamlin commenced with a lecture. He said stars didn't just wink out—they went up in a ball of fire, don't you know—and Ira couldn't have seen any such thing.''

"Milton was a retired librarian,'' said Darlene. "I guess he figured sheer proximity to all those books made him about the smartest man in the world.''

"Turned out later, he didn't know the first thing about astronomy.'' Betty sighed, as though her aggravation with the deceased Milton Hamlin might be ongoing.

"I thought maybe Ira might've miscounted his stars. But Darlene had never known him to miscount anything, so she took the boy's side, and then so did I. Well, Milton was livid. He went on and on about how Ira was just an ignorant little boy, and he had certainly not seen a star go nova. The old fool embarrassed that child no end.''

Betty was warming to her story now, leaning forward to

touch his arm and alert him that this was the good part coming up. "Well, the very next evening, Tom Jessop shows up on the porch after dark, with his clipboard and all these official-looking papers. Bless him—he wrote down Ira's account of that missing star. Tom was dead serious. Asked Ira if he could borrow the star map."

Betty smiled at Darlene. "Tom was a handsome man in those days, wasn't he?" She turned back to Charles. "But I'm digressing."

She rocked a little faster as she picked up the pace of her story. "Milton came out on the porch just as Ira was showing Tom the place where he had last seen his lost star, and the sheriff was writing down every word. Well, Milton laughed at the pair of them, and it hurt Ira all over again—poor little thing. So the sheriff says, 'You're right, Ira. Any *fool* can see that star is gone.' Now he said that to the boy, but he was staring straight at Milton Hamlin, and it was a look to freeze blood. Milton didn't say another word—not that night anyway."

She was rocking faster now. "The following evening, just after supper while it was still light, the sheriff stopped by to tell Ira that his star was coming back. 'Tonight,' says Tom, 'and that's a promise.' "

Betty slapped her hand down on the arm of her rocker. "Well, Milton nearly bust a gut laughing over that one. The sheriff stared him down, and you would have thought Tom had pulled his gun on Milton—the old fool shut his face that fast."

Betty ceased her rocking and pointed to the edge of the porch. "Ira sat right there on those steps. Sat there for hours, watching that empty place in the sky. And Cass Shelley's little girl, Kathy—she was only six then—she was right beside him. Ira believed in Tom Jessop, and so did Kathy. The kids were waiting—you see?"

Charles did see. He was staring at the porch steps. Even if he lived to be a very old man, he knew he would never lose the image of two small children sitting there, side by side in absolute faith, waiting for a star to come home.

"That very night," said Betty, "*damned* if that star didn't come back—just like Tom Jessop said it would! There it was, and right in the place Ira said it should be. So then Tom, Kathy and Ira were all huddled together on the steps, real quiet, just admiring that star for the longest time."

He smiled, knowing that Malcolm Laurie would have thought the sheriff a fool to give away this miracle for free. Charles understood what Tom Jessop had done, and how, and why. He was only having difficulty squaring the man who loved children with the man who had used an insane dog to torture Deputy Travis and Alma Furgueson.

"So it was a variable star, an eclipsing binary." Charles said it softly, in the manner of thinking aloud.

"Why, yes." Betty smiled with pleased surprise. "That's exactly what it was."

Darlene was also smiling. "Tom called the observatory. He was thinking Ira might've seen a satellite or a comet. But they told him a dark star had moved across the face of a bright one and hid its light."

Charles nodded. The eclipse would have been only hours long, but atmospheric conditions could have obscured the star for several days. So the sheriff had used that knowledge to put on an elaborate magic show for Ira and Kathy.

"It was called Algos," said Darlene.

"But we call it Ira's star." Betty wagged one finger to end her story with a flourish. "And that old fool Milton Hamlin was dead within the year," she said, as if this might be a fitting penalty for humiliating a small child.

HIS WAY WAS brightly lit by headlights from a long line of cars stretching from the highway to the fairgrounds. Though it had been a bit of a hike from Henry Roth's house, Charles was making better progress than the traffic on wheels. Always ahead of him was the lure of the giant glowing sign, screaming in neon, MIRACLES FOR SALE, and casting its red light on the canvas panels of the circus tent.

He passed the dirt parking lot, already filled to capacity, and entered a crowd of people walking toward the tent. A woman shrieked and pointed up to the center pole.

A ball of fire circled over the tent in the trajectory of a lost and disoriented shooting star. Charles recognized the illusion from his cousin's store of magic tricks. Squinting, he could just make out the guide wire in the wake of the flames.

He remembered a visit to another evangelist's performance in the different seasons of childhood and summer. One warm night, on an open prairie, Cousin Max had given away the details of this trick to repay the hospitality of an aging minister on the tent-show circuit.

Charles's smile was bittersweet.

So Max's illusion had been passed along through the years, handed down from showman to showman. Would he find other vestiges of Max inside the tent?

As he reached the wide entrance, a young man, no more than five feet tall, pressed a sheet of paper into his hand. Charles accepted it with a thank you. It was a schedule of New Church seminars under the headline of "Financial Miracles," and it was printed on paper the color of money.

He folded the sheet into his suitcoat pocket and paid more attention to the smaller man. He could not miss the Laurie resemblance in this young face, but that was a common thing in Owltown. The little man was outstanding for his shoes, which were miles too big for him, his overlarge shirt and baggy, rolled-up pants. The ensemble reminded him of the grab bag mix of clothing worn by New York's homeless people.

Charles held out his front-row pass. The young man seemed mildly annoyed, for his job was handing out papers—not receiving any. His solution to the problem was to ignore it as he handed a green sheet to another man, and then another. But all the while, Charles's pass continued to dangle in the air just in front of him. "Excuse me?"

"Yes, sir," said the young man, shoulders sagging a bit in resignation, for this problem showed no signs of going away.

Charles handed over his pass, leaving the man no choice but to accept it. "Malcolm told me to give this to someone at the entrance."

"I wouldn't know about that, sir." He called out, "Uncle Ray!"

Another Laurie face approached them. This was a man with the graying hair and wrinkles of late fifties. "What's the problem, Jimmy?"

Jimmy handed him the pass, and now the older man turned to Charles. "Well, you must be Mr. Butler." Ray Laurie's smile promised everlasting friendship, but it dimmed as he turned on Jimmy. "You should've taken Mr. Butler right in and seated him."

Now the older man grasped Charles's arm and gestured toward the entrance. "You'll have to excuse Jimmy. We never give him anything too complicated. He has trouble concentrating."

Charles found that odd, for the younger man's face showed more signs of intelligence than his uncle's placid expression and sluggish eyes.

Ray Laurie introduced himself as Babe's brother.

"I'm sorry for your loss," said Charles.

Ray Laurie's eyes blanked for the time it took to wonder what loss that might be. When at last he understood, he smiled and nodded. "If you'll just follow me?"

Charles was escorted to a front-row seat cordoned off with a velvet rope and a reserved sign. His view of the stage would have a slightly sidelong angle, and Ray Laurie hoped Charles didn't mind.

"Not at all." Charles had to shout to be heard above the crowd. There must be a thousand people already seated, and perhaps twice that many outside, awaiting admission. "So will Malcolm be carrying on with his brother's ministry?"

"Well, Mal was the preacher right along, Mr. Butler. Now Babe was a real big attraction, what with his psychic predictions and healing power—I wouldn't take that away from him. But Malcolm always did the real preaching. He's a thing to behold."

Charles was staring up at the stage when a mass of red drape was pulled away from the large board at the rear.

"Now that's new," said Ray Laurie, pointing up to the enormous photograph of the late Babe Laurie. The image was bigger than a highway billboard. "You would not believe what it cost to have that made up on a rush order. But Mal wanted to do up the memorial service with style. I think Babe would've liked it a lot."

Charles had already guessed that this giant portrait was not the standard fixture. From his vantage point to the side, he could see a portion of the older prop. All that was visible was the large bloodied hand of Christ nailed to the arm of a giant crucifix, and now displaced by the full-color blowup of Babe's face.

New icons for old.

The vacant seats were filling quickly as an army of people poured through the large opening in the canvas and filed into the rows of folding chairs.

Vendors with bright orange vests moved among the faithful, loudly hawking souvenirs and charms, shouting to be heard above the restless babble. For fifty dollars, one could buy a lock of Babe Laurie's hair. The bargain price of five dollars would buy a severed bird's foot on a key chain to protect a body from his enemies. For that same price, small feathered bags of herbs would cure ills from arthritis to cancer. For a few dollars more, one could have bits of quartz shaped like pyramids, blessed by Babe Laurie himself, and guaranteed to hasten miracles of all kinds. A beer was four dollars, a hot dog was three. And here, brothers and sisters, was the best bargain in the offering, a bit of heaven itself—a pink cloud of cotton candy, swirling on a paper cone, could be had for *two*—count 'em—only *two* dollars.

And now, with a little prompting from the barking men in the orange vests, the crowd began to chant a mantra.

"Babe, Babe, Babe!"

A gospel choir, dressed in deep purple robes and a mix of dark and light skin, assembled beneath the giant portrait and, a cappella, they sang to the chanting crowd, which took the part of a deafening, rhythmic chorus.

"Babe, Babe!"

"Oh, when the sa-a-a-a-ints—"

"Babe, Babe!"

"—come marching i-i-i-n—"

"Babe! Babe!"

"—Oh, when the saints come ma-a-a-rching in—"

"Babe, Babe, Babe!"

The music of a Dixieland band preceded the musicians,

who now marched onto the stage and took their place beside the choir, displacing the chants with rousing trumpets, one clarinet and a trombone. The crowd's chanting dissolved into cheers and applause. The rhythm of the hand-clapping became a single clap of thunder. The brass sparkled, and the horns hit their highest notes.

The music ended before the song was done, heightening anticipation as the houselights dimmed. One spotlight illuminated a small circle on the billboard at the rear of the stage. The crowd screamed and clapped. The circle of light grew in size and intensity until it was a burning sun.

Too bright. Charles looked away for a moment, and then he turned back with the oh's and ah's of the crowd to behold a petty miracle made of dry ice and boiling water, as a slow crawl of ground fog rolled across the stage.

And now Malcolm Laurie appeared at the center of the bright circle. His costume had more spangles than a matador's suit of lights. The low boil of stage fog obscured his legs below the knees as he moved forward in the smooth glide of an artful dancer, and one could believe his feet were not touching the floor. The spotlight dimmed, but Malcolm glittered and gleamed. Smiling a row of dazzling white teeth, he raised his hand for silence. The screams died out in a sigh breathed round the tent.

The litany began, amplified by a wireless microphone and accompanied by the soft croon of the choir. ''Brothers and sisters, are you *tired* of being poor? Say, amen!''

''*Amen!*'' the crowd yelled.

''Are you *tired* of your misery? Say amen!''

''*Amen!*''

''I know what you're wondering, brothers and sisters. *Why?* you ask, oh why has Babe Laurie died and forsaken you?''

The light blazed up in high brilliance. When it blacked out, Malcolm was gone.

Now the spotlight reappeared closer to the front of the stage, and Malcolm came walking out of the light. ''Babe is not gone. He is here! My brother is with me. He is with all of us tonight."

His hands reached out to the crowd, his fingers trembling, his voice soft as a lover's. "Can you feel it? Can you feel his love? Open your hearts wide and hear me. I sleep, but my heart waketh: it is the voice of my beloved that knocketh, saying, Open to me, my love." He strutted from one end of the stage to the other, gazing over the flock, leaving the impression that he had made a profound connection with every pair of eyes.

"My beloved put his hand by the hole of the door." Malcolm's hand went to his heart as he sank down on one knee. "And I rose up to open to my beloved." Malcolm stood up slowly. "My hands and my fingers dripped with sweet-smelling myrrh, upon the handles of the lock." His voice was softer, lower, saying, "I opened to my beloved." He threw out his hands as though to embrace them all. "Let him kiss me with the kisses of his mouth: for thy love is better than wine. A bundle of myrrh is my well-beloved unto me: he shall lie all night betwixt my breasts."

Charles recognized the more erotic lines from *The Song of Solomon*, more or less intact, with verses out of order. Malcolm stole from the best as well as the least. Charles turned to an elderly woman seated in the row behind him. Her eyes were trained on the evangelist as though he were her lover. And of course, he *was*.

Malcolm glistened with sweat and sparkled with light. His honeyed voice rolled over the crowd. The preacher was giving the audience holy, sanctioned sex. He was reaching out to all of them, men and women alike, stroking them with his eyes, his voice, touching all the soft places, and exciting them to a roar of *"Amen!"* He was the image of a rock star, raw sensuality in the service of the Lord.

"Brothers and sisters!" Malcolm cried out. "I can feel Babe inside of me, filling my body with the fluid of love, the power of God Almighty. I got the power!" One closed fist shot out, angling toward heaven.

"Amen!" screamed the crowd with renewed fervor.

Charles stared up at the giant portrait and listened to them intoning the name of Babe, over and over, as their hands shot out and pulled back, again and again, in mimicry of Malcolm.

So this was the New Church, borrowing a bit from the Bible, a bit from Hitler.

Charming.

Malcolm was handed a glass pitcher and a crystal goblet. He poured a clear stream of water into the goblet, but the crystal vessel filled with rich red liquid, and a thousand people gasped for breath.

Malcolm had dared to turn the water into wine.

Charles had seen this done before, but never in religious context. The colored crystals had been hidden at the bottom of the wineglass in that portion obscured by the hand.

The man drank deeply, and then turned his back on the crowd as he looked up to the monster image of his brother. The glass went crashing to the floor. His arms rose in the crucifixion pose and his body began to shake with convulsions. The crowd was hushed. When Malcolm turned around again, he was altered in every way. His mouth was larger, pouting more lower lip, eyes wider, hair slicked back with sweat, and there was a cruelty in this new arrangement of his features.

He strutted from one end of the stage to the other, cock of the walk with the suggestion of a limp. At center stage, he ended his pacing. His jaw jutted out as he drew his body up, puffed out his chest, and arrogance exuded from every sweating pore of skin. His eyes were wild as he staggered to the rear of the stage and back again to the edge. His hands shot out in a gesture of supplication. And then, every spangle on the suit of lights left its own bright track in the air as he writhed and jerked his body in spasms.

"It's Babe!" screamed a man in the front row. All about the tent was the sudden intake of breath, and then the release of a soft sigh. Utter silence now, all eyes were on the stage. The multitude was mesmerized by the resurrection and the light.

And now, abruptly, rudely, the show moved on to borrow a bit from the legendary P. T. Barnum, a more flamboyant showman than God. The professional geeks were being brought out on the stage: a woman whose arms flew about in an uncontrollable palsy and a man who walked on his hands and dragged his legs behind him. All that was missing was the dog-faced boy and the bearded lady. The band played them onto the stage, limping, crawling, shaking violently. The reincarnation of Babe Laurie laid his hands on them one by one, and then the band played again as the halt and lame danced off stage, healed and whole.

When the fakirs were gone, the less dramatic but genuine ailments came out of the crowd, imploring Malcolm to heal them. One by one, they were brought center stage. Malcolm pressed his hand to the forehead of a man supported by two canes. The man fell backward into the waiting arms of the body catchers. Malcolm dramatically broke the canes across one raised leg, and then the man limped back to his seat, unhealed and falling once before he reached the chair. No one noticed, no one cared. All eyes were riveted on the stage.

Then began the straggle of elderly arthritics, who seemed genuinely shocked when Malcolm laid his hands on their heads, compelling them to be healed in the name of Babe Laurie. One of Malcolm's hands went to the small of an elderly woman's back. He pressed on her forehead and she flew backward to the arms of the catchers as though propelled by lightning. She made her way down the stairs in shock, stunned and weaving from the assault. But her expression might be taken for exaltation, for her eyes were wide and brimmed with tears of pain.

Done with minor wonders, the program moved upscale to the collective miracle—each heart's desire—preceded by collection plates.

"Do you believe?" Malcolm had shed his brother's skin to pace the stage with his own charisma. "Say, amen."

"*Amen!*"

"Then give all that you have. Every dollar in your wallet, every dime in your pockets. Give everything you have and you shall receive more than all your gifts combined. Do you want a miracle? Say amen.''

"Amen!"

Piles of cash were growing in the plates. People in the first row were indeed emptying their wallets as they chanted the name of Babe and fixed their eyes on his billboard image. They prayed to Babe now. He was a god, and Malcolm was his priest on earth.

"It's time to demonstrate your faith. Do you want to buy a miracle?''

"Amen!"

"Then empty those wallets. Give no thought of the morrow.''

As Charles recalled, Christ had said this last phrase to Judas, but only to deter him from passing the hat at a similar gathering.

"Let go of that cash, and it will come back to you a hundredfold and then some. You will live in the light of faith and every good thing in life will be yours. I guarantee it. In proportion to your faith, you will receive your heart's desire.''

Now Charles had found the escape clause in the warranty of Malcolm's covenant. If the miracle did not occur, then the petitioner was obviously lacking in devotion and belief. Not Malcolm's fault, and no refund for those of little faith.

"I want you to dig in those pockets and come up with all your bills and coins. This is where it begins. If you lack the faith, you have wasted your time here. Open those wallets and pour your faith into those collection plates for God's work. As we help one another, we participate in the flow, and it flows right on back to us. It's a holy circle, you cannot stop it, you cannot prevent it from flowing back to you—so long as you believe. You must demonstrate your faith. You must walk out into the night with nothing *but* your faith. Say, amen!''

"Amen!"

"You women!" He stomped his foot on the stage.

"Empty out those purses. I say *dig* for that money. You don't want to get home and discover that you have held back a single coin. Your faith will surely crumble to dust, and you will be dogged by the misery of this lost chance for all your days."

Charles looked around him. Well, the curse was a nice touch. Two seats away in the third row, a formerly reticent woman was digging deeper in her bag. And to his left, and one chair down the second row, another woman had emptied the contents of her purse into her lap. Tissues and gum wrappers spilled to the floor. Charles stared at the store of pharmacy bottles in the spread apron of her skirt. Her hands were malformed, ugly knots of flesh. She was young for such an advanced case of arthritis—such desperation.

He looked into the faces of the surrounding believers. Hunger was here, an ocean of it. People all around him were rising to their feet and groaning with the power flowing through them in Babe Laurie's name. They shouted their amens, and Charles felt an electrical current which shocked him and hooked him up to his fellow man, as surely as if they had all been touched by the same jolt of Saint Elmo's fire.

"Do you believe?"

And the crowd roared with one voice, *"I believe!"* screaming as one devout petitioner with one desire.

They were plugged into Malcolm, charging him with light and energy—all save Charles, who detached himself to sit with his fears, at odds with the enormous animal roaring and rearing up all around him. At any moment, the crowd might discover the unbeliever in their midst.

He knew all the darkest things about crowds—mobs.

Malcolm was gathering size, growing with the love of the multitude, towering over them on the stage, energy flowing out to them through his extended fingertips. They fed one another, Malcolm and the faithful.

The elbow of a fervent prayer knocked Charles's head to one side, and now he saw Henry Roth standing in the wide center aisle, searching the faces of the front row, where he knew Charles would be seated. Charles only had to stand up to be noticed above the people of standard sizes. Henry waved to him, and his hands began to speak, to tell Charles that he must come away and right now. There was a great urgency in Henry's hand movements and in his eyes.

When they had cleared the opening in the canvas and traveled as far as the parking lot, the lights of the tent went out behind them. Charles stood in the center of the road. He could imagine what was going on in the blackness of that vast space. Unity would be displaced by fear in the dark, and that would grow to panic.

Henry pulled on his sleeve and formed the letter *H*. His hand moved up and down quickly to say, *"Hurry."*

As they moved into a jog, Charles looked back over one shoulder at the silhouette of the tent against the evening sky. The crowd was dispersing to its individual parts, each seeking the way into the light. He watched them pour from the tent opening, ant-size and antlike. And then the tall poles caved in on one side, and the canvas structure listed like a great wounded animal, deflated by the sudden flight of Malcolm Laurie's flock. Headlights came on in pairs, and a slow caravan of cars led away from the tent, moving toward the highway.

As Charles and Henry cleared one block of Owltown, the lights at their backs went out, and the night snapped shut behind them. The same thing happened on the next block.

And whose little miracle was this? Oh, just a guess, a shot in the dark—could it be Mallory?

Of course she had done it. She had hacked into the computer of a local utility company. He could think of no other explanation for the timing and selectivity of the power failure—and Henry's appearance at just the right moment.

So, in addition to joining Henry's list and the sheriff's list, the Lauries now had Mallory's attention as well. What a worthy opponent for a family of evangelists—Our Lady of Cyberspace. That irresponsible brat. Someone in that tent might have been killed.

Charles stopped at the windbreak of tall trees and turned back. Car headlights illuminated the fleeing mob. Henry pulled at his sleeve again, and they moved through the streets into Dayborn Square. As they passed the fountain, Henry slowed their pace to a comfortable walk. When they stepped outside the boundaries of the square, all the street lamps and window lights went out, and Charles felt somehow responsible.

He cast his eyes over the woods on the other side of Upland Bayou and wondered what tree she perched in, watching their progress, switching off the lights behind them.

When Charles and Henry had crossed the bridge, the lights came on again, and the distant telephones of Owltown began to ring, all of them, ringing constantly, until one by one they were taken off their hooks as people returned home, almost as if their phones were calling them back to their houses and trailers.

As they were crossing the bridge over the bayou, Charles said, "Poor Malcolm. The collection plates never finished the first row."

Henry smiled. *"Then he didn't make the cost of raising the tent. The first row is stocked with relatives."*

Herd instinct? Of course. Family members put all their money in the collection plates, and the rest followed suit.

A gunshot exploded in the woods beyond the bridge. Henry seemed unconcerned.

"It's only Fred Laurie shooting owls again. I saw him go into the woods. Or maybe it's Augusta shooting Fred Laurie. It's a big mistake to fool with her owls."

FRED LAURIE SEARCHED the woods, his brown eyes alighting on each dark shape that moved. He raised his rifle and squeezed the trigger again. He crept closer to his target, and now he could see it clearly. He had killed yet another leaf—shot it straight through the heart. This was the third such bit of vegetation he had murdered while his brothers were playing to the crowd back in Owltown.

Jane's Cafe had been a fund of information. In an overheard conversation, he had learned that the sheriff wouldn't allow Jane to carry a dinner tray to the prisoner's cell, and the lunch tray hadn't been touched. The sheriff was twice as mean as usual, or so Jane told Betty Hale, and that useless new girl wouldn't even look her in the eye when Jane asked if something was wrong.

Betty had allowed that not much got past Jane, and maybe Tom Jessop should have made *her* the new deputy.

Then the postman had chimed in with his bit of news: The sheriff had been driving the roads all day, looking for somebody, scanning every tree he could see from the car windows. But first thing this morning, he had torn out on the road to the old Shelley place like a bat out of Augusta's attic.

The prisoner was gone all right, vanished. Everyone in Jane's Cafe had agreed on that. "Just like her mother," Jane had said.

Fred had searched the old Shelley place, hunting Cass's brat, but found no trace of her. She would not have gone into the swamp around Finger Bayou. No one but Augusta could navigate that mire in the dark. This wood was the likely place. This is where *he* would have gone.

He emerged from the trees and stopped in a clearing to light a cigarette. He would not have found the dog's body if he had not tripped over the canvas parcel concealed by broken branches. He struck another match and held it over a hollowed-out log. Black leather protruded from the opening. He didn't have to pull it out to know it was the duffel bag that had sat for three days in the sheriff's office. It belonged to her, as did this damned dog stiffening in the canvas shroud.

He blew out the match. Footsteps? Yes, someone was coming this way.

Fred moved quickly to replace the branches over the dog,

and then he pulled back into the woods. He slung the rifle over one shoulder by its strap and reached up to a tree branch. He pulled his body up and into the cover of dense leaves before the woman entered the clearing.

She was soft-stepping like a deer. Every now and then, she stopped and listened, just as a deer would do. The tan of the deputy's uniform was light against her dark flesh. When she paused against the black bark of a tree, the outline of her skin lost all definition, and there was a heart-stopping moment when Fred believed her uniform was haunted by a woman he could no longer see.

His heart was beating again, and harder now. He could swear he heard it thumping on the wall of his chest as her gun glided out of the holster, and the barrel pointed skyward. Though she never looked up, twice she had aimed the gun straight at him, and he forgot to breathe. Now she was very still, listening again.

Could she hear it—his heartbeat?

No, that's crazy. But he held one hand over his chest.

Finally, Deputy Beaudare ran off into the woods, stopping once to look back, then running on, graceful as any animal he'd ever killed.

CHAPTER
13

THEY STOPPED BY the telephone pole near Henry Roth's cottage. Henry motioned him to stay, signing, *"See you later."* Then he walked off and left Charles standing in the middle of a dirt road.

Later?

A familiar voice called out to him. "Look up, Charles."

His eyes followed the pole's long line high into the air. Silver spikes sprouted from its sides, and in the dark at the top of the sky, the thick shaft spread out wooden arms laden with thick cables and blinking lights.

Going on faith that Mallory was up there, he began to climb the silver ladder. When he neared the crossbeams, he could see her silhouette working over the wires. Closer now, nearly there, he grasped one arm of the pole, and then they were face-to-face. Her hair was luminous in the dark, curls catching light from a waxing moon, and where the strands strayed into wisps, the stars shone through them.

She gave him a brief smile in lieu of hello. She didn't like to waste her words, or perhaps she didn't understand the average human's need of them. She had always preferred the company of machines, which were quiet, efficient and disinclined to argue. Behind her back and to her face, the officers of NYPD had called her Mallory the Machine.

"Hello, again." He made the mistake of looking down at the tiny road below them and the toy town in the distance. He hugged the crossbeam and focussed on her face. "I see you're still working without a net."

She seemed quite comfortable seated in her leather sling bearing the name of a local telephone company.

"I assume you stole that."

She nodded absently, taking no offense. She was intent on her handiwork with exposed wires. "I worked for the phone company's computer operations up north."

She reached across the nest of wires to undo his tie and pull it away from him. With one hand she undid the buttons on his vest and laid open his white shirt. Up here in the stars with Mallory—it was probably the most romantic moment of his life. He waited to see what she would do to ruin it.

She pointed a small dark box at his chest and sent out a projection of light. He looked down at the crisp computer screen glowing on his shirtfront and said, "I see you solved the resolution problem."

"Uh-huh. I translated the pixels to analog waves. But it still sucks too much battery power."

He gathered the backup battery must account for at least one of the wires running out of the tiny computer and into the pocket of her blazer. The image on his shirt changed as she bent her head over the minicomputer in the palm of her hand and worked the small keyboard with a silver pick. Her face was awash in reflected blue light.

It troubled him only a little that he was now conversant in computer jargon, though he loathed high technology. He was particularly well versed in this prototype of hers. A year ago, she had talked about little else. He so loved the sound of her voice, he had listened with rapt attention to the buzz words that were her poetry, as she explained the schematics for customized components which passed for high art in her world. The conversation had been one-sided then. It was so rare to hear her expend more than the necessary amount of words, he had not wanted to interrupt, to argue, to end it.

Now that he had finally been incorporated into her computer as a living screen, he wondered if she would look on him with greater affection. ''I suppose your next project will be an electronic book.'' This was his growing fear, that the beloved, friendly handheld book would turn into a creature with megabytes.

''You have to let go of the twentieth century, Charles. It's almost over now.''

''So you don't care for my theory that the Luddites will inherit the earth?''

No, they both knew that she was the inheritor, this strange child of high technology. Look at her now, glowing with electronic light—wires running in and out of her clothes.

He looked down at the projected diagram on his shirt. ''What's that?''

''You're looking at a power company grid. I worked for them for a while, too. Watch this.'' She turned toward Dayborn below. The lights went out again, and so did those of Owltown beyond it. Now the streetlamps switched on and off, one by one. And then all the lights of Dayborn came on at once. Owltown remained in the dark, as did everything on this side of Upland Bayou.

''Neat trick? It was a lot of work planting independent switches.''

So now he knew where she had been all these months from spring into autumn—laying traps, planning, scheming. ''And how long did you work for the tax assessor?''

''Very good, Charles. But I downloaded what I needed during the proficiency test. I didn't stay for the job interview.''

The tax records would tell her which citizens had lived here seventeen years ago, who had died, and who had moved away. By now, she would have bank records and credit reports. She would know what debts they owed, and who tithed to church or charity and how much. She had probably been listening to the phone conversations of Dayborn for months, gathering information, planning her homecoming. "The tax base helped me with my list."

"Your list? Does everyone in this town keep a damn list? It's the mob, right? All the people who killed your mother."

Mallory was staring at him. "Who else keeps lists?"

"Well, Henry has a list. The sheriff keeps one, too. Henry didn't tell you that?"

"We haven't had much time to talk. I've been busy."

"I can see that."

She touched his hand to prompt him. "The sheriff's list?"

"Jessop never stopped investigating your mother's murder. He's been torturing his suspects. Well, actually, only two that I know of—Alma Furgueson and the deputy."

"Travis? The sheriff thinks Travis was in that mob?"

"Yes. And he's been making the man pay for it all this time."

And now he thought he saw a regret in Mallory's eyes. But he had never seen it there before, and he was uncertain. "You didn't know he never gave up, did you?" No, she hadn't known; he was sure of it. "Well then, you're both on the same side really. You don't have to hide. You could—"

"Charles, he's a cop, and I'm not. I left my badge in New York. I thought you understood that."

"What are you planning, Mallory? A little vigilante justice? Henry tells me there were nearly thirty people in that mob. You can't get them all."

"Oh, sure I can." And in the same tone, she said, "Hand me those pliers, will you?"

He picked up the pliers from the crossbeam and held them out to her. "I would think the next logical step would be to find out who killed Babe Laurie. Then once you're clear of suspicion—"

"Why should I care who killed Babe Laurie?"

"But don't you wonder *why* Babe was killed?"

"No. It doesn't matter." Her voice was in the irritation mode. But she quickly shifted out of it with a sudden change of subject. "So what did you think of the show tonight?"

"Yours or Malcolm's?"

"The circus, Charles."

"Well, the magic act needs work. It's a little crude for my tastes."

"Not up to Max Candle's standards?"

"Not at all. Too much flash. Malcolm has no polish." And now Charles looked down again and remembered that he was on top of a telephone pole. The earth seemed to shift, or was that his stomach?

"Did your cousin ever dabble in icons and religious miracles?" Her tone was so offhand he might have taken it for small talk, but she never did small talk.

"Well, no, but Max knew the trade." He looked down at his shirt again as she flashed through an array of diagrams, finally settling on one she liked.

"Could you give Henry a few pointers for a small-scale religious miracle?"

And now he beheld a Mallory miracle. She touched the keyboard and then there was light in Owltown.

"This interference with the electricity, won't they trace that back here and—?"

She looked up at him, affronted. "The power company will send a crew out to check the lines. Ten miles down the road, they'll find the problem on a main line. Then they'll figure the backup circuits kicked in. I left a squirrel on the exposed section. He's burnt to a crisp."

"You didn't—"

"Charles, would you feel better if I told you the squirrel died of natural causes before I fried him?"

Her sarcasm was light, but it exposed a nerve. He knew he must seem like a clown in her eyes. "I was about to say, you didn't overlook a thing. And now if you'll excuse me, it's been a long day, and I'm tired of playing the fool."

He was climbing down when he felt her hand on his arm. "Stay," she said.

He hesitated.

Well, it was not quite the command she would give to a dog. The inflection was slightly different. In fact, coming from Mallory, that single syllable could almost be construed as an apology.

Her hand tightened on his arm, as if she needed force to restrain him. She didn't—she never did. He had a sudden clarity of sight, a hyperawareness of Mallory. She leaned across the dangerous cluster of exposed wiring. The electrical meter in her hand was aglow with pulsing red lights. Her lips grazed his cheek, his ear, and she whispered, "I won't kill another squirrel—I swear."

Before he could be insulted anew, she covered his mouth with her own. He was very still, not wanting to lose this connection with her. Had he been standing on knife points, he would not have moved. He could hear the humming in the phone lines, and feel the vibrations where his legs embraced the pole, throbbing in time to a blinking red light, an electronic heartbeat. His eyes closed to the computer-blue wash of her skin.

It was all too brief. She pulled back, but only a little. As the euphoria ebbed away, he wondered if she fully understood the effect she had on him; he thought she might. He would lose sleep wondering why she had kissed him, toward what ulterior motive.

No, actually, he wouldn't.

He didn't care why she had done it. And he would cheerfully fly down from the pole and kill a score of squirrels for her if she asked. He knew she would ask something.

"I want you to go back to New York, Charles. Go tonight."

Why couldn't she want something simple like every last drop of his blood? He had no problem with dying for Mallory. But he could never abandon her. She mustn't expect that. Going back to New York without her was unthinkable. He was shaking his head.

"Henry can help me with everything. Okay? I don't need you, Charles."

"Well, thank you very much."

"You don't know this place. You can't—"

"Good night." He began climbing down the pole. The metal spikes were cold under his hand. He fixed his eyes on the pole and strengthened his resolve not to look at her again. If he didn't see her tensing for the strike, then she had no power over him.

Yeah, right—as Mallory would say.

"Where are you going?" Her tone rebuked him for the temerity of going away without being dismissed.

Well, tough—another Malloryism. He had learned a lot of them over the years of abuse at her hands; the abuse mainly consisting of him loving her, and Mallory loving no one.

"Charles? Where are—"

"I'm going to find out who killed Babe Laurie."

"Charles." Her voice was faint in the growing distance between them.

He was doing so well. He made his way along the dark road and didn't look back. As he approached the artist's cottage, it was dark. Mallory, sitting on her telephone pole, tapping at her computer, turned on all the lamps in the house, all at once, to light his way.

AFTER A QUIET hour of housebreaking, Mallory returned to the woods with a shovel from her mother's garden shed. She wondered what the sheriff would make of her recent visit to his empty house, and what she had left behind. The tool case was slung on a shoulder strap and thumping against her side as she moved through the trees, guided by a narrow golden beam. The penlight exposed every root and rock lying in wait for her. When she brushed a fern away from her face, the penlight shone on one hand, and she froze.

Her long red fingernails were torn and broken, and the

polish was flaking away. The flesh showed scratches, raw red knuckles and blue bruises. She stared at this damage for a moment, incredulous, as though such things as chipped nails were inconceivable in her universe. And this was true.

From the age of ten, she had been compulsively neat, never suffering any chips in her facade, nor one thing out of place in her environs. Her foster mother, the late Helen Markowitz, had prized a neat, clean house. Young Kathy had worshipped Helen and made this ethic part of her religion, which did not include God, but certainly every type of mop and brush, every solvent and powder known to God and professional cleaning women. Back in her New York condo was a pantry, where each can, each bottle and jar stood at attention in the perfect formation of little soldiers in the service of the obsessively tidy Mallory, who was marred only in the places where it didn't show.

Until now.

She leaned the shovel against a tree and covered her face with the ruined hands. So tired, deflating now, as if the air had been let out of her lungs and the blood from her veins. If she could just sit down in the cool darkness and not get up again. This day had been years long, painful and difficult, but she had only come undone at the sight of chipped polish and broken fingernails.

No—it was not quite that simple.

Everything had been lost—all the family she had ever known, and she had also lost important memories. She had not been able to remember the name of the dog when he lay dying. And now she was alone again, in a state she had always believed preferable to the company of people who would eventually leave her, every one of them, by death, or on foot, as Charles had left her tonight.

Mallory turned off the penlight and stood in the dark, taking deep breaths and quietly rebuilding herself. Had there been light enough to see by, there would have been no trace of pain or any other emotion when she picked up the shovel and moved on.

She entered the clearing where she had left her dog. After pulling the loose branches away, she knelt down beside his body and pulled the black leather duffel from a rotted-out log.

The penlight was trained on the hollow in the wood, where insects scrambled over one another to escape the sudden brightness. Behind the duffel, she had stored a canvas bag with a cache of electronic equipment. She pulled it out and opened it to stash her leather sling, the tool kit and her minicomputer safely inside the metallic lining.

When everything was well hidden again, she picked up the shovel and began the sad work of digging a shallow grave. Later, she could come back and properly weight the animal's body down. Now it was only important to her to see him into the ground. It would be harder to do this in the daylight, not for the danger, but for the look of him in age and death. In the dark, it was easier to picture her dog in his prime, when they had loved one another and gone everywhere together.

Good dog.

There was only time enough to drive the spade into the earth before the gunshot exploded behind her.

She was hit, and the shovel was falling to the ground.

Her gun had cleared the shoulder holster before she spun around to fire one shot into the tree. She had no target in sight. The leaves were a mass of blackness. Aim was guided by the intuition of a new creature in the world, all reflex and instinct, detecting form in utter darkness, just as game animals distilled sound from the hunter's idea of silence.

Fred Laurie's body dropped from the tree—dead weight with a large bullet hole in his chest.

She nodded, approving the shot. She had selected the .357 magnum over the police-issue .38 for its improved stopping power—a good choice. This was what went through her mind as she stared down at her kill and appraised the hole in the target that was once a human being.

Mallory the Machine was back.

When she holstered her gun, she felt the wet slick of her own blood on her left shoulder and found the exit wound. She looked down at the rifle lying near the man's body. It was a .22.

Well, that would certainly mess up a frog. He should have used a different gauge for hunting humans.

Fool.

There was no pain from her wound yet, but it would come soon enough. She felt around the back of her shoulder. Exploring fingers found the wet entry wound. So there was no bullet to dig out. On the downside, there were two holes to lose her blood by. Still she could manage. When she was a little girl, Tom Jessop had once told her there were more than a dozen small animals running through these woods carrying bullet wounds from idiot Laurie brothers, and yet living to a ripe old age.

She waited, listening for the first sound of footsteps coming to investigate the shot. She saw nothing, heard nothing, yet she was aware of a body twenty feet in front of her. Mallory bolted away from the dog and the duffel bag and the dead man.

SHE HAD LOST Mallory in the trees, but that was not a problem. Lilith was running past the point of fatigue. Racing in that comfort zone where she gave up the struggle, doors opened in her mind. She knew where Mallory was headed. They were connected, moving through space in tandem.

Lilith paused at the rim of the cemetery. Cass Shelley's angel towered over every other monument. It was magnificent, poised for flight. She walked around the unfurled wings to the back of the statue, and there she met the angel in the flesh. The statue was twinning. The stark white face of Mallory emerged from the stone folds of the flowing robe, and in the next instant she was gone, and blood dripped from the marble as though the stone had been wounded.

The deputy streaked after her, running across the grass, skirting graves in her path. Mallory was disappearing into the woods beyond the cemetery, her gold hair shining through the leaves and then gone, blotted out by the dense foliage. Lilith screamed into the night, "If you keep running, you'll lose what blood you got left."

And now she became unhinged as the sound of laughter came back to her. Lilith ran faster now. The gold hair was in sight again, and she was closing the distance between them. And then Mallory folded and sank to the ground. Lilith was drawing ragged breaths when she came to stand over the fallen body. She drew her gun and held it in a two-handed posture as she had been taught to do.

Mallory groaned. She was bleeding from a wound in her back. Lilith knelt beside her, raising her gun barrel to the sky and freeing one hand to roll the body over. "Who did this to you?"

She was startled by the sight of the gun in Mallory's hand. In an unreal expansion of time, she watched the trigger finger pulling back in a slow squeeze.

"Back off," said Mallory, and Lilith did as she was told. But her gun barrel was lowering.

"*Careful*, Rookie."

Lilith went rigid, her gun still aiming elsewhere. It was not quite a standoff. Mallory would have the edge—if it came to trading shots.

"I wasn't put on this planet to raise you from scratch," said Mallory, leaning on one arm. "When will you learn?"

"It cost you a lot of blood to run like that. You'll die before you clear these woods."

"What's that to you, Rookie? It's not as if you were a *real* cop." Mallory was smiling now. "I know the feds recruited you from the state police."

"You don't know—"

"Don't I?" Mallory was sitting up now. "Any idiot could've worked it out. The feds keep track of every cult in the country. Or they like to think they do."

"I don't have any—"

"And you're so green. You probably bought that old line about a bright future with the FBI. Am I right? Well, surprise, Rookie. They lied. They do that a lot."

Mallory was on her feet now, while Lilith remained in a frozen crouch. "The FBI will never take you, and you can't go back to the state police, can you? They cut your orders. They know you're cooperating with the feds behind the sheriff's back. Why should they trust you? Your career is over, Rookie. Or maybe not. You could still salvage this."

Mallory tilted her head to one side. She had to be in pain, but she seemed not to notice the holes in her body and the streaming blood. Her voice was less sarcastic now. "The last thing you want is the sheriff bringing me in. Even you can see that."

But all Lilith could see was the blood from the shoulder wound. Mallory paid it no attention, and that was maddening. How much blood could she lose before she—

"Feeling a little sick, Deputy? Maybe you're thinking about that moment when you get caught, when you have to face the sheriff while he spits on you." She leaned her body into the conversation, standing easy, with nothing in her face to agree with the bullet wounds in her body, no sign of feeling. So cold.

"Deputy, I'm going to get you out of this mess. When you know what I know, the dirt on the feds, they'll have to take you in and move you along. I inherited my dossier from a master of dirt collection. Do you want my help or not?"

The deputy gripped her gun tighter as she nodded, rising to a slow stand.

Mallory altered suddenly, every muscle tensing to fire a bullet point-blank into Lilith's head. The deputy allowed the aim of her gun to drift farther afield, and Mallory eased back to a more relaxed stance.

This woman could kill her; she was sure of that much. The only thing Lilith doubted was herself. Her television image of a cop had died in the first few days at the police academy. The fantasy and the facts of life had warred.

Doubt had won. It had moved into her consciousness and followed her everywhere. It was with her now, standing off to one side like a haunt. *Could you kill Mallory?* it whispered. *Could you kill anyone?*

No—maybe. She had wanted to be a cop all her life. That was all she was certain of. Now it was all falling apart. And yes, she did feel sick. If it came to trading shots—

"Point the gun toward the ground while we talk," said Mallory. "It'll give me less reason to blow your face off." And now she smiled to say, *Nothing personal in that—no hard feelings, okay?* "I'm going to put your life back together." Mallory leveled the gun at her eyes. "Point the gun down."

Lilith slowly turned the gun barrel toward the ground. It was not fear that made her do it, but logic. Mallory would not play the waiting game, not while she was losing blood. Lilith looked down at the gun in her hand. She would not give it up, no matter what.

She was raising her eyes just as Mallory fired the shot. Lilith believed the world had banged to a close and she was dying. Every muscle in her body was loosening, knees buckling, arms flailing, and before her eyes was the after-image of a bright flash of powder. She felt the breath of the bullet, the rush of it speeding by her flesh. She had felt the heat of it. But the bullet had missed her. All these deductions were made in only a moment—just a single flying second.

When the ball of fire imprinted on her retina had faded and no longer obscured her view, she was staring at her own Colt revolver in Mallory's hand—for the second time in one day.

Shit.

Doubt, that old familiar haunt, was standing behind her, laughing at her. *So you want to be a cop, Lilith?*

"You keep losing this," said Mallory, holding up the Colt.

"Don't look so tragic, Rookie. You just learned one

more valuable lesson—don't believe anything a suspect tells you.''

''You were never gonna give me the dirt on the feds.''

''No, of course not.''

''So if the sheriff does get you, you're gonna tell him about the FBI.''

''No, Rookie, I lied about that, too. It's better if he hears it from you.''

Lilith was coming to grips with the odd and backward ethics of Mallory. There was a code here, but damned if—

''Take the speedloader off your belt and throw it down.''

Lilith unhooked the heavy weight from her belt and dropped it. It rolled to a stop at Mallory's feet. The woman holstered her own gun and trained the Colt on Lilith as she picked up the speedloader. ''You'll never need this, and it slows you down. Now take off the silly nightstick. And the rest of that garbage, the radio and the flashlight. That's more dead weight.''

The truncheon was unhooked and fell to the ground at Lilith's feet, followed by the rest of her gear.

Mallory scrutinized her. ''Now you look like a cop instead of a damn amateur.'' She dropped the speedloader into the pocket of her blazer, and now she held two revolvers again. ''I'm going to do you one more favor—so you won't have to explain how you lost the gun.'' Mallory tossed the .38 Colt into the thick foliage. It was a surprisingly long throw, and Lilith lost track of the flight of gunmetal against the dark trees.

''That should keep you busy for a while.'' Mallory pointed to the deputy's flashlight lying on the ground. ''I'm sure you've got fresh batteries in that thing.'' She smiled. ''You check them every morning, don't you?'' Unspoken was the word *fool*.

Lilith's hands balled into fists as she stared at the break in the trees where her gun had disappeared. Every other emotion was displaced by anger, and it was in her voice as she said, ''So, Mallory, maybe I'll chase you down again— *real soon*.''

When she turned back to the place where Mallory had been standing, there was no one there.

"Yeah, right," said a voice in the dark.

NEAR THE EDGE of Finger Bayou, Mallory waded through the waist-deep water and the morass of floating plants. She grabbed at exposed roots and saplings along the bank to drag herself forward. It was slippery work, a real fight to keep her balance. Her feet had no traction in the slime. The blood ran freely from her wounds. It trickled down her body and mingled with the black bayou water, leaving no track to follow.

Shock was working on her, slowing her steps as she weakened with the loss of blood. She had no warning that her legs would fail her. She fell to her knees, not feeling the cracked branch on the bottom of the bayou cutting into one leg of her blue jeans and her flesh. She reached out for a sapling and missed, falling back into the water. Now she was out of reach of the shore. She tried to make a stand, but her feet were sliding undirected with the loss of handholds. She floundered in eerie silence, making no splashing noises, but gliding this way and that, tiring more, losing more blood, and finally— exhausted. Her eyes were closing as she fell forward and lay facedown in the water.

When her eyes opened again, she lay on solid ground. Rough hands were pressing on her back, and water streamed from her open mouth. Her eyes closed again. She was only vaguely aware that her heels were making ruts in the grass as she was dragged along the ground.

FOR AN HOUR, the woods were lit with stalks of electric-yellow flashlight beams waving through the trees. Finally the quest was abandoned for the night. Malcolm and Ray Laurie had given up on finding Fred. They cursed their brother for a bastard as they made their way back home, preparing a story for Fred's wife, something to keep her from jumping to the conclusion that he was shacked up with a peep-show bimbo, which they figured he was.

The woods were quiet again, but for the owls and smaller creatures. On toward morning, another pair of men broke the silence, walking the gravel path of the cemetery, spooking the field mice and the night birds who hunted them. With great stealth, the men approached the stone angel. They bound her wings with ropes and pulled her to the ground. Then she was also dragged away in the dark.

CHAPTER

CHARLES BUTLER HAD lost his tie and gone native. The soft denim shirt was a bit tight at the shoulders, but otherwise wonderfully comfortable, as were the blue jeans and the hiking boots. The owner of Dayborn's dry goods store had been thrilled to unload all the giant-size clothing, for there was a dearth of giants in St. Jude Parish. The storekeeper had despaired of ever selling this stock until yesterday, when Charles had walked into the shop, the top of his head just grazing the eighteenth-century doorframe.

Today, Charles sat on a wooden bench and stared up at the skylight in the chapel studio, watching all the stars that were left in the early morning sky and sipping fresh coffee.

"It's an obscene hour," said Henry Roth. *"But this kind of work is best done in the dark. I appreciate the help."*

"My pleasure."

Charles followed the sculptor and his rolling pallet to the ramp at the back of the studio. A single bare light bulb hung over a group of white-shrouded figures, all in a circle on the platform which had once been an altar. Charles counted eleven draped pieces in staggered sizes. "Is there some reason why they're covered?"

"It's my private collection."

Henry began to pull the sheets away. A procession of tall statuary emerged from half the circle, their backs turned on Charles. The tallest angel must be at least nine feet high. And then the coverings were pulled from the smaller statues facing him.

Winged children.

Stunned, Charles stepped into the ring of stone figures to see the faces of the larger angels. And now he revolved slowly, watching Mallory grow from a cherub to a full-blown avenger with a sword in her hand.

THE SHERIFF WAS kneeling in the wet grass, looking down at the blood. The trail petered out three yards from Trebec House. In sidelong vision, he saw Augusta at the kitchen windows flanking this side of the brick foundation. After he heard the door slam in the basement wall, he gave her a few seconds more to come up behind him and commence a tirade on the damage he had done bringing his car across the grass, stinking up her air with his exhaust and frightening her birds. It was always the same exchange between them. She had gone to a lot of trouble to block the old road with trees. And *why*, she would ask, did he take it as a challenge to scratch the paint on his car working around all her obstacles? How many kinds of a fool was he? And then he would have a few choice words of his own. But today this old game would be a bit different.

He looked up to see her calm face, which never gave away a damn thing.

"Why're you creeping around my yard, Tom? You can't knock at the door like a normal person?"

The game had already been altered. So Augusta must have bigger things to worry about today.

"Fred Laurie's wife came in this morning. Said he never came home last night."

"Well, good for her," said Augusta, in a rare good mood

that didn't quite ring true. "That must be the first peaceful night she's had in twenty years."

He stood up and smacked the loose grass off his pants. "I guess you heard the gunfire late last night." Of course she had. Augusta was a chronic insomniac, and everyone knew it. "I sent Lilith into the woods to arrest him for trespassing 'cause I didn't want you to find him first. Lilith said the man just disappeared. Couldn't find a trace of him, and she was looking for a long, long time. But now I gotta wonder if Fred left the woods feet first, maybe with a hole in him."

"He's probably in the next parish, sleeping it off in a strange bed." She might as well have been talking about the morning rain.

"Using what for cash? You know Malcolm never gives those idiots any money, and I don't think a church voucher would buy him anything outside of Owltown."

"So you're thinking foul play?" Augusta was grinning. He had several categories for her grins. Some were downright evil, and some were dangerous. But this one was only malicious.

"If his wife shot him," said Augusta, "then I owe that woman an apology. I've sorely underestimated her, taking her for a mouse all this time." She shook her head. "The way that bastard beat on her. You sure he was here last night?"

"Oh, yeah. Two people saw him go into the woods with his rifle. I found bullet holes in a few trees, but I'm pretty sure the trees didn't put up much of a fight."

"I see where you're going with this. Well, if he shot himself, this is the last place he'd come for help."

"Damn right." He pointed to the trail she had been tactfully ignoring, as if she might be accustomed to seeing her grass splattered with bloodstains. "Maybe that's not Fred's blood. Maybe that fool actually hit something this time, and whatever it was, it came here. Is that Kathy's blood, Augusta?" He was careful in his wording. If it *was* Fred's, he didn't really want to know.

She never looked down. "I do hate to spoil your fun. That's nothing but blood from one of Henry Roth's chickens. You knew my cat was a thief. Now I'm gonna pay Henry for that chicken, so you have no business here."

The sheriff walked around the side of the house. The door between the staircases stood open a crack.

"Planning to arrest the cat?" Augusta was right behind him.

He walked toward the house. Augusta moved faster. She was there before him and barring the way.

"Tom Jessop, don't you set foot in my house without an invitation. Your father was a lawyer. I know he taught you better than to do a thing like that without a warrant."

He ignored her and pushed his way through the door. She caught it on the slam bounce, and followed him inside. "You let six million gnats into my house." There was nothing in the timbre of her voice to tell him she was anything but angry.

He left the long hallway and entered the kitchen. He looked up to the top of the refrigerator and engaged the yellow cat in a staring contest. Augusta was standing beside him now. He looked down at her and saw her eyes round out a bit as she stared at the gun in his hand.

He looked back to the cat. "You're fond of that animal, aren't you, Augusta?" He took aim. "Is that Kathy's blood in the yard? I'm waitin' on a straight answer."

The old woman put up her hands defensively, as if she were the one he meant to kill and not the cat. Then she waved her arms and shrieked. The cat's eyes narrowed and the ears flattened back as the animal sprang from the refrigerator and sank claws into the flesh of his chest and teeth into his shoulder. He could hear the horse screaming through the kitchen screens, and birds took flight from the shrubs lining the bank of windows, all screeching and flapping, blotting out the sky and the grass. Teeth sank deep into his hand. He dropped his gun and batted at the cat. He pulled at the pelt and felt his flesh rip. "Augusta, call it off or I'll break its damn neck!"

Augusta picked up the gun, threw open a window screen and tossed the weapon far into the grass. And now the cat released him after she had enough blood to suit her. The animal leapt to the slate counter and then back to the top of the refrigerator. She crouched there, bunching up her muscles, ready for another round.

He looked at the wound to his hand. These were not the pointy marks of a cat's teeth. The bite mark was Augusta's—almost human.

She pointed at the drops of his own blood on the floor. "Now don't forget where that came from, Tom. I don't want you getting confused again."

He was out of the kitchen and heading back down the hall when Augusta said, "Where you going so fast, Tom? I think you can take that cat two falls out of three."

"I'll be right back," he said, ever so politely. "I can't shoot that animal without my gun, can I?" The door slammed behind him.

He found his weapon shining through the tall grass twenty feet from the house where he had parked the car. He was wondering if the stains on the grass might not be chicken blood after all—or maybe it *was* Fred Laurie's blood.

What the hell?

He watched the horse race around the paddock. Now the animal reared up on his hind legs and knocked the crossbar off the fence. Hooves crashed down on the fallen bar and splintered the wood. The birds had picked up a contagion of panic and the volume of birdsong was building.

When he turned around, he was staring at a single-shot derringer, and Augusta was right behind it with her finger on the trigger. He stood up slowly and holstered his gun. His eyes never strayed to the derringer as he said, almost casually, "You wouldn't shoot me."

"Oh, Tom. You know better than that," she said sweetly. "Of course I would." She grinned wide and evil. "Do you really want to spend all damn day at the hospital while they pick this slug out of you?"

The dark idea crossed his mind that she would shoot anyone who threatened an animal on her land. Might she have found Fred in the woods? If that was what she was covering up, he wasn't sure he wanted to catch her before she had time to dispose of the evidence. As Augusta had pointed out, Fred's wife probably needed a rest from the beatings. "I guess I don't need to kill a cat today. But I do need to find Kathy, and real fast. If you get in my way, I'll forget how long I've known you, old woman. I'm too close to let—"

"It always comes back to Cass Shelley's murder, doesn't it?" She lowered the gun; the game was done, and she was not smiling anymore. "Revenge is a real sickness with you, Tom. This isn't what your father had in mind for you. Sheriff of St. Jude Parish should have been your *first* political office, not your life."

"Well just look at you, Augusta—the damn queen of revenge. It's your whole reason for living."

"Oh, but I do it so well—with gusto and style. I make it a fine art. With you, it's just an ugly occupation. Now move off my land or I'll let fly with a bullet." She lowered the short barrel of the derringer to his kneecaps. "Think you can catch that little girl with one lame leg?"

He backed up and eased himself into the car. When the wheels were spinning in a wide grassy lake, she fired the gun into the trunk.

God damn it!

In his rearview mirror, he could see her reloading just as the wheels found traction on more solid ground. Instead of driving forward, like any man who truly wanted to live, he backed up the car until he was abreast of her, and then he leaned out the window.

"Augusta," he said, touching the brim of his hat in salute. "Don't ever change."

Her laughter followed after him as the car rolled away.

· · ·

BEFORE HE WAS close enough to read the chiseled legend, Charles recognized the face on the new tombstone in the cemetery. Babe's photograph was encased in a cheap wooden frame fixed to the stone. This would be the smallest of graves, only a hole in the ground for the urn. No tomb for Babe Laurie, nothing so grand.

"So when will they inter the ashes?"

"He won't be cremated till after the big party at the end of the week," said Henry, looking down on the rough work of a cut-rate craftsman. *"It's a poor thing, isn't it? Malcolm spent a fortune renting a fancy glass show casket for the wake, and almost nothing on the marker. Babe would have hated this. When he was alive, he thought he was king of the world."*

Charles nodded. He had encountered such a man when he was the freak child at Harvard, eleven years old in his sophomore year. In the course of research for his behavioral science project, he had observed a patient in a local hospital. The old man was ravaged by syphilis and given to shouting, "King of the world am I!" But he had walked in an unkingly way, graceless, ungainly, and sometimes stumbling.

The old man had demanded that young Charles bow and use the proper title whenever the boy addressed him. A doctor had been present and explained to Charles that it was a hospital rule never to yield to the whims of dementia. The boy had dutifully complied with the policy and refused the king his due. Toward the end of this study period, the child had even had the temerity to explain to the old man that this was for his own good.

The old man had disagreed, and a fit of temper had been followed by convulsions. Then the doctor had gently pushed Charles from the room and turned back to his patient, who was screaming and being tied down with restraints.

The following day, the boy had returned to the old man's room, bearing flowers as a peace offering—bright blooms of every color, a veritable palette of apologies. But Charles found the room empty, the bed stripped of its sheets. The king of the world had died the previous evening.

The doctor and his nurse spent the next hour calming the hysterical little boy, trying to convince Charles that he had not killed the old man. Then, speaking to the brilliant child as equals, they had carefully explained the hell of the disease, the damage they could not reverse because treatment had come too late, and finally, the mercy of the old man's death as a release from suffering. The tantrum and the convulsions, they said, were merely behaviors common to *dementia paralytica*.

Eleven-year-old Charles had responded with behaviors common to childhood. He had cried, thrown down his guilty flowers and run away.

Now Charles, the grown man, hunkered down by the tombstone to look at Babe's portrait, and a young king of the world looked back at him. The symptoms the old man had endured might have been in this younger man's future had he lived another fifteen or twenty years.

"Henry? Who do you think killed Babe Laurie?"

"I don't know. Does it matter?"

Charles was about to speak when Henry signaled for silence. He could hear voices from the bridge over Upland Bayou, and Betty Hale's was the loudest.

"NOW STAY TOGETHER," said Betty, shepherding her flock of ten guests across the bridge. One damn fool was veering off on the side road. "You don't want to go in that direction, Mr. Porter. Three feet off the path and you're into Finger Bayou."

Mr. Porter was entranced by the worn wooden arrow pointing the way to the old Shelley place. Perhaps he took it for a traffic sign, for she could see he was longing to obey it despite the No Trespassing sign posted on a near tree.

"Is the bayou very deep, Mrs. Hale?"

"Well, no. But you could break your backside trying to

get yourself out of there.'' Yes, he would definitely crack his ass if he fell on his face.

"Now if you'll all gather round, please.'' Betty pointed up through a break in the trees. "That house is where the bats come from.'' Cameras began to click photographs of the roof and its round window as souvenirs of last evening's bat races.

"It's more than a hundred and fifty years old,'' said Betty. "It was built by the Trebec family. Miss Augusta is the last of the line. When she dies, the house passes over to the state of Louisiana.''

"So she's leaving it to the state as a historical site?'' asked the woman from Arizona.

"No, her father arranged that in his will,'' said Betty. "He put all his money in a trust fund. Augusta only got a caretaker's salary.''

"Some caretaker,'' said an elderly woman, eyes focussed through field glasses. "There are holes in that roof.''

"Oh, the whole place is a wreck,'' said Betty. "The roof is the least of it. It's a damn shame to see one of those beauties go to ruin that way. Augusta Trebec is the Antichrist of the St. Jude Parish Historical Society. They invoke her name every time they cuss.''

The line got a smattering of laughter, and Betty decided to leave it in the tour speech.

"The house has quite a history, and I—''

"Could Cass Shelley be alive?'' Mr. Porter was asking.

"Not likely. Now Augusta became the mistress of Trebec House under very sinister—''

"Are there any alligators in that bayou?'' asked the intrepid Mr. Porter. "You think maybe an alligator could've eaten her body?''

Though she wanted to stuff a sock in Porter's mouth, Betty smiled on him with benevolence. "A gator *could* eat you whole. When he clamps down on you, he goes into a death roll and drags you under.'' She liked that image of Porter. "But if the gator isn't hungry just then, he'll stuff your body in some underwater hole or a cranny in the bayou wall.'' Either way the gator went with that, Porter would be just as dead. ''And then he'll bide his time till your body rots up real tender.''

Now she had everyone's attention. Bloodthirsty bastards, bless their little hearts and credit cards. ''But an alligator didn't eat Cass Shelley. Fred and Ray Laurie killed every single gator in these bayous a long time ago. Finger Bayou runs up near Trebec House. Before Cass died, I used to take my tour groups up there. Augusta won't allow strangers on the place anymore, though. I guess the stoning spooked her. She stopped the herbicide on the bayou, and now it's choked off with water hyacinth, impassable by boat. You see those plants floating on the water? And most of the land surrounding the house is swamp, infested with poisonous snakes. So I *repeat*, you don't want to stray off on your own. Now what was I saying before we got off on gators?''

''The house,'' said the man from Maine.

''Right. Now the house and a few acres was all that was left of the original plantation. The town sprung up, lot by lot, as the Trebecs sold off the land.''

''You said the house was ruined,'' said the man from Maine. ''So Miss Trebec is too poor to maintain it?''

''Poor? *Augusta?* Oh, no.'' Betty laughed. ''She's a master of shady land deals. She owns all those cane fields out by the highway. Bought her first forty acres with seed money inherited from her mother. Then she sued a chemical factory for fouling the water on her land. That gave her cash for more land near *another* factory. Over the years, she's filed lawsuits against most of the chemical plants along the River Road. They always settle out of court. Today, Augusta owns most all of St. Jude Parish, except for Dayborn and Owltown.''

''Could you lose a body in that bayou?'' asked Mr. Porter, impatient to get back to the subject of murder. ''Maybe sink it down with weights?''

''No, I don't think so,'' said Betty. ''The sheriff was all

through Finger Bayou dragging for that body. He would have turned it up.''

''I can understand her not wanting to spend her own money on a house that isn't hers,'' said the man from Maine, still trying to make sense of the ruined mansion. ''But if the woman is rich, there's nothing to keep her here. So why doesn't she just leave?''

''Oh, Augusta won't go till the house falls down. She could set a match to it, but that would offend her sporting nature.''

The man from Maine gaped. ''You mean she *wants* it to—''

''What about quicksand?''

''No, Mr. Porter,'' said Betty. ''There might be a bog or two back there in the swamp, but even a bog will yield up a carcass eventually. Of course, only a Cajun could walk that swamp—or Augusta. She's what you might call a Cajun without portfolio.''

The rest of the group had their binoculars trained on the top window of Trebec House. One scrawny woman from California was shaking her head sadly. ''Surely the historical society will restore the house when this crazy woman dies.''

''Can't,'' said Betty. ''It would take too much money. They waived their rights in favor of Augusta's proposal for a bird habitat. Those ornithologists won't waste a dime on Trebec House. They'll just watch it rot. That's the deal they made with Augusta.''

''So what do you think happened to the body?''

''It *is* a mystery, isn't it, Mr. Porter?'' And if it were ever solved it would cut into her business, now evenly divided between bird-watchers, amateur detectives and the visiting New Church seminar suckers.

''Is it possible to lose a body in that swamp, say if you sunk it in a bog, and—''

''What goes into this ground will come up again, Mr. Porter. I'll show you what I mean.''

She led them through the skirt of trees and into the cemetery. "We generally bury bodies aboveground. If we sink 'em in the earth, they just rise again, and it doesn't matter how many stones you put in the coffin to weight it down. Now some of these bodies here were buried in a traditional manner, but you see that big slab of concrete? That's to keep the coffin belowground."

"Couldn't there have been *one* alligator hiding in the bayou?" asked the hopeful Mr. Porter.

"*No!* Sorry. No, the closest thing we got to a gator around here is Augusta. When she smiles, you can see the resemblance, and if you get on her bad side, her eyes will go dead on you—just like a gator. Oh, and just because a gator's dead, that doesn't mean it's safe to approach one. An alligator can bite you two hours after it's been killed. I plan to be several hours late to Augusta's funeral when she goes."

"But suppose there was just *one* alligator."

Betty's smile was broad, but her teeth were grinding. "Cass Shelley died this same time of year. Even if there was a gator in there, he would have been hibernating. Cass *did not* end up as gator food. Now, Mr. Porter, if we are done with the alligators?"

She pointed to the monument which towered over all the others. "That's the back of the angel. She's the image of Cass Shelley, God rest her soul. And the little girl in her arms? That's Kathy. She's come home again and murdered Babe Laurie."

The first of the tour group stood in front of the angel while Betty brought up the rear. "Now you just gather around. As I was saying, the little girl in the angel's arms—"

"What little girl?" The California woman was looking up at the angel.

"The little girl *in her arms.*" What kind of blind fools did they make up north? They shouldn't allow idiots to travel; there ought to be a law. "Later, I'll take you into the alley alongside the sheriff's office and show you where her jail cell is." No point in telling them the fugitive was on the loose. That might result in some empty rooms. "She might even come to the window, so take a good look at the little girl."

"*What* little girl?" asked the very sensible man from Maine.

Now Betty came around to the front of the statue to point out the little girl you couldn't fail to notice even if you were just this side of legal blindness.

But the stone child was gone.

The angel was alone on her pedestal, eyes cast down and holding out her empty arms.

"Oh, my God. It's a miracle." Betty walked up to the angel and stared into her eyes. "Oh, my God."

"She's crying," said the man from Maine. "The statue is crying."

Ten cameras shot the angel simultaneously.

AUGUSTA WONDERED IF sleep had been induced by the herbal concoction to stave off infection. Or had the girl passed out from the pain of irrigating the bullet wounds? Well, better that she slept.

All around the room were soggy towels and windings of gauze. Augusta picked up the bloody debris and put it into a plastic garbage bag. When she had washed her hands, she sat down in a chair by the bed and removed the bandages. She pulled the packing from the back wound and replaced the poultice. The girl slumbered on as Augusta taped the poultice in place and then turned the body over to clean the front wound in the shoulder.

With no warning, one white hand snaked out and held Augusta's arm in a surprisingly strong grip. The cat leapt onto the foot of the bed and made a low growl. Augusta hushed the cat and looked back at her patient and deep into a pair of very angry young eyes.

"What did you give me to make me sleep?"

"Nothing I didn't grow in my herb garden," said Augusta. "Now do you mind if I get on with this? It's a *big* hole.'' She bent low over the wound, ignoring the tight squeeze of her arm, and finally the hand fell away. ''Must have been a hollow-point bullet. This exit wound was real good for drainage.''

Augusta's patient looked down at the new packing in her flesh. ''Is that what I think it is?''

The old woman nodded. ''Spider silk resists bacteria. I wrap herbs inside it so the medicine releases slowly. Takes a lot of silk to make a good packing, but my house is a damn factory of spiders spinning webs.''

Augusta unraveled a long strand of cotton gauze and clipped it with a pair of shears. ''You were lucky. It's a soft-tissue wound. Missed the joint and the bone. No permanent damage.'' She wrapped the gauze over the naked shoulder to cover both wounds. ''This is a pressure bandage. I know it hurts, but the greater the pressure the less you bleed.''

''How long will I be laid up?''

''Not long at all, now that the bleeding is under control. In fact, the sooner you begin moving this shoulder the better. It won't be so stiff later on if you use it now. But go easy—you don't want to do anything to start the bleeding again.''

''Why are you helping me?''

Augusta looked up to the greenest eyes she'd ever seen, and they were drilling holes in her. Strange child.

''Real estate,'' Augusta said, bending to the work at hand, winding another layer of gauze over the holes. ''I never lose an opportunity to do a real estate deal. If you die intestate, it could take more years than I got left to tear your mother's house loose from the state.'' And now she risked another glance at her patient.

Not good enough, said the girl's bright eyes, narrow with suspicion. ''Why didn't you let the place go for back taxes?''

''And pay top dollar in a bidding war at auction?'' She put one hand to her breast to say, *What kind of fool do you take me for?* ''I tried to buy this place from your grandfather in a fair deal, but he wouldn't sell. Then after he died, and your mother moved back to Dayborn, she wouldn't sell either. But now I got you, don't I? I think you'll like my offer, Kathy.''

''Call me *Mallory*.'' This was not a suggestion, but clearly an order.

''All right then. You know, your mother never did say who your father was. That name you took—*Mallory*. Might that be his name?''

The younger woman only stared at her, impassive.

Well, there was silence, and there was silence. Maybe she did know who her father was, and perhaps she also knew how to keep a secret.

Augusta pointed to the corner. ''There's your bags over there.'' She had recovered them from the woods and made it back to the house not ten minutes before Tom Jessop had pulled into her yard with the patrol car.

''What about my dog?''

''I slipped him into the bog at the top of Finger Bayou. Fred Laurie too. Those bodies won't stay down forever, but I guess we can worry about that later. I hope you don't mind the dog keeping company with Fred. That animal deserved better, but it was as good a burial as I could manage on short notice. Poor demented dog, his dying was a mercy,'' she said in lament for the dog and passing over the incidental death of a man.

Augusta continued to wind the bandage tight. And all the while, Mallory and the cat exchanged looks of suspicion, two distrustful beings taking one another's measure, resolving into a standoff. And then the cat curled up in a ball, perhaps intentionally insulting her adversary by closing her eyes while the larger animal, Mallory, was still within harming distance.

''What was my dog's name?''

''You named him with your first words,'' said Augusta, tying off the bandage and binding it with adhesive. ''You wouldn't talk till you were three years old. It drove your mother nuts, but not me. I always figured you *could* talk—

you were just taking your own sweet time.''

Augusta picked up the old bandages and dropped them into the garbage bag. ''So, one day, I'm out in the yard with your mother, making her a *very* good offer on the house, when Tom Jessop comes by with a birthday present for you. He put that little black pup in your arms and asked what name you would give him. Well, you and your dog locked eyes and fell in love.

''Then your mother ripped into Tom for giving you a pet without first discussing it with her. Cass was mad, and Tom was real confused. Men always know when they've done something wrong, but they're never sure just what it is. So all he can think of to say is, 'But Cass, it's a real good dog, papers and everything.' Your mother was backing him up to the wall, explaining the error of his ways in simple words a man could understand. And then, clear as a bell, you said, 'Good dog,' and Cass's mouth dropped open. She'd never heard the sound of your voice until that second. Tom laughed and said, 'Good Dog it is.' And Good Dog was his name from then on. And you never did shut up for the rest of that day.''

Augusta stood up and turned her back on Mallory as she sorted through the bottles and jars of herbs on the bedside table. ''I know why you came back. You want to kill them all, don't you? Everyone in that mob.'' She turned back to Mallory. ''Ever kill a man before? Not counting Fred. I mean a complete man, an actual person.''

Mallory said nothing and turned her face to the wall.

Augusta surmised that this was not a guilty reaction; it was just too humiliating for the girl to admit she'd never killed anyone *but* Fred Laurie. The old woman wondered if this child might not be the most damaged creature she had ever dragged home.

''I'm talking to you the way your mother would if she were here. She would say, 'Now, Kathy, you know mass murder is wrong.' However, speaking for myself, a little revenge is a necessary thing.''

She leaned over Mallory and tenderly pushed back the

damp tendrils of golden curls. "You can still do evil things to them, child. If that's what you want, I will show you how to have a real good time. I'll tell you who's afraid of the dark, and who's afraid of the light. When you know where all their soft spots are, you can drag it out until you're bloated with revenge, until you've sickened on it. Now won't that be fun?"

Mallory nodded. There was a terrible purpose in those cold green eyes, but no detectable soul.

"Did your mother ever mention that I was the one who delivered you?"

Silence.

"No? Well, your mother overdid it the day she moved back into the house. Too much heavy lifting brought on an early labor. The phone wasn't hooked up, and there was no time to run for help. You were just demanding to be born. Your little head was crowning before your mother had time to say, 'Oh, shit!' She said that a lot during the delivery."

Only silence.

"Well, you're a quiet one, aren't you, Kathy?"

"*Mallory,*" she said, correcting Augusta.

"You know, you were *born* quiet. Oh, you were breathing normal enough. Your little fists were balled up, all pissed off at the cold air and the bright light outside of your mother's body. But you were stubborn—you wouldn't cry. Now that terrorized your mother. Cass was lying on the bed in a bath of sweat and blood, screaming, 'Why doesn't she *cry*?' But despite that, I didn't slap your new-born bottom. Though, privately, I thought you had it coming to you."

Finally, Augusta had pried a smile out of her, but then it ghosted away so fast. Well, at least it showed that Cass's child was still human—that was promising. So the damage had not gone bone-deep. And now there was time to wonder about the soul, and whether it might be hovering somewhere close by, searching for a way back into Kathy.

WHEN DETECTIVE SERGEANT Riker walked into the reception area of the sheriff's office, there was no one minding the store. A man's deep voice came from the next room. Riker looked through the open doorway of the private office, but the only person in sight was a pretty woman with long red hair and a tight dress.

Riker sat down on a wooden bench with a carved backing a little higher than a church pew. A toilet flushed behind a door on the other side of the room. The door swung open, and a small boy of six or seven emerged, stuffing his T-shirt into his jeans. He had the pretty woman's red hair, but not her large blue eyes. The boy's eyes were small, brown and curious.

"Are you a bum?"

"No, I'm a cop."

The boy's mouth went up on one side, and the jut of his chin said, *You're lying.*

Riker looked down at his tie, spotted with souvenirs of past meals. The old gray suit had been creased by the long train ride. It had been merely rumpled before he had gotten on that train. His scuffed shoes had not been polished since the last funeral he attended. He looked up at the boy, who was sniffing the air and no doubt detecting the beer scarfed down with lunch. "I'm an undercover cop," he lied.

"Cool." The boy sat down beside him and scrutinized the two-day growth of stubble on Riker's face. "It's really good." And now the child took in every detail of the shabby apparel, down to the scruffy shoes. "Great disguise."

"Thanks, squirt. So what're you in for? You didn't kill anybody, did you?"

"Well, no," said the boy with some regret. Then he smiled and leaned deep into the zone of conspiracy, whispering, "But I think my mom did."

"No kidding," said Riker, very impressed.

"The Georgia police arrested her. Then they put us on a plane back to Louisiana. Sheriff Jessop's in there with her now. He's gonna make her confess."

Now Riker and the boy listened together.

The sheriff's voice was asking, "You think Fred might've had a hand in it?"

Riker thought the man's tone lacked the passion of a good grilling. The sheriff might as well have been asking his suspect where she bought that tight dress. The woman's response was too soft to carry distinctly, though Riker and the boy strained their necks in unison to catch the words.

"Sally," said the sheriff, "I'm not looking at conspiracy theories here. Babe was no Jack Kennedy, and his death ain't that big a deal."

The woman said something in a low rush of words. All that was intelligible was a slight tone of indignation.

Riker leaned toward the boy and whispered, "Who's Babe?"

"My father," said the boy, brightly. "The bastard's as dead as a doornail."

And now Riker really was impressed. Even New York children were not so blasé about the demise of a parent. "I guess you didn't like your old man that much."

"He creeped me out, and my mother hated his guts."

Now Riker looked up to see a man his own age with a gold star pinned to his dark linen sports jacket. The sheriff was taking his own turn at eavesdropping.

The boy followed the train of Riker's eyes to the other man's face. "Sheriff Jessop, are you gonna lock up my mother?"

Riker honestly could not tell if this would be good news to the boy or not.

"No, Bobby. You and your mother can go whenever you like. Who's your new friend?"

"My name is Riker," he said, standing up and extending his hand. "I'm a cop. I was—"

"And you're from New York City," said the sheriff, taking his hand in a firm grip.

Riker opened his wallet to display the NYPD gold shield and ID. "How'd you guess?" As if he didn't know how thick his Brooklyn accent was.

"Oh, just a damn shot in the dark." The sheriff held Riker's ID at arm's length to read it, and then handed it back. "If we get any more of you New York boys out this way, Betty's gonna have to add another wing onto the bed and breakfast."

The boy's mother appeared at the door. Riker suppressed an appreciative whistle when she passed him by without a glance, as every pretty woman did. She sat down on the bench next to her son and ignored the sheriff when he spoke to her.

"Sally, when my deputy gets back, you tell her I said to take you out to the airport." He gestured to the open door of his office. "Come on in, Sergeant Riker. Or should I call you Detective?"

"Just Riker is fine." He settled into a comfortable chair opposite the sheriff. The clutter on the desk between them was amazing. His skill in reading upside down gave him an overview on the formidable paperwork for the Georgia extradition. Apparently, the Georgia boys had dragged their feet on compliance.

The sheriff lit up a cigarette and moved a handful of

papers to expose a generous ashtray. Riker smiled and reached for his own cigarettes. So far, he liked this little town a lot. He had been in motion for two days on a nonsmoking train, only stopping for a quick lunch in the town square. He had wanted to kiss the floor of Jane's Cafe at the sight of an ashtray on every table.

"So, Riker, I hear you New Yorkers ain't number one in crime and murder anymore."

"Oh, sure we are. And you would know that, if our police commissioner wasn't the best liar in fifty states." Riker exhaled a cloud of smoke and felt utterly at home, despite the trappings of another century.

"I don't know about that." The sheriff tossed a match and missed the ashtray. He eased his feet up on the desk, knocking files down to the floor, and winning Riker's heart as a fellow slob. "Miami seems like a real up-and-comer in the killing trade."

"Well, Miami's real competitive. They claim to kill more tourists than we do, but that's a damn lie."

"According to the newspapers, you New York boys doubled the drop in crime nationwide."

"That's slander," said Riker. "The top cop decentralized the department, and the mayor fired the press liaison. The reporters had no way to check the stats." Riker draped one leg over his chair and dropped a long log of ashes on the pantleg of his suit. "It's all politics. New York has the best politicians dirty money can buy."

"Sorry, Riker. That happens to be our state motto. But you can be forgiven for bragging. We do admire that down here."

And now Riker wondered why the sheriff had not asked him about his business in Dayborn. Just how slow did things move in this part of the world?

"There's a friend of yours in town," said the sheriff. "A man named Charles Butler."

Well, that explained a lot. How much damage could Charles have done by now? "A friend of mine? This guy says he knows me?"

"He's from New York City, too."

"New York is a real small town, Sheriff, only eight million people. And you'd think we all know each other on a first-name basis, but we don't."

"What about the man that owned this?" The sheriff fished in his shirt pocket and pulled out a pocket watch. "Louis Markowitz? That name ring any bells?"

"Never heard of him," said Riker, denying the friendship of three decades, and never going for the bait—not looking directly at the golden disk swinging from the chain in the sheriff's hand. He made a mental note to rag Mallory about the sentimental mistake of not ditching that watch with the rest of her identification.

"If you think this Markowitz is from New York, I'll run the name through the department and see what they turn up." New York had more Markowitzes than Israel did. Riker was confident that he could find one who had not been the former commander of NYPD's Special Crimes Section.

"Thanks, Riker. I'd appreciate that. But you *are* here about the prisoner."

"I'm here because you sent the FBI a serial number on a Smith and Wesson revolver. NYPD has a match. The gun was used in a fifteen-year-old homicide."

And that much was true. Riker remembered the day, four years ago, when Mallory had pocketed the revolver during a rookie's tour of the evidence room. She had wanted a gun that would make bigger holes than her police-issue .38. "It's an unsolved case." And that was a lie. The case had been closed when both robber and victim had died in a deli shoot-out.

The sheriff seemed skeptical. "Riker, if your homicide was fifteen years ago, it couldn't be my prisoner. She wouldn't have been but nine or ten years old then. I can't see a little girl doing murder with a gun."

"No, of course not," said Riker, with somewhat less conviction. He pictured Mallory at the age of ten, when he was still allowed to call her Kathy. Yeah, he could see the kid with a gun. However, Inspector Markowitz and his wife had eventually broken their foster child of all the worst habits and crimes against humanity. "I'd like to talk to your prisoner and ask her where she got that revolver."

"And of course, you'd like to have the gun back. That's a lot of paperwork."

"NYPD doesn't want any noise, Sheriff. Nothing over the computer, nothing on the phone and *no* paper trail. The old homicide could be federal jurisdiction. If the FBI finds out that gun is connected, they'll be all over this town, and they'll have a warrant for your prisoner. I don't think you want that any more than I do."

And now he could see that the sheriff did not want that, not at all. Riker knew he could always count on mutual law-enforcement contempt for the martinets of the FBI, though he owed one of them a favor for withholding Mallory's fingerprints. He was only a little uneasy about the payback on that highly illegal good deed.

"I can't help you, Riker."

"Can't or won't?"

"Don't like to waste words, do you? Well, I can see your interest in—"

"Save the folksy crap for the tourists." Riker leaned over and smashed out his cigarette in the ashtray. "You bet your ass we have an interest. Now I'm not gonna play village coot with you." He stood up with the pretense of stalking out. "You don't want to give us the gun? Fine! If you make my life miserable, then maybe I'll call in the feds myself. You think I won't push back?"

The sheriff smiled and exhaled a lazy stream of smoke. "The prisoner and the gun are gone. You wanna join me for a drink, Riker?"

"Don't mind if I do."

DEPUTY LILITH BEAUDARE waited until the sheriff's car pulled away from the Dayborn Bar and Grill. Tom Jessop was alone at the wheel, so the man from New York must still be inside.

She stepped out from the doorway and crossed the narrow side street to look through the front window. The room was filled with men. There was not one female in sight. So this was still the place where men went to be with their own kind. She suspected that had always been her father's attraction to the bar. Each time her mother had asked why he would go to a dive like that, he had smiled with a guilty secret. It was not a place where his wife would have gone, nor any of her sex.

Lilith walked in the door, and the conversations all around the room fell off as men turned their heads to have a long, hard look at her—all of her. She didn't belong here. She knew it, and they knew it.

Then the mantalk resumed, silverware clattered on plates and glasses thumped on the tabletops.

Some of Guy Beaudare's best stories had originated here. This was the first time she had ever seen the interior, though she knew what it would look like, even down to the details of the fish tank behind the bar, the sawdust and the peanut shells on the floor. It smelled of sweat, tobacco and beer. The jukebox played a Cajun fiddle tune, and against her will, her body picked up the lively rhythm of the music as she moved among the men, causing them to lift their faces and follow her with their curious, probing stares. She knew what they were doing to her as she passed each table, naked now, disarmed, undressed and barefoot in their eyes.

She was looking for the man Bobby Laurie had described, a New York cop disguised as a bum. She walked up to the unshaven man at the bar, the man with the messy suit and the bad slouch.

"Detective Riker? I'm Deputy Beaudare."

He smiled amiably, flesh crinkling at the corners of warm brown eyes. "Well, pull up a stool, Deputy."

"You think we might sit at a booth? Doesn't look right, sitting at a bar in my uniform."

"Sure, kid. Come on." He picked up his glass and led

the way to a padded booth at the back of the room where the daylight petered out. Most of the illumination came from a candle in the neck of an old Jack Daniel's bottle.

She took the seat opposite him and waited until he was settled comfortably into his drink. "It's about your friend."

"What are you—the second team? I've been through this with the sheriff. This guy Charles Butler may be from New York, but—"

"No, not him—the prisoner." She looked around her, making sure there was no one within earshot. "Mallory."

"So now the prisoner is a friend of mine?" And his smiling face said, *Fat chance.* "Your act needs work, kid. The sheriff does it better. He ran that one by me, too."

"Then how do I know she's a rogue cop?"

He threw up his hands in surrender, still smiling, as though he thought she might be the best joke in the world. "I give up, Deputy. How do you know? The sheriff says he has no idea what Mallory's been up to for the past seventeen years."

"*He* doesn't know anything."

"Meaning you do?"

"I know she's a cop."

"How do you figure that?" He put a small cloud of cigarette smoke between them.

"My mother says it's rude to tell people what they already know."

The man was silent. He was letting her hang out in the breeze, just watching the show and appearing to enjoy it a lot. This was not the scenario she had rehearsed in her head. Lilith sat back, not rushing her words any. "Mallory never mentioned you by name, but I know you work with her in New York City."

"The prisoner told you she was from New York?"

Lilith nodded, secure in the belief that she lied very well.

"If she talked like a New Yorker, I think the sheriff would've picked up on that," said Riker. "He spotted my accent five words into the conversation."

"But she doesn't have any accent. She sounds like the

television newspeople from Nowhere, USA.''

"Deputy, I hope you'll excuse me for being rude and pointing out the obvious. The sheriff tells me her prints haven't come back yet. Now that should tell *you* something, unless you're a rookie fresh out of the slot. If the prisoner was law enforcement, they would've had a match on her prints a long time ago." He drained his beer glass and set it on the table less than gently. "That's it, kid. School's out." He was looking toward the door.

"She's a cop," Lilith insisted.

Riker shook his head. "The sheriff would've known. Take my word for it, that bastard is smart."

"Not where she's concerned. He still sees her as a little girl. She used to live in this town with her mother."

"I know. The sheriff told me the whole story. In fact, he told me a lot more than I ever wanted to know about this town. Ask me any damn question about Dayborn. No, really, go ahead. I even know *this* is the freaking bar where Babe Laurie had his famous syphilis party—quaint custom." He slumped back against the padding of the booth and spread his hands, palms up with questions. "No trivia quiz? You don't wanna play? Okay, let me ask you one. Did you ever tell Jessop this theory of yours about the rogue cop?"

"Detective Riker, do you trust the sheriff?"

"So you didn't tell him." There was a slight disapproval in his voice. "Why tell me? What are you after, kid?"

"I might be looking for a job in New York City. So I help you, and you help me." *Slow down,* she told herself, *you're gushing.* She took more time with her next words. "You don't know this part of the country—I do. I can find her, and you can't."

He looked so tired when he smiled, as if he had heard all of this before. "Deputy, I don't think you'd like New York City." His voice was softer now. "Whatever mess you've made here, I'd advise you to stay and clean it up."

She sat up ramrod-straight. Her lips parted, but nothing came out.

He shook his head. "No, kid, I didn't read your mind," he said, reading her mind. "Rookie cops think every screw-up is the end of the world. I guess we've all been there. Whatever it is you've—"

"I can help you, Riker." Was that high pitch in her own voice? "You need me." Did she sound a little desperate? *Shit!* She lowered her tone. "The sheriff won't have to know I'm working with you."

"Stupid move, kid. If the sheriff can't trust you, why would I? Why would *any* cop trust you?"

And now that he had hit her between the eyes with that bat, he leaned in close to complete the kill. "You're young, Deputy. I guess I can overlook one small indiscretion. We'll just keep this between the two of us. The sheriff doesn't have to know you were gonna sell him out. I think we understand each other, don't we, kid?"

Yes, she did understand.

She had just sold herself to the cop from New York City, and she had gotten nothing in return. But Riker had not done so well either, for he was only getting sloppy seconds from the feds, who had bought her first with promises—all lies, if Mallory could be believed.

He was rising from the table, gathering up his cigarettes and matches. "If you do run into Mallory, ask her where she got the gun. Tell her I'll make a statement at her arraignment on the jailbreak charge. It's a standard deal. Any judge will give her points for cooperation." He pulled a dollar bill from his pocket and dropped it on the table for a tip. "And if I need anything else from you, I'll let you know."

She followed his progress across the bar and through a bright rectangle of daylight. Then the door closed behind him, and despite the crowd, she was alone in this place, dim and dank as a cave, watching clouds of smoke expelled from the lungs of men. She inhaled their secondhand breath with the mingled smells of their bodies and the leavings on their plates. The music from the jukebox died.

Lilith stared at Riker's half-filled glass and then slid it

over to her own side of the table. She sniffed the liquid.

Bourbon.

She tasted it.

Cheap bourbon.

Over a graduation drink in a New Orleans bar, her father had told her that cheap liquor was the mark of an honest cop. And Guy Beaudare had this on the word of his old friend, Tom Jessop, so he knew it must be true.

Lilith downed the glass in one long draught.

It wasn't the stifling air of the bar or Riker's bad bourbon that made her sick.

CHAPTER
16

JIMMY SIMMS PASSED through a patch of soggy ground, but one of his father's overlarge shoes had not moved on with him. It was stuck fast in the mud. He dropped a bulky laundry bag in the grass at the side of the road, and then he did a crane dance on one foot as he pulled the shoe out of the muck and slipped it back on. He settled down beside the cloth bag on the grass and tightened the shoelaces, as though that would help much.

And now he eyed the heavy bag, a gift from Darlene Wooley. If there was a God in heaven, there would be a pair of Ira's castoff shoes in there.

He had helped Darlene change the oil in her car, doing all the messy work at her direction. Then she had taken him into the house and cleaned his hands, as though she thought he could not do this for himself. Or maybe she thought he was as lame as Ira.

And perhaps he was.

No matter. He had relished this warm, mother contact, closed his eyes and made believe that his own mother was doing this small service for him. Darlene had scrutinized the oil spots on his clothes, lamenting that those stains would never come out. She had then sat him down at the kitchen table and made him a cold lunch. She had admonished him to drink all his milk, while she stuffed the bag with laundry-faded clothes, saying Ira wouldn't wear them anymore. All of Ira's shirts and socks must be bright red, she told him, and her boy would only wear dark blue jeans.

Darlene had also given him a crisp five-dollar bill. He had used part of it to buy a treat for Good Dog. A fine square of cooked meatloaf from the Levee Market was still warm in his pocket.

Jimmy riffled the bag, hands roaming over T-shirts, jeans and socks. He grasped one white leather running shoe and pulled it out, examining it in amazement. There was not one sign of wear. It was not even scuffed. He quickly found its mate, but there was nothing amiss with that one either. What had Darlene Wooley been thinking of? This pair was just a few months shy of new. He pulled off one of his father's shoes, and slipped on the new-old shoe of Ira's.

It fit. It was nearly new and *just the right size.*

He didn't want to muddy them, so he put his father's shoe back on and carefully tucked Ira's pair into the bag with the rest of his treasure.

Jimmy was unreasonably happy, and he was crying. Not wanting the dog to see him this way, he wiped his eyes as he made his way along the dirt road, limping on the foot with the worst of the blisters.

When he was standing in the yard of Cass Shelley's house, he found the bowl of food and the pan of water were empty. The dog was nowhere in sight.

"Good Dog," he called, over and over.

No response.

But the dog never strayed from the house—never. Well, Kathy had broken out of jail. Maybe the animal had gone off with her for a while.

He left his gift in Good Dog's bowl, regretting that it would be cold when the dog found it, and hoping that the old black Lab would know where the meatloaf had come from.

And now Jimmy wondered about the commotion in the cemetery. The voices were excited. Prayers and hallelujahs carried through the trees and up the winding road.

A FEW OF the remaining people from the tour group were still snapping pictures of the statue. Betty had quit the scene, running past Charles and Henry and not even noticing them.

Henry explained, *"She has to be first to tell the story of the miracle. Her reputation for gossip hangs on it."*

Charles stole a quick glance around the corner of a tomb. More people were coming into the cemetery, and some had brought rosary beads. "This is going to upset Malcolm—a miracle with no admission charge."

Henry handed him a piece of cold meat from a wicker picnic basket. Charles bit into the crispy cold skin and he was reborn. "This is wonderful. Is it one of your own chickens?"

Henry nodded.

"Does Augusta know you're killing birds?"

Henry put down his lunch to talk with his hands, to tell Charles that as a bird lover, Augusta was no purist, not when it came to chickens. *"She doesn't recognize them as true birds. She calls them 'gumbo ingredients.' One thing Augusta and I agree on—the only good chicken is a dead one."*

Charles was looking at the roof of Trebec House and seeing it in the new light of Betty's tour ramble. "I had no idea Augusta's father disinherited her. But still, I can't believe she's allowing that beautiful mansion to decay just for spite. Was Betty right about that, or is there more to it?"

Henry shrugged. *"The house is Augusta's business. She can do what she likes with it."*

"Can you at least explain Augusta's animosity toward the sheriff?"

"She blames him for the death of an old friend."

"And who was that?"

"The man Tom Jessop could have been, if only Cass had lived."

"There was something between them?"

Henry nodded. *"Ira's not the only one who communes with the angel. I've seen Tom out here late at night. And I've heard him too—sloppy drunk and sorry for all the things he never said to her. But he's said it all to the angel. In a way, there is more between Tom and Cass now than there was when she was a living breathing woman. But the love of stones is highly unnatural, and from what I have seen of it, I don't recommend it. I hope nothing happens to Kathy . . . for your sake."*

Charles pulled his long legs back behind the stone house as another straggle of pilgrims passed down the alley of tombs on their way to a miracle. And now he noticed one woman standing alone at the edge of the cemetery.

For a moment, his eyes had been fooled into believing that she was real. The statue stood well apart from the other monuments, deep in the lush shadows of dense foliage, picking up a green cast of life in refracted light. This was the statue of a wingless, mortal woman, small and slender, wearing a long dress and standing on a broad pedestal. She lacked the angel's drama and the baroque quality of motion and flowing robes. She appeared to be only pausing among the trees. So great was the sculptor's talent, her stance evoked the feeling that she might eventually continue on her way through the woods.

Charles pointed to her. "Henry?"

"Augusta's mother. She committed suicide. The church wouldn't allow her to be buried in consecrated ground. That's why she's out there on the edge. Originally, there was only a slab of concrete. Jason Trebec wouldn't pay for a tomb or headstone."

"She seems more delicate than Augusta."

"Nancy was a very gentle woman. Augusta is more like her father, ruthless and hideously single-minded." He regarded the statue with loving eyes. *"I entered that piece in a competition and won a scholarship to study in Rome for*

*four years. It was a wonderful time to be young and alive.
I think of Rome almost every day.''*

"Why did you come back to Dayborn?"

*"I was born in the rear bedroom of my house. The pull
of home is very strong. Look at Trebec House. That place
is Augusta's* raison d'être.''

"But she lives for its destruction."

*"I was the beneficiary of some of that destruction. Did
you see the broken tiles in the ballroom? Augusta ordered
new marble for repairs. The bank trustee didn't know the
difference between a receipt for marble tiles and a solid
block of stone. She gave me that block and my first com-
mission—Nancy Trebec's monument. I was only fifteen
years old. Augusta changed my life.''*

"But her own life was ruined by revenge."

*"Ruined? What gave you that idea? Augusta has had
more than her fair portion of fine wines, good lovers and
fresh horses. She always had a wonderfully greedy appe-
tite.''*

"But the house and all those beautiful, irreplaceable
things."

*"You look at her house and you see the ruined ballroom
floor. You don't see a young girl riding her horse through
the rooms, breaking the marble at a gallop. I was there.''*

With his hands, Henry made Charles see Augusta as she
was, half a century ago, her face flushed with heat, her blue
eyes unnaturally bright. She made the horse dance on two
legs, then on four, pounding, crashing across the marble
tiles, cracks opening in the wake of hooves. The horse
seemed to step in time. *"And I believed that I heard music,
I swear. But it was only Augusta laughing. I would not part
with that memory for the whole earth. Augusta has nothing
to regret.''*

It was Charles that Henry Roth felt sorry for. This was
not imagination; he could read that much in the artist's face.
This was the second time that Henry had suggested something might be passing Charles by, some portion of a life.

A gunshot was fired behind them, and then another shot

and another. It seemed as though the leaves of the trees were being blown away, but it was only clouds of birds taking flight from every branch. A man bearing Laurie features was shooting the statue.

The sightseers ran along every path leading out and away from the cemetery. Deputy Lilith Beaudare rushed through the line of trees. She put the muzzle of her gun to the man's mouth while she held a handful of his blond hair and made him scream until he dropped the rifle.

Where had she come from? Had she been watching—

"That makes eight," said Henry, unfazed by the violence, as though he had been expecting it. He wrote the man's name on a page of his notebook.

After the deputy had taken the handcuffed gunman away, Charles was about to rise, when Henry restrained him with one hand on his arm. The sculptor pointed to a figure on the path leading into the cemetery from the bridge road. It was Alma Furgueson, the woman with purple highlights in her black hair. A few days ago she had run from the square in tears, and now she was slow-stepping toward the angel, and her face was a study in horror. The woman fell to her knees and said. "I'm so sorry, so sorry . . . sorry."

And now a young man, clutching a cloth bag in his arms, entered the cemetery. He was gaping at the angel, moving closer, flapping his oversized clown shoes. His rolled up pantlegs were coming undone.

"Oh, Jimmy, she's crying." Alma extended a hand to this young man. "Come pray with me, Jimmy. We'll ask her forgiveness."

"I've seen that man before," said Charles. "He was at the tent show. Do you know him?" He looked down at Henry's notebook as the artist was adding the name Jimmy Simms to the list. Henry slipped the notebook back in his shirt pocket so his hands could speak.

"He's a small-job man. Every town has one. He washes windows and sands floors. Most of the time, he just walks around the town, waiting for the day to end."

"He's homeless?"

"No, the sheriff arranged a room for him in the back of the library. I think he sweeps the floors for his keep."

Jimmy Simms reminded Charles of Ira: both were young men walking on the edge of a life.

Once more, Alma begged the young man to join her in a quest for atonement. The man seemed more like a child in his oversized clothes and his shattered face—a child who had just been brutally slapped. And now he did what all children do when they are badly frightened—Jimmy ran away.

And Charles died a little.

Alma went after him on her knees for a bit, and then she stood up and came back to the angel. Her legs were unsteady, and now she fell.

What had he done? Charles was moving toward her when Henry blocked his way and shook his head.

"Now what's that all about?" said a familiar voice behind them.

Riker?

Charles whirled around to see his old friend standing there. The detective was staring at the prostrate woman, and he was not happy. "Charles, why do I think you've been picking up bad habits from Mallory?"

The three men watched in silence as the woman made an awkward stand and walked aimlessly through the city of tombs, careening toward the perimeter, arms outstretched, seeking balance, crying.

Now Riker reached up to tap Charles's shoulder, and in his face was the question *Why?* He was probably alluding to the maiming of an unarmed woman.

Riker turned his face away from Henry Roth and spoke in low tones. "I told the sheriff I never heard of you or Mallory. Will the little guy play along with that?"

And now Charles realized that Riker had been watching them long enough to see Henry use sign language, and he had assumed the man was deaf as well as mute. Charles didn't correct this impression when Riker turned his back on Henry to hold a more private conversation.

"Henry is an old friend of Mallory's," said Charles. "He wouldn't do anything to—"

"Good." Riker put one hand on Charles's arm and guided him over to the angel. There were chips in the marble. One ear was gone and the tip of a wing had been blown away by the recent gunfire.

"What a travesty." Charles looked down at Henry. "It was a beautiful piece of work."

"Oh, I especially like the tears," said Riker, staring up at the angel's moist eyes. "I know a guy in SoHo who specializes in weeping icons. Only two bills a miracle. So what did you use—calcium chloride?"

"No, nothing that sophisticated. My secret ingredient is beef fat. In a proper mixture, it liquefies in the first hour of sunlight."

"So you timed it for the tour group?" Riker turned to see Alma at the edge of the cemetery. She fell down again and did not get up this time, but crawled down the path on her hands and knees. "Very effective, but a bullet would have been quicker and cleaner."

Charles jammed his hands into his pockets, and lowered his tell-all face to hide his thoughts from Riker. He stared at the ground, as though he might find salvation there.

"I understand," said Riker, sounding almost genuine in his consolation. "It's not your fault. The devil made you do it, right? And just where *is* our little Princess of Darkness?"

"The truth, Riker? I don't know. I don't think she'd trust me with that information." And now he let Riker see his face as naked proof.

"But you can get a message to her, right?" Now Riker smiled, gleaning an affirmation from Charles's silence and averted eyes. "I have to talk to her, and real soon. The kid must have been in a hurry to pull information out of government files. She got sloppy. The feds found her little footprints in a highly classified computer. That's a federal rap, but they're willing to cut a deal."

"But you know she's compulsively neat. So, our government said Mallory was sloppy, and you *believed* that?"

"Nice try, Charles. Tell Mallory to get in touch while I can still run interference for her, okay?"

"I don't think she'd appreciate interference just now. Perhaps if you—"

"How many people do you figure that kid has on her hate list, Charles? Twenty? Maybe thirty people? That's bad, real bad, because Mallory wouldn't waste time hating anyone she couldn't destroy."

Charles didn't consider the import of these words beyond wondering if Riker knew he was mangling a quotation of Goethe's. He had always suspected Riker of being much more than he let on. Beneath that incredibly awful suit, the badly spotted tie, the slovenly, crude, unshaven veneer, was a—

"I've known her longer than you have," said Riker. "I watched her grow up. You know how much I love that kid, don't you?"

"Of course I do."

"Then believe me when I tell you, for the last time, Charles—Mallory is a freaking sociopath. I know at least one of your degrees is in psychology, so why do you still have so much trouble with that? And don't give me any of that 'little lost soul' crap. She doesn't have a soul."

"She does."

"Doesn't! She lost her soul before Lou Markowitz found her. Lou's wife tried to knit her a new one, but the kid wouldn't wear it."

Charles was casting around for some defense of Mallory, and failing in this, he offered, "But did you know that she could play the piano when she was only six years old?"

Riker looked up at the sky for a moment. And then he shrugged in surrender and inclined his head as a bow to the absurd. Without another word, he turned around and walked away.

Now Henry was standing by Charles's side, words flying off his fingers, asking why this man said all these things about Kathy. *"I've only known her to tell one lie. She said she was seven years old while she was still six.''*

"She told a similar lie to a friend of mine," said Charles. "When he was filling out papers for her foster care, she told him she was twelve when she was only ten. They compromised at eleven."

However, that had not been her best piece of work. Louis Markowitz had brought the child home one night, after arresting her for theft. It was to be a one-night arrangement for his own convenience, or so he said. But he was a very warm and decent man, so that part of his story had always been suspect.

By Louis's account, when young Kathy appeared at the breakfast table the following morning, her glittering eyes were cold, and she wore a very unnerving smile. His wife had stood behind Kathy's chair and explained to Louis that he would not be taking the little girl off to Juvenile Hall, or anywhere else—not ever. Kathy was here to stay, Helen told him flatly, and that was that. And then poor Louis realized that the baby thief had casually pocketed his wife and one mortgaged wood-frame house in Brooklyn.

Until the day Louis died, he never underestimated Kathy Mallory again. Or so he said.

WHEN TOM JESSOP came home to visit his bed for the first time in thirty-six hours, he walked in the back door and found a package was sitting on his kitchen table.

How did it get there? The cleaning woman was not due back for days, and the evidence of her absence was the load of dishes in the sink, the hamper filled to overflowing and dirty socks trailing out the door of the bathroom.

Distrustfully, carefully, he untied the string and opened the brown paper wrapper. Now he looked down at the gun he had lost to his erstwhile prisoner. A sheet of paper was rolled around the barrel. He spread the curling paper flat on the table. He was so tired, his eyes were closing to slits as he read her letter:

You wanted to know what my mother said to me when she was dying. She wrote a lot of numbers on the back of my hand and told me to run to the public telephone on the highway and dial that number. She said a woman would come for me. Most of the phone number was smudged, so I never did get through to anyone. I just kept running. I wanted to run to you, but she said, 'No, don't go near the sheriff's office, you'll get hurt.' So I always figured you were part of it. Until tonight, I didn't know the deputy was in the mob that stoned her. That must have been why she wanted me to stay clear of your office. She was afraid Travis would hurt me before I could get to you. If I could get to you now, I would—because I want my pocket watch back.

He slipped the gold watch from his shirt pocket, opened the case and speculated on the name engraved above hers. Was this the man who had raised her? She must have loved him, she prized his watch so much. So it was Louis Markowitz who had been there for her when she needed help. It might have been himself, if only he had stayed in town that day. But Cass had known that he wouldn't be back before dark—not in time to save her daughter.

A cascade of images overwhelmed him: the blood on the floor of Kathy's bedroom, the small red handprints inside the closet, Cass's flesh on the rocks in the yard. And now he saw Kathy as a badly frightened child, all alone on the road and grieving for her mother.

He walked around the house in the slow shuffle of a much older man, closing all the curtains. It wouldn't do for any passerby to glance in a window and see the sheriff crying.

CHAPTER
17

FEW CREATURES BEGAN life in November; it was largely a killing season. But in the hour before dawn, owls and bats were folding up their wings. Insects and small animals enjoyed a respite from the carnage before the balance of power shifted and the daylight predators opened their eyes.

The cemetery was at peace, but one of its angels was missing.

The chilly air of a sudden cold front had mixed up a low-lying fog, and the sheriff's feet disappeared in the mist as he stood before the bare stone pedestal and read the dates of Cass Shelley's life and death. Seventeen years ago, he had meant to add a line to this engraving, a bit of poetry perhaps, but the right words had always eluded him. All these years later, he was still thinking about this unfinished business.

He turned to his deputy, who blended so well with the dark. Lilith's ghost-white father had been the most superstitious man Tom Jessop had ever known. If old Guy Beaudare had been here yesterday and seen that angel weep, he would have been down on one knee in a heartbeat, rattling rosary beads and chanting prayers like a madman. Apparently, Guy's daughter was more at home in the solid world and not a big believer in miracles.

"So you figure they're coming right back?"

"It'll be a while," she said. "They have to lay boards in front of the pallet to move the statue over the ground. It's slow work."

"But real quiet and no tracks or ruts. So Mr. Butler never left town. Good job, Lilith. I guess you earned your pay this week."

"You're not going to fire me?"

"Never occurred to me. I knew I could depend on Guy to raise his daughter right."

"You knew all along, didn't you?"

"From the first day. But it's good you told me." Though he had only set eyes on Lilith three times in her life, it would have been awkward to fire the girl. He had so many years invested in drinking with her father, and an ocean of beer was a damn strong bond.

"I'm gonna tell the FBI to go to hell."

"I like the sentiment, Lilith, but you might want to re-think that. Twenty years ago, they came to me with the same deal."

"My father said you told them where to get off."

"But after that, there were times I could've used their help. You can learn a lot from my mistakes."

"So why did you turn them down?"

"They made my skin crawl with their little dossiers on the New Church crowd. Granted, Malcolm's pulled off some shady deals, but the feds didn't know anything about that. They just wanted to collect information on another church. They're a lot like insects, collecting things without a brain to tell them why, collecting for its own sake. I wasn't about to help them. So they asked my deputy if he'd like to make a little extra cash."

"Travis worked for the feds?"

"Not Travis—that worthless idiot. No, they used the real deputy, Eliot Dobbs. He's long gone now. Got a better job up north. What with the other towns going broke and folding left and right, I didn't really need another deputy, so I never replaced him. But I did miss the connection to the feds.''

He walked down the gravel path, inspecting tombs and looking for a likely place to hide. At his back, Lilith was asking, ''How did you find out Eliot was working for them?''

''He asked if I would mind having a spy on the payroll. Said he had a baby on the way and needed the extra money. Hell, I used to help him spin lies for his reports. And then when I needed help, the feds came through for Eliot. A boy from Dayborn had run off. Jimmy was just a little kid then—way too young to be on the road. The feds helped us trace him to New York City, and I brought him back home.''

And New York was where Kathy had run to. He was sure of that now. Did every damn road in the world lead to that hellhole? The cop at the Missing Persons Bureau had told him there wasn't a state in the union that had not contributed a child to the streets of New York. When Jimmy Simms came home again, he had probably flooded the whole school with tales of the city, hiding out and foraging for food. But Jimmy was a good five years older than Kathy when he made his run.

''I guess Eliot was gone when Kathy disappeared,'' said Lilith.

''That he was. But it didn't matter. The FBI wouldn't have spent any time looking for her. We all figured she was dead. There was so much blood.''

He picked out a monument decked with cherubs. It offered good cover and a view of the empty pedestal. ''This is as good a spot as any.''

The deputy put one finger to her lips and pointed east.

The angel was coming.

And she was magnificent, wings spread for flight and carrying a sword. The ground-hugging clouds obscured the hem of her robes and the pallet. She appeared to float along the path between the tombs.

Lilith crossed herself, and the sheriff decided his deputy did have a bit of Guy in her after all.

The sheriff pulled back to join her behind the monument just as Henry Roth appeared in front of the angel to set down two boards in her path. The planks immediately disappeared into the white soup of low fog. The angel veered left down another alley of tombs, heading toward the pedestal, and now the sheriff could see Charles Butler behind the wings, his shoulder bent to the stone, slowly moving her along.

Butler wasn't wearing his three-piece suit. He was filling out a pair of jeans and a denim shirt like a regular working man with some muscle on him. Jessop liked the man better this way.

As Butler and Roth passed behind one of the low tombs, they were lost from sight and only the head of the angel and her sword floated past the pitched roofs with their crosses and crucifixes.

The sheriff and his deputy watched in silence as the angel came into full view again. Now she was rising straight up in the air. The two men worked a jack on each side of the pallet until she was level with the top of the stone platform. Butler was surprisingly strong. He stood on the pedestal and rocked the angel to dance it into place.

And now Butler jumped to the ground and picked up the heavy pallet and the planks. He did it with such ease, it might have been only a bundle of matchsticks he was carrying. Henry collected the jacks, and they left the cemetery together.

The deputy stood up and stretched her legs. "You really think this is Mallory's idea?"

"I know it is. And now I got her connected to Charles Butler. Your cousin's in it with 'em. She backed up that story Butler gave me."

The sheriff walked up to the statue and admired this new incarnation of Cass Shelley. The angel was so fierce, just like Cass when she was on the opposite side of an argument.

Lilith stood beside him. "Why is she doing this?"

"She wants them to know she's coming for them." And it showed a lot of style, this threat carved in stone. The girl really knew how to hate. "Now I need a way to head her off before someone else gets killed."

"You don't think Mallory killed Babe, do you?"

There was something a tad anxious about her tone, like she had a lot riding on his answer, and he had to wonder about that. What might Lilith be holding back?

"You said there were quite a few locals with a grudge against Babe," she said, in an offhand manner, as though it didn't matter, and now he was sure that it did.

"So you don't see any reason to consider out-of-town talent?"

"What about Babe's widow? She hated her husband, didn't she?"

There was a trace of hope in her suggestion of an alternate suspect, and this bothered him.

"Sally Laurie didn't do it," he said with finality and the positive authority of hard fact.

Did Lilith crumble a little? Yes, she did.

"Sally made a pile off the Laurie connection," he said. "Malcolm gave her a house on prime waterfront property. It was a bribe to stay married to Babe. But her source of income was IRS money. Those tax boys have a real keen interest in the New Church."

"Why? Churches don't pay taxes."

"Nobody in the Laurie family pays taxes. Malcolm makes a healthy donation to the town treasury to stay on my good side, but no Laurie ever pays any taxes. Turned out to be legal, and after a while, the IRS took Sally off the payroll."

"How did you know Sally was working for them?"

"I saw her spending cash in the next parish. Nobody in the New Church gets any spending money. They donate all their time to the church, and the church owns their houses, their VCRs, their dishwashers and every stitch of clothes on their backs. Even their groceries are bought with church vouchers.

But Sally had cash—a lot of it. She was a first-rate business-woman.''

"That gum-chewing bimbo?"

"Sally Laurie was also your predecessor with the FBI."

Well, that set his deputy back on her heels. He smiled. "It was my idea. When IRS stopped her paychecks, I told her it was a shame to waste a perfectly good government résumé. IRS gave her a nice recommendation to the FBI. She made out real well selling lies to those suckers. You should see the size of her bank account."

"She told you all this?"

"Sally and me were good drinking buddies for years. I was the only one in town that hated the feds and the New Church as much as she did. Who else was she gonna talk to? I do admire that woman. But here's the best joke. Travis used to be a member of the New Church, and everybody thought *he* was the FBI mole."

"What about Fred Laurie? He skipped town, too. Could he have killed his own brother?"

"I *would* like to know what happened to old Fred. Though I'm not all that curious in any official capacity. I've got enough murder on my plate right now."

"You think he's dead?"

"Oh, yeah, he's dead all right. He didn't take any clothes, and he didn't have any money. Where was he gonna go? Maybe there was more than one gun in the woods that night. Maybe he just annoyed the wrong person. Augusta walks that land every night, checking the feeders and counting her owls. She wouldn't have tolerated Fred out there with a gun."

"Augusta? You're crazy. That old lady couldn't—"

"Now don't you sell your cousin short. Remember, Augusta has killed before."

Lilith smiled, as though this were a cozy memory of baking brownies instead of a murder in the family. "She was a pistol in her younger days."

"She still is. So try to stay on good terms with her." The ground fog was dispersing, and his feet scattered the wisps as he moved along the path. He was wondering how far to trust his deputy. "I'm meeting that New York cop for a beer at the Dayborn Bar and Grill around noon. You know the place?"

She nodded, but failed to mention her recent visit there and the long chat with Riker. The bartender had been unable to tell him what the conversation was about. The man could only say for a fact that Lilith could down a drink even faster than her father.

She kicked up some gravel as she walked alongside him. "Dad spent some memorable nights in that bar."

"That he did. I remember the night you were born. Your father came in with four boxes of cheap cigars, and the place just stank for days after that."

He and Lilith's father had celebrated all night long. Toward morning, Guy Beaudare had begun to cry; it had suddenly occurred to him that the entire universe, from the Big Bang to the last evening star, was one great conspiracy of heaven to birth the beautiful and perfect Lilith. A drunken young Tom Jessop had taken exception to this theory, as Kathy Shelley had been born several years earlier.

"Every man in that bar was relieved when your father left town. We were so sick of hearing about the latest cute thing you'd done. And I never met a man with so damn many wallet photos of the same kid."

No need to mention that he had matched Guy, story for story, "Lilith's so smart" for "Kathy is smarter." And then Kathy had disappeared, and the sheriff had not listened to Guy's stories anymore. He had learned to drink alone, shunning all talk among men with children, believing that Kathy was dead.

As the sheriff and the deputy were walking toward the bridge, Lilith was saying, "If those two split up, you want me to keep an eye on Henry Roth or Charles Butler?"

"Neither. There's something else I want you to do."

The sky was lightening in the east, clouds flaming in advance of the sun. A blue jay opened its eyes to the tasty sight of a beetle and devoured it alive and squirming. Over-

head, a hawk was circling on the air, watching for ground-
lings. Every waking thing in St. Jude Parish was scurrying
into motion, hunting food or running from sudden death.

A new day.

CHAPTER
18

THE AIR WAS foul, and the only light came from bright holes in the rotted fabric covering the windows. Mallory pulled aside the heavy velvet drapes and threw up the sash. A cold breeze gusted over the sill and whipped through the room to set a storm of dust motes spinning in the bright shaft of sunlight. Now she could clearly see the bat droppings on the floor and the insects crawling off to the more hospitable shadows in the corners of the room.

Mallory's strong aversion to dirt and disorder had become numbed on the upper floors of Trebec House. She was also losing her fanatic compulsion about time. Force of habit no longer drove her to reach for the lost pocket watch ten times a day. She only knew that it was still morning, and only by the low-riding sun shining in the east window. As she laid a bundle of clothing down on a cedar chest, she caught a movement in sidelong vision and turned to face the intruder in a far dark corner of the room.

It was a woman standing barefoot in the shadowy glass of a full-length mirror. She wore an antique poet's blouse and pale blue jeans. Time was slipping by Mallory, seconds melding into minutes as she drank in this soft, feminine

image so like her mother. The face in the mirror was stained
with glistening tears.

Footfalls in the hallway brought her back to the solid
world. Mallory's hand passed over her face to erase the
evidence of crying.

But there was none—her face was dry.

She stood very still, staring down at her hand. There was
no trace of—

The footsteps were coming closer.

Get a grip.

"The temperature is dropping like mad," said the old
woman, coming through the doorway, her arms filled with
clothing.

Apparently, canny Augusta could ferret out the invisible
tracks of phantom tears, for her voice was gentle now.
"You'll need a coat. I've got one here. I think it's your
size. Now those running shoes were just ruined. Couldn't
do a thing with them." She held up a pair of riding boots
for Mallory's approval. "How do these suit you?" The fine
leather was black, and the detailing was western.

"Perfect. And I already found a coat."

Augusta cast a dubious eye on the garment draped over
the cedar chest. This long black coat had been more fash-
ionable in the days when overland travel was on horseback.
It did fit well with the period blouse, but Augusta had hit
on its more useful quality. "Yes, that would blend well
with the dark, wouldn't it? I can't believe that old duster
is still hanging together. It's a lot older than I am. Well,
it's yours if you like it so much."

The old woman opened an armoire and began to pull out
boxes from the top shelf. "There's a hat that goes with it,
if I can only remember where it was stored. My grand-
mother wore it when she went riding." A large round box
came apart in her hands, and the black hat tumbled to the
rug. Augusta picked it up and turned it over in her hands,
smoothing out the low flat crown and the wide brim.

"It won't cover up all that bright gold hair." She reached

back to the shelf. "But I guess we can do something with this." Augusta held up a black bandanna.

Mallory pulled back a pair of red drapes from another window. Light washed through the room, killing every corner shadow. She turned to the mirror again and appraised the white linen blouse. The romantic flow of material was far from her own severely tailored tastes, but the billowy lines hid every trace of her bandages. She pulled on the harness for her shoulder holster and winced as the leather strap crossed her wound.

Augusta stood behind her and spoke to the reflection. "You'll have to find some other way to wear that gun. That left shoulder is gonna be sore for a while. You won't have full strength or mobility for another week or so. But I guess I pulled that yellow cat through worse wounds than you had."

Continuing a conversation that had begun over breakfast, Mallory asked, "Why did Ira's father commit suicide?"

"Suicide? Oh, now don't go making more of that than it was. Ira's daddy never was the best driver in town. That car had a lot of dents in it long before it ever hit that phone pole." She pulled open a dresser drawer and rummaged through the musty clothing. "Maybe we can fix your holster to a regular belt."

"The insurance company contested the settlement," said Mallory. She had raided the local agent's computer, but the investigator's report had been sloppy and incomplete. It contained only bare bones of dates and physical evidence. It had been no more helpful than the data she had stolen from the sheriff's computer.

"The company man did make a fuss at first. But he finally paid the claim in full." Augusta held up a narrow strip of leather. She looked at Mallory's large gun and discarded the flimsy belt with a shake of her head. "Darlene had to use all the policy money to buy her own house back from the New Church. Seems her husband had signed over the deed as a donation and a tax deduction."

"I thought the New Church was all Laurie family."

"Most but not all. I don't know that Ira's father was that religious. I think he was just looking for a way to avoid taxes. If you gave up your house, you got to live in it rent-free till you died." She had found a broad belt with an ornate buckle and held it up to the light. "Now that's promising." She handed it off to Mallory. "That was how Malcolm wound up with all that prime property on the lower bayou. He convinced a lot of fools that the best way to hold on to something was to give it away, and the best way to save money was not to earn any."

Mallory threaded the belt through her holster. "But why did the insurance company contest it? There must have been—"

"It was just a formality is all. It's a common thing when there's an alteration in the paperwork a few days before a death. The original policy favored the New Church, and then he changed it to name Darlene as the sole beneficiary."

So Ira's father had a falling-out with the New Church before he drove his car into a telephone pole, head-on, according to Deputy Travis's accident report. He had made no attempt to break his speed.

THE AIR WAS colder this morning. Charles buttoned up his new denim jacket as he stood on Darlene Wooley's porch and watched the town square coming to life, people walking by, cars slowly driving past the fountain, friends hailing friends, open and gregarious in asking after one another's health.

Ira would never be part of that flow, not entirely. Autism was the cult of one, the self-involved, but Charles wondered which of these outward-looking folk would have noticed the loss of one of their stars, if not for Ira.

The door opened behind him. He turned to see the tired but smiling face of Darlene Wooley.

"Well, Charles Butler. I thought you'd left town." She opened her door wide and stepped back to allow him to pass into the foyer. "I was just getting ready for work. Can I offer you a cup of coffee? It's already made. Won't take a minute to set out another cup."

"Yes, thank you." He followed her into a wide room of perfect symmetry. The couch and coffee table were placed dead center against one wall and flanked with a balance of identical armchairs. Matching incidental tables were centered on the side walls, and paintings were hung with an eye to pattern, large pieces accompanied by smaller works of equal size on each side. Mallory would have approved, for it was very neat, each thing in its place, though some pieces of furniture showed wear at the arms and the cushions.

"I'd like to see Ira, too, if you don't mind."

"Of course I don't mind. He remembers you very well. He says 'sandwich man' over and over, every time we have lunch at Jane's. Well, you have a seat, and I'll get us some coffee."

He settled into a large armchair with a prominent darn in the upholstery.

"This house hasn't changed in twenty years." Her voice was apologetic. "I never redo the furniture or move anything around. It makes extra work for Ira. If you were to move something just a hair out of place, he would notice that, and then he'd have to memorize the room all over again. When he's not at school, he spends most of his time in the house."

"I've seen him in the cemetery."

"That used to be his favorite place. Until recently, the stones never moved."

"He's seen the statue?"

"No. I told him to stay away for a while, till the sheriff can figure out what's going on out there. So you came to see Ira. Well, isn't that nice. I don't think he's had a visitor since he was six. Back in a minute." Her voice trailed off into the kitchen. As she had promised, a minute later she was back and handing him a cup of coffee. "Black, with three sugars, right?"

"Yes, thank you. Actually, I have a professional interest in Ira. I've been on the phone with the director of the Dallheim Project in New Orleans. They explore the gifts of the savant with a view toward learning more about the brain itself. They have a young adult program for autism. It would take years of work, but he might have an independent life."

"I know all about the Dallheim people." She sank down on the couch and stared at her coffee cup. "That was my big dream, Ira with a life of his own. The way he is now—" She looked up at him, her face sad, casting around for words. "If anything should happen to me, he'd wind up in an institution. I begged those people to take him. They told me not to come back until Ira could hold simple conversations."

"The director told me Ira never sang for them."

"No, he only does that when he wants to. It's easy to get him to play the piano. He did that real nice. He played Chopin for them."

"I told them about his singing. Multiple talents made Ira more interesting. There's still a long waiting list. It may be months or even a year before they take him, but I have to get his paperwork in before his twenty-fifth birthday. That's the cutoff age for the program."

"There's no point in taking him back if he can't talk to them."

"You don't have to take him anywhere. I have the credentials and their permission to do another screening test—right here."

"He won't talk. He might talk *at* you, but it's nonsense."

"Not entirely. Sometimes the echolalia is an effort at direct response. When he echoes what you say, don't you feel he's communicating?"

"Well, yes, and I did tell them that, but they said it didn't count."

"I faxed them pages from Cass Shelley's journals on Ira's therapy. He was remarkably articulate for a small child. No difficulty with personal pronouns—that's atypical. He showed a normal grasp of grammar and syntax. She rated his intelligence in the upper ten percentile. The Dallheim people didn't know about that, either."

"But the screening test—"

"One simple conversation. There's a way to get a quick result. It's a method Cass Shelley used when Ira had his setback. She forced him to talk. It may be very rough on him. I have to get him to focus for a while, but I won't do anything Cass wouldn't have done. The director suggested I go for a traumatic event, like the violent death of his doctor. He'll talk to me just to make it end, to get rid of me, but he *will* talk. I only need a few direct responses to questions and the screening requirement is satisfied."

Anyone would talk under torture. Given Ira's fear and revulsion of the human touch, what he planned to do to the boy was very cruel.

She nodded, looking more hopeful now. "But he stopped talking before that happened. It was the faith healing that did the damage. Cass was real upset with his father for taking him to that freak show."

He had agreed with the sheriff that it would be a bad idea to mention the certainty that Ira had witnessed the murder. But this should have come out long ago. Ira could not wait forever.

"The death of a mentor is a major trauma, but I could try another approach. I understand Ira lost his father within a year of Cass Shelley's death. That would have been a devastating event."

"No, not really. That last year, his father didn't spend much time with him. He tried taking Ira to a doctor in New Orleans for vitamin therapy. When that didn't work, I guess he just gave up on the boy. He gave up on everything."

"And you? Have you given up?"

"No. I guess I—" She looked down at the tight fists in her lap. "You have to put your hands on him, don't you? Cass did that. You know that's like real pain to him? He can't stand it—it terrifies him."

"I know that. It's your decision."

Darlene shook her head, more in indecision than a negative response. "He's happy in his own world. I don't think he'd like this one much, do you?"

"He might never fully appreciate being—"

"Human?" She seemed tensed for a fight, or at least a reproach.

"He's always been that. I think Ira's only more intense about day-to-day life than we are. It's not that he's unaware of the world around him. Ira is frighteningly aware of every detail of the universe. It's threatening to overload his consciousness. He must pull the plug, shut the world down now and then, or he could not survive. And he knows this. Ira is a very sophisticated human being."

And because of Ira's gifts and his strange vision, Charles found him to be exquisitely beautiful.

"The program you have him in now is tailored for the mentally retarded. I'm sure he's making progress, but that type of school has severe limitations." He produced the faxed forms with the Dallheim letterhead. "Perhaps you could fill in the medical history while I talk to Ira. It's worth a try, isn't it?"

Before they reached the door to Ira's room, the boy had begun to sing. Charles recognized the aria from the cemetery concert. Darlene put her hand on the door and hesitated. She smiled as she hovered on this periphery, basking in the music of her mysterious child. Then the door opened, and Ira, suddenly alarmed, stopped singing.

THE DOOR CLOSED, and Ira was left alone with the sandwich man. His large visitor sat down on the bed and talked softly for a while, as Ira rocked back and forth on his heels, not listening, blocking it out and searching for a safe place inside his head.

The man stood up and came toward him.

No! Don't!

Ira backed up to the wall. The sandwich man grabbed him by the shoulders and repeated the words until they became real, intruding on his mind with sense and weight. He was using Dr. Cass's words.

He remembered Cass's face before him, forcing the jarring contact of the eyes, holding him by the shoulders, insisting. *"Say one thing that is real, that is you, just one thing, just for me."*

Now he said to the sandwich man, "I am afraid."

The man dropped his hands away. He reached into his pocket and pulled out a photograph of Dr. Cass. "Look at this, Ira. Tell me about the day she died. I know you were there. What did you see?"

Ira said nothing. The sandwich man grabbed his shoulders again. His face was coming closer. His eyes—

"Rocks!" Ira screamed. And then he went rigid, waiting for the man to keep the old rules of the game.

The sandwich man released him. An hour passed in this way. The big man would come toward him, and Ira would concentrate on the words. If he spoke, the sandwich man would back away.

"Who threw the rocks? Do you remember the deputy being there? Deputy Travis?"

Ira started to flap his hands. The man advanced on him. Ira covered his ears and began to rock frantically. The sandwich man pulled Ira's hands away from his head. The man's voice was louder now. "Was the deputy there? A man in a uniform?"

Ira nodded, but the sandwich man still held on to his hands, for nodding was not good enough. There were rules.

"Did he throw rocks at Cass?"

"He threw rocks at the dog."

The man let go of Ira's hands and lowered his voice. "Did you see people throwing rocks at Cass Shelley?"

"They listened to the blue letter. Cass never said a word. And then she was red. The dog lay down in the dirt. He cried. The deputy hit him with another rock. He didn't move again. Cass was all red. They left. All quiet."

He had run from the house, from the bleeding bodies, dog and mistress. He had departed from the road and waded into the thickness of the water, slapping himself, testing the parameters, finding out where his body ended and the bayou began. He kept falling, water filling his mouth and choking him. Then as the muddy liquid was coughed back to the bayou, he knew the edges of self and the beginning of water, even before his father screamed in anguish and rushed into Finger Bayou to drag him back to the solid ground, and finally to home and bed, saying all the while, "Ira, what were you doing there?" But Ira couldn't answer his father. He was still seeing images of Cass mingling her blood with the dog's.

The sandwich man came toward him again. "I need a direct answer to a direct question, Ira. Do you know who threw rocks at Cass? Did you see—"

"Daddy." He began to rock, harder and harder, consoling himself as only he could do. He had never looked outside himself for comfort. Outside was only pain.

"What?"

"Daddy threw the first rock at Dr. Cass." Ira beat his head against the wall.

The sandwich man restrained him. "Your father was part of the mob?"

"Yes!" he screamed, his back sliding along the wall. He sank down to the floor. "Daddy! Daddy threw rocks at Cass!"

"That's *enough*!" His mother stood by the open door, hands covering her face, and she was shaking.

"Mommy, make him go!"

And his tiny mother did make the large man go. She pushed the sandwich man out of the room and slammed the door after him.

Now she came at Ira, falling to her knees in front of him, as he drew in his legs and made himself into a ball. Her hands danced all about his face and body, never touching him, wild to get at him, but fluttering only, like terrified birds that could never light on any branch of arm or leg for fear of causing him fresh pain.

CHAPTER
19

WHEN CHARLES KNOCKED on Augusta's door, Henry Roth admitted him and made the common sign for silence. *"Augusta has company."*

Charles entered the kitchen as Riker was holding out his identification and detective's shield for Augusta's approval.

She bent low and squinted over the small card bearing the detective's photograph. "I need my eyeglasses. I won't be but a minute." She gave Charles a curt nod in passing and hastily disappeared into the other room across the hall.

Glasses?

She had never needed them before. In fact, on the day they met, he had found it odd that she could read the fine print on his business card with no trouble at all.

Now he turned to Riker, who was looking around the room with great interest.

"Let me guess," said Charles. "You've been following Henry."

"Yeah." Riker turned around to face the sculptor. He spoke slowly for the benefit of the man he believed to be a deaf lip-reader. "Not your fault, pal. You were pretty good at shaking off that rookie deputy, but you didn't figure on a second cop, did you?''

Augusta returned with a pair of glasses set low on her nose. The antique frames and thick lenses must have belonged to some ancestor with badly impaired vision. Her eyes were greatly magnified.

Curious.

"Now let's have a good look," she said, leaning closer to Riker's identification card. Now she was staring intently at his face. "Well, that's a real good picture of you." She introduced him to Henry and Charles, adding, "Mr. Butler's been kind enough to help me with a few legal problems settling an estate."

It was an interesting moment in the complications of deceit. Riker had not acknowledged him, in keeping with the lie that they were unconnected; Augusta was maintaining the executor's ruse; and Henry appeared to be keeping everyone's confidence, or, in plain parlance, he ducked. Charles elected to follow suit as he shook hands with Riker.

Augusta went to the stove and began to stir the contents of a pot. "You'll all stay for lunch, I hope."

"I don't want to trouble you, ma'am." said Riker. "I'm looking for information on the sheriff's prisoner. Her name is Mallory."

"Well, I can direct you to the sheriff's office. You go through the cemetery and come out on the road back to the bridge and—"

"I've already seen the sheriff. He says the prisoner broke jail, ma'am. Day before yesterday."

"Oh, my Lord." She turned slowly and walked back to the table in faltering steps. Alarmed, Charles moved toward her. Standing just behind Riker, Henry Roth motioned him to back off.

Augusta sank down to a chair at the table, and Henry's hands flew into silent explanation. *"It's the strategy of the southern woman. She can lift her weight in canned goods, but right now she's trying to convey that she is fragile."*

She seemed to be conveying it rather well. Riker's face

was filled with genuine concern. He only saw the gray hair, the lined face, the greatly enlarged blue eyes of a woman who must be half blind to need such thick lenses.

"I'm sorry, ma'am," said Riker. "I didn't mean to frighten you."

Augusta waved the air weakly, as though fighting for breath. "Water?"

Riker flew to the sink to fetch a glass and fill it. He brought it back to her and then pulled up a chair on the other side of the table.

"Why, thank you." She gripped the glass with both hands and sipped the water. "I can't imagine it. A murderer loose in Dayborn."

"I don't know if she actually killed anybody," said Riker. "I don't think you're in any danger."

"Now that's a real comfort. Do you think you'll catch her soon?"

"I don't have the authority to arrest anybody, ma'am. I'm just visiting in Louisiana."

Augusta's hand delicately fluttered up to her face and she smiled almost shyly. "Oh, well isn't that *nice*."

Henry's hands were flying with the translation: *"Dithering ambiguity to avoid tipping her hand or taking up sides."*

"I think this Mallory woman can help me," said Riker. "You see, I'm working on a homicide case."

Augusta's hand covered her mouth. "Oh, well isn't that *awful*."

Henry explained that this was a companion tenet to "Isn't that nice," and had about the same meaning.

"I understand her mother was killed by a mob. Do you have any idea what—"

She moaned and put the back of her hand to her forehead. "I can't bear to think back on that terrible murder."

Henry explained that this rather antiquated maneuver was called "the vapors." It was used to table a discussion, and bide time.

"I'm sorry to put you through this, ma'am," said Riker. "But I really need your help."

"I'm so flattered that you think I *could* help you."

Charles looked at Henry, who shook his head. *"She would never give aid and comfort to the enemy, not even if Riker was bleeding to death."*

Since Charles was standing in plain view of the detective, he could not return the courtesy of apprising Henry of Riker's reactions. It was clear that Augusta had gone too far with her cliché when she picked up a sheet of paper and began to fan herself, casting her eyes up to heaven. Riker's eyes flashed with understanding and a silent *Gotcha!* The detective was reappraising Augusta as an adversary now.

Riker scanned the kitchen, eyes flying from one surface to the next. He breathed deeply, taking in the odors of cleaning solvents. And now Charles also looked around the room.

Yesterday the kitchen had been relatively tidy, but today it was immaculate. The glass of the cupboard doors was invisible now, free of the yellow tobacco tinge from Augusta's cheroots. Inside the cabinets, all the canned goods and boxes were perfectly aligned. The copper pots gleamed and lustered. Even the herb pots on the windowsill had been shined up, and now each one was equidistant from each other. Most unnerving, all the plant leaves gleamed as though they had been recently washed. This cleaning job was definitely beyond the norm, nearly deranged. She might as well have left her fingerprints on the sparkling, stain-free porcelain sink.

So Riker had found Mallory.

"You know, ma'am, I'm not surprised that you're upset," said Riker, very sure of himself now. "Sleepy little burg like this. Now back in New York, we take this kind of thing in stride. We got a thousand fugitives on the loose, and every one of them would cut your throat for spare change. Things move faster. It's a deadly place to live."

He leaned toward her and smiled with the artful suggestion of a dare. "You gotta be quick."

Augusta returned Riker's smile and inclined her head slightly to acknowledge that the rules had changed. They were onto a new level of gamesmanship. Knives and guns had not yet come into play—but they might.

"You only *think* New York is dangerous, Detective Riker." She removed her glasses. "We got five varieties of poisonous snakes, and deadly spiders. Our alligators are longer than two New Yorkers put together, and you can throw a saddle on the average mosquito."

"In New York, we got rats that could run on a racetrack at Belmont. We got a gridlock of automobiles from Harlem to the Battery, and two rivers full of dead fish and murdered taxpayers."

Augusta slapped one hand flat on the table. "We can outpollute you *and* outkill you. You seen the chemical plants along the river? We got those cancer factories on a signed legal contract with Satan and his elected minions. And it didn't cost us one extra cent to have 'em poison the wind and the water. Ain't that a deal and a half? We don't accept corruption here—we *demand* it. All you've got, Riker, is a little pissant island with a bad traffic problem. I know all about New York City."

"Miss Trebec, I think I'm in love."

"Then you must call me Augusta." She smiled with exquisite insincerity, a second cousin to flirtation.

Riker melted a bit. Admiration was in his eyes, but that did not prevent his closing shot. "You're tough, Augusta, I'll give you that. So when Mallory came to the door, you just chucked a rock at her, and she ran off, right?"

Riker sat back in his chair and lit a cigarette. The room was so quiet, his burnt match made an audible ping against the glass ashtray, landing among the butt ends of her cheroots. "I need to talk to Mallory. It's important. Tell her that." He blew a cloud of smoke into the air and stared at the door to the next room, as if he could see Mallory standing on the other side.

Augusta lightly drummed her fingers on the table. "I don't think she'd come here. I like to believe my reputation for ruthless brutality precedes me. But if I do see her, I will certainly shoot her for you."

"She can reach me at the hotel in the square."

"Or the sheriff's office," said Augusta in the tone of an accusation.

"Yeah, there too. But I wasn't planning to mention this little conversation to the sheriff," said Riker, his light sarcasm implying that he could do some damage if he wanted to.

"I have no secrets from the sheriff," said Augusta, clearly unimpressed. "I've had one or two occasions to swat his bottom and wipe his runny nose. So maybe I'll tell him myself. Oh, I'm sorry. I didn't stop to think. Would that create a problem for you—if Tom thought you were holding out on him?"

Riker rose from the table and made a mock bow, graciously conceding the win to Augusta. Then he did something so out of character, Charles was startled. Riker leaned across the table, took up her hand and kissed it.

Charles walked outside with him. "Looks like you've met your match."

"Yeah, she's something." Riker glanced back at the door between the staircases. He put one hand on Charles's shoulder and led him farther away from the house. His tone was more confidential now. "I had a look around that chapel—your friend's studio? Charles, would you say the little guy was fixated on Mallory and her mother? Maybe dangerously fixated?"

"That's absurd. He's a very gentle man." A man who kept a grisly list and cheerfully entered into a plot to torture residents of Dayborn, but still, a gentle soul. He shook off Riker's hand. "I can't see Henry killing—"

"Ease up, Charles. I'm just asking. If you were thinking straight, you wouldn't be looking at me as the enemy. You know it and I know it. This is Mallory's work."

"You don't know what you're talking about. I haven't

spoken to her since you came to town. You think you know her so well, and here you are maligning her on—''

''Yesterday, you asked me if I knew she could play the piano. I heard her play once. It was a surprise party for Lou Markowitz. The musicians had gone home, and so had the families. It was only cops in the hall, and the party wasn't slowing down any.''

Charles knew he was being softened up, suckered into a warm moment of shared intimacy. But Riker told stories so well, he fell for this, time after time.

''So Lou calls out, 'I want music.' ''

This was when life was still good to Louis Markowitz. His wife, Helen, had not yet been killed by the cancer. Louis was a family man with a cop for a daughter. His father and grandfather had been cops, and that tradition was going to continue. The old man was in high spirits that night. ''He wanted the party and the music to go on and on. He was standing by the piano, yelling, 'Can't any of you bastards play?' ''

Mallory sat down at the piano and began a child's study piece. ''It was a tune my niece played when she was taking lessons. Just a simple little song, pretty and sweet. And now a hall full of drunken cops quiets down—no noise at all— only the music.''

But what Riker remembered best was the look on Louis's face. He had raised her from a child of ten and never knew she could play the piano. She had always been so secretive about her past. But that night, Mallory played for him. This was a gift for her father. It was an elegant gesture, for she only played that one time, only played for him, and never again.

''Lou Markowitz really pissed me off when he got himself killed. Now I'm afraid for his kid. I lose a lot of sleep worrying that she'll spin out of control if there's nobody to care about her and keep her grounded. I know how you feel about her, Charles, and so did Lou. I think her old man was counting on you to give his kid a little ballast in the wind. But you screwed up. She's here to hurt a lot of people, and you're helping her.''

"That's unfair, Riker.'' It *was* unfair, wasn't it?

"I was at the hospital last night. I wanted to see the deputy, but he couldn't have visitors. You remember that woman who crawled out of the cemetery yesterday? Her name was Alma Furgueson. They were bringing her in the door as I was leaving. The ambulance driver told me she slit her wrists.''

"My God.'' Charles kissed his soul goodbye as it was edging away from him, trying to avoid association by proximity.

"They got her to the hospital in time. She's gonna pull through. But what if she'd died? You came real close to killing a woman for Mallory. How much further will you go?''

How far was he prepared to go for Mallory? Oh, straight down to the center of the earth, where he imagined hell must be. He anticipated being barred from heaven because of what he had done to Alma.

Before he could answer to Riker, the sheriff's car came spinning out of the trees and across wet ground from the direction of Henry's cottage. It stopped in a wide lake in the grass and spun its wheels, then freed itself and pulled to a stop twenty feet from Riker and Charles. The car was splattered with mud and fresh scratches from low branches.

The sheriff leaned out the window and yelled. "Riker, if you still want to talk to Travis, you better come quick. He wants to make a confession. The doctor says he's not gonna last all day.''

"We'll talk later,'' said Riker in a low voice.

"Maybe I'll see you at the hospital,'' said Charles. "I think I'd like to visit Alma Furgueson.''

"Good idea.'' Riker walked across the grass toward the sheriff's car. The passenger door was hanging open.

When the car was out of sight beyond the trees, Charles heard the basement door open and close behind him. He turned around, not really surprised to see Mallory standing there. But he was unsettled by the changes in her. The running shoes had been replaced with boots, and she wore a flowing white blouse from another era. A dark bandanna covered her throat. There was nothing to cover her gun. A heavy belt dipped low on her right hip with the weight of the revolver—in the best tradition of a gunslinger.

WHEN THEY HAD cleared Augusta's yard, the sheriff's car pitched into a lake of rainwater flanked by trees. The wheels turned while the car went nowhere.

Riker leaned over to light the cigarette dangling from the sheriff's mouth. "You don't think it would have been easier to leave the car at Roth's place and walk to Augusta's?"

They were rolling forward again.

"Yeah, but I do like to annoy that old woman. She thinks she's got her place locked off from the rest of the world. So I come through in the car every now and then, just to thumb my nose at her. Most days she yells at me, and it's a lot more fun. You know small towns. We're all so easily amused."

Yeah, right. "How'd you know where to find me?"

"Oh, my deputy tailed you out to Augusta's."

"The deputy was on *my* tail?"

"Well, yeah. Real early, she caught on that you'd seen her, so she started to follow Henry instead, just to throw you off. Then she let Henry lose her so she could double back and pick up on you again. Don't let it bother you, Riker. She did say that for a city boy, you did a good job of staying with Henry. I understand he took a real snaky route."

Now Riker had to wonder if the deputy's act in the bar had been a double blind. The sheriff was that convoluted.

"So Travis is dying," said Riker. "You've been waiting for this a long time, haven't you?"

"Seventeen years. I thought that little bastard's heart would never give out. Glad to have you with me, Riker. I need a witness if that deathbed confession is gonna carry weight in court.''

The car turned onto the wide highway.

''Oh, by the way, Riker.'' The sheriff was grinning. ''When you see your old friend's foster daughter, you tell Detective Mallory she can have her pocket watch back anytime she wants to come and get it.''

Riker slumped down in his seat and stared out the window. ''Okay, you got me.''

They rode in silence for another mile. There was a comforting monotony in the endless fields of sugar cane, the flat landscape with nothing higher than a tree. No surprises out there.

''Professional courtesy, Riker, cop to cop? Is Kathy a good detective?''

''She's as good as it gets. You're not half bad yourself, Sheriff. I suppose you ran Markowitz through the back door—a warrant call on a New York car registration?''

''Yeah, but that only told me he was a dead cop. I got the rest from Jeff Mckenna in Missing Persons. You know him?''

''Sure. That old bastard's been around for a hundred years.''

''I met him eighteen years ago when I was hunting a runaway. I knew the boy was in New York, so I called Mckenna. He found him a month later when the kid got picked up in a drug sweep. I met the man when I went up north to fetch the boy home.''

''So you called Mckenna and asked after your old friend, Louis Markowitz, who you never met in your life.''

''That I did. And Mckenna breaks the news that old Lou is dead. Then I asked what became of Mallory, and he says she's still on the force, and she's got a detective's shield now.''

''And then you asked about me?''

''Oh, he had a lot to say about you, Riker. Yeah, good old Mckenna—memory like an elephant. He even remembered the name of the boy he tracked down for me. We were lucky to get the kid back as quick as we did. He was sick as a little dog, but no holes in him bigger than a needle, thank God. Interesting town you got there, Riker. Children getting stoned on drugs, people pissing on the walls, perverts cruising Forty-second Street, looking to buy little boys. Must get you down after a while.''

"Yeah, you're right. But now I've found the Lord in Louisiana.''

The sheriff smiled. "I heard you were drinking with the New Church roadies in Owltown. Pick up anything useful?''

Riker pulled a crumpled pamphlet from his pocket, held it out at arm's length and read from it. " 'You are on a long journey over perilous ground. You can take the tortuous road, or buy a miracle and fly.' '' He wadded the pamphlet and tossed it to the floor of the car to join the debris of empty beer cans. "I don't get it. A religion based on fortune cookies and airline commercials?''

CHAPTER
20

THE WALLS HAD been painted the color of an orange Popsicle in a cheerful attempt to brighten the hospital room. But the framed pictures of budding spring flowers were a bad joke on Deputy Travis, who lay dying. Yet he seemed to play the good sport. His mouth was set in a grimace of pain that passed for a bizarre smile.

His skin was sallow and filmed with sweat. The tubes in his nostrils tied him to an oxygen unit in the wall. More tubes were plugged into his body, running down from an IV pole where Riker counted six hanging plastic bags of fluids. The lead wires for the pacemaker were sutured to the man's skin. His breathing was labored, and his erratic heartbeat was graphically displayed by three waveforms on a monitor screen. Cross-wired machines were gathered near the bed like consulting physicians in discussions of lights, beeps and lines.

The smell rising off the body was earthy and dank. Decay prevailed over the medicinal smells from the collection of bottles on the bedside table. Over the past thirty years, Riker had become something of an expert on the smell of death.

On the opposite side of the bed, a young man with a stethoscope and a white coat was talking in an arrogant, high-pitched Godspeak, explaining to the sheriff that this interview was against his professional advice. He had counseled Travis to cancel it. He was sworn to protect his patient at all cost, and his authority superseded the law's. So he must insist that the sheriff collect his friend and go. *Now*. That was an *order*.

The sheriff moved closer to the doctor, who was a smaller man with narrower shoulders and no gun. Tom Jessop explained, in a somewhat larger voice, that the younger man had best back off. *Now*. That was a *suggestion*. Or they might need to roll Travis over to make room for the doctor on that hospital bed.

Riker watched the doctor's face go slack and noted the general shakiness in the younger man's stance—all the signs of a virgin mugging victim. The doctor glanced at his patient, reconsidered his oath and backed off to the far side of the room to slump against a friendly orange wall.

Riker checked Travis's chart for recent doses of painkillers which might void his confession. Rules of evidence demanded lucidity. He also scanned the dates and times for a series of resuscitations by violent shocks from a crash cart. And now Riker wondered if the young doctor had ever read this chart. Above another physician's signature was a shaky scrawl that must be Travis's own hand. It said, "No more." And another doctor had signed her name after the words "no code," the instruction not to resuscitate one more time.

The sheriff leaned over the deputy's bed and read from a card. "Travis, do you make this confession in the full knowledge that you are about to die?"

Travis looked up at the sheriff, stunned. He had clearly not expected this, despite the six times he had already died and his own written plea not to interfere with his next death. The deputy's wide eyes had suddenly taken on the fixed and dulled aspect of a corpse, and so Riker was disturbed by the tears.

Tom Jessop repeated the question, and Travis slowly moved his head to indicate that he believed it *now*.

The sheriff's face had no emotion as he crumpled the card in one fist, dispensing with formality. "Were you in that mob? Did you murder Cass Shelley?"

"I threw a rock at the dog. He was coming for me. I don't even know where that rock came from. It was just in my hand, and the dog was coming for me."

"You were there when she died."

"I didn't go there to hurt anybody. Cass was going to accuse me of—" His hand rose to make weak circles in the air. "It was all in the letter—the lab tests. She was gonna hang me with science. I knew it was a mistake, and I was gonna tell her that. I never hurt a kid in my life. And I didn't want to hurt Cass. But Christ, you just whisper a thing like that in a small town—" He stopped with a look of sudden pain.

An alarm went off, and a line on the monitor broke into jagged spikes. The doctor approached on cat's feet, and the sheriff pushed him away without needing to touch him, only nodding him back to the wall.

Now a nurse appeared at the bedside. She was a large woman, dark and round. One pudgy hand held up a syringe and squirted fluid into the air. Now she bent over her patient to probe him for a likely vein among the bruises on his arm.

"What's that?" Jessop demanded.

"Morphine for the pain," she said, looking up at him as though he had just crawled out of a roach trap. And now her glare included the doctor at the wall in the same sentiment.

"You can't give him that!" Jessop shouted at her, moving forward. "Drugs invalidate the—"

"Fuck off," said the nurse. And then she shot the needle home.

Riker gave the sheriff points for recognizing the voice of ultimate authority in this room, and for having the grace to know when to quit. The man kept his silence for all the

minutes it took the nurse to satisfy herself that the drug was
doing its work on her patient and destroying a prime piece
of evidence.

Riker marked the nurse as a class act when she refrained
from spitting on the doctor as she majestically sailed out
of the room.

Travis's face was relaxed. His mouth sagged open and
his words came slowly. ''Then the rocks were flying, and
the dog was coming for me.''

''Tell me about the letter.''

''That's all I know about the letter.''

''Who else was there?''

''Ira's father. Then I had a rock in my hand, but I never
picked one up from the ground till after I threw that first
one at the dog. I never—''

''Who else? Was Babe Laurie there?''

Travis nodded.

''You saw him throwing rocks?''

''No. He could've, I guess. I was busy with the dog.''

''Malcolm and Fred Laurie?''

''Not Malcolm. Fred was there, and I did see him chuck-
ing rocks. Malcolm had walked off before Jack Wooley
threw the first one. I picked up more rocks to hit the dog.
He was still coming at me.''

''Forget that dog. What about Alma Furgueson?''

He was drifting for a moment. The sheriff grabbed his
shoulder to call him back, and then Travis nodded.

Riker leaned in and asked softly, ''Did Babe Laurie ever
threaten you? Did he have anything to do with your heart
attack? Were you in a fight with him the day he died?''

''I had nothing to do with that. I never killed a living
thing in my life. I stoned the dog, but the dog lived.''

''What brought on the heart attack?'' asked Riker.

''I was out at the Shelley house to pick up Good Dog
and take him to the vet. Henry Roth always helps me with
that, but he wasn't there yet. And the dog was jumping up
and beating his head into the window glass. Then I had the

pain in my chest. I was driving back to town, when I saw her walking in the road.''

''Mallory?'' asked Riker.

''Kathy,'' said Travis. ''She looked just like her mother. Then I felt like I'd been stabbed by lightning, and I ran the car off the road. Kathy saved my life. She should've let me die.''

''You got that right,'' said the sheriff. ''Why did that mob murder Kathy's mother?''

''I don't know. It was me Cass was after. But it was a mistake—I swear to God. She barged into the meeting and said—'' His hands were rising, flailing about.

''What meeting?''

''But I'd never hurt a kid. I don't know why she—''

''I don't think that mob assembled to save your sorry ass from a charge of child abuse. I want the *truth*, Travis!''

''You might as well go ask the dog.'' Travis's eyes closed.

The sheriff reached down and grabbed him by the shoulders. ''Don't you die on me, you son of a bitch!'' He shook the deputy's thin body with real violence. ''Why did they murder Cass?'' He was yelling to be heard above the scream of the monitor alarm.

The question went unanswered. The monitor's flat line and loud noise said that it was now wired up to a corpse, and the other machines agreed that the heart was no longer beating. The doctor stepped to the bedside. He flipped all the switches to the off positions and cut the feed on the oxygen line. Then he looked at his wristwatch and penned a note on the chart, marking the exact time when the technology died.

CHARLES SLOWED THE car just beyond the gas station. Mallory turned to the rear window. ''The car is stopping. It's not a tail. Gun the engine, Charles.'' She kept the gas station in sight for another few minutes as they barreled down the road and joined the highway.

All around them, sugar-cane stalks were moving with the wind, rippling like water on the surface of a vast green sea. The car sped toward an unnatural structure on the horizon; it bore the logo of a chemical company. Waves of stalks lapped up against this skeletal monster of towering dark steel pipes and girders, a specter from the future, a taste of world's end. White smoke plumed from the stacks and joined up with the wind. Charles knew the whiteness was deception. What was smoking into the air was not something Augusta's birds should be breathing. He better understood her ruthless ambition to give them sanctuary.

It was a good fight.

He pulled off the highway and onto a side road marked with the hospital sign. "What makes you think they'd keep the records this long? Don't most hospitals toss them after ten years or so?"

"Not anymore. Computers solved the storage problem." The hospital was in sight now, a bland building of straight lines. "Augusta's favorite cashier at the Levee Market has a part-time job scanning the old hard copy into a data bank. If she'd only worked a little faster, I could've lifted everything I wanted from my laptop."

He slowed down and pointed out the sheriff's car parked near the entrance. "We could come back later."

"No, I need this stuff now. Don't worry about it, Charles. They won't ask questions. You told Riker you wanted to visit Alma, didn't you?"

"But what about you?"

He didn't hold out much hope for this disguise of hers. She would have seemed less out of place on horseback in another century. The long black duster was wide in the shoulders and covered most of her body, stopping short of the riding boots and a bit of the blue jeans. The black hat was also an antique, short in the crown but wide enough in the brim to resemble a cowboy hat. Beneath the hat a black scarf covered every strand of her hair. The incongruous aviator sunglasses made her look even more dangerous.

He thought the costume was actually more revealing of her character than disguising of person.

"Seriously, Mallory? You don't think Jessop and Riker will notice you the second you walk in the door?" Could a bright red fire engine be less conspicuous in the hospital lobby?

"I'm going in through a basement window."

Oh, of course. He had forgotten who he was dealing with. Any fool could go in by the front door. He pulled into the visitors' parking lot and rolled along the side of the building. "Just stop me when you see a window you like."

"It's the last one at the rear." Mallory consulted his wristwatch. It was safely past the hour when the clerk went off shift. "Augusta says this woman always complains about the view from the back end of the parking lot. Pull up here. And park the car close by." She handed him a piece of paper. "And get this prescription filled at the pharmacy. It's for Augusta."

He stared down at the paper in his hand. "This has my name on it as the prescribing physician."

"Well, you're a doctor."

"I'm a Ph.D., not a medical doctor."

"You are now. I gave you a New Orleans physician's number. You'll be on the pharmacy computer. Don't worry about it."

She crept out of the car, and he gave her cover while she opened the basement window. He had expected her to whip out an elaborate tool kit with delicate lockpicks. Instead, she opted for expediency and used a rock.

RIKER CHANGED HIS mind about going outside for a smoke. Charles Butler had just entered the lobby, bearing a huge bouquet of brilliant flowers. Though he usually attracted some attention for his size and height, he walked through the crowded area without turning a head. In the aftermath of a highway accident, people in hospital garb were moving with urgent purpose. The civilians were haranguing the personnel at the front desk, and others sat, worried and waiting, filling all the chairs and couches scattered about the lobby. All around the giant in blue jeans, people were preoccupied with matters of life and death.

Only Riker noticed Charles approaching the pharmacy window and handing a piece of paper over the counter. The gray-haired pharmacist looked at the paper, nodded and held up five fingers, to say this transaction wouldn't take much time.

Charles had only walked a few steps away from the counter, when he was roughly shouldered by a speeding nurse, who bounced off of him. Riker could read the body language of Charles rushing to apologize for what *she* had done to *him*. The nurse gently touched one of the exotic blooms in Charles's bouquet and nodded. Now she pointed down the hall where Charles would find Alma Furgueson's room and her visitor, the sheriff.

Riker had begged off that interview. He hadn't wanted to see the sheriff's interrogation style applied to the woman who had crawled from the cemetery on her hands and knees.

He felt around in his pockets for cigarettes and matches as he walked outside. Charles's Mercedes was nowhere in sight. He strolled around the side of the building and spotted the silver car at the back of the lot, though there were a dozen spaces close to the front door.

Now that was interesting.

He walked toward the car, but stopped when he came to the window with the broken pane of glass. It put him off for a moment because this was not her style. Well, maybe the brat had been in a hurry.

He turned to the metal doors under the sign for the service entrance. They should open onto a freight elevator. He tried door pulls—locked tight and no signs of a pick. She had definitely gone through the window. She probably wanted to avoid meeting staff in the basement halls.

He tested the door of Charles's car. Not locked. Good.

He had never hot-wired a Mercedes before, but it shouldn't be much of a challenge.

Riker forgot the urge for a cigarette and returned to the hospital lobby. A young woman was entering the door next to the pharmacy window. A few minutes later, the old man with the glasses was heading down the hall marked by a sign for the cafeteria.

Riker walked up to the window, gave the young woman Charles Butler's name and asked her when the prescription would be ready.

"Oh, you're in luck. He finished that one before he went to lunch." She slid the bag over the counter. "That'll be thirty dollars and twenty-five cents, Dr. Butler."

Riker paid her and opened the bag. *Doctor* Butler? He read the labels for drugs which were all too familiar. One he recognized as an anti-inflammatory. The second bottle was antibiotics. And the Percodan would kill the pain.

He strolled over to the basement door as an orderly parked a wheelchair by the wall a few steps away. And now the rest of the plan fell into place as the orderly disappeared into the men's room.

Riker opened the basement door and surveyed the deserted stairwell. He rolled the wheelchair through the doorway and down the stairs. The lower floor was a labyrinth with no helpful signs, and no elevator in sight. He knew he was facing east as he rolled the chair down a corridor which turned a corner and sent him south. He reoriented himself with every turn, hunting for the room to match the window with the broken glass. This section of the basement was pin-drop quiet, deserted in the lunch hour.

He settled on a door at the end of a long hall. On his way toward it, he passed the freight elevator which would open onto the service entrance in the parking lot. This was just too good to be true, and he flirted with the idea that God was on his side in this plan to batter a woman, to knock her senseless and carry her away.

He parked the wheelchair in front of the door at the end of the hall. Hunkering down, he used both hands to block the overhead bulb from the wide crack at the threshold. No light shone through from the room beyond. He pulled out a handkerchief and unscrewed the bare bulb over the door so the light from the hallway wouldn't give him away in silhouette. Beneath the doorknob was a standard lock, nothing formidable. He applied all his strength to a twist of the knob to force the flimsy lock. The door opened quietly.

The long room was almost black. There was hardly any light from the rectangle of the broken window in the far wall. While his eyes adjusted, he was guided by the small penlight in Mallory's hand.

She was completely absorbed in the contents of an open file drawer. He made out the dim shape of a desk lamp to her right. One of his hands went out to the lamp switch, and with the other, he grabbed Mallory by the shoulder and spun her around. And then there was light, but he was more startled than she was.

"Well, if it isn't Jesse James," he said, staring at the wide-brim hat shading her eyes. Her coat was laid open and now he could see the gun belt. "You got your geography mixed up, kid. This is the Deep South, not the Old West."

Her face turned up and now he met her eyes. She was blinking in the light and wincing with real pain, her fingers working frantically to pry his hand from her shoulder. As his hand dropped away, the pain in her face lessened. He pulled the coat back and felt the bulk of the bandage beneath her blouse.

"Ah, Mallory, you took a bullet, didn't you?"

She shook him off, saying nothing, only showing him she was not all that happy to see him again. He held up the pharmacy bag. "Dr. Butler's prescriptions? I thought this crap looked familiar. Now what's going on, kid?"

She took the pharmacy bag from his hand and checked the contents, as though she thought he might have stolen something. He knew she was stalling for time, hunting for a good lie.

"I'm looking for missing lab work my mother ordered

on a patient. Any blood work would have been done here.''

That could be true. Mallory sometimes told the truth just to confuse him. Sheets of blue papers protruded from the oversized pockets of her long black coat. ''What've you got?''

She ignored the question as she slid open another file drawer and continued her pilfering. It was awkward work, for she would not turn her back on him, and thumbed the files from the side of the open drawer.

Now that she was on her guard, he had no hope of taking her by surprise, and he couldn't rush her with the file drawer blocking him.

''How've you been, Riker? You look like hell.''

''So? I saw the mug shot of you in the gingham jailhouse uniform. Now that was terminally cute.''

No reaction; she was deaf and blind to him.

Well, it took better bait than that to get a rise out of Mallory. ''The FBI found your footprints in a classified system, kid. That's a federal rap, real jail time.''

Now he had her.

She smashed the pharmacy bag into her coat pocket. ''I did not leave tracks in that computer. Those bastards have been trying to nail me for years.'' She slammed the file drawer. ''But they *can't* prove illegal access—no way. If they can't prove it, I didn't do it.''

''Oh, yeah?'' He pointed to her left shoulder where the wound was. ''That was pretty careless, wasn't it? But we'll let the bullet hole slide, okay? The sheriff used your pocket watch to backtrack Markowitz. That was another screwup, kid, not ditching the watch with the rest of your ID. And then I saw the broken window—not your usual neat style. Was it your idea to park Charles's car close enough to flag it for me? Oh, yeah, I can believe you got sloppy. I think the FBI does have something on you, maybe enough to prosecute.''

That put a small dent in her facade. The smallest doubt was all he needed to work with. ''The feds send their compliments, and they want whatever you got on the New

Church. You don't give them what they want—they flood this burg with agents, and your own little scheme goes up in smoke.''

''They're running a bluff. They don't have enough probable cause to flood a Dayborn phone booth with agents.''

He leaned one arm on the file cabinet, testing the waters. She didn't move away from him. ''Mallory, they did me a favor. They held back your prints and they're not looking to prosecute the computer break-in. Now I owe them one. You know this game.''

''You can tell them the New Church isn't planning to overthrow the government. There are no assault weapons, no explosives, nothing bigger than a squirrel rifle. So they really have no excuse to blow up the town.''

''I need a little more than that.''

''The feds have a twenty-year-old file on the New Church. It may have dawned on them that it's all bullshit.'' She spoke to the open drawer as she pulled back file holders, stopping now and then to take one out for a closer look. ''They had a profile on Babe Laurie as a brilliant and dangerous cult leader. Maybe they just found out he was the town idiot. If they did, they read it in his obituary. You wouldn't believe how much the FBI paid for bogus information. I'm sure they tried to get better data from Internal Revenue, but IRS would never let them near an ongoing investigation.''

He knew Mallory couldn't string that many words together without telling at least one lie. So there was no IRS investigation.

And now she was putting some distance between them, drifting away from the file cabinet.

''Okay, kid, tell me what IRS has.'' *Yeah, tell me a story*.

''I can't do that without admitting I was in another classified computer. Like you said, Riker—that's a federal rap. Real jail time.''

''So? I'm gonna rat on you?'' The distance between them was growing in tiny increments. He took one step toward her, and she brushed aside the long black duster to settle one hand on her right hip, exposing the gun. He recognized this as Mallory's idea of being subtle.

You wouldn't shoot me, would you, kid? Aloud, he said, "Give me something I can take back to the feds."

"It's a tax fraud scam. Babe Laurie's brother is liquidating New Church assets into a financial holding pen. It's all set up to feed into a foreign account."

"So we're talking big-time embezzlement?"

"It gets better. Malcolm is planning to skip out on the family. He just did a deal on all the lower bayou property. Sold it out from underneath his own relatives. They'll be homeless and on the dole at the end of the month."

"So that's why you had to come back now. You didn't want the locals to scatter till you nailed everyone in that mob."

And now—time out for a little heartache.

She was coldly regarding him as a stranger, armed and dangerous. Was she seeing the same thing in his own eyes? Of course she was.

"So you figure Babe Laurie was in on the scam?"

"No," she said. "Babe was a fool. Malcolm would've been crazy to tell him anything."

"Suppose Babe found out about it? Good reason for Malcolm to do away with his little brother." *Tell me someone else could have done this murder. I'll believe in you— even if I don't believe you.*

"Malcolm didn't do it," she said. "He wouldn't do anything to call attention to himself right now. Neither will IRS. But when he tries to leave the country, they'll arrest him for tax fraud, embezzlement and flight to avoid prosecution. If the feds spook Malcolm and mess up that operation, IRS will turn them into roadkill."

He moved toward her, and that was a mistake. She backed up and planted her feet wide to make a stand. He didn't believe she would draw the gun on him just yet; he'd done nothing to provoke that.

"Mallory, it's not like I think you'd leave me hanging

out in the breeze with the feds, but is any of this IRS crap true?''

Was she smiling? He could barely make out her face, though her lower body remained in the dim circle of light from the small desk lamp.

"IRS *does* have an open file on the New Church," she said. "And they *are* running audits."

Her head turned to the door.. He stepped to one side and neatly blocked that exit. And now he realized she had just confirmed the impending betrayal.

It was a strain to keep his voice casual. "So IRS is suspicious. So what? They suspect everybody. But they're not really planning an arrest, are they?''

"After you report back, the FBI will ask IRS about the investigation." Her voice was machinelike, no trace of stress. "IRS will say they're not running one—force of habit. But IRS keeps tabs on every organization, so the feds will figure that's a lie, and then they'll believe an arrest is in the works. Ten minutes after the feds clear the room, IRS will start a criminal investigation. They'll bank an arrest warrant on Malcolm against the audit findings." She was retreating into deeper shadows. "So the truth is just a little bit out of order, okay?''

He moved on her before he could lose the light on her gun belt.

"That's close enough, Riker."

At no time in his life was he more aware of the heavy weight in his shoulder holster. The lamp was behind him now, and he was only a dark shape to her. His hand moved slowly inside his coat, reaching for the gun. If he could only show her the gun, Mallory might not draw on him. She might bow to the laws of ballistics which dictate that a drawn gun is faster.

If she drew first, he was a dead man. Sentiment would not get between Mallory and what she wanted most—payback for a murdered mother.

"Mallory, the sheriff's got his motive. He knows Babe Laurie was in that mob. He can build a case against you.''

Her hand was rising, stopping short of the revolver on her belt, hesitating in the air—waiting.

He was touching his gun now. He eased it out of the holster, working slow, no sudden movements to make her draw. She was so much younger, years faster; he would have to cheat to beat her, and he was counting on the dark to give him an edge. The only light shone on her. "I know what you're planning. All those people. You can't do it, Mallory."

"We're done, Riker." Her gun hand flashed out.

"Kathy!" he yelled in a pure reflex, forgetting he held a weapon, trying to get to the child he knew, before this strange woman could kill him.

The basement was plunged into blackness. Mallory's hand had found the fuse box. She had only killed the light. Seconds later, Riker was alone in the room.

CHARLES'S THOUGHTS WERE with the old king of the world when he looked down at his bouquet, another apology of flowers. When he entered Alma Furgueson's hospital room, the sheriff was gone and another visitor was sitting by her bed. The large proprietress of Jane's Cafe was mashing delicate wildflowers between her thick fingers as she arranged them in the water glass on the bedside table.

"Hello, again," said Jane. It was the warm welcome of an old friend, though they had never even spoken to one another. "I heard you were back in town. So you come to visit with Alma. Well, isn't that nice." She bent down to the woman on the bed and reiterated this, as if Alma had no eyes and they were not trained on the enormous man looming over her.

"Say hello to your visitor, Alma." Jane took the flowers from his hand and began to arrange this larger bouquet in the water pitcher, brutally snapping the long elegant stalks to better fit the short length of glass, bruising every petal as she forced them into the narrow container. The overflow of water spilled out on the table, smearing the ink on

Alma's only get-well card, which was signed by Jane.

"I'm so sorry about all this, Miss Furgueson." He pulled up a chair and sat on the other side of her bed. "I know it had something to do with the angel in the—"

"Oh, no it didn't," said Jane, answering for Alma. "She does this at least once a year. She's pixilated, you know. Now you just call her Alma—everyone does."

Charles began again, speaking to Alma. "I was in the cemetery when you—"

"Wasn't that a sight?" said Jane. "I guess everyone in town's been up there. But angel or no angel, Alma was due for another round of slashing and bleeding."

And now Charles looked down to the bandaged wrists. Older scars protruded from the line of the white bandages. It was true then; this was a ritual with Alma. That assuaged his guilt only a little. Suppose she had died?

"I understand you're a member of the New Church," he said in a game attempt at making conversation with the woman on the bed.

"Well, everyone in Owltown belongs to New Church," said Jane. "I did try to talk Alma out of that. She was a staunch Catholic, you know. It was pure insanity to deed her house over to the *New Church*." She made a distasteful moue as she spat out the last two words, and for a moment, Charles thought she might spit on the floor.

Alma was staring at him. He couldn't fathom her expression. Was she frightened or glad of a visitor? Again, he looked down at the history of mental illness in the old scars above her bandaged wrists.

"Would you like me to go?" he asked Alma.

"Certainly not," said Jane.

Alma's eyes never left his face. When he smiled at her, she smiled back. Well, lunatics liked him. That was his curse in life. There was something about his foolish smile that made them believe he was one of their number.

He covered Alma's hand with his own. "Perhaps you should be resting."

"Now don't you worry about her," said Jane. "She's

only a little peaked because the sheriff was in here upsetting her with a lot of questions about a meeting. 'What about that meeting?' he yells, like she's deaf or something. And poor Alma turned white as a sheet. But she's all right now.''

"What sort of meeting?" He spoke to Jane this time.

"Oh, nothing special," said Alma. "Just a business meeting for the board members. And I told him that. We were talking about repairs on the tent and budgets for the mail order catalogues. And then Cass walked in."

Now Jane chimed in. "Alma bought herself a place on the governing board of the New Church when she deeded over her house."

Charles looked at Alma. "What was Cass Shelley doing at that meeting?"

Alma looked to the glass and pitcher, both filled with flowers. "Jane, could you get me some water?"

When Jane had gone off in search of flowerless water, Alma touched his arm. "Jane says you're real tight with Malcolm."

"We met in her cafe. I don't—"

"And I saw you in the front row at the memorial service the other night. You were in the chair with the velvet rope." Now she clutched his wrist, her nails dug into his skin and she smiled with fever-bright eyes. "I never told the sheriff anything about the letter."

The letter again. What had Ira said about the letter? "You mean the *blue* letter?"

"Yes, it was blue." And now she smiled, very pleased with him, as if he had passed a test of sorts. "Tom Jessop's not a believer, you know, not one of us. He knew I was there when Cass died, but he didn't understand the importance of her ascendance into heaven. Now she's come back to take me away. You know, Cass always wanted to do that. She would get all her legal papers together, and then Jane—Oh, doesn't Jane love a good fight. Jane would get a legal-aid man out of New Orleans to say that there was no cause to take me anywhere. But now Cass is back, and this time she will bear me away.''

Yes, Alma was quite insane. And someone *should* send her away, but he thought that was unlikely. Every notch cut into her wrists represented a lost opportunity to get her the help she needed. He could see her future now. One day she would get it right, and she would die alone. What a friend she had in Jane.

''What do you remember about the meeting?''

''Cass came in as we were talking about mending the tent for the next road show. She was real angry. Her office had been robbed. I know the sheriff was out of town, but I don't know what she expected us to do about it. And she was waving that letter. Now she said that it was stolen, but there it was in her hand.''

''Could it have been a copy?''

''It could have been. Now that would make more sense, wouldn't it?''

''Do you know what was in the letter?''

''Yes, of course I do. She wanted to take me away. I told you that.''

''All right—the meeting. Did that have anything to do with the stoning?''

''No, that was God's work. The stones came out of the sky like rain, and one fell into my hand. Not hard, mind you, but it just settled there in my hand. I took it home with me, and I keep it under my bed. It was so quiet between the fall of one stone and another.''

Alma's voice was shrill now, and her eyes were very bright. ''Cass didn't scream or anything. That was part of the miracle. You wouldn't think a woman could die in silence while her body was being broken that way. It was a test. But she understood what was happening to her.''

Alma clutched his arm with one hand and raked the other through her hair. ''And the rocks only rained on Cass. It was a miracle the way she died.'' Tears were streaming down her face and her voice was louder, almost shouting. ''And now she's back, going about His work. She's come for me. I was afraid once, but no more. It's my time of atonement for all my sins.'' She looked to the ceiling, and screamed. ''I'm so sorry! I have offended Thee!''

''What have you done?'' Jane pushed the door open with one meaty elbow. Her hands were filled with a pitcher and a glass. ''She's not supposed to be upset. Maybe you'd better leave, Mr. Butler.'' Behind Jane, a nurse's voice seconded this opinion. When Charles stepped into the hallway, the door was slammed behind him.

Riker was leaning against a gurney, an unlit cigarette dangling from his mouth. ''Have a nice visit, Charles? Sounded like a prayer meeting. Is Alma worried about going to hell for what she did?''

''I'm not sure she did anything. Alma says she did have a rock in her hand, but she took it home with her. She's not lucid, but I believe that much.''

''Did the rock just appear in her hand?''

''How did you know that? She thinks it fell from the sky.''

''The deputy had a similar story, and he wasn't the least bit crazy.''

''I don't think Alma will stand up to any more questions, if you're—''

''I'm not here for that. I think you should wait till the sheriff leaves before you pick up the brat.''

''Pardon?''

''Cut the crap, Charles. I just gave Mallory the pills from the pharmacy. She was down in the basement stealing files. Do you know what those pills are for?''

''For Augusta.''

''That's what Mallory told you?'' Riker gave him a pity smile. ''She's got a gunshot wound in her shoulder, Charles. *That's* what the pills are for. I have to get her out of here before she takes another bullet, and I need your help. I'll tell the sheriff you're giving me a lift back to town. We can load her into your car and just keep driving.''

A bullet wound? Charles shook his head in disbelief. It couldn't be. How could she—

"Charles, you know she killed Babe Laurie."

"No I don't, and neither do you."

"Well, let's see what I got to work with here," said Riker. "I got one dead mother killed by a mob. And that wacko religious cult fits nice with the mob concept, doesn't it? According to the feds, Babe Laurie led that cult. And this bastard gets his ass murdered within an hour of Mallory hitting town. You wanna play connect-the-dots?"

"That's enough, Riker."

"Or maybe a fast round of blindman's bluff? I'll wear the blindfold first, okay? I'll pretend I can't see her killing a man just because he stoned her mother to death."

"Mallory wouldn't use a rock."

"Why not? That's the way her mother died. You gotta admit the kid has an interesting sense of justice."

"Put a lid on it, Riker."

"The sheriff still has good memories of a tiny little girl who couldn't even lift a gun. If she stays much longer, it'll be too late—he'll have her jacket from NYPD, maybe psych files too. Do you want that man to find out what Mallory's really made of?"

"So you want to lure Mallory into the car, and—"

"Yeah, I owe it to Lou Markowitz. He'd do the same if he was alive. Hell, the old man would toss her in the trunk and drive straight through till morning. I just want to keep his kid alive and out of prison. Help me, Charles. You want me to beg? Okay, I'm begging. Lou would be down on one knee if he was here."

Of course Riker couldn't do it without a trusted friend to betray her, to lead her into the car, where Riker would be waiting.

"No." Charles looked down the hall as Tom Jessop was walking toward them. "I think the sheriff's ready to leave now. Goodbye, Riker."

Riker turned to the sheriff and called out, "Two minutes." The sheriff waved and walked off.

"Why don't you sleep on it, Charles. We'll talk again

tomorrow. If I have to do this alone, I might have to hurt her, and I'd rather not do that.''

''I don't believe you could hurt her. And I know you couldn't force her to go with you, not by yourself. Did you ever try to take Mallory *anywhere*?''

''Yeah, I did,'' said Riker. ''Once I took her to the Bronx Zoo. She was eleven. The animals in the monkey house didn't wanna play with her. I think the kid made them nervous—they wouldn't come anywhere near the bars. She didn't take rejection very well in those days. So the kid points to the monkeys, and she looks up at me and says, 'Shoot 'em.' ''

''You're making that up.''

''But you're not sure, are you?''

CHAPTER
21

"I LIKE THIS one best," said Malcolm Laurie, in admiration of the statue wielding a sword over his head.

Sergeant Riker was startled. He had not expected company from that direction, not in this predawn hour.

"Good morning," said Malcolm, as if it were the most natural thing in the world to find a New York City detective crouching in the grass behind a tomb. "You left the bar too early. I was just about to break out the good stuff." In his hand was a flat silver bottle.

Riker stood up and accepted the hip flask, breaking his time-honored rule of no hard liquor before breakfast. After one sip of whiskey, he pronounced it very good stuff indeed. Averting his eyes from the angel and her stone sword, Riker's gaze wandered over the surrounding faces of more passive, unarmed sculpture. "Never saw so many angels in one place. It's a damn convention."

"There are sixteen of them. Seventeen, if you count Nancy Trebec." Malcolm walked over to the marble woman standing off to one side of the cemetery, all but lost in the trees. He pulled out a gold cigarette lighter and flashed the flame in her face.

What a pretty face, full of sorrow.

"No wings," said Riker, returning the flask.

"A fallen angel doesn't need wings. She's not going anywhere." Malcolm leaned one arm on the statue's slight shoulder as he tipped back the whiskey for a long draught. "No room for a suicide in Catholic heaven."

"Why did she kill herself?"

"You didn't take Betty's tour?"

Riker turned back to look at the angel with Mallory's face and a lethal weapon. "The statue broke up the party when it started crying."

"Well, Betty tells it better, but I can give you the short version." Malcolm stood back from the statue and regarded it with a half-smile. "Jason Trebec wanted a male heir to carry his name. But after Augusta was born, Nancy couldn't have another baby. She was barren. And Catholic—no divorce. Jason was a cruel old bastard, and every last day of Nancy's life, he found some new way to punish her for not giving him a son."

"The old man was nuts. I've met Augusta. She's twice the man I am."

"Oh, you don't know the half of it." Malcolm had seemed cold sober only a moment ago, and now he split his face with the wide smile of a happy drunk. "Augusta has balls, all right." He grabbed his crotch. "They used to be *mine*."

He was laughing as he sank down to the stone pedestal at Nancy's feet. "Augusta snipped them off me in court. Sued me for damaging a bird habitat. Then she moved on to the chemical plants, snipping off trophy testicles in courtrooms up and down the Corridor. Now she has enough balls to set up a damn pool table."

Riker sat down on the cold stone slab at Nancy Trebec's feet. "Naw, I don't think that's Augusta's style. I see her banging 'em across a net with a paddle."

Malcolm nodded as he considered this. "Or baseball?" He nudged Riker's arm. "Splat with a bat?"

Riker winced and leaned back against the statue. In the

benign afterglow of a long night's boozing, he studied the man beside him. When they had first met over a watered-down whiskey in Owltown, he had not known what to make of Malcolm. But very quickly, the personality had jelled into a man's man with a taste for Riker's unfiltered cigarettes and an unlimited capacity for drink. Riker's approval had grown with each glass he downed on Malcolm's tab.

And now the hip flask came back to him again. The scotch was smooth, and it warmed him. Life was good.

Ah, wait. Here's a snag. He upended the silver bottle and one golden drop hit the ground. "Aw, you killed it," said Riker, perhaps ungraciously.

"That's no problem." Malcolm took it out of his hand. "I'm in the resurrection business." He turned his back and said a brief prayer to Bacchus. When he offered the hip flask to Riker again, it was full.

"Praise the Lord," said Riker, wishing he could remember the words to Malcolm's prayer so he could try this stunt at home. "I've seen the light."

"Sooner or later, they all do."

"I hear you've got quite an act, Mal."

"Well, I've been working on it for thirty years."

"You don't look much over thirty now." According to the roadies, Malcolm was only a few years his junior. In the better light of an Owltown bar, he had searched for signs of a face-lift, but found none. "What's your beauty secret?"

"Clean living," said Malcolm, tilting back the flask. "Got another cigarette?"

Riker fished in a side pocket where the package had fallen through the torn lining. Impatient, Malcolm plucked a cigarette from the air. He snapped his fingers, and a flame appeared to spurt out of his thumb.

Riker was about to say he had seen Charles Butler do that same trick a hundred times.

Well, he had definitely had enough to drink for one night. Not wanting to lose face with a fellow boozer, he put the silver bottle to his lips but didn't drink before he handed it to Malcolm. But after a few more passes, the flask hadn't lightened any. And now Riker realized he had been drinking alone tonight.

Shit.

Either that or Malcolm was the Second Coming.

"The roadies tell me you can turn water into wine." *And cops into babbling idiots.*

"Yes, sir. Now that's a real crowd pleaser."

"But they think you're really making wine out of tap water. These guys go on the road with you. They do the setups for the act, right? So how can they believe it's for real?"

"Most every religion demands faith in impossible acts." He pointed to the crucifix on the tomb next to them. "People believe that man on the cross was begotten by a god. He could heal the sick and raise the dead. How magical."

The pointing finger moved on to another stone house. "That's the tomb of a local woman in the same trade." The walls were marred with graffiti and the base was littered with colored bits of broken glass, ribbons and pins. "The drawings are voodoo symbols. The things on the ground are religious offerings. She's a hundred years dead, but some people believe she's still got the power."

Malcolm stood up, his arms lifting into a crucifixion pose, and his hands spread wide on the rising wind. The air was blowing cold, and his long hair flew back to reveal the shape of his skull. As he spoke, his smile was dazzling—even in the dark. "This part of the world is ripe with magical thinking."

A MORE PRAGMATIC, enlightened thinker of the late twentieth century, Charles Butler, Ph.D., stood at the edge of the cemetery, holding a jar of blood—still warm from the recent sacrifice of a chicken's life.

He waited in uneasy silence. Finally Malcolm walked down the gravel path and through the circle of trees with one arm thrown around Riker's shoulders. Evidently, the seduction was a great success, for Riker was laughing as the salesman of wonders led him away.

Charles turned to face Henry Roth, and together they moved on to the avenging angel and proceeded to bind her wings with rope. They worked quietly through the next hour, exchanging one piece of sculpture for another. They worked faster toward the end of the hour, for it was getting light, and the believers would be coming soon.

How disappointed they would be.

Henry wiped the sweat from his brow as he walked back to the tomb of Jason Trebec and turned an old-fashioned key in the lock on the door. He stored his tools alongside the chicken blood and a block of dry ice.

Charles was staring down at the sad face of barren Nancy Trebec.

"Henry, do you think Babe Laurie could have been sterile?"

"Possible. Most of the Lauries are as prolific as rabbits, but Babe's only child was a bastard."

"What do you think of a bastard child as a motive for murder? Suppose Babe took it out on the boy, Fred's son? Maybe Fred retaliated?"

"Ugly things have been done on account of bastards." He looked up at the bas-relief of a man's crumbling face above the door. *"Jason Trebec once hauled his wife into court and tried to have Augusta declared illegitimate."*

"Do you believe Augusta was a bastard?"

"No, and neither did the judge. The resemblance was so obvious. If this stone portrait was in better shape, you could see it, too. I think Jason just wanted an annulment so he could get on with the business of begetting a son by another woman."

For a long time after Henry had gone home, Charles was still searching the stone likeness of Jason Trebec, looking for traces of Augusta. He found them in the shape of one uncrumbled eye and what remained of the mouth.

He turned away and walked along the path heading east.

The sun was a pale white disk behind the cloud cover. The birds had begun to sing again, but he discerned another sound above the racket, footsteps on gravel. He glanced over one shoulder.

Riker was back, slogging down the path, as though his legs weighed a hundred pounds each. The sky was light gray now, and so was the detective.

"Hey, Charles. Given any more thought to helping me with my problem?" Each word was very distinct. The man took great pride in never slurring his speech, no matter how much he'd been drinking.

Charles regarded the slack face, the poor color, and wondered why his old friend didn't fall down. Between the liquor and the chain-smoking, Riker had never been in the best of shape. "You need to get some rest."

"I take that as a *no*." Riker was suddenly in thrall to the angel recently restored to her pedestal. "Oh, Jesus. Charles, you gotta stop this. It's weirding me out."

Distant thunder rumbled in the west. And the gray sky was bright for one split second.

"It's over now," said Charles. "That's the original angel."

Riker stepped closer to look at the child in the woman's arms. He turned back to Charles, who nodded. "It's Mallory. Six years old, going on seven."

"She's really into this, isn't she? The bastards must be going nuts wondering when she'll make her move." Riker drew the collar of his suitcoat close about his neck and folded his arms against the cold.

"I suppose it's a bit unsettling," said Charles.

"Unsettling? A woman tried to kill herself." Riker was shivering in his flimsy suit.

"Don't throw that up to me again. And don't ask me to turn on Mallory." Charles sat down on the grass, suddenly very tired. "Why must you do this to me?"

"I have to get her away from here before Babe Laurie's crowd finds her. Travis placed Babe on the scene of the stoning, so Mallory has the best motive in town. The sheriff probably—''

''You're tired, Riker, and off your game. You should know by now that nobody cares what happened to Babe Laurie.''

''Except the people from the mob that killed her mother.'' The first drop of morning rain found Riker and stained his suit with a small circle of a darker gray. ''They'll wonder how she knew Babe was one of them. They'll see her as a threat.''

''A very smooth recovery. Much better logic.''

''But no sale?''

''No, I don't think so.''

The rainfall was light, but the incessant birdsong stopped, and every more sensible creature ran for cover.

''Charles, the sheriff wants her to go. This might crush the brat's ego—couldn't hurt to try—but I'm not so sure the jailbreak was Mallory's idea.''

''You think the sheriff set her up for that?'' *Not likely.* On the day of the jailbreak, the sheriff had seemed very determined to get her back again—assuming that the sheriff wasn't lying.

Riker shrugged. ''There's no warrant for her arrest. Interesting, huh? No cop outside this parish knows she's missing or wanted. If we take her out of here right now, I don't think anybody's gonna come after us.''

Assuming that Riker wasn't lying.

''She has a right to investigate her mother's death,'' said Charles.

''And when she's got the complete list of names? What then?'' Raindrops streaked Riker's face. They looked like tears.

But they're not. Only the rain.

It was coming down harder now, pelting the leaves of the surrounding trees. Riker's hair was wet. ''You can't go on blind faith. You got no idea what she's planning. Suppose more people die?'' He reached into his pants pocket and pulled out the gold pocket watch. ''Here, take it. The sheriff wants her to have it back. And then he wants her to go.''

Charles quickly grabbed the watch and closed his massive hand around it in a tight fist to keep it from the rain. ''Why can't you be on her side? All she wants is a little justice.''

He was walking away from the detective, crossing the circle of tombs, half blind with the rain slanting into his face.

Riker said to his back, ''I gotta figure she came back to destroy maybe twenty, thirty people.'' His voice was rising to cross the distance between them. ''I don't want you to be too disappointed in the kid . . . when she actually pulls that off.''

And Charles kept walking.

''DOES ANYONE KNOW where the sheriff was when Babe Laurie died?''

''Charles, you don't really think he did that.'' Augusta presided over the kitchen table. It was laid with plates of sweetbreads and bowls of steaming concoctions, mingled aromas of saffron and chicken, sweetmeats and vegetables. Augusta was spooning a broad array of food onto Charles's plate. ''Tom Jessop wouldn't take time out of his day to talk to Babe, let alone kill the man.''

''But the sheriff has a history of violence. I understand he beat up Fred Laurie for taking shots at the dog.''

''Oh, that was years ago. Now Tom was there, but I was the one who beat up on Fred.''

''You, Augusta?''

''With a shovel. I hit him in the gut with the first blow and whacked his hands with the next one. Tom was busy checking the dog for holes. He looks up at me and down at Fred, and he says, 'Augusta, that's rude.' But he didn't say anything when I hit Fred alongside the head. Tom isn't given to repeating himself.''

He looked at Henry, the source of this story, but Henry

was concentrating on his food. Charles turned back to Augusta. "I'm sorry. I was misinformed."

Deliberately?

And now Charles became lost in speculation. Henry could have been shielding Augusta. Or she might be shielding the sheriff. One of them was less than truthful. And now he pondered the etiquette of lies within this company of liars he had joined. And then he considered the well-intentioned lie versus the lie for personal gain, the general ranking of sin.

"So Fred told people Tom did that?" Augusta did not look pleased. "Well, that isn't right, giving Tom all the credit."

Now Henry lifted his face and his hands to say to Charles, *"I thought you were more interested in the old murder. Getting hit with one rock doesn't have the same cachet as a stoning by a mindless mob."*

"A mob is not mindless," said Augusta, passing Henry a plate of butter. "You don't remember that lynching in Arkansas?"

She turned to Charles. "Three boys were jailed for murder. One of them had a change of heart and run off before the man was shot and his wife was robbed of her jewelry, but all three were arrested. Next day, a rumor spread all over town that the woman had been raped—though she never was. That night, a mob dragged the boys out of the jailhouse and lynched them—all but the one. They were putting the rope around his neck when someone in the crowd yells out, 'That boy had no part in the murder.' The rope was taken off, and the mob returned him to his cell."

"She's right, Henry," said Charles. "The mob has a goal and a guiding intelligence. It even has an awareness of right and wrong. But something has always bothered me about *this* mob. It's just wrong somehow."

"The lack of noise? The lack of passion?" asked Henry.

"Yes. It was done in cold blood. That's one oddity. But I don't think Travis or Alma knew what was going to happen before they got to the house."

"It wouldn't make sense to do a cold murder in a group," said Augusta, "unless they were all in on it. Otherwise someone would talk."

"That *is* a problem," said Charles.

"Not a problem at all." Mallory stood in the doorway of the kitchen, holding a carrier cage full of white doves. "They have a lot in common." She set the cage on the slate counter. "One murder charge for all of them, whether or not they threw the rocks. Bloodshed makes the bond real tight."

Augusta set out a plate for her, saying, "Now how did you charm those doves into the cage?"

"I threatened to break their little legs if they didn't cooperate." She sat down at the table. Her back was turned on the cat sitting on top of the refrigerator. "How's it going?"

Augusta ran one finger down the list. "Henry's favorites are the women. But if you don't count Alma, every one of them has an admirable mean streak. Not a weak sister in the pack. I could make the same claim for most of the men."

"Most?"

"Well now, this name is a surprise." She pointed it out for Henry. "Are you sure about this one?"

"I'm positive."

"I wouldn't have thought he had any violence in him at all."

"He's the one I want," said Mallory.

The cat was only staring at the captive doves, her eyes wide, and perhaps disbelieving.

"You don't know he did anything," said Augusta. "Alma never threw her stone, and Travis only stoned your dog."

"If you believe them."

When Charles turned back to the cat, it was standing on top of the wire cage, staring at the docile doves, which apparently had never seen a cat before. There was a great deal of eye contact, but no violence yet.

Mallory, unaware of the impending massacre, was saying, "I don't care if he threw rocks or flowers. He was there, and I'm gonna break him."

"Maybe not," said Augusta. "You don't know the first thing about these people. You could pummel this one all day, and he'd just take it."

Charles was raising his hand to point to the cat's paw dipping in between the wires, when cage and cat tumbled to the floor, the door banged open and the doves flew upward in tight formation, all of one mind in their desire to live.

"Damn cat!" Mallory was on her feet. "It took me hours—"

"I'll take care of it," said Augusta.

The cat was in pursuit of its lunch, and Mallory was reaching for her revolver. Augusta grabbed the wrist of the gun hand and stared the younger woman down, eyes hard and unwavering. "Don't even think about it, little girl." Each word had the same weight, the same amount of menace.

The cat was leaping joyfully from countertop to refrigerator and down to the floor again in pursuit of each new roost of a dove. But the birds were quicker. White feathers were flying, and some were drifting to the floor as the manic chase went on.

Augusta still held Mallory's wrist in a tight grip, and her expression was conveying that the younger woman would be dead meat if she dared to shoot that animal. And that was a promise.

The cat was closing on a bird, stealing up from behind and hyperventilating in happy anticipation. A squeak of excitement escaped from the cat and warned the dove into flight.

Mallory's expression was somewhere between anger and incredulity. This old woman had no weapon, no—

Augusta assured her with a slow nod that she could and would make good on a threat. If Mallory wanted to go round and round, the older woman was up for it.

Charles was only a little shocked to note that Mallory was clearly weighing this proposition. Then she sat down.

HE SIPPED HIS coffee and watched a fish hawk dive for its dinner as the gulls screamed and circled over the river. Charles was viewing nature in a less than pastoral light these days. He smashed an insect on his wrist and left a red smear on his skin. Another bug made a clean getaway with his body fluids, and who knew what was going on among the flightless insects and the small animals in the long grass extending out to the levee. And what of Augusta, nature's local custodian?

Mallory leaned against the veranda rail, and stared down at the pocket watch in her hand, oblivious to any violence not of her own making.

He had asked her a question ten minutes ago and was still waiting for a response. "You're not going to tell me anything, are you?"

She wouldn't even look at him.

He felt his relationship with her had reached a new growth point, for she pissed him off so easily these days. "You don't trust me. You think I'd give it all away."

She slipped the watch into her jeans pocket. "Do you trust *me,* Charles?"

"You want blind faith? Like Malcolm's little flock?" He hadn't meant to say that aloud. It was only an echo of Riker from the back of his mind. "When were you going to tell me about the bullet wound in your shoulder?"

"Never."

Well, so much for trust.

"I want you to find Riker," she said. "Just go from bar to bar, you'll turn him up. I want you to give him a story, send him off to the next parish to keep him out of my way."

"Riker thinks you've come back to destroy all those people. Have you?"

"I came here to collect evidence in a homicide."

"Not just any homicide."

"It's like any other case, same—"

"Mallory, you're not really going to play the blushing virgin, are you?" He noted the sudden widening of her eyes, and he nearly laughed. "You always said I didn't have a face for poker. Well, you don't have the face for righteous indignation."

She was angry now. *Good.* Before she could speak, he put up one hand. "I should warn you, I can not only out-virgin you, but even though I'm not from the South, I can outsouthern you too. I've learned a lot from Henry and Augusta."

"Yeah, and you were going to find out who killed Babe. How much did you learn about that?"

He didn't care for her sarcasm either. "Well, according to the sheriff, to know Babe was to have a motive. What did you turn up at the hospital yesterday?"

"Nothing."

Right.

"Charles, are you going to help me with this or not?"

"What you're doing is just another variation on torture. That's the sheriff's method."

"It was Markowitz's method too."

"No, your father was a good and decent man."

"And a world-class cop. When Markowitz didn't have any hard evidence to use in court, he worked the perps into a frenzy. He lied like the devil, and scared them shitless. If Markowitz had been here, he would have done it the same way, or maybe gone me one better."

"Riker says this is—"

"Riker will say whatever it takes to get you working against me. He came here to bring me back to New York, like I'm some runaway kid."

"He worries about you. I think his biggest fear is that you're only—"

"I came here to do a job, and I will finish it. So *don't* help me, all right? Just don't get in my way." She stalked to the staircase.

"Mallory, wait. I don't think—"

"No, you're not thinking at all—you've got Riker for that." She turned on him. "He's got you blindsided." She came walking back to him, not with her usual stealth, but with boot heels hitting the boards hard. "He's a fine one to quote the rule book. You don't think he's ever gone over the edge to get a confession?"

She stood over him now, arms folded. "Once I watched Riker slap a child molester on the back and smile. Then he commiserated with the pervert—'What a tease that four-year-old kid was, huh, pal? Yeah, she had it coming to her.' Oh, did I mention that the creep killed the kids when he was done with them?"

Charles lowered his head, and she shot out one hand to lift his face to hers. "No cop can stomach the rape of a child. It's the lowest crime, and this insect also killed them. Not because he was sick—he just didn't want any witnesses—it was that cold."

Her hand fell away. "Riker was the child killer's best friend. The perp was so smitten with his new buddy, the cop. He led us to every little corpse—all for the love of Riker. As we went from one child's grave to another, Riker held the perp's hand in the back of the car. It was a love affair. Are you disgusted, Charles? You think there was a righteous way to get that confession?"

His eyes stayed with her as she paced to the staircase and back again.

"Did Markowitz try to stop it? Did he say, 'No, Riker, don't get down in the dirt with that creep'? No! The old man watched Riker develop the suspect as a witness to his own crime. Riker went around with this pervert for days and days until we'd collected seven very small bodies. The techs would dig up a little kid, and Riker would hug the pervert and say, 'Good job, pal.' And then they'd pick up their shovels, and we'd all go on to the next shallow grave."

She hunkered down beside his chair. So close. "By comparison, I don't think Riker found *you* much of a challenge." She stood up and turned her back on him.

Charles felt drained, as though he had run a mile. He looked down at a flower blooming through the rail near his chair. Its vine had twined up fifteen feet of brick foundation to get at the wood. The flower was flame-red, so beautiful, fragile. A dark, twitching beetle crawled from its center as Mallory came to light in the chair beside his own.

"Forget that the victim is my mother." Her voice was so calm, so utterly detached. She went on, with no inflection to give a meaning beyond the dry words. "The crime is old. A cold trail is the hardest one. No evidence, no witnesses, unless you count Ira, and I don't. I'm keeping him out of this. And Alma's crazy and useless."

Now her voice was on the rise, but still no emotion, as though she had merely turned up the volume on a machine. "I have to develop a witness to testify against the rest of them. I plan to break the bastard any way I can—whatever it takes."

Mallory's face was inches from his own. Her hand wrapped around his arm, fingers digging in. All her emotions came out to play now. There was real pain in her face, her voice. "And then I'm going to tell the creep that my mother had it coming to her! That the bitch *deserved* to die!"

His head jerked back as though she had slapped him.

Her voice softened. "I'll tell him any filthy lie he needs to hear." She whispered, "That's what cops do."

And now she was rising, going away from him again. She stood by the rail and leaned back on her hands, all cold to him now, and mechanical when she said, "So Alma Furgueson slit her wrists. Alma's still breathing. My mother is dead. Time to choose up sides, Charles."

She hovered by the staircase, undecided whether to go or stay. "Has Riker won you over?" She set one boot on the steps. "Are you throwing in with him or me?"

"I would never—"

"Are you in or out, Charles?"

"I'm in." After all, Alma *was* still breathing.

CHAPTER

22

THE SHERIFF SAT back and evaluated his young deputy over the rim of his beer glass. Though Lilith Beaudare still had a lot to learn, she had been broken of arrogance—just as he had broken Eliot Dobbs before her. Deputy Travis had come to him prebroken, and was no damn fun at all.

"Very soon, things may get ugly, Lilith." And how would she react? "Could you kill somebody if you had to? If you can't do it, you might wind up dead, or someone else will. You'll only get one second to find out what you're made of."

And now he knew he had hit on a soft spot. She lowered her eyes—a bad sign. Had she already been tested under fire? There was nothing in her file to say she'd ever been involved in gunplay.

"Have you ever killed anybody, Sheriff?"

He approved. Distraction was a good move on her part. But her brains were not in question today. "In all the years I've had this job, I've never had occasion to fire my gun in the line of duty."

"That's not what I asked."

"I do believe we'll have the time to know each other a

little better, Lilith, but that time is not here, not yet.'' Well, that knocked her down again. ''So what is it you're not telling me?''

Her hands wormed around her glass as she dropped her eyes again, casting around for some better diversion. Soon he would have to teach her not to give so much away.

She looked up again. ''I think Mallory might be a cop. It's just a—''

''A good guess. She is. Detective Sergeant Kathleen Mallory.''

''How did—''

''Well, if it isn't the man from New York City.'' He pointed toward the door of the Dayborn Bar and Grill.

Charles Butler was blocking out most of the sunlight streaming in behind him. The door swung shut, and now he was in that disorienting passage from bright light to dim.

While the man was still half blind and vulnerable, the sheriff called out across three tables, ''Mr. Butler! If you're looking for your friend Riker, you just missed him. He's gone off to New Orleans.''

The sheriff gathered that Butler had elected not to bluff his way out, but to ignore the remark. The man was smiling as he joined the sheriff and his deputy.

''Call me Charles, please. Actually, I was looking for *you*, Sheriff.''

Tom Jessop was working hard to suppress a grin, for now this poor bastard had to come up with a reason for his impromptu visit.

''I was just wondering if you had any men on your suspect list yet. So far you seem to favor women.''

''Still do, Charles. I'm nothing if not politically correct.'' He turned to his deputy. ''Ain't that right?''

Lilith smiled as she rose from the table and left with explanations of places to go and things to do. Out of respect, Charles stood up to see her off. Tom Jessop remained seated for much the same reason.

''So, Sheriff, you don't think Fred Laurie could have done it?''

"He could have." And he did like the idea of a dead man as a suspect. Fred was probably in the ground by now and in no condition to whine about being maligned.

"I also wondered where *you* were when Babe Laurie died."

The sheriff grinned. "You have real good instincts. If I'd known what Babe did to Ira, I might have been your best suspect. As it is, I still like the ladies. And now you're probably thinking I missed Augusta, but I didn't. I just didn't want to ask her on the off chance she might confess. As I'm sure you know, letting Augusta get away with murder is a tradition in St. Jude Parish."

"You're speaking figuratively, of course."

So Charles didn't know. "Didn't you take the tour? Betty tells the whole story to everyone who comes through here."

"I've been rather busy."

"You must be the only visitor in fifty years who didn't know that Augusta murdered her own father."

Charles only shook his head from side to side, smiling now to say this must be a joke. "She couldn't have done that."

"She dragged it out, too." The sheriff caught the bartender's eyes and held up two fingers. "Not a neat clean death. 'Course, I know the details better than most. My father was her lawyer. Augusta would be happy to tell you the story herself. It's not like she ever tried to deny it. Fact is, she took a lot of pride in that murder. She's a rare one. Most southern women would favor slow poison for the alibi factor. They'd want to be three counties gone before your body hit the floor. Not Augusta. Hell, she wanted the credit."

Two beers landed on the table, cold gold on the inside, cold sweat on the glass. "Put it on my tab," said the sheriff. The bartender nodded and walked off.

"Thank you," said Charles. "So, she confessed? There was a trial?"

"No, it never went beyond the coroner's jury. The ruling

was accidental death. You gotta remember that she was fifty years younger then—nineteen, almost twenty years old. The coroner's jury was all men. Not a one of them wanted to see her hang for murder. And to be fair—she meant to shoot the old bastard, not push him down the stairs in his wheelchair.''

"Was it the money? I know he cut her out of the will.''

"Oh, hell no. That's Betty's theory, but Augusta didn't care about that. She could have married more money and a bigger house if that's what she wanted. You just don't know what a beauty she was. People from Nashville to New Orleans had heard of Augusta Trebec.''

"I know her mother committed suicide. Was it—?''

"You could say it started with her mother's death. The local doctor—he was also the town drunk—he said Nancy's suicide was insanity. Old Jason probably figured her blood was tainted. Now suppose Augusta went crazy, too? What would happen to his precious house? That's all any of the Trebec men ever cared about—that damn house. And what if Augusta married? His property would pass to another family. So Jason had his own daughter neutered like a cat.''

"Augusta wouldn't have allowed that.''

"She didn't know. Old Jason and the doctor made up some bullshit story about her appendix. She was only sixteen. Well, he'd killed off his last chance for an heir with Augusta's surgery. He was a sick old man in a wheelchair, and in no shape to make another baby.''

"So he made the house into a historical monument to himself.''

"Right you are. By the time Augusta turned nineteen, the hack doctor who butchered her was dead. It never occurred to Jason that the drunken old fool left medical records on Augusta's surgery. So another doctor took over the practice, and he told Augusta what had been done to her.''

"And then she killed her father?''

"Didn't waste any time, either. She came home that very

day and went after him with a pistol. The sight of the gun scared him so bad, he backed up his wheelchair—backed it right down the grand staircase. But he didn't die right away. He was lying there all broken up and screaming in agony. Augusta decided it would be a damn shame to put him out of his misery. So she stayed with him until he died. It took the better part of two days.''

''Are you telling me she didn't call a doctor?''

''No, she didn't. But she had the presence of mind to call a lawyer. That was my father. That's how I happened to be in the room the night she finished the old man off. I was five years old.''

''Your father brought you into a thing like that?''

''He had no idea what she wanted him for, and it was late at night. He couldn't leave me at home. The housekeeper was gone, and I didn't have a mother. So I was there when Augusta hurried up Jason's demise. Half the bones in the old man's body were broken. My father called for an ambulance the minute we got there. I suppose Augusta was afraid her father might pull through. So she leans down and tells Jason she's gonna bury him in the family plot where he can have a good view of the house he loves so much. The old man smiles. And then she yells, 'So you can watch it *fall down*! I'm gonna let it *rot*!' Well, the old man turned red, and then he turned blue and died.''

''But you said she confessed. How could the coroner's jury bring in a verdict of accidental death?''

''It was a bit of a stretch, but their reasoning was pretty sound. They figured if she was gonna lie about him backing his wheelchair down those stairs, then she would have lied about her original plan to kill him with the gun. So they decided she was truthful about that fall. And it *was* sort of an accident, if you look at it with a legal squint.''

''But she let him lie there in agony for *two* days.''

''Now that did trouble the jury. So my father solved that problem for them. He swore under oath that Jason Trebec, late in life, had converted to Christian Science and didn't want a doctor—so Jason and Augusta had spent those two days praying together.''

''And the coroner's jury bought that?''

''Don't you see? They *wanted* to believe it. They were smiling the whole time Dad spun that lie. But then, when he finished his testimony, Augusta burst out laughing. Well, Dad stepped down from the stand, cool as you please, and he slapped her face. He told the jury she was hysterical with grief. And then he strong-armed her right out the door before she could do any more damage.''

''Your father was in love with her, wasn't he?''

''And fortunately, so was her doctor. He backed up my father's story on the witness stand. So, you see, she could have killed Babe Laurie. But I don't ever want to know that for a fact, so I never asked.''

''She had no motive to kill him.''

He liked Charles's loyalty, and he was satisfied in the man's character. Augusta's friendship spoke well of him, considering that he had no feathers or fur.

''Augusta presides over every matter of life and death north of Upland Bayou,'' said Jessop. ''I don't think much has got by her since Cass was murdered. She took that killing very hard. She blocked off Finger Bayou and the road to the mansion, locked up her land just like you or me would lock up a house. So there was Babe on that road to Cass's place, lying in wait for Kathy. And I know that's what he was doing. I found three of his cigarette butts near the spot where he died.''

''But how would Augusta know that? You would have to assume that she knew all the events leading up to the death. That's really reaching, isn't it, Sheriff?''

''If she didn't do it, I'd bet good money she knows who did. Don't you understand it yet? Augusta can see everything from her attic window, and she spends a lot of time with that spyglass. You think she's only watching her birds? We're all part of Augusta's aviary.''

CHAPTER

23

JIMMY SIMMS SAT tailor fashion on an old plaid bedspread, hunched over his book, and resplendent in his new-old clothes. His feet were encased in Ira's castoff socks.

The wooden crate beside Jimmy's cot held the rest of Darlene Wooley's charity. T-shirts, jeans, a sweatshirt and a denim jacket were neatly stacked in laundry-faded stripes of red and blue. Jimmy was a rich man now. Beside his cot were shoes that fit his feet perfectly.

The rough surface of the crate held one can of soda, a pack of doughnuts, and a lamp with no shade. The bare lightbulb was warm as a hand on the back of his neck, and this illusion of human contact counted as an additional creature comfort.

His small room had once been a storage area for books, and now it was home. Disowned and unhoused at seventeen, he had taken to making his bed alongside the sleeping drunks on the streets of Owltown. One chill night, as winter was coming on, the sheriff had picked him up off the sidewalk and dropped him into this safe harbor at the back of the library. For the past thirteen years he had been content in this place. Augusta Trebec had given him the first odd jobs, and Tom Jessop had scared up more work. Between the all-seeing eye of Miss Augusta's attic window and the gruff attentions of the sheriff, Jimmy had lived with the delusion of aloof but constant parents.

Now, beyond the door, the telephone was ringing in the main room of the library. He ignored it, taking the call for a wrong number. It was always a wrong number in the evening hours when the library was closed. When he was still a teenage boy, he had run into the main room each time it rang, believing his mother was calling.

But she never called.

When he missed her terribly, he would show up on the front steps of the house, and she would bring him inside quickly, lest the neighbors should see him and tell his father. Then his mother would give him hot soup and a warm meal—mother food. And she would wash his clothes, just like a mother, and give him more clothes, miles too big, to take away with him. She would pack extra food in a paper bag, the way she had once packed his lunch for school. But once he was gone, she forgot him again. She never called. So he had learned not to answer the library phone in the night.

His eyes went back to the page of his book. But the ringing was persistent, and there seemed no way to end it but to take the phone off the hook. The main room of the library was not heated, and so he pulled on Ira's denim jacket as he left his bed and walked out to the front desk.

Wind came through the old window frames in a gusty sigh, and he could feel the room's cold breath on his face and neck. The century-old building creaked with elderly joints of wood and plaster, and he could hear mice creeping in the walls.

Jimmy stood by the ringing telephone, keeping one eye on the dark rows of bookshelves. The headlights of a passing car made the globe by the window cast a moving shadow the size of a child. He looked away quickly and picked up the receiver of the ringing telephone. Before he could lay it down to break the connection, a woman's voice said, "Jimmy?" He stared at the receiver and the voice called out again, "Boy, are you there?"

He held the phone close to his ear now, caressing it. "Mom?"

"No, Jimmy, it's Augusta Trebec."

Of course.

"Yes, ma'am."

"I got a small job for you. It has to be done tonight. Shouldn't take more than an hour. I'll pay you ten dollars for your time. Does that sound about right?"

"Yes, ma'am, ten dollars sounds just fine." And he could use the money.

Jimmy was staring at the library window facing Dayborn Avenue. The light of the streetlamp was haloed with misty fog. Not a night to go walking, especially if he wanted to skirt the cemetery, and he did. The new shoes would be ruined by the alternate route over rain-soaked ground, and he had thrown his father's old pair away.

"Why don't I come in the morning, ma'am. First light?"

"That won't do me a bit of good, Jimmy. I need this errand run tonight. You understand?"

"Yes, ma'am, I do."

"There's a bit of fog out there. Why don't I meet you at the bridge? I know every hole in that dirt road. I won't let you fall."

MISS AUGUSTA WOULD not like to be kept waiting on a cold night. He walked along the sidewalk at a fast pace, heading for the bridge over Upland Bayou. Jimmy could only see twenty feet into the mist, and he took comfort in every normal thing in that small field of vision. Sturdy telephone poles and fire hydrants were markers of the solid world he hurried through, as were the streetlamps and the yellow windows of the houses. As he approached the bayou, every landmark beyond the near shore was lost in the fog.

Miss Augusta was waiting for him at the foot of the bridge. Her white face floated above a long dark shawl. She nodded a greeting and turned away, crossing the bridge in silence. He walked behind her, making no attempt at conversation. Small talk was neither his strength, nor hers.

Good as her word, the old woman led him around each rain-filled hole in the road. He could see the dull glow of lights through the trees. So people were still visiting the angel. Though, only this morning, he had heard that the long lines had petered out to nothing and the miracle was over.

As they entered the cemetery, a dense ground fog rolled up to meet him. It was thick as he had ever seen it. His shoes disappeared below his ankles. His eyes strayed to Cass Shelley's monument. He could only see the back of her wings and the votive candles on her pedestal.

He scanned the grounds for Miss Augusta. She was farther down the alley of tombs, and he feared losing her in the mist and the turn of a corner on the gravel path.

But he had to look back one more time.

Cass's wings ruffled lightly like the feathers of a living bird. It was only an illusion created by the flickering play of candlelight. He knew that for a written-down, scientific fact—but belief was a different matter in the dark.

He was hurrying by the tombs, in a rush to catch up with Miss Augusta, when he heard the sound of stone crunching on stone. He looked back. Had the statue moved? No, that was not possible. He was only looking at it from a different angle. The great spread wings still hid her body from sight.

He turned back to the alley of small white buildings. The old woman had probably veered down some other street in the city of tombs and vanished.

"Miss Augusta?"

Behind him, something heavy had hit the ground. He felt the vibrations through the soles of his shoes, but he would not turn around, not for anything. And now, something in his sidelong vision moved. He would not look directly at it; he could not. He turned to Cass's angel for reassurance.

Her pedestal was bare. He looked down the alley where the old woman had gone. Miss Augusta had returned for him. She was standing just beyond the periphery of clear vision. It must be a trick of the mist that made her seem so much smaller.

"Miss Augusta?"

A woman's voice called to him. "Jimmy." He felt a hand on his shoulder and his knees began to liquefy. And then the hand was gone, and he was running toward the hazy figure of Augusta at the end of the path. He stopped short, kicking up gravel, backtracking until his legs locked and he froze like an animal trapped in the fascination of an onrushing train light. It was another angel, smaller than the one which had left its pedestal. It was the statue's missing child, and now she had wings of her own.

The little girl moved toward him on heavy stone feet. He could hear the pounding on the ground as she drew closer. Her hands had blood on them, and there was blood on the rocks in her small arms.

She stopped her forward motion and slowly rose in the air. He could see her tiny feet above the ground fog. He sank to his knees. The child was drifting toward him, floating, as if she weighed nothing, though she carried a heavy burden. All those rocks.

"I didn't do anything," he said. This was a lie. And the stone child knew it. She would have kept track of his sins.

"Cass was going to tell," he said with his hands splayed on the air, asking the child for understanding. "She was going to tell *everyone*."

The child hovered on the air, as though listening.

He covered his face with both hands. "I'm sorry, I'm sorry."

She called to him in a soft small voice, "Jimmy."

His hands dropped away from his face, and he opened his eyes.

She began to revolve in the air, and all the rocks flew out from her arms in a spiral, spinning off into the mist, making no sound as they fell. The stone child was whirling faster and faster as he screamed.

She slowed her revolutions, then stopped, only hovering now.

He brought his hands together, as if to pray.

She exploded into flight, the stone wings were in motion, beating on the air, and she was rushing at him, hitting him with her small body, her wings. She was not stone anymore, but warm, a pulsating child with a real heart beating against his chest, and then, in seconds, she was gone, flown off.

Lost feathers drifted to the earth.

He clawed at his eyes and fell forward, prostrate on the ground with his face in the gravel, small jagged bits of stones jutting into his flesh. He raised his head and looked back to the end of the alley. Cass's angel had returned to her pedestal. From this vantage point, he could see that it was the old angel, and the wingless stone child was back in her arms once more. He began to weep over the strange reunion of Cass and Kathy. And then he began to wail as the dog had wailed, lowering his head now, kissing gravel and crooning to the earth.

"Howling mad," said the voice of Augusta Trebec.

The thick ground fog was rolling away—more magic. The old woman's feet were close to his head. And now there were others gathering around him. As he was slowly raising his eyes, he wondered if these people would have rocks in their hands.

WHEN THE HYSTERICAL rambling had subsided to ordinary tears, Augusta knelt down by the shivering young man. "Now, Jimmy, you come along with me. I'm gonna fix you a nice strong cup of herb tea." She took one of his arms to pull him up, and Mallory slipped the black bandanna from her face and took the other arm. As the women walked the small man toward the path leading to Trebec House, Augusta was saying, "Everything is gonna be just fine."

Riker guessed the old lady was lying through her teeth.

He stepped out from behind the tomb and crushed one of the papier-mâché stones underfoot.

Charles wore a black cloth draped over his body, looking more like a priest than a magician. He was staring at the gun in Riker's hand with something approaching horror.

Riker holstered his revolver, as he watched the odd trio walking away. That frightened little man was the kind of suspect he always prayed for in every case with no physical evidence.

He looked at Charles. "You were right to believe in her. I was wrong."

Charles didn't seem to take any joy in this win. He only nodded as he pulled the black drape away from the statue of the winged child.

Riker picked up the velvet cloth. "So that's how you made her disappear." A second drape fell from the raised pallet. The fake fog was still escaping from the mobile platform in stray wisps. "There wasn't enough fog tonight? You had to rent a fog machine?"

Charles shook his head. "It was only dry ice and hot water."

When the last of the gas cleared away, Riker could see all the wheels and gears that made the angel rise and spin. He guessed that Charles had made the heavy footfalls of the stone angel's walk. "But what was the guy raving about? All that babbling crap about the angel flying? I saw the birds fly, but I never saw the statue take off."

Charles bent down to the small statue and gently cleaned the blood off her hands lest it stain the marble. "I don't know what that was about."

"Take a guess."

"It was supposed to be a very simple illusion, one thing changing into another. When I released the birds and draped the statue, he should have seen the stone turn into a flight of doves. I didn't expect the birds to fly straight at him like that. How could I know they were going to attack him?"

"I still don't get it, Charles."

"It was an accident of his own mind, a collision of illusions. The birds took the form he expected to see. He must have been very frightened. He's half crazy now."

Riker nodded. He was reminded of magical eyewitness testimony, the bane of every cop. If the witness heard a shot, he would swear under oath that he had seen a gun—whether it was there or not. And sometimes the gunshots were not real, either. Yet the witness was truthful.

"Don't beat yourself up, Charles. Cass Shelley was terrified when *she* saw the stones fly."

"Jimmy Simms was only thirteen years old when she died."

"Killer kids get younger every day. We got one back in New York who's only nine."

Of course, this was no comfort to Charles, who only wanted the workings of the world to be sane and fair. He was constantly being disappointed.

"You know, Riker, Jimmy never actually said he threw the stones."

Riker smiled at this. Charles was still hanging in there, pitching a case for civilization—another illusion. *Welcome to the new world, the animal planet.*

"It was a great technique," said Riker. "I've spent days breaking a suspect down to a puddle, and you guys did it in under ten minutes. I really thought Mallory would drag it out more—turn those screws a little tighter. So Jimmy's the future state's witness in her mother's homicide. Am I right?"

Charles nodded. "Yes, you finally got it right."

There was still more work to do. Riker knew this night would be uncommonly long. He lifted one hand in a farewell to Charles, and then he followed after the women and their captive.

He turned back once and saw Charles putting his shoulder to an angel, tipping and jogging her on the pedestal until she was facing south again. Henry moved along the path, rolling the pallet of a lesser angel, a copy of the little girl Riker had known as Kathy Mallory.

The small group ahead of him was leaving the wide oak lane, crossing open ground toward the house. Riker walked through water, soaking his shoes before he learned to follow Augusta's zigzagging example and avoid the puddles.

The suspect fell, and the two women knelt down to help him up again. Augusta stroked Jimmy's head as if he were a dog.

Riker gave them lead time going into the house, and then he opened the door slowly, minding the possibility of a creak.

He reached the end of the hallway and peered into the kitchen. *Aw, Mallory, no—not this way.* This was all wrong. It sickened him.

The two of them were seated at the table, where a tape recorder was glowing with a green ready light. Mallory had one hand on the suspect's shoulder; it was almost a caress. And she was trying to show the man how much she really liked him.

It would have been easier on Riker if he had found her crying. Mallory's strange attempt at a smile was hurting him so much more.

Riker cleared his throat. She looked up, and he gestured for her to join him outside the kitchen—right now.

When she stood before him near the front door, her arms were folded. Though it was dark at this end of the hallway, he could see that she was angry.

"Stay out of my way, Riker. Get out of here."

"I'll do it myself," he said. "I'm better at this than you are."

"Get out!"

"I should be the one to do it, Mallory. You know I'm right."

She turned her back on him and would have walked away, but he came up behind her and put his hands on her shoulders to keep her with him. "Just hear me out, kid. You've got to turn this perp around. There won't be another chance. If you blow it, the rest of them will scatter."

He felt her go rigid under his hands, yet she stayed.

When he spoke again, it was in a soft tone of voice he could never use if she were facing him. "In every homicide case, you learn too much about the victim. Some strange woman is lying dead on a slab, and you're using her name fifty times a day, talking to people who knew her, learning intimate details her own family doesn't know."

He bowed his head close to her ear and said, very gently, "Then comes that moment when you realize you're calling a dead woman by her first name—like she was an old friend of yours. And then it gets a little harder, doesn't it? It's more personal. But this time, Mallory, you call the dead woman *Mommy*. It's the only name a little kid has for her mother, the only name you ever called her by."

He held her closer, and every word he breathed disturbed the strands of her hair. "You know why you can't do this, kid." He didn't want her to hear his voice break. He slowly measured out his next words, pausing in the places where they strained and cracked. "I'm going to turn him around for you. . . . I'll hold his hand, and rub his back . . . and tell him it was perfectly natural . . . to break your mother's body with rocks, to knock out her teeth . . . to leave her lying in the dirt, bleeding to death."

Mallory nodded.

The deal was done.

His hands dropped away from her shoulders, but she would not turn around. Though Mallory made no sound to give away any emotion, he was careful not to look at her face as he moved around her and walked back down the long dark hallway toward the light of the kitchen.

CHAPTER

24

"THIS IS THE last of it." Augusta moved a stack of papers to one side and set a mug of hot coffee on the kitchen table. "I'll have a fresh pot in a few minutes."

Riker sat semi-upright, elbows propped on the table, hands covering his ears to block out the constant torture of cheerful twittering and chirps. The birdcalls had penetrated the kitchen with the first light of morning through the bank of tall windows. He missed his New York lullaby of car alarms and fire engines, screams and gunshots.

Different country—different songs.

"Don't those damn birds ever shut up?"

"No. They sing all day long." Augusta switched on the coffee maker and cocked her head toward the hallway, listening. "That's Charles at the door. He's got a soft way of knocking."

When Augusta had quit the room, Jimmy Simms stirred in the chair next to Riker's. The young man was snoring lightly, head pillowed on his arms. His sleeping face was unlined, so innocent.

Well, what's in a face?

Riker rubbed his red eyes, and then rushed the caffeine

into his bloodstream, hardly pausing to taste the coffee. He knew he was too old for these all-nighters, but he had even better reasons to quit his job. He wondered if he would ever feel clean again, for he had recently made himself at home inside the younger man's head, and lain back among the creepy crawlies. Jimmy Simms's mind stank, and Riker wanted to take a hundred showers.

"Morning, Riker." Charles Butler had a way of filling up a room. He seemed to understand this and sat down immediately, almost apologetically, to meet Riker at a more egalitarian eye level. "Mallory's not up yet?"

Riker swallowed his envy of the well-rested man. He looked at his watch. It was just past eight o'clock. "Well, the kid had a busy day."

"And I spiked her supper with passionflower and valerian," said Augusta, staring at the coffee machine, as though watching it would make the carafe fill up faster. "The girl wasn't getting enough rest. She'll be out for the rest of the day."

"Nice work," said Riker, grinning. "Can I have the recipe?"

Charles surveyed the spread of paperwork in front of Riker. "Is this all of it?"

"The whole case." Riker picked up a small stack of blue papers, each bearing the letterhead of the hospital laboratory. "One of these has to be a copy of Alma's blue letter." They were all addressed to Dr. Cass Shelley in her adjunctive role as the St. Jude Parish health officer. "Along with Jimmy's confession and everything Mallory got from the computers, it's enough for a grand jury to indict the whole pack."

Riker bundled all the paperwork together in one pile. "I'd say it's a wrap." He looked down at the sleeping Jimmy Simms, and then to Charles. "Did you ever have one of those days when you just didn't know where to put your hate?" Now he realized he was talking to the wrong person. He turned back to the stove where Augusta was stirring her pots, and she said, "Amen to that."

He ran one hand through his graying hair. So tired. "Charles, why don't you go back to Henry's and get the car out of hiding? I'll walk Jimmy over in a few minutes. I don't want anybody to see the state's star witness until he's in lockup."

"Now don't you run him off yet." Augusta put a mug of coffee in front of Charles. It was followed by plate after plate of foods, cooked and cold.

Riker, a coffee-and-toast man, was horrified. But eventually he was seduced by Augusta. She coaxed him with the aroma of hash browns, and she spoon-fed him tastes of batter cakes running with cane syrup. Then, when he was stuffed and couldn't eat another bite—just for fun, she buttered a warm biscuit under his nose, and he was letting out his belt and reaching for another.

Throughout the meal—the damn orgy of breakfast—Riker could see that Charles wanted to say something, but the man was silent until Augusta had finished her coffee and left the room with a sack of birdseed for the feeders. He was not accustomed to seeing suspicion in Charles Butler, but there it was. Charles was listening to Augusta's footsteps in the hall and the close of the front door. Now what could the old lady have done to deserve this?

"Do you have to turn Jimmy over to the sheriff?" Charles's voice was low and conspiratorial.

Another odd note.

Riker lit a cigarette and paused a moment, waiting for the nicotine to kick in. "You got a problem with that? Is there something I should know?"

"Well, Mallory put this case together very quickly, didn't she? And the sheriff had seventeen years."

Oh, great. Everybody wants to be a detective.

"Okay, Charles. You figure the sheriff had something to hide?"

"It's a reasonable conclusion, given that—"

"This is Mallory's work." Riker stretched and yawned. "You've got acolyte fever—I know the signs."

So Mallory had finally infected Charles. This was serious

damage. He preferred the old Charles Butler, a very nice man, who genuinely liked people and suspected the best of them. Not the makings of a good cop, but a first-rate human being.

Damn Mallory.

"I'm using straightforward logic," said Charles, somewhat defensively. "She has nothing to do with this."

Riker rested one hand on the thick pile of paperwork. "The kid didn't do all of this in a day. She's been hacking into classified computers for months, chasing down leads without warrants, circumventing the Constitution of the United States, and lying like a maniac."

He pulled out the blue sheets. "These reports on the lab work? She *stole* them during illegal trespass and destruction of state property. Oh, and she was there the day her mother went down. I'd say she had an edge, a little bit more to work with than the sheriff had."

"But Jessop actually knew who some of those people were."

"He *suspected* them. Big difference. He couldn't have sweated a confession from one of those bastards—not the way I did it. He could never suck up to vermin. The man just wasn't made that way. And you've gotta be real convincing to make the scum love you."

"He could have gone after them and—"

"He wore them down the best way he could. Without evidence, he couldn't make one solid arrest. If he'd brought in a suspect, the rest of them would've scattered. It's a toy town, Charles. Jessop doesn't have the resources to track down out-of-state runners."

God, are you listening? Save me from the amateurs.

"He tracked down Babe Laurie's widow," said Charles. "He had her extradited from another state."

"Yeah, but he got no help, zero cooperation. I saw the paperwork. Those Georgia politicos jerked him around six ways from Sunday. If Sally Laurie hadn't waived her rights, it could've taken another six months."

"Other police officers do it. They cooperate with—"

"The feds? According to my source, Tom Jessop won't play nice with the FBI—flat out refuses to spy on his neighbors. Can you imagine that? I got twenty bucks says the feds leaned on the Georgia boys to slow the man down."

Now Charles seemed a little off balance. "But what about Babe Laurie? Everyone assumes he was lying in wait for Mallory. Don't you find it—"

"And you think the sheriff had a hand in that? Screw Babe Laurie."

And now, time for a little therapy, my old friend.

"If you're on Mallory's side, everyone else is the enemy. I know you bought into that, and look what it's done to you. You can't recognize an honest man anymore." Riker stubbed out his cigarette. "You're a *blind* man now. That's what it cost you to stand by Mallory."

He was lying of course. The truth was less flattering. The blinding of Charles Butler was the damage just for getting in Mallory's way. She had succeeded where Riker had failed in his own attempt to maim this man.

"The only criminal thing about Jessop is that he never got over Cass Shelley's death. He just couldn't get past it." Riker watched his cigarette smoke curl up to the ceiling. "Poor bastard. And you thought he could've been part of a murder? Maybe a cover-up? You suspect Augusta of something, too, don't you? Who's next? Henry?"

Charles's lips parted, but nothing came out. Mallory had rendered him sightless, and Riker had struck the man dumb. But he was not done yet.

"Here's the real kicker, Charles. Even Mallory—who trusts nobody—*Mallory* would tell you this idea of yours is bullshit. How do I know that?" He leaned forward for the last shot. "It might take her more time than most, but even that amoral brat can recognize an honest man, and God knows she's no Diogenes."

Charles sank down in the chair, deflated and defeated.

And now Riker believed there might be a future in the miracle business, for lo and behold, the blind man could see once more.

Praise the Lord.

Ah, but wait—there was a downside to this healing trade. The sad giant was seeing too clearly now.

"It worked out for the best, Charles. You stood by her, and now the kid finally gets a little justice for her mother. That must be some consolation."

But the big man was unconsoled.

"What do you want, Charles? You want absolution? Well, you got it." Riker waved his cigarette to make the sign of the cross in the air.

JANE WAS STANDING at the cafe window when the silver Mercedes pulled up in front of the sheriff's office. The two men from New York City were helping somebody out of the backseat. Was it a man or a boy? He had a jacket pulled up over his head—just like the celebrity murderers on the evening news.

The cashier, Charmaine, joined her at the window in a cloud of cheap knockoff perfume. "Well, who is that?"

Jane shook her head, wishing Charmaine would go away. She turned to the empty porch of the bed and breakfast. Betty would probably be in the cemetery with her little troop of tourists by now. So this event belonged to Jane alone.

The man in the middle of the trio was slender and small—that narrowed it down some. And now that he had cleared the body of the car, she could see the red shirt below the hem of his pulled-up jacket. Oh, and now she had a clear view of the trademark red socks.

Now, don't that beat all. Who would've thought—

"Well, that's the idiot," said Charmaine, stretching her neck and seconding her employer's unvoiced opinion. "Is he under arrest?"

"Looks that way, don't it?" said Jane. "The man with the bad suit is a New York City detective."

"I wonder what that idiot's done. That mother of his—letting him roam around town at will, bringing him in here for lunch every day like he was normal. Didn't I tell you he was dangerous, didn't I, Jane?''

"Yes, Charmaine, I believe you did mention that." *Twenty times or more, you slovenly, bleach-blond bitch.*

"What do you suppose he's done?"

"It wouldn't be Christian to speculate. Poor Ira. And my heart just goes out to his mother." Jane's smile conveyed no such charitable sentiment as she walked over to the buffet line and began to load up a tray. "I think the new prisoner will be needing his lunch."

"But it's not even eleven o'clock." Charmaine was looking at her watch, which she swore was gold, but it wasn't. "Kind of early for lunch, isn't it?"

Well, Charmaine always had been a bit slow.

THE SHERIFF FOLLOWED his deputy into the reception area to greet Charles Butler and Detective Riker. Another man was sitting on the bench behind them. A denim jacket covered his head.

Well, aren't you the shy one.

Tom Jessop decided to let the man sit for a while, let the fear ripen a bit. And he did not mind dragging this out a little longer. For the past seventeen years, anticipation had been everything to him.

"Me and my deputy was wondering when you were gonna bring in the witness."

"It was supposed to be a surprise," said Riker. "You're takin' all the fun outta this."

"You can blame Lilith for that. She was in the cemetery last night—saw the whole show. Is Kathy coming in?"

"Well, technically," said Riker, "she's still a fugitive from justice."

"I guess she's better off at Augusta's."

Charles Butler smiled. "Sheriff, is there anything you don't know?"

"I don't know how you made that statue fly." He lightened up on the sarcasm for his deputy's benefit.

Lilith Beaudare turned on him. "I know you don't believe me, but I'm telling you, I saw it."

It was a hard story to swallow, even given his past history with her father. Guy Beaudare had never conjured anything so imaginative as an avenging angel rising off the ground, stone wings flapping to beat the devil, and attacking a man with the wrath of God. But it was a good story, and Guy would be proud of his daughter.

But Charles Butler seemed stunned, and now Jessop had to wonder if there might be something to the story.

Lilith gave Charles a pleading look. "The sheriff says the trick can't be done, not even with wires. Please tell him how you did it. He thinks I'm crazy."

Charles and Riker exchanged glances, as if debating this question of Lilith's sanity. The detective shrugged, deferring to the larger man in all things magical.

"I do it with mirrors," said Charles, as if bringing stone to life were an everyday thing with him, and not worth a bit of Lilith's wonder.

"Right," said the sheriff, turning to his new prisoner. "Well, let's see what we got here." In the spirit of opening a long-awaited present, he pulled the jacket away from the man's head and stepped back. It took a moment to see past the disguise of different clothes, the barbered hair and beardless face. Jimmy Simms was all dressed up like a normal person on the verge of rejoining the world.

Tom Jessop felt suddenly very tired. This was the last thing he had expected. "You were right, Lilith, he's got the Laurie family resemblance all right. This is Babe's nephew."

Jimmy bowed his head to hide his face.

The sheriff put one hand on the younger man's shoulder and shook him lightly. "You saw that killing, and you never said a word to me?"

"He was part of it," said Riker, holding out a bulging manila envelope. "It's all here. A signed confession and all the names."

The sheriff waved the envelope away and backed off

from the prisoner. "I want to hear it from him. Lilith, take the boy into the conference room." The man was thirty years old, but Tom Jessop would always see him as a runaway boy, and he didn't trust himself to touch Jimmy Simms, not yet.

They all filed down the hallway and through the last door. The sheriff remained standing while the others sat down in metal folding chairs pulled up to the long table. This back room lacked the antique warmth of the reception area. The walls were cold white and held contemporary maps and bulletin boards with papers dangling by pushpins. Riker was seated at the head of the table, flanked by Lilith and Charles. Jimmy Simms sat alone on the other side.

And now the sheriff hovered behind the prisoner. "Let's hear it, Jimmy."

The younger man only looked down to the end of the table, where Riker was coating half of it with official-looking papers. The sheriff put one hand on the prisoner's shoulder to prompt him. "You told it to Riker, now you tell it to me."

Jimmy stared at Riker, who didn't look up, but continued to cover the table with evidence, pieces of a murder. Now Riker did look up as he pulled a blue sheet of paper from the envelope, and held it up to the prisoner.

Jimmy spoke as if he were reading the words. "Cass took me to the meeting at the New Church. She dragged me right into that room. She was so angry, waving her letter around and yelling at people."

The sheriff bent low, his head close to Jimmy's. "What was Cass angry about?"

"I don't remember what she was saying. I just wanted to crawl away and die." Jimmy looked at Riker, who smiled gently and nodded, making a rolling motion with his hand. Jimmy continued. "She was gonna tell the whole town. She was gonna tell *you*. The last thing she said was, 'The sheriff will be back in the morning, you bastard.' "

"Who did she say that to?"

"My uncle." He sank down in his chair and covered his face with his hands.

Riker waved a hand to caution the sheriff. "Don't get him off on that. He'll cry, and it'll take an hour to settle him down again." To the prisoner, he said. "Go on, kid."

"My father must've put it all together, 'cause he was looking at me real strange, just staring at me like I'd crawled out from under some rock. After Cass left, Dad told me to wait outside while the grownups talked."

"Talked about what?" the sheriff prompted.

Riker handed him two blue sheets of paper, hospital lab reports on blood tests for a twelve-year-old boy. "The ID number matches Dr. Shelley's case file number for Jimmy."

The sheriff scanned the first line. "Hepatitis?" He looked at Riker. "I knew he had that. Cass treated him for it when I brought the boy back from New York." But apparently, she'd treated him for a more serious ailment as well. On the next blue sheet was the positive test for venereal disease. "Jesus." That might explain the downslide of the boy's life from the day he had brought him home to his parents.

"There's more," said Riker.

Jimmy was staring at the blue sheets and crying softly.

"All right, boy." The sheriff put one hand on his shoulder. "Never mind that now. Get on with the rest of it."

Again, Jimmy looked to Riker for his instructions, and the detective nodded.

"We all gathered at the Shelley house. At the time, I didn't know what for. I remember accidentally kicking a stone loose from the flower bed around the big tree in the front yard. So I stooped down and put it back. Dr. Cass was particular about her flowers."

She loved her flowers. They bloomed all around the house in every season.

"Then I saw the blue letter again and people were talking in whispers. They were going to fix everything so no one would know."

By killing Cass, who never did you any harm and never would.

"Somebody threw a rock and hit her on the side of the head. She never cried, never said a thing. It didn't seem real—like TV with no sound. Another rock hit her in the shoulder. Then somebody put a rock in my hand. It was just there in my hand, and this voice whispering in my ear, 'Do it, do it.' And I threw the rock and hit her in the knee. That one brought her down. She fell so quiet."

"And then what did you do?"

Jimmy looked up at the sheriff, with faint surprise. "Well, I went back to the flower bed to get another rock." As if that were the most obvious answer, the most natural thing to do, for he had thrown his rock and needed another one, didn't he? Jimmy turned to Riker. "And that second rock was the one that broke her front teeth."

Riker smiled and nodded in approval.

Behind Jimmy's head, the sheriff's hand was rising like a club. Hate was everything now. Charles Butler was getting up from the table. Riker only touched the sleeve of the large man's shirt to restrain him. "Stay out of it, Charles."

Jimmy looked up to see the sheriff's large fist hanging over him. He stared down at his own hands neatly folded in his lap as though he were on best behavior in church. His shoulders stiffened, bracing for the beating. His voice was calm and reasonable when he said, "I'm sorry for it now, but I didn't want them to know what he did to me."

The sheriff's hand was suspended in space.

In the same reasonable voice, Jimmy said, "The dog forgave me."

Riker held up more blue sheets. "The kid was raped. He says his uncle did it—a lot." He passed the papers down the table. "It didn't stop till he was thirteen. There were other kids, too."

So that was what Jimmy had run from, and what he had delivered the boy back to. Now the sheriff read a blue sheet with an account of the blood workup for a six-year-old boy, identified only by a number.

"Another case of hepatitis." And now he looked at the other sheet for the same child, bearing a later date. It was a positive test for syphilis. "Why would Cass test a six-year-old boy for VD? How did she make the jump from hepatitis? We've had hepatitis in the schools before. It's pretty common."

Charles said, "Not the blood-borne variety. Small children get a highly infectious form transmitted with clumsy toilet habits. Even that one would be rare in the upper grades, Jimmy's class. You'd have to be sexually active or shooting drugs to fall into a high-risk group for hepatitis B. It was a glaring marker for abuse in a six year old."

The sheriff turned to the last sheet, a positive VD test for a nineteen-year-old man. He looked up at Charles and held out the sheet. "There's no name. You're sure this one is Babe?"

Charles nodded. "It matches Cass's patient file number for previous treatment."

Now he looked from one sheet to the other. The six year old was the most recent infection of syphilis. Jimmy's was older—second-stage and apparently not contracted during his brief flight from home.

"Babe's infection was the oldest," said Riker, "even at the time of his famous VD party at the Dayborn Bar and Grill."

"I gather he never completed the treatment," said Charles. "That would explain the advanced case at the time of his death."

Riker was talking, explaining the remaining evidence to support the motive for murder, the illegal activities which would not stand up to any investigation, and the pedophile with a preference for small boys.

The sheriff was not listening. His rancor was curiously absent as he picked up another set of papers from the table. This was the handwritten statement of Jimmy Simms. At the bottom of the final page, all of Cass Shelley's murderers appeared in a neatly printed column. His eyes moved listlessly from one name to the next, and then the sheets dropped from his hand and landed on the table.

This was not the outcome he had been anticipating, *feeding* on for all this time.

What a cheat.

He had expected something larger, more on the grand scale of Lilith's stone avenger in flight. The long-awaited moment had finally come, and it was not enough.

Lilith remained to guard the weeping prisoner. Tom Jessop left the room with the hollow feeling that he had missed a meal. No—a great many meals—years of them.

He led Riker and Charles back down the short hallway to the reception area, speaking mechanically, all business now. "Me and my deputy are gonna take Jimmy out the back way. I think he'll be safer in a New Orleans lockup. We might be a while. I've got to scare up warrants for twenty-three people, and I don't know a single judge that owes me a favor. Riker, could you mind the store and stay close to the phone? I might need the backup if a judge is gonna buy this story."

"No problem," said Riker.

As the small group entered the reception area, they encountered Jane's smiling face. She was seated on the bench by the door and holding a covered tray on her lap. "Hello, Tom. I saw your new prisoner come in. I thought you might want to feed him."

"No need, Jane. I turned him loose ten minutes ago. But you just send me the bill for that tray, all right?"

Jane's smile was undiminished, and that told him she wasn't going away with nothing for her trouble but the price of the tray.

When the door closed behind her, he turned to Riker. "Whatever she heard, it's gonna be all over town before lunchtime."

"How fast can you get the warrants?"

"Not fast enough. Babe's funeral is tonight in Owl-town—just family, but that's at least a hundred drunks. It's a better idea to move in real early tomorrow morning with state troopers. We'll pick up the suspects when they're all hungover and sick.''

AT ONE O'CLOCK, Charles returned to the sheriff's office, carrying their lunch and coffee in paper bags from Jane's Cafe. "I didn't hear any gossip going around. Maybe Jane didn't hear anything either.''

"Fat chance." Riker's eyes never left the window on the square as he groped in the brown paper bag and pulled out a sandwich. He was staring at one of Jane's customers. The man had just walked out of the cafe, and now he slowly turned to face the sheriff's office.

Charles was in good spirits as he sipped his coffee. "So Mallory did it by the book.''

"I count three felonies in the paperwork gathering. Whose book are we talking about?''

"Well, she didn't hurt anybody.''

Didn't she?

Riker said nothing. The sandwich lay on the desk, untouched. He was intent on the man in the square, who had been joined by a friend. There was no conversation between them, nor any curiosity. They were only keeping watch on the sheriff's door—sentries.

"Riker, you don't still think she—''

"Mallory came back here to get those bastards, and now she has a complete list." He slumped back in the sheriff's chair and put his feet up on the cluttered desk. "I wish you'd go back to Augusta's and keep her occupied for a while.''

Another man had joined the watchers in the square. They moved back to the fountain and perched on the rim of the basin like a row of Augusta's birds on the paddock fence.

Riker turned away from the window to face Charles, his next problem, and such a large one. How to get rid of him?

"Why can't you trust her?" Charles was pacing now, unaware of the watchers, but adding to the tension. "You know she won't do anything to compromise this case.''

"Charles, what does it take to get through to you? For Christ's sake, she's telegraphing everything." It was a fight to keep his eyes from straying back to the window, to the watchers. "You've seen the gunslinger outfit. You think Mallory's playing dress-up? She's the real thing, Charles—the genuine article."

"That's ludicrous."

Riker only glanced out the window, as though he might have a casual interest in the weather. Malcolm Laurie was leaving Jane's Cafe, stopping for a moment to exchange smiles with the men by the fountain, and then passing on. Charles was looming over the desk, waiting for a return volley.

"I'm not gonna argue with you, Charles." Riker flicked through the sheriff's Rolodex, then picked up the phone and dialed the number for the hotel across the square. "Hi, I wanna book a room for Charles Butler. . . . Yeah, that one." As if there might be two giants with large noses. "He'll be by in a few minutes. . . . Fine. Thanks."

When he set the phone down he looked up at Charles. "No offense, Charles. I like your company, but I need to get some sleep. I don't want anybody to see that car going over the bayou bridge, so leave it in front of Betty's. Sign the register and go straight on through to the back door. Then go back to Augusta's and sit on the brat till morning." And now for the closing shot. "But don't get any ideas about taking the gun away from her. She'll hurt you just for trying."

Well, that made him angry, but at least he was leaving, silently and quickly. The outer door slammed. Bless Charles's misplaced loyalty to Mallory.

Riker looked back at the small gathering of men. Their heads turned in unison to watch the silver Mercedes drive down the street, turn the corner and roll to a stop on the opposite side of the square. When Charles had disappeared into the hotel, the men turned their attention back to the sheriff's office. They were joined by two more men.

Riker checked the bullets in his gun and debated calling

in the state troopers. What would he say? "There's a crowd of smiling good ol' boys gathering in the town square, and they scare the shit out of me." And then the state cops would ask what he was drinking.

"Excuse me, neighbor." A man his own age was standing in the office doorway. Flab hung over the belt of his jeans. His smile was wide; his eyes were dull and stupid. "My name's Ray Laurie." The man was walking toward him with one hand extended.

Under the cover of the desk, Riker shifted the gun to his left hand and offered Ray Laurie his right.

Ray pulled up a chair across the desk from Riker. A new visitor was standing in the doorway, and there was another man behind him. When Riker glanced back to the square, the sentries were moving toward the building. Underneath the desk, Riker was pointing a .38 automatic at Ray Laurie's midsection.

More men filed into the office. Riker counted eight of them, and now the gun in his hand became meaningless. They stood all about the room, and one of them moved to the window next to the desk. Another man used this distraction to move to the wall behind the desk. He listened to the heavy feet climbing the stairs to the lockup, and then running down again.

This man appeared at the door. Catching his breath, he looked to Ray Laurie. "The place is empty. Maybe she heard right and they did turn him loose."

Riker never heard Ray's end of that conversation. He was struck from behind. When his eyes opened again, he was on the floor. He drifted in and out of consciousness as he floated through the back door of the sheriff's office.

"I don't buy it. Idiots can't even write," said the man who held his legs to the man who held his arms. If there was more to this discussion, Riker didn't hear it.

Nap time.

•   •   •

THE BATS HAD flown from Trebec House in the sunset hour. Ira tracked them across all the sky he could see from the circle of trees around the cemetery. And then he turned back to the statue of Dr. Cass.

His mother had been wrong. This was the same old statue of Dr. Cass with Kathy in her arms, and she was standing right where she always did. But there were changes to deal with. There were wheel ruts and spills of gravel on the grass, and broken twigs on the low-hanging branches.

The birds were flying up from the trees, and the rush of wings created a breeze all around him.

"So you're the witness," said a voice behind him, only sound without real meaning. Alarmed, Ira turned to see a man striding down the gravel path between the tombs.

"So you're the witness," said Ira, not comprehending, only making the required response as he was backing up to the angel, pressing into the stone folds of her robe, looking there for sanctuary.

The man came closer, growing larger, his hands rising in closed fists. Ira slumped down to the grass. He drew in his arms and legs and tucked in his head like a turtle. The first blow was nothing to him, only an unwanted intimacy. Fistfalls rained harder, and soon the pain seeped in like the color red knifing into pure white paint, cutting a clean sharp edge into his brain.

He was being kicked now. All his fear had become a bright ball of fire, and now it was diminishing in its brightness, the light was going gray, going out. His face was wet. He had blood in his eyes.

He understood what was happening. Babe had yelled at him and swatted his head when he played a familiar handful of notes on the piano. And then Babe had broken his hands. But when the music had ended, the pain ended, too. And now he began to hum the notes that had played all the while Cass was dying.

This infuriated his assailant and the blows were heavier and faster, more vicious.

A strange intimacy, this.

And now Ira reached out to his attacker with the rest of the music. He had learned the entire song, and he crooned it now, his voice becoming horn and flute in an accompaniment to pain, a musical score for violence.

And when his song ended, and he lay quiet, not moving anymore, the violence stopped, just as Babe had stopped.

Ira had learned his lesson well.

EVEN WITH HIS eyes shut, Riker recognized the trappings of the Owltown bar where he had spent some time as a guest of the New Church, boozing with the faithful. He could feel the rough wood under his hands and his face. The night before last, he had listened to the same bad music on the jukebox. Now the song was slightly muffled, and he knew there was a door between his prone body and the outer room. The stale smells of beer and sweat were not muted at all. He kept his eyes closed while he counted the voices in the air—three men.

"Wake up, Sunshine." This greeting was punctuated by the nudge of a boot in his rib cage.

Riker opened his eyes and focussed on the only window and a patch of dusky sky. He had been unconscious for at least five hours. This enforced rest was not such a bad trade for the small ache on the side of his head.

Two men sat at a small square table. Ray Laurie was standing over his body and cracking the seal on a bottle. "Mr. Riker needs a drink—a lot of drinks." He filled a shot glass with whiskey from the bottle as he spoke to the man with the rifle. And now Riker noticed his own .38

automatic in the hand of the second man. "Now don't let him nurse his shots. This shouldn't take all night."

Ray leaned down and handed the glass to Riker. "Just drink it."

"Sure, why not?" Riker pulled himself up to a sitting position and drank from the glass. "Not bad. Not bad at all." And he meant that. He looked around at his companions and smiled. "You know, this was always my big dream, being forced to drink good whiskey at gunpoint."

They all smiled back—no hard feelings here, no animosity whatever. He recognized the two men at the table. He had spent some time drinking with them on his last excursion to Owltown.

Ray Laurie was lining up the bottles on the table. "Just keep pouring till the job is done. 'Night, Riker."

When the door had closed on Ray, one of the remaining guards lifted the rifle barrel slightly. "Drink up, friend."

"That's a lot of liquor." Riker admired the labels, all beyond his means. What was served out front was watered-down swill, and he guessed these homeboys had never seen the undiluted article in this bar. The collection of bottles on the table must be Malcolm's private stock. "I don't think anybody'd notice that I wasn't drinking alone."

The two men looked at one another, and then at the virgin bottles.

"Go ahead," said Riker, pretending not to see the rifle barrel as he climbed into a chair at the table. "Would I rat on you guys?"

He slugged back the rest of the whiskey and threw the empty glass across the room. Suddenly a rifle and a gun were pointing his way, aiming at his head. Overlooking this blatant rudeness, Riker grabbed up the open bottle. "Let's get down to some serious drinking, boys." He put the bottle to his lips and tilted it back. Then he passed it to the man on his right, the one who was holding on to his .38.

The man accepted the bottle from force of habit, but now he looked to his friend across the table for further instruction.

The man with the rifle shrugged and said, "What the hell." And then it became a warmer, friendlier group drunk.

As the bottle was passed around the table, Riker wondered if these men knew they were dealing with a full-blown alcoholic, a professional drinker. He assessed the two men as lesser artists. After they had demolished two bottles, Riker began to slur his words, and he dribbled liquor from the corners of his mouth. He considered falling out of his chair, but dismissed the idea as overacting.

MALLORY'S SHOULDER WAS stiff and sore as she raised herself to lift the shade of the bedside window. The sun had gone down and all the plants she could see were the mute green of the twilight hour.

She had lost a day, a whole damn day. How could that be?

The yellow cat was sitting at the edge of the bed, hissing. Mallory was slow to grab her pillow, giving away her intentions. The cat emitted a low growl. She tossed her pillow at the animal, missing it by a good two feet.

Not possible! How could she have missed such an easy target?

And now the cat came stealing back, perhaps sensing weakness in a slow reaction time, a foggy brain at work, and best of all, a bad aim.

Mallory threw back the covers with the certain knowledge that she had been drugged and that her next target would be Augusta.

She had pulled her jeans over the nightshirt before the cat crawled out from under the mangled sheets.

She found Augusta in the kitchen, stacking plates and bowls in the dishwasher. Charles sat at the table, poring over a sketchbook, his empty plate pushed to one side.

"Well, hello," he said.

But Mallory only had eyes for Augusta. She glared at the old woman, the herb queen, her personal enemy of the hour. She had already forgotten how much she hated the cat.

"Well, my, don't you look rested," said Augusta, well armored against glares of all kinds.

The message in Mallory's eyes was unmistakable. *I'll get you for that.*

Unimpressed, Augusta turned back to the more pressing business of stirring a large pot on the stove. "Now you go sit down and I'll heat up your dinner."

Mallory was thinking it might be a comfort to break something—or someone. She looked at Charles, but he had done nothing to make her angry. She pulled up a chair at the table. "Where's Riker?"

"Holding down the fort at the sheriff's office," said Charles. "The sheriff and the deputy are taking Jimmy Simms to New Orleans."

"That's smart," she said. "But what are you doing here? Why is Riker by himself?"

Charles shrugged. "He told me to leave. I think he wanted to get caught up on his sleep. He thought I might be more useful here."

"Doing what?"

Charles had no answer for that, but she could guess that this was a baby-sitting detail. And she knew Riker was not sleeping. If he had been planning to close his eyes even for an hour, he would have kept Charles around to wake him in case of trouble.

Augusta put a bowl of aromatic rice and meat on the table in front of her. Mallory looked down at it with deep suspicion.

"Did you want me to taste it first?" Augusta laughed, as she sat down to join them. She poured herself a cup of coffee from the pot on the table and grinned very wide, the better to frustrate the younger woman.

Mallory ignored her and looked out the window. Not dark enough yet to give her cover. "I want the car keys."

"The car isn't here," said Charles. "Riker told me to park it outside of Betty's and leave by her back door.

Thought it would be best if no one followed me back here.''

That didn't sound like Riker. He was too laid back to be that neurotic about security. ''So there was a leak?''

''Well, not a big one,'' said Charles. ''Jane might have overheard something, but nothing important.''

''That's the worst possible case,'' said Augusta. ''She'll make up what she doesn't know. So the word is out. Count on it.''

Then why would Riker get rid of Charles? ''Tell me what was going on right before you left him.''

''Nothing. It was very quiet. The phone didn't even ring the whole time I was there. So it's over.''

The hell it was. But Charles believed it. He wasn't holding out; he didn't know anything. Mallory turned to Augusta. ''Did Riker know you drugged me?''

Augusta's smile said it all. So Riker had not sent Charles back as a baby-sitter. Why then?

''The only mystery left is what happened to your mother's body,'' said Charles. He was speaking to Mallory but looking at Augusta. ''That must have driven the mob crazy, not knowing where the body was.''

Mallory nodded, though her mind was elsewhere, fighting back the fog of too much sleep.

''I thought the mob made off with the body.'' Augusta pushed the bowl closer to Mallory's hand. ''It's safe. Trust me.''

Yeah, right.

Augusta read her mind and laughed out loud. But Charles was not even smiling. Something was definitely wrong. What was going on here? And what did Riker—

Charles touched her arm to get her attention. ''Is that the way you see it, Mallory? The mob took the body away?''

''No.'' Mallory shook her head and decided to risk a cup of coffee—Augusta's cup. The old woman gave it up with no protest. ''That would only make sense if there was some attempt to cover up the crime, and there wasn't. All the evidence of a murder was lying around in plain sight.''

She was more curious about Riker than her mother's missing body. When she looked up, Augusta had vanished and Charles was walking out of the kitchen.

Mallory looked into the pot on the stove. It held enough food for several meals. The old woman was obviously cooking in bulk. So she wouldn't have tampered with the whole pot. Mallory bent over the garbage disposal, scraping her plate of Augusta's serving. She picked up the pot ladle.

Something was wrong.

Her head was clearing now. She dropped the ladle into the pot and walked back to the other room where Augusta kept her telephone. The door at the top of the stairs was just closing behind Charles.

The yellow cat circled around her as she dialed the number for the sheriff's office. She listened for four rings.

Riker, pick up the phone.

The cat jumped up on the table and sent the telephone crashing to the floor. Mallory and the cat stared at one another. The receiver in her hand was dead, and its frayed, broken wire dangled to the floor. The cat vanished. Very wise.

CHARLES TRAILED AUGUSTA through the rooms of the house and up the stairs to the top floor. The bats had flown, and there were no malingerers in sight when he passed through the midsection of the attic, holding his nose and guided by the electric light from the room behind him. More light streamed through the cracks in the wall ahead. He passed through the door to the last segment of the attic, where she kept her telescope. A cool breeze was rushing through the holes in the roof, and the air was almost fresh.

A bat lay in a cardboard box stuffed with shreds of newspaper. One wing was extended and sporting a large bandage. Augusta was kneeling on the floor, lifting the creature in her hands, and now Charles saw the red metal band that marked this animal as the old man of the colony. Augusta unwound the gauze covering most of the wing. The bat

screeched, and she paused to feed him liquid from an eye-
dropper. He went limp, and she worked over the exposed
wound with no further distractions.

Augusta could not help but be aware of him standing
only a few feet away, yet she didn't look up. The silence
was stringing out like a taut wire. How to begin?

"It must have driven them crazy, not knowing where the
body was."

"You're repeating yourself, Charles." She kept her eyes
on the delicate membrane of the bat wing.

He sat down in the dust beside her. "They could never
be sure Cass was dead. They'd never feel safe. And a missing corpse would keep the mystery alive."

Augusta nodded. "Everybody loves a good mystery. It's
been a boon to the tourist trade. So you figure Betty Hale
stole the body? She does have a good head for business."

Charles was silent until she met his eyes. "Don't you
think it would comfort Mallory to know where her mother
was buried?"

"No, Charles, I don't. She's a wonderfully compact creature. Not an ounce of sentiment to carry around with her
and weigh her down. It's enough for her to know that her
mother is dead. I'm sure she does know that much. Kathy
would never have left Cass while the woman was still
breathing."

She ran one light finger across the mending tear in the
wing.

"And you're not at all curious about the body, Augusta?"

"No." She basted the wound with the foul-smelling contents of a small dark bottle.

"Because you know where it is. Finger Bayou literally
points to her grave, doesn't it? Is that why you became the
executrix? So you could stop the herbicide on the water
along her property line? When the water hyacinth ran wild,
it choked off the bayou and made it impassable by boat.
And then you planted trees on the road to Trebec House to

discourage visitors. Betty does have a way of whipping up the tourists' curiosity.''

"It's an interesting theory. I guess I've heard worse logic over the years." She layered fresh gauze on the wound and set the bat back in the box.

"It's your style, Augusta. You watched Cass Shelley grow up in that house—and then Kathy. And then when you saw what had been done to that woman, ordinary justice wasn't good enough, was it? Not for an artist like yourself. What an original revenge.''

"And when did I have time to do all of this? Henry was the one who found the body.''

"He reported the murder on the following day. You had all night to dispose of her body.''

"I never heard that mob, and that's the truth.''

He believed that much. "The mob never made any noise, but you can hear a dog howl in pain from quite a distance. You would have wondered about that howling. You would have seen the dog from this window and gone to help him. You'd do anything for a wounded animal.'' The cat gave away her character. It was a natural enemy of her precious birds, yet she had saved the creature. And now she was working over a bat she had once characterized as owl food.

"You're talking through your hat, Charles.''

"As Mallory said, all the evidence of the murder was lying around in plain sight. No one had attempted to hide the crime. But the sheriff told me the back stairs had been cleaned. I don't believe Mallory knows about that. If she did, she would have put it together before I did. You took the body down those stairs, and then you erased your tracks—and the smaller tracks Kathy made when she ran from the house.''

"The sheriff was all over my land, poking and digging.'' She gently prodded the bat with one finger until the animal was roused from his herbal sleep. "Tom even dragged Finger Bayou. It was a damn thorough job.''

"You put Cass's body in a temporary hiding place. Later, you had all the time in the world to bury her in ground he'd already covered. She's probably lying under something heavy enough to keep a corpse from rising—say, a pile of rocks. You were standing on a pile of rocks on the day you fed the alligator."

"You have a flair for spinning stories, Charles."

"I wonder if the sheriff could do anything with my guesswork. I think he might go to a lot of trouble to find out where Cass Shelley is."

"If you start spreading that story of yours, you'll cause Mallory more grief than you know."

Oh, very good shot, Augusta. She knew the pressure points.

"That's Cass Shelley's grave at the tip of Finger Bayou, isn't it?"

She was grinning gloriously, unintimidated, unafraid. Might she be laughing at him? And now it crossed his troubled mind that Riker was right, he'd been altered somehow—blinded. Here he was, virtually threatening Augusta, who had done him no wrong. Quite the opposite, she only had helped him, and then she had trusted him with the secret of the alligator.

Her smile was more subdued now, and he could see that she was already forgiving him.

"Charles, I know you wouldn't do anything to hurt Mallory. So I know you'll keep all this wild speculation to yourself—and without ever knowing why. It'll drive you crazy at first, but everybody needs a little mystery in their lives." She tilted her head to one side as she studied his face. "I'd say you need it more than most."

IT WAS DARK when Mallory left the house. The birds were louder than usual, when they should have been settling down for the night. And it was well past time for Augusta to put the horse in his stall. But there he was, racing back and forth in the paddock, rearing up on his hind legs.

The long black duster whipped around her boots as she walked down the oak lane. What was spooking the animals? Her eyes scanned everything in view, hunting for the thing out of place. She used the mini cell phone to call the sheriff's office again. No answer. She was on the path leading into the cemetery when she heard the woman.

Mallory was through the skirt of trees, following the sound of crying. Her gun was drawn as she slowly cleared the ground, stopping at each small side street of tombs, watching for movement, then moving on.

She found Darlene Wooley kneeling near the south rim, leaning over Ira's body and cradling his bloody head in her arms. Ira allowed it. He was past his fear of the human touch, but not yet dead.

"So you're the witness," said Ira, as Mallory bent over him, scanning the blood, and wondering how much real damage had been done to him.

Darlene looked up at her. "He was late for dinner. I came to get him for—"

"So you're the witness," Ira said again.

Mallory pulled her palm computer and its electronic bundle from the deep pocket of her duster. She detached the mini cell phone from the battery pack and dialed the emergency number. When the dispatcher answered, she handed the phone to Darlene. "Just tell them you need an ambulance."

Darlene nodded, and Mallory set to work on Ira's wounds. He had all the signs of a deadly beating; most of the damage would be internal. She wiped away the blood from his mouth. No broken teeth, but there was a bad head wound, and one arm was broken. "Everything will be all right, Ira." She walked to the oldest tree and gripped a dry branch, cracking it straight down and pulling it from the tree. Now she tore a cable from her battery pack and wound it around his arm, binding it to the branch to keep him from moving it and causing more damage.

Ira stared at her quietly, his eyes large and full of trust.

She smiled down at her old playmate, humming the music she remembered from their brief childhood. He began to sing as Mallory ripped off a section of his torn red shirt and his mother cried into the telephone.

After a few minutes, Darlene put her hand over the mini-phone and spoke to Mallory. "They're out on a call—all of them, ambulances, fire trucks. One of the chemical plants went up in a ball of fire and torched a cane field. The dispatcher is patching me into the sheriff's car."

"Don't mention my name." Mallory wound a bloody strip of Ira's shirt around the bloody head wound. She couldn't smell any smoke. The fire must be miles down the road.

Now Darlene broke the connection and closed her hand over the tiny phone. "The sheriff is pulling off the highway. He'll be here in a few minutes."

Mallory checked Ira's pupils. He was holding his own. Darlene was not doing so well by half.

In her own strange way of offering comfort, Mallory said, "I know who did this. I'll kill him for you, okay?"

Darlene was shaking her head in confusion. "No, Kathy." She was talking in the mother tone now. "Cass wouldn't want that, and neither would I. It has to end, don't you see?" Her hand wound around Mallory's arm. "The damage can't just go on and on. All these years, all this damage."

Mallory gently pried loose Darlene's restraining fingers and stood up. As she was moving through the cemetery with slow deliberation, Darlene called out after her, "Kathy, don't kill anybody."

Mallory recognized the same worried intonation her own mother had once used to caution her not to touch a dead bird she had found in the yard. As she walked, she checked the chambers of her revolver, and ceased to hear Darlene.

She was on her way to Owltown.

AUGUSTA FIXED ONE eye to her telescope. Studying the wildlife? Charles thought not. "You aren't bird-watching, are you, Augusta?"

"Not at the moment, but I do find birds more interesting than people. Killer humans are definitely the more gentle species. Now you take the way Cass was killed—no passion. You should see the owls and hawks rip and tear the meat. But death is quick. If you blink, you miss it."

"I'm sure you manage to keep abreast of all the killing around here." What was she looking at?

"Oh, I don't know about that. I spend some of my time watching the stars. But there's a kind of violence out there too. This whole world is careening through space with a real wicked spin. I try to lay back and roll with it, and I recommend that to you."

But her telescope was not trained on the stars tonight. "I think you're a bit less passive than that. You don't just watch, do you? You're a player."

"You've been listening to stories, Charles." She smiled, but never took her eye from the telescope. "They're all true. I'm a murderess. Killed my own father."

"I wasn't thinking about that."

"Your friend Riker is in trouble. They're closing in on him."

Charles ripped the glass from her hand. Augusta patiently helped him refocus on the fairgrounds where the tent used to be. Now the most prominent thing on the field was a large truck with a long, flat bed strung with Christmas tree lights and the brighter spotlights perched on stalks of steel. At the center of the truck bed was a glass-domed coffin. It reminded him of a display case for a preserved insect.

Perhaps a hundred people milled and reeled around the truck waving bottles and paper cups. The women were laden with gaudy jewelry and they wore bright party dresses of shiny materials. Even some of the men wore sequins, and here and there was a costume more appropriate to a Mardi Gras parade than a funeral. A band of musicians stood off to one side and a stilt-walker moved among them with bright silver streamers in both hands.

In addition to the coffin, there was a chair on the truck bed. It was gold and elevated like a throne. Malcolm Laurie sat there, dressed in his suit of lights. He pointed toward the center of the crowd. The people stepped back to clear a wide circle, and there at its center, Riker stood alone, out of place in his drab gray suit.

CHAPTER
26

CHARLES'S SHOES HAD only hit on every third step in his descent, and now he ran the length of the hallway to Augusta's back room. He was lifting the antique telephone receiver when he saw the note lying on the table: "I'm going to the sheriff's office to check on Riker. *Stay where you are!*"

Her last phrase was so heavily underscored, Mallory was virtually shouting off the page.

He was examining the broken telephone cord when Augusta hurried past him on her way to a chest of drawers in the far corner.

"There's a pack of men coming over the bridge." She was ripping through the top drawer, and articles of intimate apparel were flying. "We got to leave, and fast." She pulled out a very small handgun and slammed the drawer. She held the weapon out to him. "It's only a single-shot forty-five, but better than nothing." She stuffed it into the pocket of her dress and ran from the room. The cat seemed to grasp the sense of it before Charles did, and now the creature was following its mistress.

Charles quit the room and ran down the hall, racing the

yellow cat. He closed the outer door on the animal, and it
began to growl, not frightened at all, but genuinely pissed
off.

"Let the cat out," commanded Augusta.

He opened the door and the cat sped past him. Charles
looked up at Augusta, astride the white horse and without
a saddle. She danced the stallion closer to the courting staircase. "They'll be at the cemetery by now. Get on or you're
a dead man."

"Wouldn't it be better to—"

"I know a lynch mob when I see one, Charles. Want to
live? Get on!"

Charles stepped on the second stair and swung one long
leg over the rear of the horse to mount behind Augusta.

"Hold on tight as you can!" she yelled. They galloped
across the wide grassy lawn.

He had not been on horseback since he was a child, and
then he had sat in a proper saddle. Now he felt that he
would fall in every passing second. The horse's massive
muscles were elongating and contracting as they flew over
the long grass, heading for the great earthen dike, pitch-
black against the sky.

He held Augusta by the waist and leaned into her neck
to yell, "We're going along the base of the levee, right?
Around the tip of Upland Bayou?"

"Can't," she called back to him, heading straight for the
great looming barrier. "Too many bad patches and wet
ones," she yelled into the wind. "The horse would lose his
legs in the dark before we even got to Henry's place."

"When will Henry be back?"

"Not till late. Wrap your legs tight and dig in with your
heels. We're going the way the horse knows best. He's been
this route a thousand times."

And now they were moving up the embankment. Skill-
fully she led the horse into a slanted approach to the road
atop the levee. Charles held on tight, knees and heels to the
horse's hide, arms wrapped around Augusta, and certain
that he would slide off as the horse faltered on the steep

slope of Bermuda grass. But the animal never lost its forward momentum, finding purchase in the worn areas of dirt
scumbling out beneath his hooves in a brown spray as he
climbed up to the stars. Now the horse was running full-
out across the levee road, along the top of the earth where
it met the sky.

Charles looked back to the mansion. A small army of
ants with pale white heads and hands emerged from the oak
alley and converged on Trebec House.

THE STILT-WALKER'S BAGGY pants obscured the glass-
domed coffin as he tottered back and forth alongside the
truck's flat bed. Every one of the hundred mourners was
dressed for a blowout party of free booze. A few men in
the crowd had disguised their eyes with bright costume
masks. Some wore feathers and capes. Gaudy colors
bobbed and weaved as the liquor flowed and spilled, and
cheap jewelry flashed in the beams of spotlights on tall
metal stands around the truck. But Malcolm's suit of lights
outglittered all of them. He had forsaken his throne to strad-
dle the coffin, riding it like a nightmare, waving one hand
in the air, hailing his subjects and laughing.

Only the Dixieland band was silent. The musicians stood
by the float, exchanging glances, shifting on their feet and
wanting to leave now. Clark Kinkaid, the trumpet player,
put up his horn and nodded to the others. They began to
back away from the truck. One of the Laurie brothers
stepped in the path of the man with the sax. Old Ray was
stern as any chain gang boss, and carrying a rifle.

The musicians thought better of leaving. A pretty woman
danced by with a full bottle for the band to pass around.
The drinking had been well under way for an hour, but the
funeral had yet to begin.

Clark cradled his trumpet in one arm and looked toward
the pile of gas-soaked rags wound on sticks. They should
have been lit long ago to signal the start of the torchlight
parade down the main street of Owltown. But the crema-

torium truck had arrived only to be sent away empty. Apparently, Malcolm had plans to expand the evening's entertainment.

Well, this was not part of the deal.

Clark had arranged another gig for his band, figuring this would be a done thing before eight. So when was the show gonna get on the road, and who was that old guy in the center of the loose ring of drunks? Men and women closed ranks to tighten the circle and block his view. Clark stepped onto the truck's bumper and hoisted himself up on the fender for a better look.

Every pair of eyes was trained on Malcolm Laurie as the man swung one sequined leg over the coffin, stood up and held out both his hands for silence. "This man, Riker." Malcolm had real anger in his voice as he pointed to the man in the gray suit. "This staggering drunk, this subhuman garbage, was found in the cemetery, naked from his waist to his ankles—standing over the idiot's dead body."

Obscenities and moans rose up all around the truck.

"Look at this man, so drunk he can hardly stand. His victim did not die easy. The boy was raped and beaten to death. Poor helpless idiot. It's like the rape of a child."

"You ought to know, Malcolm," yelled Riker, not the least bit inebriated. "Your brother raped Ira Wooley when the kid was only six years old. Does it run in the family? Is that where your expertise comes from?"

"Shut him up!"

A man stepped forward to put a fist in Riker's face and do just that. Riker fell to his knees. His lip was split open and blood ran into his mouth. Malcolm was livid. Something had gone wrong, and Clark wondered if it had anything to do with Riker's sobriety.

Malcolm waved his fist to the sky. "Three witnesses found him—"

"That's why Cass Shelley had to die!" Riker stood up. "She had the hospital reports. Babe raped Jimmy Simms, too. That's why he ran away when he was only twelve years old."

"Shut his lying mouth!"

But no one stepped forward this time, except Jimmy's father, Dan Simms, all rapt attention. Malcolm turned to his brother Ray, who nodded back his understanding and moved into the crowd to do the job right as Riker was saying, "She couldn't figure out how a six year old could contract a junkie hepatitis. Then she ran the test for syphilis. Remember Babe's syphilis party. He—"

Ray Laurie had both his hands on Riker's windpipe.

Dan Simms was a larger man and had no trouble clearing Ray's fat fingers from Riker's neck. Simms looked down at the shorter Ray Laurie and backed him off with only a rising fist. Simms turned to Malcolm. "This ain't the story you gave me, Mal. Now I want to hear this man out."

Malcolm strutted to the edge of the truck bed, shaking his head in pity, and pity was in his voice. "Dan, how can you listen to a man who was caught with his pants around his ankles assaulting that poor idiot?"

"But you said he was drunk too, and he don't seem all that tight to me," said Dan Simms. He turned to Riker. "Go on, mister."

"Cass had all the blood work," said Riker. "She matched up the stages of syphilis. Babe's was the oldest, then Jimmy's, then Ira's. That's what she was trying to tell you when she crashed that meeting. But Malcolm drove her off and covered it up."

"Lies, all lies!" said Malcolm.

"And what kind of lie did you tell Ira's father?" Riker was louder now. "I know he threw the first rock. You put it in his hand, didn't you?"

Ray Laurie was standing behind Jimmy Simms's father, saying, "Now Dan, you know that's a lie. Malcolm was gone before the first stone flew."

Simms turned to look up at Malcolm. "Well, how did he know Ira's father threw—"

It was done quickly with the butt end of a rifle, and Simms fell. A second blow sent Riker to his knees again.

Malcolm strutted across the truck bed passing in front of

the coffin. "He would tell any lie. He would spew any filth. All we know for certain is that Riker raped and killed that poor idiot. Maybe he was afraid we wouldn't turn him over to the sheriff. Maybe he thought we would be so outraged by what he had done, that we would pluck out his eyes and flay his skin and stone him to death. And I could not blame any man or woman for doing this." He pointed to the torches. "Take up these torches and shine the light on him. See this monster for what he is."

Riker staggered to his feet again. Malcolm pointed one finger at the musicians. "Play," he commanded them.

They stared at one another. "Play loud!" Malcolm screamed, and then Ray was there with his rifle leveled on the bandleader. Clark jumped down from the truck fender and lifted his horn with the rest of the band, and they began to play.

"Louder!" yelled Malcolm.

The band played, Riker screamed out in pain. Malcolm Laurie jumped down from the truck and walked away across the fairgrounds, heading for the lower bayou.

ALL THE LIGHTS of Owltown went out, followed by the strobes positioned around the truck. This was Charles's only clue that Mallory was not yet in the fray. He held fast to Augusta. She was not frail. Where he encircled her waist, the body was firm and well muscled. Her hair was flowing over him like a soft river, and to his left was the mighty Mississippi and the long sloping fall to night-black water. He could feel every pounding, jarring meeting of hoof and earth. They had cleared Upland Bayou and Dayborn township. The torch flames from Owltown were still match-size from this distance.

Augusta screamed, "We're going down now."

The horse was descending, flying down from the road, his massive heart pumping fast. The animal stumbled badly, and they were falling. Charles's stomach was rising, and his body was flooded with the chill of adrenaline. He watched the ground coming up to meet him as the horse went into a roll. Charles held Augusta closer, raised his knee and braced his foot on the horse's back to push off with one leg. Then he and Augusta were flying through the air, clear of the horse, which now lay screaming in the dirt, rolling the rest of the way.

Charles hit the ground on his back with Augusta on top of him. She was first to her feet. The horse was struggling to rise, and falling back in a fresh agony of screams with every attempt. The moon was brilliant. He could see the broken white bone shining through the skin and the blood of the horse's leg.

Charles moved toward Augusta and put his hand under her arm. She waved him off, scowling at him and pulling the derringer from her pocket. "Look out for your own damn self. Get on. I have to do this."

As he was turning toward the far edge of the fairgrounds, Augusta knelt by the horse, one hand on the muzzle, the barrel of the derringer behind an ear. Charles was on the run when he heard the gunshot. The screams ended. His steps faltered, and then he ran on toward the firelight of Owltown.

The first person he saw was Malcolm, walking away from the mob while the band played on.

Charles ran into the crowd. He had no difficulty forcing his way through the crush of smaller people. He found Riker at the center of the mob, lying on the ground amid a scattering of rocks. He covered Riker with his own body and absorbed the blow of a stone to his back, then another hit one leg. He did have the sense to tuck in his head. He had learned a great deal from turtles.

The mob parted long enough for Charles to see Augusta standing by the truck's rear wheel. By the light of a passing torch, he watched her feed a rag into the gas tank. The cloth darkened, soaking with gasoline. She looked up and caught the eye of the trumpet player. She struck a match and showed it to him. The musician dropped his jaw and nudged the sax man standing next to him, and then all five musicians fell back from the truck. Augusta touched her match to the rag and calmly lit a black cheroot as the flame traveled along the rag and into the tank.

Ray Laurie stood on the bed of the truck, overseeing the mob, while Augusta walked steadily into the enfolding darkness, and a Dixieland band ran across the deserted fairgrounds toward the parking lot.

The explosion rocked the ground. Charles felt the impact of the waves of energy exploding outward in a wide spray of flying bits of metal and flame, leaving a vacuum at the core of the blast. A roar of fire rushed back inward in a ball, then plumed up in a mushroom cloud of bright orange heat. Ray Laurie's body shot straight out from the truck, and spikes of flame licked him in flight to set his hair and clothes afire. The man stood up and screamed, as the horse had screamed. He ran into the crowd, and the people backed away from the human bonfire. Ray fell to earth and writhed at their feet. The crowd had grown deathly still. A wicked whiff hung in the air, and Charles was stunned to realize that burnt human flesh could initiate hunger.

So this was hell.

While the crowd was in thrall to the spectacle of Ray Laurie burning to death, Charles was on his knees, pulling one of Riker's limp arms around his neck. He was rising to a stand with one arm circled around the man's waist, and now he dragged Riker's unconscious body along with him. The toes of Riker's shoes made ruts in the dirt behind them, and their progress was slow.

Ray Laurie had ceased to scream, to flail, even to twitch. The crowd turned its attention back on Charles and his heavy burden. He could feel their eyes on him, the heat of the flames at his back, and the tension growing with the sound of slow shuffles as a hundred pairs of feet were set into motion.

Though there was nothing spoken, no signal, they moved in unison, walking toward him, fanning out to form the next stoning ring. One by one, a head bowed down, low to the earth, and a hand shot out to snatch up a rock.

Charles braced himself for the next blow. He was preparing to lower Riker to the ground, to lie across his friend's body and give him cover.

"Look there!" A woman standing at the fringe of the crowd was pointing to the other end of Owltown's main road flanked by darkened shabby storefronts.

Only one streetlamp was lit. Standing in the pool of light was a lone figure wearing boots and a horseman's duster. The face was shaded by the brim of a black hat.

CHAPTER

TOM JESSOP STOOD by the nurses' station in the hospital corridor, holding Ira in his arms. Other cases were rolling by on gurneys, each one an entourage of emergency personnel. Darlene was crying, the public address system was issuing orders, and the harried triage nurse was looking down at Ira's swollen, bloody face as she checked his pulse and pulled back the lid of one eye.

"I'm sorry, Sheriff. We're stacking up critical cases in the halls. It'll be a while before a doctor can see him. The chemical burns are first priority."

He knew what she really meant. The boy's breathing was a ragged whistle, and his color was edging toward a blue pallor. He had seen this before in the aftermath of road accidents. Ira was dying, and the nurse was more interested in the patients who might be saved.

She hurried off to examine the next victim coming through the emergency entrance. The new arrival had bubbly skin and blood-soaked clothes. Half of the woman's long dark hair had been burned away. The sheriff watched the nurse shake her head over this patient too, condemning an unconscious woman to die alone by the wall where the gurney was pushed.

Well, he had not broken the sound barrier getting Ira to the hospital in thirteen minutes flat just to lose him in the waiting line for a doctor. He turned to Lilith. "Get me one of those little bastards with a stethoscope. I don't care how you do it."

The sheriff laid his burden down on the long counter of the nurses' station. All around him was a desperate energy of noise and motion, blood passing by in plastic bags on metal carts, and more blood on the people wheeling down the hall on the way to the operating rooms at the far end.

Darlene hovered over her son, her head very close to his. She was listening for breath, ready to breathe for Ira if he should stop.

The sheriff looked up to see Lilith walking down the hall with a stalking gait, and he could guess where she was heading. Her father could go directly to that place in the trout stream where the fish gathered to exchange secret handshakes and plan strategies to outwit fishermen, and Guy never came home without a trophy. Apparently, his daughter knew the source pool of doctors.

A door swung open and he could see the cloud of cigarette smoke, the vending machines and furniture a damn sight more comfortable than the plastic junk in the lobby. Lilith was smiling as she snagged a doctor on his way out.

The man was angry at first, but then he smiled, openly appraising the young woman in front of him, taking inventory of her parts and pausing awhile at her breasts, as if he had the right. She leaned in tight to whisper something in the man's ear. Tom Jessop was certain the doctor meant to cover his balls with one hand, but the motion was aborted as Lilith grabbed his arm and propelled him down the hall.

The sheriff smiled at his deputy and mouthed the words "Nice catch."

The doctor leaned over Ira, and assessed the damage. "Definitely a collapsed lung. I need a nurse and an OR, but—"

"You got it, Doc," said Lilith, slipping away down the hall in search of a nurse to terrify and an operating room she might commandeer.

While Ira was being prepped for surgery, the sheriff was leading Darlene to the waiting room, another kind of bedlam, voices rising in hysteria and tears, shouts and laments for the dead and near-dead. He settled her in the only empty chair. She had been crying softly all this time, but now the fingers of one hand slowly opened, and she was staring down at a tiny cell phone in her hand. Her head snapped up with some new anxiety.

"Kathy," she said.

And now Darlene had his complete attention.

"Kathy's gone to Owltown." She gripped his arm tightly. "I know she means to kill somebody."

"I might be able to give her a hand with that." Before Darlene could say any more, he was striding across the lobby. He pushed through the glass door, and crossed the driveway to his car. As he was pulling out of the parking lot, the passenger door flew open and Deputy Beaudare piled into the front seat.

THE COFFIN HAD been thrown clear in the blast. It lay cracked open in the dirt just short of the paved road. The glass dome had shattered to tumble the corpse of Babe Laurie onto the ground. Flames from the truck had reached across nine feet of strewn rubble to find him. The suit caught fire and Babe's face was passive as the flames lapped at his head and ate the mortician's wax from the cracks of his broken skull.

But the mob was oblivious to Babe. They were all staring down the dark road where only one streetlamp was lit. It went out. Farther down the street, another lamp switched on, and there was Mallory again. And so she moved toward them, in and out of the dark. The last lamp at the foot of the road went on, but the pool of light was empty. Yet the crowd was riveted, staring at it, waiting for her.

But she was already among them, passing through their ranks while they were looking for her in the light.

Mallory stepped out from the thick of the crowd, and stood at the rim of the stoning circle. The men closest to her backed away as she lifted the side of the duster and swept it back over the holstered gun riding low on her hip. Unhurried, almost casual, she walked toward Riker's unsupported right side. She flung one of the unconscious man's arms over her shoulder and encircled his waist.

Mallory was facing the road ahead as she spoke to Charles. "Go forward, don't stop for anything." Her free hand gripped the gun in its holster.

Four men moved into the road in front of them. All held rocks in their hands. One greedy man held three, and this one stepped forward, grinning as he bent his arm back to throw his first rock.

Her gun cleared the holster.

The man had heard the bang of the bullet that ripped open his thigh, and he had seen the flash of the gun, but now he only stood there looking down at his ruined leg and wondering if these events might be connected. And then the commonsensical laws of gravity and insupportable limbs kicked in. He fell to the ground and dragged himself off, crying, still shaking his head in disbelief. The crowd parted to let him pass, but showed no signs of helping him and no fear of the gun in her hand.

Slowly, Charles and Mallory walked forward, dragging Riker's body between them. The mob was not so concentrated now. They had spread out, walking on either side of them. A woman in a red satin dress screamed obscenities at Mallory and tossed a bottle. It missed Mallory by three feet, but she drew her gun on the woman and fired. The woman looked down on the black hole in the sleeve of her dress, and her face waffled between outrage and confusion.

Of course she would be astonished. A moment ago, this woman had been invincible. But now she was a naked target in a red dress.

Mallory raised the gun again, and the wounded woman ran screaming between the gray buildings.

They walked forward into the lull. One teenager ran in front of them, and the next missile was a brick. It hit Charles's shoe, glancing off and doing no real damage, but Mallory drew on the assailant. Though he could only be fourteen or fifteen years old, the boy understood immediately that his tender age was not going to shield him, that when she leveled her gun at his head, she meant to kill him. He melted back behind the adults on the sidewalk. In the bar behind the boy, a wide front window broke in an outward burst of flames and flying glass. The crowd rippled in jerks and starts.

"They don't have a leader," said Mallory. "They'll take their cues from us. Stay cool, Charles."

Oh, right.

A small barrel-chested man appeared in front of them, and his rock hit Mallory in the shoulder. Retribution was swift. She leveled her gun and fired it as the man was running away. The little man fell, screaming and clutching his side where the blood was spurting between his fingers. Another rock came from behind a car. She put her next bullet through the vehicle's window. An anguished man stumbled away from the car, one hand to his shoulder where the red stain of blood was spreading down the front of his shirt.

She fired another round into the crowd, at random this time, and then another shot.

Now they all stopped, beginning to sense their individual mortality in this strange lottery of bullets. She only had to raise her gun this time, and more of them fell away. By Charles's count, her six-shooter should be out of bullets now. There were only stragglers hanging on the fringe, but at least twenty of them.

A rock hit Mallory between the shoulder blades. She turned and took aim at the man who had thrown it. He put out his hands as though this might stop a bullet, and then he faded back into the heat of the growing fire.

"Charles, take Riker's weight for a second and don't

stop moving." She swung out the speedloader from her belt and jammed the bullets into the free chambers of her gun. Then she picked up her share of Riker's weight again.

Charles felt the heat at his back, and his head was turning when she said, "Don't look. The buildings are burning. There's nothing else to see."

Ah, but there was, and only Charles could see it. He looked over the heads of the crowd to follow the quick lean figure with flowing white hair moving away from the most recent fire and on to another building. Augusta was carrying a gas can and a bottle with a rag stuffed in its mouth.

Another rock flew to Mallory, hitting her in the leg. Cheers came up from the crowd, hurrays for a strike. She raised her gun and fired into the clot of men on the sidewalk. One of them screamed and the rest moved away from this victim, as if bullets might be contagious. Mallory was still looking that way when Charles saw another arm rise to hurl a rock in their direction. But now this man was himself hit in the head with a rock. A light laughter was heard in the dark. The tone was young, sweet and high, but Charles knew it was Augusta.

Two rats crossed the porch of a near building, running in advance of the black smoke hugging the boards as it crawled forward. But then, the smoke sipped back under the doorsill, as though the wood structure had inhaled it. In the next second, two front windows blasted outward in a hot spray of fire and glass shards. Rolling waves of flame quickly covered the outer wall.

The fire might have been Augusta's pet when it started, but now it went where it wanted to, spreading to the roof. A tongue of flame licked straight up in the air. He could feel the heat on his face, and his eyes stung. The wind washed over him and carried the smoke back toward the lower bayou. The acrid stench remained. The fire roared.

It was feeding.

"Don't be afraid." Mallory spoke in an easy conversational tone. "There's no point in it anymore."

He understood. He had given himself up for dead the

moment he had lain down to cover Riker's body. Mallory had given him all these remaining minutes of life—a gift she bought at great cost. And he had bought nothing for her. But while he understood that fear was pointless and almost ungrateful, his heart was racing. His body was still afraid and pounding out adrenaline.

Two young men stood close to the burning building, passing a whiskey bottle between them and laughing at the fire. They didn't realize it was alive and hungry.

Charles knew; he could hear it eating things.

A flame stabbed straight out and ran its tongue around one man's head, searing his flesh and setting his hair afire. They ran away together, one man madly slapping the head of the other, batting out the flames. The burning man screamed, yet he would not let go of the whiskey bottle in his hand.

For the rest, they hardly noticed the fire. They were drunk on liquor and drunk on the moment, reeling and cursing alongside Charles and Mallory, all moving inexorably along the road.

Mallory's gun banged off a shot and cast a wider protective circle around Charles and Riker. The crowd hovered at the edge of this unseen line and came no closer, menacing only with raised fists and their mouths twisting in ugly shapes. The mob screamed, the fire roared. Mallory's gun shattered the night and scattered them again.

But they came back, the mob and fresh fire. Another building bloomed with yellow flames as they passed it. Charles looked back over his shoulder. The blaze was beautiful, dazzling. A bottle hit the side of his head, but he hardly felt the blow. He was exhilarated; he was scared out of his mind.

A man's shirt caught fire and he rolled in the dirt alone, left behind by the wall of people who moved with them up the Owltown road. The liquor bottles in all the bars were bursting glass bombs. But Mallory made the biggest noise of all, her gun exploding with authority.

Charles watched two large boys, nearly man size,

perched on the rail of a porch, keeping to the shadows, dark as crows and watching, waiting, moving their lips in unison. And now Charles realized they were counting off her shots.

The next rock fell short of the mark. Mallory fired an empty gun. They were almost at the end of the road when the bird boys flew from the porch rail and ran forward with rocks in their hands.

"On your right," said Charles.

She watched them for a moment and then threw the gun at the boy in the lead, clipping his head and drawing blood. The other boy stopped for a moment to look at his friend, who was sinking to the ground, blood dripping on his shirt from the head wound.

"Take Riker," she snapped, "and keep going." Mallory went after the boy who was still standing and holding a rock in his hand. She grabbed one of his arms and broke it over her raised leg. Charles heard the bone snap. She walked away from the boy, and left him screaming as they continued to walk, shouldering Riker between them, facing forward, both tall and taking long strides, matched horses in tandem. Charles had never felt so perfectly in tune with Mallory.

The flames were all around them now. The older men were gone, faded away in the heat. And now the younger men and a scattering of women drifted back to the edge of the road. And last, the boys, with their violent eyes and hairless bodies, took flight and entered one of the buildings.

A gunshot rang out from the upper window. Mallory talked to him across Riker's body. "Most people can't shoot worth a damn. These bastards couldn't hit a moving target to save their lives."

"I thought these people were all issued hunting rifles at birth." Charles looked up to see the long metal barrel protruding from the window on the second floor.

Another shot kicked up the dust in front of them. "Well, that's an improvement," said Mallory, in a cool critique of the shooter.

Charles caught the flight of a bottle with a fiery rag in its neck sailing through the window next to the shooter's. The interior was lit up with a burst of flames. And there were no more shots from the upper floor. He looked around for Augusta, but she was nowhere in sight.

They walked steadily, never slowing the pace. People were walking along with them but keeping their distance. He wondered why. Mallory had no weapon now.

"They don't know what to do," said Mallory. "They're pure reaction. Don't look at them."

Finally, they were at the top of the paved road, within steps of the dirt path that led through the windbreak of trees and into Dayborn, where electric lights were burning instead of torches and buildings. The energy of the mob had petered out to nothing, to wandering figures without direction.

Charles looked to Mallory and Riker. They might survive this after all.

Ah, but now a man stepped into the street, flanked by two teenage boys. Malcolm's suit of lights sparked with a million independent fires. He was holding a rifle in his arms. Two more men joined them. One carried a baseball bat, and the other man held a rock in each hand.

THE SHERIFF KEPT his eyes to the road ahead. The headlights of the car picked out the details of trees and shrubs along the way, but the moon had gone into the clouds, and everything beyond the scope of the beams was utter darkness. At the turn for the road to Owltown, he saw the flames and stopped the car, yelling, "Get out!" Lilith opened her mouth to speak.

He was faster, saying, "This is my personal business, Lilith. It may not be all that legal. Now you don't want to spend your vacation days in court, do you? Witnessing against me?"

And though he did not believe he would live to face Guy Beaudare with the tragic news of Lilith's death, he could imagine the man's pain at losing his only child. All too well, he remembered the agony of losing young Kathy Shelley.

Lilith would have a long life ahead of her, time enough to recover from this insult.

He could see she was gathering a few well-picked angry words, but before she could spit out more than "You can't—" he reached past her, opened the door and pushed her out on the road. As he sped off, he watched her in the rearview mirror as she stood up, dusted herself off and stared after his taillights disappearing down the road.

RIKER'S HEAD WOUND continued to bleed and this was the only clue that the man was still alive.

Malcolm raised the rifle. He was pointing it at Charles's face.

Riker's body hung limp as dead weight, and perhaps it was a mercy that he was unaware of what was about to happen. Charles listened to the crackle of fire and looked at the angry faces surrounding him. They were all stealing back.

He turned to Mallory. Her face shone in the firelight, and he found some comfort there. Death was surely coming, but he was beyond being frightened anymore. This tiny fragment of a day, standing on a patch of dirt at the end of the gauntlet with Mallory, this was sublime. It was the peak experience of his entire life—only one exquisite moment left.

He wondered what Mallory would do to wreck it for him—that *was* her nature.

"If you move, Charles, even a hair," said Malcolm, "I'll kill you."

And Charles supposed it was good logic to take out the largest target first, but foolish to underestimate Mallory as the lesser threat. He neglected to enlighten Malcolm, for he had finally come up with a last-minute gift for Mallory. His death might buy her seconds of diversion to run, to live.

"Malcolm, you're a real moron," said Mallory, dripping with contempt. "A rank idiot."

Charles thought this might not be the time for common name-calling. Possibly a more elegant line from—

"I understand the town idiot died," said Malcolm, smiling behind the rifle sight.

She shook her head in mock wonder. "You keep making the same mistake, Malcolm. You always leave the scene before the job is done. Ira's still alive. Screwed up again, didn't you?"

Malcolm lowered the gun, but only a little. Charles was still in the rifle sight.

"Another loose end to lead the sheriff to three more murders." Her voice was taunting, and now she had a larger audience, as more people came closer, pressing around them.

"Shut up," said Malcolm, turning the gun on her now. "Just shut up!"

Of course, this was *his* audience and he couldn't afford to lose them to a better act, not now.

"Yeah, like you're going to do your own killing for a change." Mallory seemed almost bored. "According to the witness, you walked away from my mother's house before the stoning. You let your brothers do the job. Now you might have gotten away with that murder—if it had gone to trial."

The spinning red light of the sheriff's car was barreling down the road from the highway, the siren screaming with urgency. It turned onto the Owltown road at its base and rolled toward them through the streets of flames.

"Get him!" Malcolm screamed.

The crowd moved into the road as the car was slowing. It stopped dead in the morass of arms and legs as bodies crawled over the vehicle like insects. The door was opened and the sheriff was dragged from behind the wheel. Charles saw the blood on one side of the man's head as the mob lowered him to the ground in front of Malcolm.

The sheriff's hand was slowly moving to the weapon in

his holster. A shout came out of the mob, and Malcolm turned to point the rifle at Jessop while a young boy relieved the man of his pistol.

"I called in for backup," said the sheriff. "This time, the law will be here before you can run. Give it up, Malcolm."

"I don't think so." Malcolm shook his head. "I don't hear any more sirens, Tom."

The boy who held the sheriff's gun kept his eyes on Malcolm, not quite sure of what was happening, so excited he could not stand still but danced his feet in the dirt.

Charles watched the flaming debris from a bar land on the roof of a store and spread along the shingles. Near the neighboring building, a barrel was in flames. Bright sparks flew over the roofs of other structures. A woman batted live cinders from her hair, and another woman brushed them from her skirts.

"This is the story," said Malcolm, nodding in Mallory's direction, but not taking his eyes off the sheriff. "She shot up all these innocent citizens in a wild killing spree, and she had to be put down like a dog. You died in the line of duty, Tom. I hope that's a comfort."

He lowered the rifle and pointed one finger at the young man with the sheriff's gun. "Shoot him, Teddy!"

"Don't do it, Teddy," said Mallory to the boy. There was so much authority in her command that the boy lowered the sheriff's gun and stared at her.

"Malcolm has a gun," she said, speaking only to the boy. "Don't you wonder why he doesn't do his own killing?" She turned to Malcolm. "Why let a kid take the fall? Do it yourself."

Charles thought this was not her best idea.

Malcolm glared at the boy with the gun. "Kill him *now!*"

The boy dropped the gun and ran. Malcolm raised the barrel of the rifle. "All right, I *will* do it myself."

"No you don't!" screamed a woman's voice.

Every head turned to stare up at the deputy standing on

the roof of the sheriff's car. Lilith's face was shining with sweat, her chest was heaving and her gun was pointing at Malcolm's head.

"Kill him!" yelled Mallory.

The crowd was silent, watching, waiting.

Malcolm's face was grim, eyes locked on his target, the sheriff. "Put the gun down, Deputy, or I'll shoot your boss right now." He risked a glance at the woman with the gun. "Put it *down*! Now! Do what I—"

Lilith let a bullet fly through Malcolm Laurie's forehead. Bone fragments scattered, and blood sprayed from the hole. There was time for him to register surprise, but only just. An accident of perfect balance kept the body standing for another moment, but he was dead before he toppled forward and hit the ground.

And now they heard the sirens.

A convoy of police cars roared down the road from the highway, perhaps twenty pairs of lights shining in the night. The remains of the crowd scattered, fleeing the brightness of burning Owltown.

Lilith Beaudare climbed down from the roof of the car. She was stiff in her movements. Her body had lost its fluid grace as she walked toward Malcolm's corpse with slow, halting steps. She stopped to look down at her gun, as though surprised to see it there and wondering who that killing hand might belong to.

Mallory had to call Lilith's name twice to break her trance, and now they stared at one another. The spinning lights of the sheriff's car turned their faces bloodred with every revolution. Glowing cinders swirled above them and came back to the earth in a brilliant rain of slow-falling stars.

CHAPTER
28

"BEST TO TAKE him in the car," said the sheriff. "That damn chemical plant is still pumping out casualties. We'll be here all night waiting on an ambulance."

"No problem with that." The young state trooper closed his first-aid kit and looked down at his patient. "He'll be fine in the car. It looks a lot worse than it is."

But Charles did not believe Riker could look much worse than this without being dead. Every rib had been taped, one arm rested in a makeshift splint, and a good portion of the man's face was swaddled in heavy bandages.

The trooper helped them settle Riker into the back of the sheriff's car beside Mallory. She covered him with a blanket, tucking him in like a child. He was semiconscious, opening and closing his eyes.

The police officer leaned down to the open window on Mallory's side. "I called this in to the hospital. Detective Riker's got top priority in the emergency room. If they jerk you around and make you wait for that X ray, you got a two-car escort of cops to back you up, okay?"

"Thanks," said Mallory, as if she might actually need help.

When they were alone, with Riker dozing between them, Charles said, almost incidentally, "Did you notice that Augusta was burning Owltown?"

"She's cleaning," said Mallory.

"Pardon?"

"It's her land now. She can do what she likes with it."

"You mean Augusta is the one who bought out the New Church land holdings?"

Mallory nodded, as she pulled the blanket up around Riker's face. "She owns the commercial section and all the waterfront property. She wants to redevelop it as an owl habitat." She turned to the rear window. "Ah, look at that." Behind them, another building burst into flames. "Another eviction notice."

He saw Augusta's slender silhouette moving away from the flames as the sheriff and his deputy climbed into the front seat. The car was rolling past the smoking remnants of Owltown. Charles leaned closer to Mallory. "But shouldn't we at least speak to her about—"

"There's not much left, Charles, just that one building." She pointed to the last storefront, saved from its burning neighbor by a wide gap of land. "Oh," she said, as this too went up in a roar of flames like so much kindling. "All gone." She turned to Charles and smiled. "Damn."

The sheriff swung the car around and pointed it back toward the highway, heading for the hospital. His rearview mirror was bright with the flames of Owltown. He turned to his deputy, who had not said a word since the shooting of Malcolm Laurie. "You earned your salary today, Lilith. Your dad is gonna be real proud of you."

From the backseat, Mallory said, "She was slow with that damn bullet. She still needs work."

"But she didn't give up her gun," said the sheriff in Lilith's defense. "And her aim was damn good."

"You're right," Mallory conceded. "Not your basic rookie. But she's got to shoot faster."

"Well, I can't let her practice on any more Lauries. Wouldn't be sporting. They're limping targets now."

"Where— What happened?" Riker's eyes were half open. He turned his head slowly from window to window, trying to fix his place in the world.

"It's a wrap," said Mallory. "Go back to sleep."

"Hardly a wrap," said Charles. "We still don't know who killed Babe Laurie."

"And we may never know," said the sheriff, not seeming to mind this in the least. And suddenly Charles knew the sheriff had solved that little mystery, for the man reflected in the rearview mirror was smiling contentedly. Mallory seemed unconcerned, disinterested.

"Hey, kid," said Riker.

"Stay quiet," said Mallory. "We're almost there."

"You remember when you were a little squirt, and I was still allowed to call you Kathy?"

"Yes, I remember. Rest now. Close your eyes." It was unmistakably an order, but her voice was gentle, soothing. She might have been talking to a child.

Riker did not take direction well. His eyes were all the way open now. "We've been through a hell of a lot together, haven't we?"

"Yes, Riker."

"So, can I call you Kathy now?"

"No."

Riker smiled and closed his eyes, drifting off again, mumbling something which might have been derogatory. But even now, Mallory would not let him have the last word. She leaned her head very close to his and whispered, "Sleep."

Charles toted up the damage to his traveling companions. The sheriff wore a large square bandage above his right eye, but he seemed to be in the best of moods. Riker was defying Mallory and coming back to consciousness. Mallory had shot and wounded all those people, yet she seemed only a bit tired after a long and busy day.

Lilith was another story, for she had just killed a man, and she was not fortified with Mallory's damaged psyche.

Charles watched the deputy's profile as she stared out

the side window. He caught the almost imperceptible movement of her head from side to side, fighting that slow slide
into shock. Her lips were pressed together in a grim tight
line. To stifle a scream? Her eyes, so sad, were slowly
closing.

Charles intuited a sense of loss, something spoiled.

The passenger window framed an engorged yellow moon
suspended over the sugar-cane fields. The alignment of the
car created the deceit that the moon was also in motion and
racing them along the black ribbon of highway, darting behind the odd building and reappearing on the other side.

Lilith's chin lifted slightly. Her eyes opened, and in the
dark mirror of the window glass, Charles noted a hardness
in her expression. Her gaze might have been fixed on the
same moon that kept pace with them, the same fields, but
he thought not. He believed she was looking out on an
entirely different landscape.

Death had changed everything.

CHAPTER
29

MALLORY HAD ABANDONED the boots for a new pair of running shoes. She stood apart from the rest of the party, holding an heirloom wineglass up to the window and staring at the etching of the Shelley family monogram. All the furnishings of this elegant formal dining room had been taken down from Cass Shelley's attic for this occasion. The long rosewood table was laid with antiques of gleaming silver, crystal and lace.

Charles watched as she carried her glass into the adjoining room, a library of bare shelves. He would have followed her, but his hostess stood in front of him now, blocking the way.

"She's saying goodbye to the house," said Augusta.

Charles nodded. He raised his glass and smiled. "To another successful real estate deal."

She clinked glasses with him, and behind her back, Henry Roth signed in the air, *"She'll be after my place next."*

"I hope there was a deed restriction," said Charles. "You're not planning to burn this place or let it rot?"

"Mallory made those very stipulations." Augusta

grinned and went off to see to Riker's glass, which was in danger of going empty.

The bandaged detective was comfortably ensconced in a well-padded armchair with a footstool. The plaster cast on his arm had been autographed by pretty nurses, state troopers and the lovely Lilith Beaudare. He was enjoying the role of invalid, only needing to glance at the table to have his every wish fulfilled. Augusta had taken a liking to Riker. The rest of the company were left to fend for themselves. The sheriff and his deputy poured their own wine while Augusta and Riker shared a cloud of smoke from cigarette and cheroot.

Charles looked through the wide doorway to see Mallory standing before the library fireplace. The wind rattled the panes all around the house. A draft found entry through an open chimney vent, and a small flurry of dust swirled about the brick hearth at her feet.

So you've come home again, Mallory. Was it everything you thought it would be? You have your revenge—the thing you wanted most—and what do you think of it now? You only stand there, waiting for the dust to settle in the chimney.

She was such a closed and private person.

Augusta was right. He would never have answers to all his questions, and he knew better than to voice the most personal ones. So the queries went round and round his brain, blind bats every one, all doomed to fly in endless circles.

As to why she had chosen the name Mallory, he liked his theory that it was her father's name, but she would tell him nothing about the man. Or perhaps she cared nothing for antecedents. Louis Markowitz had been her father from the age of ten, and apparently he was father enough.

Mallory turned to catch Charles staring at her. As she was walking back to him, she stopped by the doorway to pick up the carton of her mother's personal possessions. She set it down near the foyer, for soon they would load it into the car. The party was almost over.

Now that they were all together in one room. Augusta proposed a toast to the long road home. Charles turned to Mallory.

And where is home now?

Tomorrow morning she would drive back to New York with him, but how long would she remain there? He resolved that home was neither what nor where, but a person, and it was highly unlikely that she would ever come home to him; one only visited with friends. However, her friendship was no small thing, not something he settled for, but something—

Yeah, right. As Mallory would say.

Charles ceased to tell himself comfort lies and looked down at his watch. It was nearly time to pick up Riker's bags at the hotel before dropping him off at the airport.

The glasses were drained, the door was opening, and now one of Charles's unsolved riddles left the formation of circling bats and flew into the room. "Will someone tell me who killed Babe Laurie?"

Riker had not appreciated that, and did his best to pretend he had not heard it. Henry only smiled pleasantly, inscrutable, taking no sides in this matter. Tom Jessop stood with one hand on the door he had held open for Lilith, who had escaped. The sheriff was not so lucky, for Charles was looking directly at him and smiling in expectation.

The sheriff's face relaxed in good-natured surrender. "Off the record?"

"If you like."

"It was Fred Laurie. He's been missing ever since Kathy's dog disappeared. The little bastard tried to kill Good Dog once before. So I figure he took care of that piece of unfinished business before he ran. I got two witnesses to put him in those woods with a rifle."

Well, that would neatly clear up the murder of a dog. But it wasn't even—

"It works for me." Augusta was polishing an imaginary spot on her wineglass.

Mallory was examining the floorboards, saying, "I suppose Babe's son is the motive?"

"Yeah, I tend to favor that one," said the sheriff. "The boy belonged to Fred, not Babe. So one of them snapped, and they had it out on the road. I already wrote up the report and put out a warrant for Fred Laurie's arrest."

A look passed between Mallory and Augusta, but Charles could not decipher it. In another minute, he found that he could, but he didn't want to. In fact, he went to a great deal of trouble to abort an idea at the moment of creation. He managed to altogether eliminate one of the myriad questions in the bat room of his mind, and he ceased to ponder how many bodies might lie at the tip of Finger Bayou.

All he knew for certain was that Fred Laurie had not killed his brother. That much he had gleaned from the tone of liars coming to agreement on the fine points.

"What's the evidence against Fred Laurie?" asked Charles, knowing he was alienating everyone in the room. "Don't you need something besides suspicion to back up a warrant?"

"I've got Travis's deathbed confession," said Jessop. "He named Fred as the killer. Riker signed a statement to back it up."

Charles turned to Riker, who found his pack of matches most engrossing, examining them as a strange and rare artifact he had just pulled from his pocket.

The sheriff broke the silence. "Hey, Riker, why don't we get back to town and pick up your bags? I'll take you out to the airport myself."

Riker seemed to like this idea. Of course he did, and he was already moving out the door.

The sheriff turned to Mallory. "Coming back for the trial? Not that we're short of witnesses. They're crawling all over each other to turn state's evidence."

She shook her head. "I'm done with this place."

After the last goodbyes were said in the driveway, and Riker had made his getaway with the sheriff, Charles lifted the heavy carton into the backseat of the silver Mercedes.

Something had begun to tick, and it was regular as a clock.

He looked at Mallory, not suspecting that she was harboring a bomb among her mother's things, but it did tick.

"It's a metronome," she said. "The pendulum must have come loose."

As they slid into the front seat, he asked, "Do you remember Ira's piano lessons at all?"

She nodded. "We played duets. There were two pianos in the house then, my mother's baby grand and an old player piano. Sometimes Ira and I would race each other through the music."

The metronome ticked off four beats in a measure. The cacophony of birdsongs in the surrounding trees refused to conform to the rhythm.

"Mallory, why did he come to the house that day? Did your mother continue his music lessons after Ira's father stopped the therapy?"

"The therapy never stopped. Ira missed her. He kept showing up at the house on his regular schedule. His father was supposed to be watching him while Darlene was working, but he wasn't much of a baby-sitter. So there was Ira, standing out in the yard. My mother couldn't turn him away."

Charles sat with the ignition key in his hand. The metronome was slowing its ticks, filling each measure with a single note. The birds were singing louder, faster, in such a rush to get the music out. Tomorrow morning, when they were on the road and beyond the reach of Augusta's sanctuary, it would be all too quiet, miles of road and—

"You never asked me if I killed Babe Laurie," said Mallory.

"I didn't need to. He was hit from behind with a rock—not your style. Now if they'd found him with a nice symmetrical bullet hole and less mess, that would've been quite different." He turned back for one last look at the Shelley house as he put the car in gear. "But I had the feeling that

I was the only one in that room who didn't know the killer's name.''

"Not true, Charles. Riker and Augusta have their own ideas, but they're wrong.''

"And the sheriff?''

She turned away from him now. "No one cares who killed Babe Laurie. It just doesn't matter.''

"I'm so sick of hearing that. *I* care.'' The car moved out of the yard, and then he brought it to a sudden stop on the dirt road. "Are you saying the sheriff knows, and he's not doing anything about it? You know too, don't you?''

Of course she did. But she kept her silence. Why had he even bothered to ask? Well, he sometimes forgot that she still followed the children's code of not ratting on thy co-conspirator.

"Hints, Mallory? Anything at all?''

She looked at him for a moment, perhaps weighing trust, as if that were in question after everything she had put him through. The metronome made a tick. He waited for the next beat, but the seconds dragged by. Then it ticked again.

"There's no proof,'' she said.

"Fine, I'm not looking to make a citizen's arrest. But if you don't give me a sporting chance to work this out, I'll go stark raving mad.''

"I told you the hospital was storing old hardcopy files on the mainframe. When the clerk scanned Ira's first hospital record, she must have seen the old lab report for VD. She flagged his computer entry for a prior child abuse. When I hacked into the hospital computer, there was no file in the system yet, just the flag, Ira's name and the disease.''

"Child abuse? But he was no longer a child.'' He held up one hand. "No, wait—I've got it. Tell me if I'm wrong. I know Ira's diagnosis was changed from autism to profound retardation.'' In the absence of a separate facility to treat autism, that was the only way to qualify him for a state therapy program. "That and his dependency on his mother gave him the legal status of a minor child. Right?''

"Right. So when Darlene brought Ira into the emergency room with his broken hands, the abuse flag came up on the computer. The hospital was obliged to call the sheriff."

The metronome never ticked again.

RIKER HAD MASTERED the art of one-armed packing in ten minutes flat. He opened the top drawer of the dresser and wadded up his underwear the better to smash it into his suitcase. Normally, he never moved this quickly, but he was almost home free and not taking any chances. The metal clasps snapped shut. Done.

But too late.

Shit!

"Not so fast." Charles Butler was leaning against the doorframe, all but wearing a No Exit sign around his neck.

Riker sank down on the bed beside his suitcase. He wished he had a drink. He had been looking forward to a comfortable chair in the airport bar and maybe swapping a few war stories with Tom Jessop.

"About Travis's deathbed confession." Charles closed the door behind him. "Why did you back up the sheriff in a lie?"

"I think you know." But now it dawned on the detective that knowledge and belief were different things in Charles's strange relationship with Mallory, this blind friendship which kept her cloaked in innocence despite every bit of evidence to the contrary. Riker had a more pragmatic form of loyalty. If Mallory had shot an elderly nun in a wheelchair, he would assume the nun had it coming to her.

"So you still believe Mallory did it."

"The motive is pretty strong." Riker was making an effort to keep the sarcasm out of his voice. Derision was undeserved. Charles's blindness touched him as nothing else ever had. "She also had opportunity and no alibi."

"Because Babe was in that mob? The logic is a bit flawed, isn't it? Travis was there too, but she saved his life. You must realize she couldn't have had any idea who was in that mob. She was inside the house, locked in a—''

''She could hear everything from her bedroom, Charles. Listen to the birds.''

Charles turned to the closed window. The tree in the yard was indeed full of singing birds, and their voices easily penetrated the glass. And now that he paid attention, he could hear Betty on the front porch. She was greeting new guests. The voices of a man and a woman were not so clear as the birds, but he could pick out the odd word in their conversation.

''Augusta gave me a tour of the Shelley house,'' said Riker. ''I saw the kid's room. Did you notice the window near the top of the closet? I never saw a thing like that before. Augusta said the closet window was pretty common in old houses built before electric lights. Now Mallory couldn't have seen anything. It was too high up for a little kid. But you know she heard something—maybe not Travis's voice, but *something*, maybe just a few words. She wouldn't have understood what was happening, but she put it all together when she saw her mother after they were done with her. I told you the kid had more to work with than the sheriff did.''

''Travis only stoned a dog. Alma was there too, but she took her rock home with her. If Mallory heard—''

''Charles, drop it.''

''That mob was Malcolm's work, not Babe's.''

''The whole mob is accountable—that's the law. For Christ's sake, that's even *Mallory's* law!'' Riker held his silence for a moment, calling back his temper.

''You're right, Charles. Malcolm had to implicate every witness at that meeting, everyone who might've led the sheriff back to the letter, the blue letter. But even if some of them didn't throw rocks, they all watched that woman die. They never moved to help her, they never told. There are no innocent people here.''

Riker walked to the window and pulled up the sash. The sheriff was leaning against his car in the street below.

''Hey, Tom. Two minutes, okay?''

"Take your time."

Riker closed the window again, and now he turned around to finish off Charles Butler. *But gently,* he cautioned himself.

"Oh, yeah, I think she did it. That's why I backed up the sheriff on that bullshit confession. At the time, I was just so happy that Mallory didn't take out the whole town."

Oh, wait. She did take out Owltown. It was level ground now, wasn't it? Ah, but most of the human casualties were only punctured and burned.

Charles only stared at him with sad eyes.

"What do you want from me?" Riker picked up his suitcase and set it near the door as a hint that Charles might move away from the room's only exit. No good. The big man showed no signs of moving.

"I'm not gonna recant that statement, Charles. There's no point in it. The sheriff doesn't care who killed Babe Laurie. Nobody does." No one except for himself and Charles. But Mallory was well out of it now. She was going to get away with murder.

"It wasn't Mallory," said Charles. "I know that for a fact—I'm not going on blind faith this time. Does it matter a bit more now?"

Riker felt something close to that weightless moment in an elevator when the contents of his stomach rose and fell. Because he had never known Charles to run a bluff, the detective was experiencing every cop's waking nightmare. The outlaw act, that one step across the line, was about to come back on him. He would have been more comfortable with the premonition that his plane was going to crash.

"No, it doesn't matter." Riker was lying, of course. He had always been the victim's paladin—until now. Loving Mallory had cost him a great deal. "Babe Laurie raped two kids that we know about. How many more? That murder was a public service."

No, murder was never that. It was the worst crime. All his feelings for Mallory had been altered by it. He was sorry and sick at—

"Well, you only have Jimmy Simms's statement to back that up," said Charles. "You wrote it down as he was telling it, didn't you? It must have been difficult to be coherent while he was crying."

"Are you telling me I missed something?" It was the last question he wanted answered. Charles seemed to intuit this and kept his silence.

"Charles, why are you doing this to me?"

"I just wanted to be sure that *you* weren't playing the blind man this time around. So you don't want to know who killed Babe? It doesn't matter? Fine."

Charles turned to go.

"Wait. Who was it?"

"You can't have it both ways, Riker. Either you care or you don't. I'm surprised that you would even ask. Suppose it was the sheriff? You know, I rather like him. Oh, did I mention that he had motive, opportunity and no alibi? But I'm sure you'd be happy to excuse him too. Isn't that one of the perks of your job—all your friends get away with murder?"

"The sheriff? Are you saying—"

"I'm not saying who did it. I know—but you don't care."

"Who killed him, Charles?"

"It doesn't matter—your very words." He walked to the door and opened it wide.

"Don't make me nuts. Who—?"

"Have a good flight home, Riker."

The door was pulled shut.

Riker ceased to hear the birds anymore. He stood by the window, looking down on the sheriff's car. Cops could not kill their suspects, not ever—that was Riker's law. But now he finally believed in Mallory. His suspicions of the man waiting below were a lesser sickness and easier to live with.

Thank you, Charles.

•   •   •

IRA WAS ASLEEP in a soft nest of white bandages and linen sheets. His mother sat by the bed, reading a magazine. Darlene Wooley was not wearing a suit today. A simple dark skirt and blouse accentuated the pallor of her skin, and Charles wondered if she had seen the sun even once in the past four days.

Darlene looked up at him and smiled. She folded back a page of the magazine to mark her place, then looked quickly to Ira, as though this rustle of paper could have disturbed his sleep. She motioned Charles to join her in the hall outside the room.

Softly, she pulled the door closed behind them, saying, "It's his first day out of the intensive care unit. His doctor says he's going to be just fine."

"I'm glad to hear it. I have some good news for you. Let me buy you a cup of coffee in the cafeteria."

As they walked down the corridor, he noted that Darlene did not fill out her clothes anymore, and her nails were bitten down to the quick and raw.

"You know," said Darlene, "when he's awake, he lets me hold his hand. I'm sure he still hates to be touched. I think it's sort of like he's giving me a present."

Her fingers went mechanically to her mouth. Suddenly self-conscious of the ragged nails, she drove both her hands deep into the pockets of her skirt. "When Ira was little, he used to bring me flowers from Cass's garden. I always thought she made him do that, maybe as part of his therapy. But Mallory said no. When she came by last night, she told me Ira always asked Cass if he could pick flowers for his mother."

Charles thought that was a beautiful story. And if Mallory had made it up, it was even better.

The cafeteria was noisy with the rush of feet and fifty conversations, clattering dishes and silverware. The staff and visitors were all deep in their own preoccupations and taking little notice of Charles and his pale companion.

Darlene's skin was sickly in this brighter fluorescent lighting. He seated her at the nearest table. If she did not sit down, and soon, she might fall. When had this woman slept last?

"You wait here. I'll get the coffee."

He meant to bring her only that cup of coffee, all that she had wanted, but while he was in line with the other patrons, he also loaded down the tray with nutritious green vegetables, and suspicious gray meat swimming in dishwater gravy. The *pièce de résistance* was a dry-looking slice of chocolate cake encased in a cellophane bag. It was his intention to fatten her up.

When he set the tray down in front of her, she laughed.

Well, that was an improvement.

As he sat down, he handed her the letter of introduction from the Dallheim Project. She read in silence, and then the paper fell from her hands. "They want him! They want Ira!"

"Oh, yes. Now they're very excited about him. Eat something. And it's not just the multiple talents. I think it was Ira's star that finally won them over."

He had badgered the project director for days with stories gleaned from Betty, Mallory and Augusta, until Darlene's son had become a person instead of an application number. Ira had jumped to first place on the long waiting list.

"They'll take him as soon as he's well enough to travel to New Orleans. You won't be allowed to visit him for the first three months. But later, you'll be able to bring him home on the weekends."

"I understand. You really think he has a chance of making it on his own?"

"Thanks to you. If you hadn't kept up his therapy, he'd be a lost cause by now. Please eat something. It might take years of work, but in time, he *will* be able to survive outside of a care facility."

"So if anything should happen to me—"

"He won't go to a state institution."

She was happy for a few moments, even outglowing the brilliant overhead lights. Then something else must have occurred to her, for her eyes were saddened now. Perhaps she was grieving over something that had not happened yet. He could make a shrewd guess at what that might be.

"That's good—wonderful." She was more subdued now. "There's something I have to do. I only needed—"

"Try the meat, Darlene. I'm just wildly curious to find out what species it is."

She picked up the knife and fork and went through the motions of cutting the meat. Losing the last of her energy now, the knife and fork were laid down in the thin gravy.

"Not too appetizing, is it? Sorry."

"I need to talk to the sheriff," she said. "There's something—"

"Did you hear the sheriff's theory that Fred Laurie killed Babe?"

"Fred didn't do it." Her hand upset the coffee cup, and a stream of brown liquid ran across the table.

"I know." Charles pulled napkins from the metal dispenser at the center of the table and mopped up the spilled coffee. "But, you see, everyone really likes this theory. So it might be difficult to force your confession on the sheriff. Try the vegetables."

"You knew." She raked one hand through her hair, fingers thin as claws. "I wanted to tell Tom. I wanted to tell him every day. I don't sleep at night. I keep hearing that rock hit Babe's skull."

"You don't have to tell me any of this."

"But I do," she said, a bit too loud. The people at the next table turned to look at her. Darlene lowered her head. "I want to." Her voice was a whisper now. "I have to talk to somebody." She worked her wedding ring up and down her finger. "I saw Babe leave the car at the gas station. He was heading for the bridge over Upland Bayou. I went back after him while the doctors were working on my boy. But it's not what you think, not because of what he did to Ira's hands."

Her ring was so loose now, so little flesh on the bone.

Charles stared at his reflection in the metal napkin dispenser. He couldn't meet her eyes anymore. She was in so

much pain as she described the violence on the road to Cass
Shelley's house.

"I didn't know if I'd killed him or not. I screamed when
I saw all the blood, and I ran for the car. I was sure someone must have heard me or seen me. I left him lying there
in the road and went back to the hospital to wait for the
sheriff. I was so sure that any minute Tom would walk in
the door and arrest me. When the doctor came to the waiting room to talk to me, he didn't notice that there was more
blood on my suit—Babe's blood splattered over Ira's."

She buried her face in her hands, and Charles stared at
her wounded fingertips.

"Eat something." This was what his mother had always
said to him when he had been through another day of torture among normal children with average-size noses and
intelligence. Food conveyed nurture and caring, and it was
all he could think of to comfort her.

Darlene picked up her fork and absently stirred the peas
into the cranberry sauce. "I was half crazy wondering what
would happen to my boy when I went to prison." The peas
swirled round and round in the red sauce, faster and faster.
"Every single day, I thought Tom would arrest me. I even
tried to tell him once—when I thought I couldn't stand it
another minute."

The fork slipped and the peas scattered, some to the
floor, and one flew to the next table. "But I didn't tell.
Who would have looked after Ira?"

Two people seated nearby stared at the single pea and a
dot of cranberry sauce at the center of their table.

Darlene abandoned the vegetables. Peas were too difficult. She picked up the cellophane package with the cake
inside. "How did you know, Charles?"

"This is the hospital where Cass ordered Ira's blood
tests. When you brought him in with his broken hands, a
red flag showed up on the computer for the previous entry—when Ira was only six. The doctor would have asked
you if he'd completed the treatment for syphilis. The com-

puter entry was sparse and he would have wanted a patient history—standard procedure.''

''It was the desk nurse, not a doctor.'' Her hands worked over the cake wrapper, trying to tear it open and failing to find the weakness in the cellophane seal. ''I didn't know what that woman was talking about. I said it was a mistake. Ira had been tested for hepatitis that year, not *syphilis*.''

Charles wondered if it would be rude to assist Darlene with the cake wrapper, to imply that she couldn't—

''Well, it made no damn sense at all. So the nurse took me down to the basement where they stored the old health department files for St. Jude Parish.''

The cake wrapper was impenetrable. She stabbed it with one finger, forgetting she had no nails left to tear it. ''We found one file to match Ira's computer number. There were no names, only dates and statistics for tests on a boy of six—Ira—another boy thirteen, and a nineteen year old. The file clerk told the nurse they were all in that same folder because the doctor—Cass Shelley—was backtracking the infection.''

''Jimmy Simms was the thirteen year old.''

''I guessed that. And Babe had turned nineteen that year. Everybody in town knew about his syphilis party. It was a legend. And then there was the faith-healing. Ira was never the same after that. So I thought he'd raped my boy. What was I supposed to think? And he did smash Ira's hands. I had good reason to believe it, didn't I?''

''You don't seem quite so sure of it now.''

''After I killed him . . .'' Not wanting to meet his eyes, she stared down at the insoluble problem of the cellophane bag. ''I mean, later that night, I realized my husband must have known about Ira's syphilis. They have to notify the parents, don't they? And that would've explained his quarreling with Cass. Maybe she accused him of raping his own son.''

Her wedding ring fell off and lay on the table. He wondered how much weight she had lost. He longed to open the wrapper for her, to feed her.

"Had to have happened that way," she said, twisting the package in her hand, mashing the cake. "Ira's clean now. So, at least my husband had the grace to get the boy treated before he wrapped his car around that telephone pole."

"So now you believe you killed the wrong man?"

"I heard Ira tell you his father threw the first rock. Well, that's proof, isn't it? Cass was going to tell, so my husband—" Her hands were resting on the table, covering the cellophane package, too tired to fight with it anymore.

"Your husband didn't hurt Ira," said Charles, covering one of her hands with his own. "But I believe he was *told* that Cass had accused him. Something similar was done to Deputy Travis. Malcolm read him Cass's letter, and Travis thought she was accusing him of raping a boy in custody— Jimmy, I suppose. When Travis was dying, he said Cass was going to ruin him with science. He was innocent of course, but just the accusation meant ruin. The rock was put into his hand—the idea was put into his mind."

Look at the damage Darlene had done with a rock and a single maddening idea. But Travis had only stoned the dog. "Actually, there was a letter on file from the hospital lab. It was a negative report on your husband's blood test."

"That was the letter Malcolm read from?"

"I believe so. The date matches up with the stoning. Mallory found a copy of it in the hospital files. There was another letter on file, addressed to your husband—the same negative report on his tests. But by the time it was mailed out to him, Cass was dead."

"That's why he killed himself."

Suicide never made sense. But Darlene wanted the world to be orderly for a few minutes. She was coming undone, and this was a small thing to ask.

"Yes," he said. "Your husband and Cass probably argued when she asked him for a blood sample. He would have been outraged. He was innocent, but she needed to eliminate him as a suspect. So Cass had the results in her hand when she went after the real child molester that day, and she was angry."

"Then it *was* Babe. Mal was shielding his brother with that letter."

"There's no way to know for sure."

"Who else *could* it have been!" Her eyes were suddenly wide and startled, disbelieving that shrill scream could have come from her own mouth. The people at the nearest table left it, upsetting a chair in their haste to be gone. The abandoned chair rocked and teetered on its hind legs and then crashed to the floor.

"Babe had the disease before the others did!" Her voice was louder now and carrying across the cafeteria. Her hands splayed out in the air as if to call the words back and hush them down. All around them, conversations ceased, and the newspapers of solitary patrons went flat on the tables.

Her lips pressed together. She was in control again, but just barely. "I know Babe was the nineteen year old in that file. His was the oldest stage of syphilis. The nurse told me so."

And so it must be true. A man had died because of her faith in hard science.

"That chronology, by itself, proves nothing about who gave it to whom."

The cellophane package lay by her hand. The wrapping showed no signs of wear, but the cake was badly smashed. She renewed her struggles with it for a moment, and then gave up. "If only Ira could have told me."

"Children are the best of conspirators," said Charles. "They're so easily frightened, they rarely tell. Jimmy never told, and neither did Babe when it was his turn to be abused."

"Babe?"

"He had a very late stage of syphilis according to the autopsy. But there was no way for a pathologist to pin the date of infection with only a dead body to work with. The coroner didn't have the history of convulsions, the weakness in the legs, fits of temper, delusions of grandeur—it was all there."

Malcolm had supplied some of the symptoms in his impersonation of Babe on the stage. "The unsteady gait made everyone think that Babe was stoned on drugs. And I'm sure he was on some kind of painkiller. He would have been in a lot of pain near the end of his life. Those symptoms don't usually appear until a man is nearly fifty." And with all the wear on Babe, mind and body, that might have been his true age when he died at the calendar's measure of thirty-six years. "So Babe must have been a child himself when he contracted the disease."

"How could that happen? Somebody would have known." And then she froze. For she had not known about Ira, had she? Did Jimmy Simms's parents know what had been done to *their* child?

"I'm sure Malcolm knew," said Charles. "Babe would have run the gamut of symptoms. But Malcolm was hardly going to have a small child, his own ward, treated for venereal disease. There would have been an investigation."

"But Cass was treating Babe when he was—"

"When he was a teenager and it could be passed off for whoring around. Tom Jessop told me Cass dragged Babe right off the street to treat him. Lesions would have been evident by then. She didn't wait for the test results to tell her what she already knew. When Cass did get the tests back, when she realized the extent and the duration of the disease, she made the link to Jimmy Simms. His hepatitis led her to Ira. And suddenly she had a lot of questions for Malcolm."

The cellophane had burst open; the cake was in Darlene's hands at last, and it was mashed to bits. "So it was Mal she went to see at the meeting that day?"

"He raised Babe from the age of five. He had the opportunity."

Her hand closed. Chocolate crumbs leaked through her fingers. "Then Babe just did what was done to him. Well, that makes a bit of sense."

Charles could see she was desperate for something to make sense, but he shook his head. "Only attorneys make the case that their child-molesting clients were themselves abused. All the stats on that are tainted. Malcolm was always the more natural seducer. The time frame works. He probably went after his nephew Jimmy when Babe was no longer a child. And then he could've easily taken Ira at the faith healing.''

That had been the most likely window of opportunity, and it would account for the setback in Ira's therapy. The child would have been terrified when Babe did the healing act, the laying on of hands. He would have been screaming. Malcolm would have played the role of the calming influence. He would have taken the child away to some quiet place. If Ira had screamed again, if anyone had overheard, who would have guessed the real reason for it? No one— not even his own father seated in the audience that night, perhaps only steps away from his small son during the abuse.

If Darlene had followed this much, she was willing the image away, slowly shaking her head. The dry cake crumbs, crushed to a finer dust, fell from her hand to spread over the tray, the table, and some trickled to the floor.

''It must have been hard for Babe to watch Cass Shelley die,'' said Charles. ''Cass was his doctor once. Probably the only one who had ever cared what happened to him. Then Mallory appeared—the image of her mother. And Ira began to play those notes over and over on the piano. Those same notes were playing on a scratched record all the while Cass was being stoned by the mob. Babe went wild. He might have yelled at Ira to stop. But you know Ira would have blocked that out and kept on playing. At this stage of Babe's disease, he couldn't have handled any frustration. So he slammed the piano lid on Ira's hands to make the music stop. When the music did stop, the assault was over.''

''But Babe was lying in wait for Mallory.'' Louder now, insistent, ''He was going to *ambush* her!''

Her coffee cup crashed to the floor.

The room quieted for a moment. Then the other patrons resumed their conversations, but everywhere about the room, eyes were trained on the dark stain spreading across the floor and the woman who might be dangerously crazy.

"I rather doubt that Babe meant to harm Mallory," said Charles. "Perhaps he dimly saw her as Cass, an old source of comfort, an easer of pain. Or maybe he was lucid and wanted to talk to Mallory about the day her mother died. That might explain why the brothers fought in the square and again at the gas station. But we'll never know. It's always a tricky thing—second-guessing the dead."

It began with quiet tears, and then she was trembling. Stutters of breath were choked up in her throat, emerging now as racking sobs. The people seated around them had finally redirected their eyes to their own affairs. Tears were the norm in this place, and Darlene's seemed to comfort all of them, saying there was nothing dangerous here—only death and pain.

Charles patiently waited out the crying, occasionally handing her napkins. When she was composed again, he fetched another piece of cake and opened the wrapper for her.

She tried to give him a smile for the cake, and she failed. "No one gave a damn who killed Babe Laurie. Only you."

"Oh, that's not true," said Charles. "They were liars, every one of them who said Babe's death didn't matter. They all thought someone they cared about had done it."

Well, Mallory *might* have believed the sheriff had killed Babe Laurie. When pressed, she had pointed him in Jessop's direction, hadn't she? But Charles remained uncertain. It was always so hard to tell when Mallory was lying. She might have reasoned that Tom Jessop could easily fend off a false accusation; but if Darlene had gone to prison, who would've looked after Mallory's old playmate? It would be just like her to choose the expedient—

"Charles, what do you think the court will do with me?" Darlene's words were listless. She was calm now, and seemed only mildly curious about her future.

"Tom Jessop is a very decent man. He'll have a strong influence on what happens to you." Jessop would certainly support a plea of temporary insanity for the crime of mother passion. "I suppose your best outcome would be probation."

"And if you were on my jury?"

"Would I ask for a pound of flesh? No."

Babe's life would have been absolute hell if he'd been allowed to live it out. The best medical treatment in the world might have eased the suffering, but not reversed the insidious damage. "However, I do regret Babe's murder— particularly the *way* he died."

"All alone and scared," she said, nodding. "Left to bleed to death like a dog in the road."

She was in accord with him now, sharing his regret, her face set with real grief. And pity? Yes, that too. So, the death of Babe Laurie had mattered a great deal. And now the dead man was assured of one mourner, his own murderer, a woman who would certainly visit his grave to bring him the odd bouquet of guilty flowers.

EPILOGUE

THE NIGHT WAS mild, and so she was without her black duster. The pale blue jeans and white shirt had made it easy to follow her in the gathering darkness. Though Charles had trailed Mallory here, he made no move toward her, but kept to the darkest shadows in the ring of trees, silent as a parishioner in church.

She stood on a small patch of open ground at the center of the cemetery, where two gravel roads met in the form of a cross. Just behind her was the movement of something small and alive racing through the grass in a line of bowing fronds. A bird of prey crossed the sky in a glide and then descended in a lazy circle, settling to earth. In the grass at the owl's feet, a tiny animal screamed, and the night bird rushed up to the stars.

Mallory's head tilted back, and at first, Charles thought she was only following the flight of the owl. But no, something else was going on here, and it was suspiciously close to a religious act. She was looking up at the sky, not in admiration for the holy handiwork in the firmament, nor with the aspect of worship, but it definitely was a communion of sorts.

Were there obscenities in her eyes?

Whatever did Heaven read in that angry face of hers? For now, in a sudden rush of wind, it began to cover its own vast face with clouds, and the conversation was ended, debate lost by default.

Disrespecting borders, she stalked across gravel and onto the grass, moving between the carved monuments and tombs. She paused by the stone that meant the most to her, and then Mallory moved on.

Now he only followed her with his eyes until she disappeared into Henry's woods. She re-emerged, climbing the levee in long graceful strides. When she reached the top, she stood still for a moment, looking down on the cemetery. He pulled back into the circle of trees.

Though there would be days on the road before they separated, in a way, he was saying goodbye to her. Their actual parting would be more mundane; she would slip off into the canyons of New York skyscrapers and forget him. And for his part, he would cease to debase himself by following after her, doglike, growing smaller in her eyes until he altogether vanished.

The clouds were dispersing in a network of lace to expose the constellations. And now he had a small insight on the poetry of Ira's vision, freed of conceptions of space and time, mass and the radiant energy of distant lights. Low-hanging stars winked in and out with her passage across the levee road. There was no hard line of demarcation between the heavens and the high earthen barrier. In his fractured perception, she was walking across the sky.

Goodbye, Kathy Mallory.

He said her name again, aloud this time, and now another connection was taking place, almost against his will. He climbed into Mallory's point of view, an uncomfortable and cramped place to be, for she was only six years old, going on seven. The child in the closet had heard no sound from her mother, only the one voice speaking to the silent mob. The words may not have been clear, but the voice would have been recognized. Thoughts of the child were linking to Malcolm, whom those of long acquaintance called Mal.

Mal Laurie—*Mallory*.

The child had taken the name of her mother's killer. She had been plotting, even then, to come back for him one day when she had her size, when her hands were large enough to hold a lethal weapon. Each day of her life, she had been called by that hated name—so she would not, *could not,* forget the worst pain a small child could suffer and yet remain alive.

Charles stood there for a time, collecting his emotions. And then, forgetting his resolution of goodbye, he struck out across the starry night, following after Mallory. He was planning to hold her very close, to inflict comfort on her, and consolation for all her pain and loss.

He realized she might not care for that. Actually, he knew she would hate that. She would probably try to wave him off, as though he might be an annoying two-hundred-pound housefly.

Well, too bad, Mallory.

He needed to hold her; that need was very strong. And now he was forming another intention to annoy her even more: Until the end of his life or hers, whenever she turned around, there he would be.

*Turn the page for a special preview of
Carol O'Connell's newest novel*

JUDAS CHILD

*now available in hardcover from
G. P. Putnam's Sons*

UP AND DOWN the lane ran two bright ribbons of grass, still green so deep in December. Long flanking rows of pine trees ended where the modern public road met this private one of ancient cobblestones. Though there was no proper name on any map, the townspeople called it the Christmas tree lane.

Hidden beyond the west bank of evergreens, lay all the brown dead leaves of a bare-branched forest. The dry carcass of an eyeless sparrow was crushed under the man's shoe as he shifted his weight from one foot to the other. The day had turned chilly and mean. Wisps of fog hung low where the denuded woodland was protected by the windbreak of tall pines. The highest boughs of a nearby oak disappeared in the haze, and the trees behind it were only ghosts of birch and elm.

The man glanced at his watch.

Any moment now.

His fingers splayed wide and then balled into fists. The surrounding air was dead still; the brittle leaves and low lying clouds of the woods never stirred as a clean breeze whipped down the Christmas tree lane.

He took great pride in this art of selecting the time and the place. Soon, a solitary child would come riding by on her bicycle, as she did every Saturday afternoon at this same time. The little girl would be fearless, for the cobblestone roadway of trimmed grass and majestic pine trees was so different from the atmosphere of the forest, it might have been carved out of another world, a better one, where this man could not exist.

SHE SLOWED THE purple bicycle and turned around to look directly at him with the full force of big brown eyes and a wicked grin.

The boy's front wheel wobbled at the exact moment he braked to a dead stop. And then the child resigned himself to the short flight over the handlebars, all but shrugging in midair. The hard landing on the road was all the pain and punishment he had expected it to be.

Why did she do these things to him?

Though Sadie Green had never laid a hand on him outside of dancing class, one day at school she had caused him to step off a second floor landing, to fall down the stairs and cut his head—but only because the sudden sight of her had blinded him to science, more precisely, the law of gravity. For one fraction of a second, he had believed he could step out into thin air and not pay for it.

Now David Shore sat cross-legged on the cold ground near his fallen bicycle. He pulled off a torn woolen glove to pick the gravel out of his hand. Sadie's bike was describing lazy circles in the road, and by her wide smile, he could tell she was enjoying this enormously. As he plucked out one sharp bit of stone, the indent of his skin filled with a red droplet. He looked up at her.

How much blood is enough, Sadie?

Even from the distance of several yards, he could see all two hundred of her freckles jump as she laughed at him. He could still hear her laughing—like the maniac she was— as she sped around the clot of shrubs, turning off the road and into the Christmas tree lane. He was on his bike again and in motion, when her laughter stopped abruptly, not trailing away with distance, but ending, as though she had been turned off.

For the first time, he stopped his bike at the foot of the lane. On every other Saturday, he had peddled on by in the pretense that he had some business of his own farther along the public road. Now he stared down that long empty space between the two rows of evergreen trees.

Where was she? The lane was a straightaway to Gwen Hubble's house, and Sadie could not have covered all that ground so fast.

David stood with one foot planted on the road, rocking his bike from side to side. He didn't want to look into the woods beyond the pine trees, for fear of seeing her there, writhing on the ground and holding her bloody intestines in her hands.

She had done that to him before.

Sadie went to entirely too much trouble to frighten him. If she only knew how much fear she inspired whenever he thought about actually talking to her—as opposed to merely stalking her on Saturday afternoons.

He pedaled down the lane, but stopped halfway to Gwen's house, a stately white Georgian mansion locked behind intimidating iron gates. The profile of a security guard and his newspaper was silhouetted in the window of the gatehouse. But the guard might as well be posted on the moon, for David rarely spoke to people—or girls. Anxiety and hysteria froze his vocal cords each time he tried.

The boy cocked his head toward the left bank of pine trees. He heard a faint and garbled slew of sounds coming from the woods on the other side. Of course it was Sadie—baiting him. If she were carrying a spare set of pig's intestines from the biology lab, she would not want to waste them.

Well, he would play the fool for her, if that made her happy.

He got off his bike and wheeled it through the tight brace

of evergreens. One bough of prickly needles scratched his face in yet another blood sacrifice, and then he was standing in the woods, looking at the stark trees bereft of leaves, shrouded in mist and feathering out to hazy and indistinct forms in the distance.

Oh, this was Sadie Country, prime for horror. She must be loving this, wherever she was hiding.

He stood very still, tensing every muscle in his body. At any moment, she would come flying around the trunk of an oak tree, perhaps with some new weapon, another trick to cleave his poor startled brain into equal parts of terror and delight.

Two small animals ran across his path. A gray cat crackled leaves and snapped dry twigs in pursuit of a squirrel. But this was not the noise he had heard from the lane. He listened for the sound of something female, ten years old and nearly human. He rolled his bike farther into the woods, and now he saw a small metallic swatch of purple.

Everything Sadie owned was purple, even her running shoes exactly matched her purple parka.

Her bike was partially covered by a gunny sack, dirt-encrusted and blending well with the dead leaves. She was probably in a hurry and making better time through the woods on foot. He could guess where she was heading, and that would explain why she had not gone all the way to Gwen's. If they were meeting at the old boathouse, then Sadie must be in fresh trouble. The girls had not gone there since the last time Gwen's father had forbidden them to play together.

Confident that Sadie was not planning an ambush, he relaxed and took his time walking his bike around the tree trunks and fallen branches. At the edge of the woods, his vista opened to the wide lawn of St. Ursula's Academy. Grass rolled downhill to the lake, a calm mirror of the gray winter sky. The near shoreline was obscured by rock formations and foliage. He laid down his bicycle and drew closer to the boathouse. Now he could see part of the long wharf spanning the other side of the building and reaching far out on the lake. Its boards were worn smooth by the barefoot steps of generations of children.

St. Ursula's Academy was very old, and over the past century, the students had marked every bit of it. The vast green lawn spreading upward from the lake was scarred with ancient rough trails where boys and girls had worn away the grass as they departed from the normal paths. And this departure was at the heart of the boarding school for not quite normal, and some said quite unnatural, children.

He drew back when he heard the sound of a door being pulled shut. Now a single loud bark came from inside the boathouse.

Had Gwen brought her dog along this time? She had never done that before.

David didn't take up his regular post beneath the window; that might set the dog to barking again. He walked back toward the woods and sat down on a patch of ground behind the cover of shrubs. Here he would wait until Sadie came out—so he could follow her home.

The dog barked again and kept it up for a long time. Then it stopped suddenly—the same way that Sadie's laughter had ended in the lane—the dog had been switched off. Over the next hour, this was repeated three more times.

What were Gwen and Sadie doing to that animal?

Now there was another noise behind him. He shrank back behind the massive trunk of a centurion oak. A small blond girl was running through the woods: It was Gwen.

But how could that be?

GWEN HUBBLE PUFFED white clouds of breath, and her legs churned faster. The child-pink locomotive with the flapping red scarf and blue jeans ran a weaving path, skirting the trees. Her running shoes, laces undone, smashed brittle leaves to powder. Dry twigs snapped with sharp cracks in sync with her heartbeat.

The printed message on her pager had been an odd one.

"Urgent—boathouse—tell no one." But that was Sadie's style, the cliffhanger.

Gwen broke through a tight line of speckled trees at the edge of the wood. Her flushed face was scratched, and her socks fell in loose woolen rolls around her ankles. Breath came with ragged tears at her throat, and the bones of her shins were going to splinters with the hard pounding across the ground. She rounded the side of the old boathouse, her thick blond braid thumping at the back of a red parka.

She stepped onto the wharf, and as she walked toward the boathouse door, her steps slowed. A rock lay on the boards next to the rusted padlock and its crusty hasp amid the debris of splintered century-old wood and fragments of weathered paint. Well, perhaps the school had changed the padlock since Sadie had mastered the combination.

Or maybe not.

The crude breakage would be an improvement on Sadie's usual method of operations. *Yes, that must be it.* And Gwen approved. Now this was really scary.

She pushed through the door and walked into the dark.

No candles?

She braced herself for the assault. Would Sadie be waiting behind the door?

No—not this time.

Gwen's eyes had adjusted to the light streaming in the door behind her. And now she made out the small body, the familiar head of light brown hair and the purple down jacket. Sadie was lying at the center of the floor. Gwen was disappointed. After the big production of the broken lock, she had expected something more imaginative. She knelt down beside her friend and shook her.

"Hey, I'm not buying it. Get up."

The child lying on the floor made no response. Gwen looked up to see the lock on the boathouse phone box had also been broken.

"Sadie, it's not funny. Sadie?"

•   •   •

DAVID STOOD UP and stamped his feet. They had gone numb while he sat hunched and hidden in the bushes. Now his toes tingled as they came back to life. The air was growing colder. He pulled up the collar of his jacket against a sudden rush of wind off the lake.

Sadie should have come out long before now if she expected to get home by dark. He walked out onto open ground, emboldened by curiosity.

He hadn't heard the dog bark for a very long time. If Gwen had not brought her own dog, then where had the animal come from?

David moved closer to the boathouse, the better to eavesdrop. The window facing the shore was the source of all his Sadie trivia. He pressed one ear against the rough wood of the shutters, but there was no sound from within—no barks, no giggles, nothing.

The grass and the trees were all melding into the same gray hue, and the sky was darkening. The boy walked around the side of the building and stepped onto the wharf. He popped off the balls of his feet and hung there in the air for a moment, hesitating. If they caught him spying on them, what story could he give?

Oh, sure. Like he could actually get the words out. Well, he didn't need a story. He had the strongest right to be here as a boarder at the school, and they were only day students, townies.

David guessed it was close to dinnertime, and soon his housemother would be standing in the door of the cottage, calling out his name the way the real mothers did in the neighborhoods of Makers Village. But he couldn't leave yet. He had to know what was going on in there, though he strongly suspected it was another one of Sadie's traps set to scare him to death. He spotted the padlock lock and hasp on the wharf beside the door.

That was odd.

Sadie's plotting had never been so elaborate. She always went for the swift shock. A slow build to terror, and now, this violence upon private property—well, this was entirely too subtle.

He pushed the door open and went inside. Though the interior was black, but for a few feet of bad light from the open door, he knew immediately that the boathouse was empty. But the girls could not have gotten past him. No way.

David walked deeper into the darkness, memory leading him safely around the tarpaulined canoes, a sailboat and stacks of boxes. His two classmates were only impressions on the air. He sniffed the musty space to separate the smell of the lake water from the smell of dog hair and traces of girl in the faint residue of spearmint gum and talcum powder.

The boy's head snapped to one side.

What was that?

A queer, rude finger of ice stroked his spine. There it was again—a furtive shadow within shadows and the quick scratching of small feet. On some level, he knew it was a rat, but he would not believe in it. Although he owed his scholarship to a festering rat bite as much as to his IQ score, his brain was blind to vermin. They could not follow him here. They were all back there in the foster home. He had seen that place for the last time when a social worker had carted him off to the hospital. There were no more rats in the world. He would not believe in them.

The wind banged the door shut behind him, and his world went black. David stopped breathing for all the time it took to cross the wide room, to bang his legs against a wooden box and find the knob for the door. And then the boy was swinging into the air, holding on to the door handle and dangling over freezing water. He had opened the wrong door, and his long legs had overstepped the shallow stairs leading down to the sheltered boat slip. The wider door beyond this one was standing open to the remains of daylight.

David used his body, swinging his weight to bring the door close to its wood frame again. His feet, pedaling in midair, found purchase on the ladder, and he climbed back into the boathouse. Now with the dim light from the slip, he found the right door and stepped onto the solid planks of the wharf. He walked to the end of the building and stared at the lakeside doors. This was the only other exit—by water.

That had to be how they had gotten past him, paddling behind the rocks and foliage along the shore. He could count the canoes to see if one was missing. But no—he was not going back in there, not for anything.

He walked out to the far end of the long wharf where it hung on stilts over the water. The lake had become a choppy agitation of whitecaps; wind-driven waves licked and slapped the pilings. There was no boat in sight along the shoreline. David turned back toward the massive red-brick building at the top of the hill, looming there like a great authoritarian parent, five stories tall counting the two narrow rows of dormer windows set in black shingles. His own cottage was left of the main building and farther back in the woods. He longed to go there; he was aching from the cold, and very hungry.

The girls were probably home by now. It was almost dinnertime. But still he hated to leave this riddle undone. He headed back through the woods to look for Sadie's bike. She would not have left it behind.

He found the gunny sack, but the bike was gone. So they had at least not drowned in the lake.

Of course not, idiot.

They were probably at Gwen's house having a hot dinner.

Passing through the wall of pine trees, he entered the Christmas tree lane near the public road. Sadie's purple bike was parked by the bus stop, propped up against a signpost, and this made no sense at all—nothing did. First a canoe and now a bus? Why would they take the bus so close to dinnertime? What new game was this? David looked toward Gwen Hubble's home at the top of the long cobblestone driveway. The lights were going on, one by one, as though someone were racing from room to room in a great panic, in absolute terror of the dark, turning on all the lamps in the house.